One Heartbeat A Minute

By Craig William Emms

Cold Fish Books

This novel is entirely a work of fiction.
The names, characters and incidents portrayed in it are
the work of the author's imagination or are used
fictitiously.

First published in Great Britain by
Cold Fish Books 2012

Craig William Emms asserts the moral right to
be identified as the author of this work

A catalogue record for this book is
available from the British Library

ISBN 978-0-9572168-2-2

This book is dedicated to my life-partner Dr Linda Barnett. She is one of the toughest, most resourceful and intelligent people that I know, yet she also has a heart of pure gold. If it wasn't for Linda I would never have passed through the darkness to see the light again. Thank you.

PROLOGUE

Tuesday 15th October 2013
Peterborough

The man was sitting slumped on the thin plastic mattress when the door to the cell slammed open. He was six feet two inches tall with a lean, muscular body, and had spent the last four days sitting tall and straight-backed in the dock, looking the members of the jury, the judge and the prosecuting barrister right in the eye. Now he looked as though he had given up all hope. The plain black suit that he wore, with simple black tie and white shirt, seemed to hang limp from his rounded shoulders and his head was bowed as he stared down at the floor. He didn't even lift his head when the metal door to the cell sprung open with such force that it clanged heavily as it hit the wall.

The two uniformed civilian prison guards sauntered into the man's cell, one carrying a plastic tray with a plastic plate of sandwiches and a plastic cup of tea from the dispensing machine.

"Here's your lunch *paedo*. I hope you choke on it."

"Fucking pervert. You're gonna go down and when yer get to prison, them fuckers in there will sort yer out good and proper. Yer fuckin' pervert."

"My colleague here is right paedo. Do you know what the inmates favourite trick is with nonces like you?" The man still didn't look up as they moved in front of him and stood, legs braced apart as they glared down at the top of

5

his head with disgust. He once had a head of jet black hair, but now it was heavily silvered with grey and cropped close to his skull.

"Well I'll tell you, you fucking nonce; they mix up some petrol and sugar in a bottle, stuff a rag down the neck and then light it, just like a fucking petrol bomb. Then they get you all alone in your cell and throw the bottle so it smashes on your head and soaks you in flaming liquid. The sugar is to make it stick to your skin better!" They both guffawed. "And don't think that the screws will help you. They hate fucking nonces as much as the rest of them, though they will put the fire out in the end."

"Yeah. *Eventually*!" They guffawed again.

"Anyway here's your lunch paedo." And with that they leaned forward, hawked loudly, and deposited two big green lumps of snot and spit; one on the sandwiches and one in the tea. "You might as well get used to it yer fucking pervert, 'cause everyone's gonna be gobbing in your food from now on!" They creased up with laughter, shoving the tray towards the man's head.

It was then that the man looked up for the first time. They were surprised to see that there wasn't any fear in his coal-black eyes; just an emptiness of emotion that reminded them of a shark's eyes. Then he smiled, and they felt a cold chill run down their spines.

Detective Chief Inspector Alan Davies, head of Cambridgeshire Constabulary's Serious and Organised Crime Agency, or SOCA for short, sat in the cafeteria of Peterborough's Crown Court building, tucking hungrily into a plate of mixed salad with pasta. He was a slightly built man, and looked much too young to have gained his responsibility and rank. In fact he was quite young, only 28 years of age, and had been fast-tracked through the police force after getting a philosophy degree at the University of Warwick, near Coventry. Next to him sat Detective Sergeant Henry Price. He was a typical long-serving copper; tall and heavily built with a paunch that hung over his trouser belt. He was 45 years old and had served for almost 25 of those years in the police. He was from the old school of policing, despised his academic boss and was hungrily taking a huge bite out of a large bacon roll.

"I don't know how you can eat that shit boss. You should get some proper food down your neck, not that rabbit-food. It's not good for you."

"It's a damn sight better for you than that plate of gristle and fat you've got!"

"No way boss. This is real food. Good for you."

They were interrupted from taking the conversation any further by the appearance of Detective Constable Helen Wright at the door to the cafeteria. Helen was 22 years old and attractive, with long blond hair that normally hung free almost to her waist; at the moment it was pulled tightly back from her face and tied off into a ponytail. She almost ran across to her two colleagues.

"The jury's coming back in boss!" She said breathlessly.

"Bloody hell! That was quick; I haven't even finished my lunch. They can't have been out for more than forty minutes."

"Forty-five boss." Said Price, glancing at his watch. "Good timing; at least you won't have to finish that rabbit food."

"Or watch you die of a fat-induced heart attack."

"It must be good news boss. Always is when the jury comes back quickly." Said Helen, excitement reddening her face.

"Of course it's bloody good news! We've got the bastard bang to rights; he's as guilty as sin. Let's get back in there and watch him go down."

"Yeah. Twenty years minimum would suit me."

"Fuck that! Thirty years would be about right for the fucking pervert. Come on!" They rushed out of the door in a gang.

Courtroom number three was bustling as everyone headed back to take their seats after their brief lunch break. The prosecution and defence teams took their places at their benches, speaking in hushed whispers to each other. As he sat down with his two colleagues in the public gallery, DCI Davies gave the thumbs up to Steve Mackay, the Chief Prosecutor of the Crown Prosecution Service, who acknowledged the sign with a satisfied smile and a nod of his head. The family of the deceased made their way, with a mixture of sobs and angry noises, to their seats in front of the SOCA team. Members of the public and a gaggle of journalists pushed in behind them.

The trial had dragged on for four days and everybody knew that John Smith was guilty of this terrible crime and that he was going to go down for a long, long time. All the evidence was there to be seen; the raped and dead body of eleven year old Mary Knightly, with fragments of Smith's skin found under her fingernails, confirmed by DNA testing. His fingerprints had also been found on her shoes. Strands of her hair had been found and identified in the back of his van, presumably where he had raped and then killed her. With all of this evidence he was crazy to have pleaded not-guilty to the abduction, sexual assault, rape and murder of young Mary, but that was what he had done and DCI Davies for one had been glad, as there would be no discount on his prison time for pleading guilty and saving the time of the court. No, he would be sent down for the maximum time allowed. Of that he was very, very sure. This would be a good day for SOCA, and God knows they needed some very good publicity.

Everybody settled down into their seats and looked on as the twelve members of the jury, six men and six women, filed into their own seats and sat down. Most of them were stony faced, but one or two couldn't keep a self-satisfied smirk from showing.

After a few more minutes everyone looked up as the door to the dock opened. They were hoping to see the look of fear on the defendant's face as he was escorted in by the uniformed guards. It wasn't him though; it was just a harassed-looking and bewigged court clerk, who almost ran around the courtroom benches as he made for the Crown Prosecutor. There was a bout of frantic whispering and then Mackay pointed across to DCI Davies in the gallery and the clerk nodded and rushed over to him.

"Can I see you outside for a moment sir?"

"Not now man, I want to stay and see justice done!"

"Please sir. It's very, very important!"

"Okay, okay. Price, come with me. Wright, stay here and keep a tab on events; I'll want to hear all about it when I get back." They followed the clerk out of the courtroom, where he looked around the semi-crowded public waiting area, spotted the half open door of an interview room at the back (indicating that it was not in use), and gestured for the police officers to follow him as he headed to it. Once they were safely inside and the door was shut, he couldn't get his words out fast enough:

"He's gone sir! He's escaped and he's killed them both!"

"Slow down man! Who's escaped and who's been killed?"

"The defendant sir! Smith! I went down to the cells to tell the prison officers that the jury had reached their verdict and were coming back into court. I didn't know what to do sir! I found them there, both of them, dead!"

"Are you saying that John Smith killed the prison guards and has escaped?"

"Oh yes sir! Yes! He's killed them both! They're dead sir! Dead!"

A few minutes later, Davies and Price were staring through the slot in Smith's cell door, where trays of food were normally passed through.

"Jesus Boss! They look dead, I can't see them breathing." Both of the civilian prison officers were lying on their faces in the cell, arms and legs akimbo.

"Where the fuck is the key for this cell?" shouted Davies, rattling the handle. "We've got to get in there!" The court clerk was standing beside them, his face a mask of shock.

"I don't know sir. The guards usually have them attached to a chain from their belt."

"Well that's no fucking use to us, is it? They're in there and we're out here! There must be a spare key somewhere?"

"I guess there's one in the room that they use at the end of the corridor sir, but that's locked as well."

"Jesus fucking Christ! Price, get on the phone to headquarters and tell them that Smith is on the loose and to get an APB out on him now, and get an ambulance here as well. You, show me where the guard's room is."

Price stormed off up the stairs that led towards the courts to make his calls, swearing to himself as he realised that he had switched his mobile off when he'd gone into the courtroom and that he'd have to wait for a few precious moments for it to get a signal. Davies followed the court clerk at a run to the glass-enclosed guard's station at the end of the corridor. He tried the handle but the clerk was right; it was locked. Peering through the glass he could see a key-box hanging partly open on the wall of the room, and could also see that there were a couple of CCTV monitors sitting on the desk. He cast around the corridor for something with which to break the glass and the clerk seemed to read his mind: "Won't do any good sir. This is reinforced glass; you won't be able to break it."

"Shit!" He hollered up the stairs at the retreating form of his DS: "Price! When you've finished with those calls get a fucking locksmith down here ASAP!"

John Smith pulled the silver Vauxhall Astra into a small parking lot at the rear of the Carpetright shop. Without getting out of the car he looked around to see if there were any CCTV cameras and finding none, he smiled to himself.

He backed the car into a bay and relaxed, prepared to wait for a while until an opportunity showed itself.

Finally, after twenty minutes that seemed like days to DCI Davies, the locksmith showed up and opened the lock to the guard's station. DS Price shoved his way past the locksmith and fumbled through the keys in the key box.

"Here you are boss. Cell three." He said, throwing the keys underhand to Davies. The DCI ran down the corridor, closely followed by two yellow-jacketed paramedics who had been standing around twiddling their thumbs for the last ten minutes while they waited for the locksmith to arrive. He unlocked the steel cell door and pushed it open to allow the two medics through. They quickly checked over the prone guards before looking up at the policeman.

"I'm afraid they're both dead mate, and it's too bloody late to try and revive them."

"How'd he kill them?"

"Well we're not pathologists," said the senior medic, "but it looks to me like they were both hit in the throat. Their larynxes are crushed. It must have been impossible for them to breath."

"Shit!" Davies punched the cell wall in his frustration. "Don't touch the bodies any more than you have to; this is a murder scene now."

"Okay mate, there's nothing else we can do for the poor bastards anyhow. We'd better get back to the ambulance station."

As the two medics packed up their gear and walked away, Davies looked down at the bodies. Even to an inexperienced eye, he could see the blue lips and bugged-out eyes of the two civilians. He imagined them rolling around the floor, clutching at their throats as they fought to take a breath that wouldn't come. He suddenly felt sick. Fucking hell; there will be hell to pay for this; not only has Smith murdered two guards and escaped; but he'd done it while I was sitting upstairs in the same building eating my

11

fucking lunch! Shit! His thoughts were interrupted by a shout from Price:

"Boss! You'd better see this boss!" He turned and headed at a run back to the guard's station. Price was standing in front of the desk with a remote control in his hand, pointing at the screen of one of the CCTV monitors. "Here's the bastard boss." They both stood and watched the grainy black and white image of a man in prison officer's uniform strolling unconcerned out of the back door of the courthouse. He was dressed in black trousers with white shirt and a black tie, wearing a prison officer's peaked cap and carrying a clipboard. A set of keys and a key chain could easily be seen dangling from a clip on his belt. Both of them recognized the tall figure of Smith. As Smith followed the contours of the building around he stopped for a second, looked directly up into the CCTV camera, and grinned. Then he walked on out of sight.

"Cocky fucking bastard!" Swore Price. "Watch the other screen boss; the second camera's covering the car park." On the other screen Smith could now be seen walking amongst the parked cars. He still had the clipboard with him, but now it was sticking out from his midriff.

"What the fuck is he doing?" Asked a dumbfounded DCI.

"I reckon he's got his other hand under the clipboard and is using it to hide the fact that he's pressing the remote of one of the guard's car keys. Look! The lights are flashing on that silver Astra over there." They watched helplessly as Smith changed direction and opened the door to the Astra, pausing only long enough to remove his cap and to throw it and the clipboard onto the passenger seat, before climbing in. A couple of seconds later and the car disappeared from view as he drove it out of the car park.

"How long ago was this?" Price peered at the timings in the bottom right corner of the screen and then at his watch, quickly calculating. "Fifty-five minutes boss."

"Shit! He could be thirty miles away by now. Make sure that headquarters get the make and registration

12

number of that car, and make sure that they get it out to every officer on patrol or on the beat within a hundred miles of Peterborough. I want this bastard caught!"

Only a few minutes passed before Smith saw just what he wanted; a single elderly man parking up his red Ford Focus in order to go to the carpet shop. He grabbed a thick coat from the rear seat of the Astra where the now-deceased prison officer had left it that morning, and got out of the car, locking it behind him. He searched through the coat's pockets as he put it on and grinned when he found a packet of cigarettes and a lighter. He put one in his mouth, lit it and inhaled deeply before slowly letting a stream of smoke out between his lips, sighing happily. That was much better. He strolled across the car park in the direction of the old man's car.

Fifteen minutes later the old man came out of the shop, carrying a large plastic bag with a heavy rolled-up rug sticking out of the top. As he approached his car, Smith stepped towards him.

"Excuse me sir, you wouldn't have a light would you?" He asked, brandishing an unlit cigarette with a friendly smile on his face.

"Sorry." Answered the man, "I don't smoke."

"That's okay." Said Smith, still smiling as he stepped in closer. "It's your car that I really want anyway." A hand with fingers as hard as steel clamped onto the old man's shoulder. "Don't make a fuss and you won't get hurt. I've no reason to hurt you, so don't give me any. Okay?"

The old man looked up into Smith's eyes. What he saw there made his blood run cold with fear.

ONE

Tuesday 15th October 2013
Huntingdon, Cambridgeshire

Three hours later and DCI Davies was sitting at his desk in Hinchingbrooke Police Headquarters. It had been the longest three hours he'd ever known in his life and he had had to take his last two paracetomal tablets to stave off a huge headache that was threatening to engulf him. He felt like shit, both physically and mentally. There hadn't been a single sighting of Smith or the prison officer's car and he was getting it in the neck big-time from his bosses, as though it was his fault for letting the bastard escape. The only bit of luck he'd had so far was that the press hadn't caught on yet. Once that happened he knew that the shit would really hit the fan.

He looked up as an equally tired and distressed-looking DC Wright burst into his office.

"The car has been found boss! One of the patrol cars recognized the registration!" Davies forced himself to ignore his pounding headache.

"Great! Where is it? Any sign of Smith?"

"Sorry boss; no sign of Smith yet. The car was in a small car park at the back of Carpetright, about 500m from the courthouse in Peterborough."

"500m? Jesus Christ, why wasn't it picked up earlier?"

"The car patrols were all concentrating on the roads leading out of Peterborough boss. No one thought that he'd abandon the car so quickly, or so close to the courthouse."

"Okay, okay. Any CCTV from the car park or the surrounding streets?"

"There aren't any cameras covering the car park boss, nor the surrounding streets. The guys are on their way out now to talk to local shop owners to see if there are any cameras in their premises that might have picked him up, or whether anybody spotted anything suspicious."

Davies sighed, rubbing at his temples in the vain hope that he could relieve the ache. "Fat chance of that. If I didn't know that this creep was just a fucking delivery van driver, I'd say that he was pretty good at evading us; either that or he has the luck of a lottery winner. Any news from the pathologist yet?"

"He's not finished the post mortems yet boss, but DS Price spoke to him on the phone just a minute ago. He says that the preliminary findings show that the two guards were struck on their throats and died of asphyxiation, just like you thought."

"Any sign of the murder weapon or how he got it into the courthouse?"

"Not yet boss. The plods are still doing a fingertip search around the courthouse and the car park, but they haven't come up with anything yet."

"Okay. Well make sure that the Astra is dragged into a forensics bay; we may find the weapon there, or some clue as to where the bastard has disappeared to."

"Okay boss."

"Meanwhile, get me a coffee will you Helen? And get someone to nip down to the police doctor's surgery and get me a packet of headache tablets."

Half an hour later the phone rang on the DCI's desk.

"DCI Davies."

"Hello Mr Davies, its Professor Schouten from the Coroner's office here."

"Good to hear from you professor. I take it you've finished the post mortems then?"

"Yes, I have. You'll have my full report as soon as we can get it faxed over to you. I'm calling because I thought it would be best if you heard the results directly from me first."

"What's up Prof? You're beginning to sound very mysterious."

"Well the results of the post mortem indicate that you shouldn't waste any time looking for a murder weapon."

"Go on."

"The two prison officers were each killed by a single blow. To be precise, they were killed by a very sharp thrust of the second knuckles of a hand, delivered as a punch straight into the larynx. Rather like a 'dragon-punch' as practiced by some martial artists; where the fist is elongated and flattened so that it can be delivered precisely between the chin and the juncture of the collar bones above the breast. I've only ever seen this type of punch used once before, and that was in a fatal accident many years ago at a martial arts club."

"Hold on a minute Prof. You're telling me that Smith killed two big, tough and experienced prison officers with just a single punch to the throat? That seems unlikely for our man. There's absolutely no record that Smith knows anything about martial arts or how to deliver a punch like that. Are you sure of your findings?"

"Absolutely DCI Davies; the imprint of the murderer's knuckles is very clear at the site of the wounds. He also delivered the blows with a great deal of force and perfectly on target; enough force to instantly crush the larynxes. I would have to say from our findings that you are dealing with a man who has studied some sort of unarmed combat for many years, and is particularly adept at using his hands as weapons."

"Okay, thank you for letting me know professor, much appreciated." Davies put down the phone. Jesus Christ! Who the hell is this guy?

He walked to his office door and shouted into the noise and bustle of the squad room: "DC Wright! Get a copy of Smith's file and bring it into my office! Now!"

Tuesday 15th October 2013
South-east of Coventry, Warwickshire.

At about the same time as Davies was reading through his file, Smith was pulling the hijacked Ford Focus onto a grassy car park surrounded by woodland. Although the woodland was only about 80 miles from Peterborough as the crow flies, Smith had taken his time and had got there by driving along minor roads, rather than using the main A14. He had used every trick in the book, and a few of his own, to make sure that he wasn't being tailed, and had avoided driving through anywhere that might have CCTV cameras installed, such as small towns. He had even avoided driving past petrol stations that might have their cameras pointing out onto the adjoining road.

The old man had spent the entire journey sitting quietly next to Smith in the passenger seat, frightened out of his wits. Every effort of his to start a conversation with Smith had been met with a stony silence, so he had soon given up trying to connect with his kidnapper. For his part, Smith had offered no more threats to the old man.

Smith broke the silence now by asking the old man to step out of the car, and follow him into the woods. Shaking nervously the old man obeyed. As they walked together into the trees, Smith relented when he saw how scared the man was.

"Don't worry old timer; I'm not going to hurt you." His voice was gentle and his smile friendly. "I'm just going to pick up something that I left here a long time ago. Then I'm afraid I'll have to tie you up and leave you here." The old man shuddered. "But don't worry. You have my word that I'll let the coppers know where you are in about an hour's time. You'll be okay; you're not my enemy, mate.

17

I'm not going to hurt you and I won't leave you here to freeze to death either."

As they walked a few hundred metres into the trees Smith kept stopping and looking around, as though seeking out landmarks that only he remembered. Eventually their route took them to a huge old oak tree that towered above the small-leaved limes around it. Smith smiled to himself, and searched a bit more until he found the decayed remnants of a very old wooden cart. The cart was now just a few bits of moss-covered timber with rusted wheel rims lying amongst the vegetation, partly hidden by a growth of bramble. Smith bent down and started scraping away at the ground with a stick that he snapped off from a tree. In just a few minutes he heard the satisfying grate of the stick against metal, and then used his hands to remove enough soil to be able to pull a small metal box from the ground. It was about two feet long and a foot wide and deep, and the old man could see that there was a padlock on the lid. Smith looked up at him.

"Okay mate, I'm afraid I'll have to ask you to sit down with your back to that tree."

He indicated a nearby tree of about a foot diameter to the old man, who hesitantly did as he was told. "Okay. Now reach back and put your hands together behind the tree. Good man."

Smith quickly undid the leather belt on the man's trousers and withdrew it through the trouser hoops. Then skilfully he used the belt to secure the old man's hands behind the tree by wrapping it in a figure of eight around his wrists and tying it off. Next he stooped down and looked the old man in the eyes.

"Don't struggle mate, you'll only hurt yourself. I gave you my word that I'll let the law know where you are and I will, so don't worry. Just stay here and try to relax. I'm sorry I dragged you into all of this but look on the bright side: at least you'll have an amazing story to tell your grandkids tomorrow, eh?"

The old man felt compelled to wish Smith good luck as he walked away with his box on one shoulder but he was damned if he knew why.

TWO

Tuesday 15th October 2013
Huntingdon, Cambridgeshire

"I don't understand this." Fumed DCI Davies to his DS. "I've been through Smith's file again and there's absolutely nothing there to suggest that he knows how to kill a man with his bare hands, never mind two of them at the same time. He's just a bloody van driver for fuck's sake!"

DS Price looked at his superior, and tried to hide the loathing that he felt for the man from his voice.

"I know boss. He's just a 52 year old bloke who's led an unremarkable life. We thoroughly researched his past before the trial to see if there was anything else that we could pin on him and found nothing of any bloody use. He was born and raised on a council estate in London; he went to a local comprehensive school and his school records show that he wasn't particularly outstanding at anything. Since then he's had a handful of long-term jobs driving trucks and vans and delivering stuff to factories and offices. He's got no surviving relatives that we could find; no girl friends; in fact no friends at all except for his colleagues at work. He's just a nobody, boss."

"Then how come he's killed two prison officers, managed to escape from the courthouse cells, and has evaded the whole of the British fucking police force into the bargain? We're missing something here. But fuck knows what."

DC Wright stuck her head through his door. "There's a call for you from a DS Thompson of Coventry CID, boss; line two."

"Okay, thanks Helen." He picked up the phone. "DCI Davies, what can I do for you DS Thompson?"

"You can shut up and listen for a start."

"Who the fuck do you think you are?"

"I know who I am Davies; my name is John Smith. You may remember me you bastard. I'm the one that's been framed with rape and murder."

"Look. I don't know who you are but you're seriously pissing me off! This is not the right time to make sick jokes!"

"Just shut the fuck up Davies. I am who I say I am." The DCI suddenly froze when he realised that the man might be telling the truth.

"If you are John Smith, then prove it." He said, raising his eyebrows to Price, who got the message and shot out of the office to try and set up a trace and to record the phone call.

"I've had enough of trying to prove things to you. Now just listen to me. To the south-east of Coventry there's a place called Ryton Wood. There's an entrance to a lane which is almost opposite the Bull and Butcher Pub, and the lane leads from the main road into the wood. You need to get someone up that lane and into the wood because I've left some poor old geezer tied up about 200m west of the car park, and I don't want him to freeze to bloody death. Have you got all that?"

"No, no. Wait a minute; I need to get a pen and paper to write it all down."

"Don't fuck with me Davies. I've already been fucked around enough by you lot. Just go and get the old sod."

"Okay, okay. Just say it all again, will you?" Suddenly Smith laughed down the phone.

"There's no point trying to trace this call you silly wanker. It's an unregistered mobile and as soon as I've

21

finished talking to you I'm going to take out the battery and throw it away. Even if you manage to get a location for this call from the nearest microwave mast it'll be too late because I'll have fucked off and be miles away."

"Okay smart-arse. Tell me this then: why the fuck did you have to kill the guards? Why didn't you just do your time for killing that little girl, you perverted little fucker?"

"I killed them because they fucking well asked for it and I'm not going to do time for something that I didn't do in the first place: I did not kill the girl."

"Okay, well if you're innocent of the girl's murder, why don't you just turn yourself in?"

"You're having a laugh! Turn myself in to the 'Silly and Disorganised Crime Squad'? You lot couldn't find your own arse to wipe it! But I'll tell you what I will do though, just to make it all a bit more interesting."

"What's that?"

"A few years ago I wrote down the story of my life. It was supposed to be good therapy for me to get everything down on paper, but it didn't work. I'll email some of it to you; I reckon you'll be interested in reading it. Maybe, just maybe, you'll realise that I'm innocent of the girl's murder and that I've been set up."

"You're fucking nuts Smith. Why would I be interested in reading about your poxy life? We both know that you raped and murdered that little girl, and now you've added two more murders to your list."

"Not everything is as it seems, Detective Chief Inspector. Those two guards deserved what they got for treating me the way they did. They were a couple of bullies and they paid the price. I'm gonna go now. Catch you later. Bye." Davies poked his head out of the door.

"Tell me you got that Price?"

"Nope, sorry boss. If you could have made him stay on the phone for a few more minutes we might have got him, but the call wasn't long enough." This time Price couldn't hide all of the disdain in his voice, but Davies either didn't notice or didn't care.

"Well make sure everything is set up in case he calls back. I want this fucker!"

From: john smith (johnsmith2223@hotmail.com)
To: SOCA@Cambspolice.org.uk
Date: 15 October 2013 21:27:58
CC:
Subject: FAO Detective Chief Inspector Alan Davies, Cambs SOCA.

Hi Alan, you don't mind me calling you Alan, do you? Not that I really care anyway. I've attached the first instalment of my autobiography, as promised. Let's see if your brilliant detectives can sort out truth from fiction, shall we?

I've had a chance to think about my present predicament, and I've decided on a positive course of action to remedy it.

You will be hearing from me again, and soon.

Regards

John Smith

THREE

I was born in a council flat close to the centre of London and was the youngest of three brothers. My family life was good and my parents were kind people who worked hard all of their lives.

When I was about four we moved from the east to the west of London, into a three-bedroom council house. I remember the excitement of the move and a huge pile of empty tea chests that we had filled with our possessions. The council estate that we moved onto was brand new and quite posh at the time, with all of the families being vetted by the council before they were allowed to live there. The house was an end terrace, with an enclosed back garden, a garage, and a large, grassed front garden. It even had central heating; quite a change from the pokey little flat that we had moved out of.

From an early age I was taken in by the idea of being a soldier and fighting for my Queen and Country. I was determined that I would join the army when I was old enough. This was about the same time that the TV series *Kung Fu* was first aired and I thought that learning Kung Fu would be a good way of getting fit and hardening myself up for the army, so I began to practice the moves that Kwai Chang Caine made on the TV. My parents, God bless them, probably saw my interest as a good opportunity to get me out of the house and enrolled me in a Kung Fu class at a local community centre. Once a week I would go to the class and learn all that I could. Then every evening after school I would practise and practise until I became really very good. My dad even helped me convert our garage into a home-made gym, complete with punching bag, and that was where I would practise for hours; exercising, stretching, kicking, punching and blocking, time after time. Eventually the classes ended and moved onto a new location that was too far for me to travel to; so I started with a different class run by a Chinese Master from Hong Kong, learning several new styles. Then I branched out even further and took up Tai Kwon Do and Karate, achieving black belt grades in both of these martial arts within a few years. As a child I was basically a tough little bastard and I was always getting into fights at school, as well as into trouble.

I worked on my fitness to the point of obsession; running miles upon miles every week, speed-marching with a backpack full of house bricks, exercising every day with push-ups, sit-ups, pull-ups and tricep lifts. All of my teenage years were geared up to my becoming a soldier and that is just what I did a few months after leaving school. At age 16 I enrolled as an Infantry Junior Leader in the British Army.

FOUR

I clearly remember the day that I left home to join the army. It was late morning when we finally arrived at Folkestone train station. Here, several hundred recruits had arrived from all over the country and there was a fleet of coaches waiting to pick us up and take us the short way to Sir John Moore Barracks in Shorncliffe, Kent.

When our coach arrived at the barracks we formed up into three ranks for the first time. What a motley crew we must have looked. Just a bunch of skinny, spotty kids dressed in an assortment of civilian clothes. All as scared and apprehensive as each other. We were marched away to have a pep talk from the battalion's commanding officer in the gymnasium, accompanied by shouts of "pick your feet up you lazy bastards!" "Swing your arms, you're not in a fucking zoo now" and "don't look at the arse of the bloke in front, you'll only get a hard on".

I don't remember much about the commanding officer's pep talk as there were so many new sights and sounds to take in that it was all a bit overwhelming. Afterwards we were marched around the camp again, to the constant shouting of our instructors, and shown where everything was, such as the mess hall and billets etc. I don't think that any of us really took in anything at this stage. All I can remember is that we were a mess, constantly out of step and struggling to carry our bags and suitcases. Eventually we were marched back to our billets. There we queued up to be issued with our kit from the company quarter-master stores. Then, carrying our suitcases and juggling a huge pile of kit we were finally shown to our rooms.

I was placed in number one platoon of Arnhem Company – the Parachute Regiment Company. In those days the typical size of an infantry section was ten men and there were three sections to a platoon, so we were split up between three rooms that held ten men each. I managed to get a bed in the corner beneath a window, which at least meant that I would be able to get some peace and quiet occasionally.

Despite all my own personal preparation and training I felt very scared. It was a hell of a culture shock to find myself suddenly thrown into the deep end. From that moment on I was a soldier, no more civilian life, no more mum and dad to look after me, no more school. I was in the army now and everything was going to be different. I don't think I was the only one to feel this way either. I reckon that every one of us was going through the same emotions. We were all scared witless and shitless.

There was one guy who was allocated to our room who immediately curled up into a foetal ball in a corner. He was suffering really badly from homesickness and in fact he had it so bad that he was discharged from the army after a few hours and sent back home. I never even saw his face. For the rest of us we began a year of training that was one of the hardest and toughest of our lives; a year that would seem to last a lifetime, but one that would leave each and every one of us with the necessary skills and leadership qualities that would make us into potential non-commissioned officers in the most professional army in the world.

The one year of training as a junior leader was split into three terms. If we survived the tough and sometimes downright brutal training then we would pass out as trained soldiers at the end of the year and would be entitled to wear our maroon regimental berets and Parachute Regiment cap badges instead of the IJLB cap badge and

28

plain black beret. But even then our training would not be over. The Junior Leaders of Arnhem Company, which was the Para's Company of the battalion, would then have to undergo a further two months training at the Parachute Regiment Depot in Aldershot, Hampshire. Here we would be mixed in with the ordinary junior soldiers of the Para's, the guys who were thought to lack leadership potential, and be put through some of the hardest physical training that the British Army can come up with, before passing out once again as trained soldiers. Then, and only then, would we be allowed to join our regular army battalions.

A typical day would begin at about 5am. We'd parade outside the company block in full webbing (about 120 lbs in weight), wearing our heavy old-style steel helmets and carrying rifles. Then we'd set out on a Combat Fitness Test, otherwise known as the 'march and shoot'. This consisted of an eight mile forced march, three miles of which was cross-country and the rest on roads. Officially we had two hours to complete the test, but our instructors always aimed to complete it in less than one and a half hours. After all we were the best; we were the Para's. After the march we would go over the assault course and then do a 100m run. The run would be done carrying our kit and weapons and also a buddy, and their kit and weapon, thrown over our shoulders in what was called a 'fireman's carry'. Then we'd swap and the carrier would become the carried for another 100m. After all this we'd end up by shooting ten rounds into targets on the 30m range. Well and truly knackered by this time we'd double march (run) back to the barracks, clean our rifles and have them inspected (and woe betide any silly bugger who hadn't cleaned his weapon until it was spotless!), change uniform, have a wash and a shave, and join the queue for breakfast.

At 8am we'd parade outside the company block again and begin a hard days training. The morning and afternoons were split into 40 minute lecture periods, with a ten minute 'smoke break' between each lesson and a short lunch break at midday. The lessons taught us the full range of knowledge that we would need as soldiers in a modern army. Subjects included weapons training, field-craft, radio-operating, first aid, map-reading, infantry tactics and foot and rifle drill. On top of this there were the endless physical training sessions which included going over the assault course, squad runs, speed-marches, circuit training, swimming and playing sports. Plus we'd have regular forays into the Army School of Education to study for our 'O' and 'A' Levels.

After our evening meal we would spend our 'spare' time cleaning our personal lockers, rooms, bathrooms and hallways. The instructors would carry out regular inspections, and our accommodation had to be gleaming. We'd also get our own personal kit ready for the next day, as we were always checked at the morning parade, and often there were other inspections made by senior officers. All in all it was a pretty busy schedule and we often worked well into the small hours. Weekends were only a little better; Saturday was sometimes a day of rest if we had done well over the previous week, but if we'd cocked up in any way (and we often did of course), or upset our instructors in any way, then Saturday would be filled with punishment duties and extra training. Even Sunday was never entirely our own time as we had to attend 'Church Parade' every Sunday morning, in our best kit of course, and after being inspected.

Looking back it's no wonder that when I went home on leave after my first 14 weeks of this training my parents walked passed me at the train station without recognising me. I'd left them as a skinny young boy, and I'd returned on that first leave as a fit, glowing specimen of young soldier-hood.

Being home on leave was where I first realised that 'normal' people (i.e., people who weren't stupid enough to join the army) just didn't have a clue about how hard it was to become a soldier and how tough the training could be. I used to really look forward to going home on leave, as we all did. But when I finally got home I'd find that no one was interested in what we did as soldiers, and they certainly didn't believe how tough it was. I always found that after a few days on leave with very little to do, all that I wanted was to get back to my job and my mates. Then, of course, the whole cycle would begin again, with me wishing that my leave would hurry up so I could go home again. It wasn't until later years that I realised that all of my mates were going through exactly the same thoughts and emotions. Being in the army is not just about having a job or a career; it becomes your whole life. As my first sergeant was fond of saying: You don't join up for 40 hours a week – in the army you are potentially available to work for 24 hours a day, seven days a week, 365 days a year. The army is a vocation, and I truly believe that unless you've experienced it for yourself you can't really know what it is like.

As the three terms went by, the training got more complicated and harder. Field-craft and battle camps became more and more frequent and realistic, often with our company being matched against other companies from within the battalion. Sometimes we even went up against other troops from the regular army and the other armed forces. On one memorable occasion we were fighting against a company of Royal Marines on Dartmoor. Our company had been drawn up in a 'patrol harbour' in a stretch of woodlands after a long forced march through the night. We set up our sentry points and *bashers* (a Malayan word for a type of shelter made from two waterproof ponchos, one laid on the ground and the other suspended about eighteen inches above it) in the torrential rain, and sent out our normal reconnaissance patrols to have a look around the area. One of them came back with the interesting news that a company of Royal Marines had set up their own patrol harbour a few miles away from us. Our instructors gave us a warning order that we would be sending out a full fighting patrol to hit their base the following dawn. We got pretty hyped up about this as the Royal Marines have a reputation for being mean, tough bastards in a fight. We had no illusions that we'd have to expect some pretty fierce hand-to-hand stuff with them. Even so, the few poor sods that were left behind to guard the camp as the fighting patrol set off around midnight were well pissed-off that they wouldn't be involved in the action.

We didn't approach the enemy patrol harbour in a straight line from our own but curved away to one flank to hit them from behind. This meant about six hours hard marching and we finally crept into position about an hour before dawn and settled down to wait before we went into the attack. It was still raining and bitterly cold but our nerves kept us warm and none of us wanted to fuck up.

As the light slowly strengthened we could just see and hear the enemy moving about in their harbour in a patch of woodland. The allotted time came and we opened up with everything we had and began our 'fire and manoeuvre' as we moved forward into the assault. Even though we were very green in those days, we could still tell that something was wrong. There were far fewer of the enemy returning fire than we had expected and as we moved through the marine's camp it became obvious that most of them were not there and only a small party of sentries remained. Where the hell were the rest of them? We were all feeling very disappointed that we weren't going to have the scrap that we had hoped for, when suddenly I saw this big hulking marine rise up as if out of the very ground right in front of me. Automatically I smacked him one with the butt of my rifle right in the face, and kicked him in the bollocks as well. He went down with a loud groan and as I side-stepped to go around him my eye was caught by the commando knife on his belt. I turned and made a grab for it, but he tried to throw a punch at me from the ground so I kicked him in the face, ripped the knife from its scabbard and just for good measure I shot him at point-blank range in the chest, before hurrying off to join my section as it reorganised on the other side of the marine's camp. It was only a blank

32

round and not the real thing of course, but a lot of heat and bits of brass are expelled forcibly from the barrel when a blank round is fired. We had been told many, many times over the preceding weeks, that you must never fire a blank-round directly at a living target, especially when your rifle barrel is only an inch or so from his chest!

After we moved back to our own patrol harbour we found out that the marines had attacked our camp at exactly the same time that we had attacked theirs! We had obviously missed each other during our night approaches. We were all pretty wound up, and it was only then that I realised that I might get into trouble for shooting and belting the marine the way that I had. The first thing that I did was to dig a small hole and bury the stolen commando knife. It was bloody lucky that I did as a few hours later we were told to go 'non-tactical' and to line up on parade with our kit on the ground in front of us. A very angry and very sore Royal Marine captain, with a bruised and battered face, a bandage wrapped around his bare chest and his partially melted combat jacket draped across his shoulders, walked up our line looking each one of us in the eyes and barked: "Was it you?" into our faces. Of course he didn't have a chance of picking his assailant out because it had happened so quickly, and let's face it we were all dressed in green with short hair and wearing camouflage cream on our faces. When he got to me there wasn't any sort of flicker of recognition in his eyes as he barked his question at me, and I answered "No Sir!" as loud as any of the others.

After he'd finished walking down the line our kit was searched for the stolen knife, but of course it was never found. I managed to retrieve it later, after the marine officer had buggered off. The only hint that any of our permanent staff instructors knew who had committed the heinous crime came after we had returned to Shorncliffe Barracks a couple of weeks later when my platoon sergeant, Sergeant Stewart, got me into his office and praised me for a job well done. When I asked him what job?

He just winked, told me that he "hated fucking marines" and then told me to fuck off out of his sight.

At the beginning of the last term, junior leaders who had proved their leadership qualities were promoted to junior lance-corporals, corporals, sergeants, and company sergeant-majors. I became a junior sergeant, the second-in-command of Number One Platoon, Arnhem Company. I'd worked hard and proved myself capable of being a bloody good soldier.

FIVE

One evening after a cold, rainy day on the rifle ranges, a young junior leader decided that he couldn't take the pressure any more, went into the toilets, put the muzzle of his rifle into his mouth, and blew his brains out. I happened to get involved because it was my bad luck to be on what we called 'fire-piquet' that night.

Fire-piquet was just another name for guard duty and everyone in the battalion took their turn at it. However, on this occasion I was extremely unlucky that the young boy had decided to take his own life while I was lying in my pit in the fire-piquet room after just completing a two-hour patrol. The provost sergeant banged open the door to the room, spied me and my oppo relaxing, pointed to us and said:

"You two, come with me, I've got a job for you."

We traipsed down to one of the company blocks and followed the sergeant inside. The army ambulance crew were just removing the body from the toilet cubicle as we arrived. I got a brief look at what was left of this poor kid's head (nothing above the jaw-line) and then I was in a cubicle myself throwing my guts up. After a few minutes of this I ventured outside again to find my mate exiting another cubicle where he had also been throwing up. The provost sergeant put a hand on each of our shoulders. For once he didn't shout and I had the feeling that he sympathised with what he was about to put us through.

"Sorry you had to see that lads. It's never easy the first time. Now I've got to ask you to clean up the mess that this wanker has made, before we get the civvy contractors in to fix the hole in the ceiling." He led us into the cubicle where the kid had blown his brains out. There was blood, snot, gore, brains and bits of bone plastered all over two walls and the ceiling, and a dirty great hole in the ceiling where the round had exited. Luckily, it had gone straight out of the building through an exterior wall on the floor above without hitting anyone else. My guts heaved again at the sight and the smell, but I don't think I had anything else to throw up, though I could taste bile in my mouth.

"The cleaning kit's in the cupboard there. I really am sorry about this; it's just your bad luck. Someone has to do it."

"Yeah, then why don't *you* do it, you fucking bastard?" Was what went through my mind. Not that it did any good, of course. We ended up scraping and scrubbing all the shit off the walls where most of it had congealed into sticky lumps, and it took us about three or four hours. We felt sick the whole time, but we gritted our teeth and got on with the job. I can't say that we left the cubicle in pristine condition after we had finished, but at least most of it had been cleaned up. If you don't count the bloody great hole in the ceiling, it was pretty hard to imagine that someone had ended their young life there in such a violent way only a few hours before.

I couldn't get the sight of that mostly headless body out of my mind for the next few days and nights. I didn't sleep well, couldn't concentrate on my training, and didn't eat much. It was just my bad luck that I decided to go out on the piss the following weekend and drown my sorrows in lager.

There was a small group of us and we drank ourselves stupid in a succession of pubs before climbing into a couple of taxis to take us back to the Barracks. Back at the main gate we staggered past the guardroom, intent on not bothering to sign in. If we had to go in front of the regimental police to sign the book in the guardroom we were bound to get some grief because we were in a right state. Across the road from the guardroom was the sergeant's mess, and in front of it was a car park. I was about as pissed as you can get and still manage to stand and I was dying to go for a pee after the half hour journey from Folkestone. Not really understanding what I was doing, I sort of staggered across the road into the car park, found a large imposing car, unzipped my jeans and began to pee onto the wheel arch. I was still standing there pissing when I heard this angry shout, and looking around I saw this huge figure marching quickly across the road towards me from the guardroom. It was the provost sergeant, but I was in such a state that I didn't really care; I just kept on pissing on the car.

"You! Yes you, you little fucker! That's the Regimental Sergeant Major's car you're pissing on! He'll have your guts for fucking garters!" and with that I was grabbed by the collar and frog-marched back across the road. That was it: I was nicked.

I spent the rest of the night sleeping it off in a cell. In the morning I was brutally awoken about 5am by a regimental policeman slamming open the cell door, and I was half pushed, half dragged out onto the road. I reckon I was still half-cut as I couldn't seem to make my legs and arms work in co-ordination as I was double-marched around the barracks a few times by a pair of sadistic lance corporals. In the end I was doubled back around to the mess where I was taken to the front of the queue of waiting juniors to be given a plate of greasy sausages, eggs, beans and tomatoes. I was very nearly sick, but I still managed to get some of it down my neck. I also managed a quick cup of tea before being marched back to the guardroom. The regimental policemen weren't allowed to double (run) any soldier just after he'd eaten, as there had been cases of soldiers having heart attacks when this was done to them in the past. But they were allowed to quick-march you as fast as they liked, and I remember this bloody Scottish regimental policeman screaming into my ear:

"Left, right, left, right, left, right, left!" With the tempo getting faster all of the time until my legs and arms were a blur. "Mark time! (marching on the spot) Left, right, left, right, left, right, left! Forward!" Around and around the barracks we went, with the regimental policeman screaming at me, and me marching like a man possessed, arms and legs moving faster and faster. Eventually I was marched back to the guardroom and into my cell, where they stood at the door for a few minutes while I marked time. Then at last they dismissed me, though I wasn't allowed to sit down or lean against the bed or the wall - no matter how much time you spent in the guardroom, you were never allowed to sit or lie down until 'lights out' in the evening. Everything had to be done standing up. Bloody hell, but I was knackered. My legs, particularly my calves, felt like they were on fire and the whole of my body was shaking from fatigue and the last of the 'too much to drink the night-before' feeling. But worse was to come. At 9am I was doubled down to Arnhem Company on company commander's 'orders'. This time I was marched down by the RSM, who was not in a good mood at all.

The upshot of all this was that I had badly damaged any immediate army career prospects. The company commander busted me back down to junior leader, so I lost the sergeant's stripes that I had worked so hard to get. I also lost two weeks pay and was detained for 14 days in the guardroom. The company commander kept telling me how disappointed he was in my behaviour and how I could have done really well in the regular army, except that now I had put a black mark on my record, which was bound to affect my future. I was feeling pretty bloody down and despondent. To top it all, when I was dismissed by the

38

company commander the RSM grabbed me by the neck and whispered in my ear:

"You disrespectful little shit! I'm going to make the next 14 days pure hell for you!" and with that he personally double-marched me around the camp for an hour or so before dropping me off at the guardroom. "I'll be back to sort you out later!" He screamed at me as I was pushed into a cell by a grinning regimental policeman. Jesus was I in the shit now!

Despite my fears, 'Jankers' (detention) was tough, but not a lot harder than basic training had been, so I didn't suffer too badly. I was really looking forward to getting out of the guardroom and back to my mates in the platoon though. Then, on my last day in detention, I had an unannounced visit.

There I was; in my cell and polishing my boots, when the door eased open and in walked a bloke in a civilian suit. He had an offer that, considering my present predicament, I would have found hard to turn down. It was an offer that any young soldier, with his head full of 'death or glory', wanting to fight for his Queen and Country, would have jumped at. Which just goes to show how stupid young men can be.

His name, or so he said, was Harry. No surname was forthcoming. He worked as an agent for the British Secret Intelligence Service (the SIS), otherwise known as MI6 or 'the firm'. He was looking for a young soldier, preferably a very good young soldier, to assist the SIS in gaining intelligence about a potential threat to the national security of the United Kingdom. He had read my personnel file and apart from the little bit of trouble that had landed me in the guardroom, it appeared that my reports were glowing. Was I interested?

Of course I was; what soldier wouldn't be – this sounded like James Bond stuff!

Okay, good, then I would be required to travel to a house in Dorset when I was released from the guardroom, where I would be fully briefed and prepared. I was not to talk to anyone, including family or close friends about this visit, what had been said and what was to happen after. He would have a rail warrant passed on to me before I was released. Thank you and goodbye. That was it, a five minute talk and I'd committed myself to God knows what for God knows how long. Did I feel any trepidation? Of course not. All I felt was a glow of patriotism and pride that I had been chosen. It didn't occur to me that my life would be in danger, and even if it had, well, that's what I'd joined the army for, wasn't it - to risk my life for my country?

I didn't wonder why the SIS had chosen such a young man for a job; after all I was only 16 years of age. It wasn't until much later that I realised that my young age was a positive advantage in the posting that I had volunteered for.

Harry was true to his word. I received the rail warrant on the day of my release. I went back to my company barracks, packed my civilian clothes and buggered off out of camp, heading towards the railway station at Folkestone. Luckily, the company had been out of barracks on a training exercise, so I didn't have to excuse myself to anyone. I also walked out of camp the back way through some woods, rather than try to bullshit my way out of the main gate.

About four hours and a couple of changes of train later, I exited the train at a small railway station in Dorset, wondering how the hell I was going to get to my destination, as I didn't have any cash, and didn't even know where the bloody place was. I needn't have worried as a bloke was waiting for me and gave me a lift in a dark green Land Rover. He didn't say a word on the journey and wasn't exactly friendly either, so when we finally arrived at a small country house tucked away in some woodland, I was as nervous as a little boy who's nicked the last sweetie out of the jar.

As it was, I needn't have worried, as everything went smoothly and I fitted right in. I was shown to my room and then attended a briefing with Harry and a full colonel from the Intelligence Corps. I was briefed on the background to the mission and what my role would be. Then after a tea break, I was filled in on how I was to fulfil my role. That first night I was so excited by what I had been told that I could hardly sleep. The next day my training began.

SIX

Three months later I found myself in southern Africa. My name was now Danny Brown. My cover story was that I was an ex-paratrooper from the 2nd Battalion, the Parachute Regiment, who had recently served a tour in Northern Ireland. As a result of a mate being shot and not being able to return fire against his killer, because of the stupid 'Rules of Engagement' for British soldiers serving across the water, I had become disillusioned and had bought myself out of the British Army. Another mate had supposedly written to me and told me how good it was out in Rhodesia, so I had spent my last cash on getting down to London for a meeting with a clandestine recruiting agency for the Rhodesian Army in a posh hotel room. I had passed their tests, been issued with a Rhodesian passport and a plane ticket to Johannesburg in South Africa. After flying out and arriving in Joburg, I had been picked up, along with a bunch of other recruits from England, and driven north across the border into Rhodesia.

The last three months had been hectic. I had been given my cover story and had to learn it inside out. This included where I was born and had lived, who my family and friends were, where I had gone to school, the names of my teachers, and finally where I had served, and with whom, in the British Army. This required a lot of reading, site visits to the places in which I had 'grown up', and hours upon hours of being questioned about my cover story by Harry and others. Once I'd become proficient enough in my cover, I'd been shipped out to attend the 'All Arms Preparachute Selection' course at Catterick in North Yorkshire, known to everyone as 'P (Pegasus) Company'.

This was a bastard of a course attended by volunteers from across the British Army who wanted to serve with the airborne forces. The course lasted three and a half weeks and was pure physical torture. I had thought that I was fit before, but the P Company course showed me just how wrong I had been. All through the course we were badgered, 'beasted', bullied, pushed, encouraged, helped and supported by a directing staff of some of the fittest non-commissioned officers in the British Army, who were all Para's of course. These guys didn't just run along at the side of us shouting their heads off (though they did this too). They also carried the same weight as us on their backs and went through the same pain; only they did it for course after course after course.

After completing the P Company course we went down to Brize Norton in Oxfordshire for the four week-long Royal Air Force Basic Parachute Course. This was a training course run by the static-line training squadron of the RAF parachute training school. Compared to P Company, the basic parachute course was a doddle; though jumping out of a plane is not as simple as it sounds. One part of this course that I distinctly remember was my very first parachute descent. This was an 800 feet jump from a platform suspended beneath a barrage balloon at a place called RAF Weston-on-the-Green, in Oxfordshire. Jumping from a balloon is a lot harder than jumping from an aircraft; it's very quiet when you're up there and you can see the ground a long way beneath you. Just launching yourself out into empty space takes a lot of nerve and a lot of guys fail on this part of the course even when they can jump satisfactorily from a plane. I was as nervous as hell and it didn't help that the Parachute Jump Instructor had a bit of a sick sense of humour:

"Do you see that cemetery over there?" He said to me just as I was about to do the leap of faith from the balloon, pointing across the flat landscape to the graveyard of the nearby village with a grin on his face. "That's where we bury all the guys whose chutes fail." I thanked him profusely for that bit of enlightening information, closed my eyes, and with a shout of "Geronimo!" I jumped.

After passing this course I got to wear the coveted maroon-coloured beret, the winged cap badge of the Parachute Regiment and my parachute wings. My cover was now complete.

However, my training was not over. The next stage of training was held at Weingarten in Germany, at the International Long Range Reconnaissance Patrol School. Here I was taught, amongst other things, about travelling along agent pipe-lines, using dead-letter drops, unarmed combat, the stages of capture, escape and evasion, battlefield survival and resistance to interrogation. When I had completed all of this training, I was as ready as I could ever be to operate as an undercover SIS agent in the Rhodesian Army.

Why Rhodesia though? What had this southern African country ever done to make it a threat to the UK? The politicians will tell you that the UK didn't support Rhodesia because they were a country ruled by a white minority and were therefore racist and not democratic. However the truth is that the African National Congress was putting pressure on the British government to help them win the war in Rhodesia, by threatening to seize and nationalise all UK assets in the copper belt. I'm not an economist but I would guess that those assets were worth something in the region of several hundred million pounds, if not billions. It always comes down to money in the end; money is God.

Rhodesia had been a former land-locked British colony in central southern Africa. It was bordered by South Africa to the south; Botswana to the southwest; Zambia to the northwest and Mozambique to the east. In size it was only about one and a half times the area of the UK but had a population of less than seven million, of which less than 5% were of European, or white origin. The Rhodesian white minority government had seriously pissed off the British when they had declared their country independent from British rule in 1965 in what became known as the 'Unilateral Declaration of Independence'. British Prime Minister Harold Wilson was so pissed off that it was rumoured he had considered sending in the Parachute Regiment to regain control of the colony. However, none of this had anything to do with me or my mission in Rhodesia. I was there for one reason only. My mission was to infiltrate the Rhodesian Army, work my way up as high as I could within its ranks and to supply tactical and strategic information back to my case officer, Harry. I have no doubt that I wasn't the only British agent who had infiltrated the Rhodesian armed forces. There must have been quite a few of us for it to be worthwhile for Harry to be posted out there full time. But as it turned out I do believe that I ended up as one of the most important and I did this within the context of the 'Bush War'.

Following the unilateral declaration of independence, in the 1960s and 1970s black insurgents had already represented a minor threat to Rhodesia. Until 1972 though, containing the insurgency was little more than a police activity. The real terrorist insurgency began with a series of scattered attacks on isolated white-owned farms. These attacks led to a lengthy armed campaign by ZANLA, the military wing of the Zimbabwe African National Union (ZANU), and ZIPRA, the military wing of the Zimbabwe African People's Union (ZAPU), against the Rhodesian government. This campaign became known as the 'Bush War' by the white Rhodesians and as the 'Second Chimurenga' (or rebellion) by the supporters of the guerrillas.

When I joined the Rhodesian Army as a trained soldier this bush war was reaching its peak. At this point, ZANU's alliance with FRELIMO (the Mozambique Liberation Front) and the long, porous border between Mozambique and eastern Rhodesia enabled large-scale infiltration into Rhodesia by ZANLA guerrillas. The governments of Zambia and Botswana allowed ZIPRA guerrillas to set up bases in their countries and the guerrillas began to launch operations deep inside Rhodesia, mainly attacking soft targets such as roads, railways, economic targets and isolated security force positions. From this time on, the white Rhodesian population began to take more serious casualties, leaving few white families untouched by the bush war. Rhodesia's armed forces included about 25,000 regular troops and police and the conscription of all white males over the age of 16 was in force. Volunteers from overseas were recruited to help in the fight, coming from a variety of European countries including Britain, Belgium, The Netherlands and Germany, and included Vietnam War veterans from the United States and Australia who had found it difficult to re-adjust to civilian life in their own countries. Most of us were young guys, aged from 17 through to 19, and we fitted right in with the young Rhodesian conscripts.

SEVEN

This was the war that I stepped into at a little over 17 years of age, though Danny Brown's papers showed me to be closer to 19. For the first couple of weeks I was based at Cranborne Barracks, just outside Salisbury.

I had opted to join 3 Commando of the 1st Battalion Rhodesian Light Infantry as a trooper or 'troopie' as they were known. This was an all-white regular airborne commando regiment and 3 Commando was where a lot of the foreign volunteers ended up. Because I had just left the British Army and was a fully trained soldier and paratrooper, all that I needed to fit into the Rhodesian Army was a short acclimatisation period to adjust to their slightly different organisation. Overall, the organisation of the Rhodesian Army was very similar to the British Army, which wasn't that surprising as they had initially been organised and trained by the Brits.

Acclimatisation started from day one in Rhodesia and I soon got a taste of how the bush war was being run. During my first week in the country we patrolled out in the bush, getting used to carrying our new equipment and weapons, and learning the tactics that were employed there. Every day for a week my patrol had passed a large bungalow on the edge of a town where an English couple lived, and every day we had been invited in for a cup of tea. Most days we had been too occupied to accept the offer, but eventually the sergeant leading the patrol had succumbed to the temptation.

So as not to dirty their carpets we all traipsed into the large fenced garden at the rear, removed our webbing and sat down in an assortment of plastic garden chairs while the woman of the house brewed the tea and served us. The English couple were in their mid-fifties and had immigrated to Rhodesia 18 months previously, when the guy had got a job as a supervisor in a local factory. They had a pleasant English-style garden with a large lawn and borders of bright flowers around the edges, and it was obviously well-tended by the couple. I couldn't help noticing though, that there was a distinctly unpleasant odour around the place, and it was obvious from the grimaces on the faces of some of my fellow squaddies, that I wasn't the only one who found it a bit nasty. After about 20 minutes of sitting there the patrol leader finally broached the subject of the pong with the couple. They replied that it had started a few days ago and was getting stronger all of the time, but they didn't know what its origin was as they'd looked around the garden and couldn't find anything wrong. One of the guys suggested that it might be a snake that had got caught in the garden fence and died, as they always gave off a hell of a stink when they were dead. I volunteered with a couple of other guys to search around and see if we could find it, but after ten minutes or so it was pretty obvious that there were no snakes caught in the fence and that the smell was actually emanating from a covered man-hole at the end of the garden. A pal and I lifted up the metal cover but the drain beneath it was quite narrow and very deep, so we couldn't actually see anything, though the stink coming from it was atrocious. Stupidly, and without a second thought, I lay on my belly and thrust my arm down the hole. It was a stupid thing to do because this was Africa, and the one thing that you soon learn not to do is to stick your bloody hand into a hole. There could be a snake or a scorpion or any number of other horrible and dangerous things down a hole. However, on this occasion I sort of got lucky. By stretching down into the dark, narrow confines of the drain I first of

48

all felt a stick with my fingertips. It was a round stick, I'd guess about an inch or so in diameter, and strangely it was stuck upright in the middle of the drain and was held very firmly by something. When I grabbed hold of it and tried to shake it lose, I found that I could only move it a few millimetres or so to each side and it was so firmly embedded that I couldn't pull it out. I let go of the stick and stretched down even further, wriggling my head and shoulders down into the hole. My fingertips brushed against something quite wiry so I struggled even further into the hole, almost gagging on the powerful stench of something that was definitely dead. I managed to grab hold of a small amount of the wiry stuff and gave it a sharp tug. At first it resisted my pulling, but then all of a sudden and with a horrible squelching sound something gave way and I pushed myself up, holding tightly onto the piece of whatever was in there.

When I got it out into the light, for a second or two I couldn't quite figure out what the hell it was, and then I knew. I was holding a piece of rotten human scalp in my hand. I flung it down in disgust and scrambled away from the hole where I commenced to throw up my guts all over the well-tended lawn.

To cut a long story short, the Rhodesian police were called out and they dragged the dead body of a young black kid out of the drain. The coppers told us a few days later that the victim had been virtually skinned alive, except for his head, which was left untouched, presumably so that he could be identified (which was what the terrorists wanted). Still alive he had then been forced down into the drain, feet first. His killers had then broken his jaw and forced a long pointed stake into his mouth, down his throat and gullet, and out of his asshole. This bit killed him of course. The coppers managed to identify the kid as a police informer from the local village. They reckoned he was about 12 or 13 years old and had been tortured and killed in this particularly brutal way either by terrorists or by terrorist sympathisers as a warning to other would-be police informers. The body had been shoved down the English couple's drain as a separate warning to them. The man and his wife apparently got the point because they moved back to England about a week later, and I don't blame them at all. I almost packed up and buggered off myself. This was only the second dead person I'd ever seen and it was a harsh introduction into how this war was being fought, with both sides committing atrocities against the other. This was not how I had imagined a war to be; there were no brave display of flags and trumpets; no courageous charges against overwhelming odds; no heroes and no villains. This was a sickening, brutal and frightening war against an enemy that you couldn't, for the most part, identify.

EIGHT

After acclimatisation I was posted to my Commando, which was deployed on 'Fire Force' duty at a base called Grand Reef in north-eastern Rhodesia. My first tour of duty lasted six weeks, after which I had twelve days rest and recuperation back at Cranborne Barracks. In total I was deployed on Fire Force for three tours.

Fire Force was the Rhodesian equivalent of the British Army's 'Quick Reaction Force', intended to arrive on the scene of terrorist activity as quickly as possible, seek them out and destroy them. We were pretty busy, with three or four deployments and enemy contacts daily. I parachuted into action eleven times, one after the other during one single 24 hour period in the course of my third tour, each time being shot at and shooting back. In total I reckon that I did about 450 parachute jumps during this period, the vast majority of them from between 400 and 600 feet, which is bloody low (about 120-200m above ground level). A lot of the time I landed in small trees (as we all did) which wasn't so bad, but occasionally I'd come a cropper by getting entangled in a big tree, though luckily I was never hurt so badly as not to be able to carry on.

While I served with them, 3 Commando were based at the airfield at Grand Reef, and contained around 70 men. On each Fire Force deployment we usually had 32 men plus the commander in the first wave, followed when needed by a second wave of similar size. The first wave was supported by four helicopters, one DC-3 Dakota aircraft that we called the 'Dak' or 'ParaDak', and a Cessna

Skymaster light aircraft, known as a 'Lynx'. The helicopters were mainly old French Alouette Mk IIIs, though Fire Force did get a few American Bell UH-1s (Huey's) later on in the war. One of the choppers was armed with a 20mm cannon and carried the commander who was usually the officer commanding the Commando, and whose call-sign was 'three-nine'. This chopper was called the 'K-car'. The other three helicopters were known as 'G-cars', and they were armed with a twin Browning .303 machine gun each. The G-cars each carried a 'stop' of four soldiers in addition to their crew. Each stop had a junior or senior non-commissioned officer in charge, two troopies and a machine gunner. The Lynx light aircraft was armed with two machine-guns and normally also had two 30 mm rocket pods and two small *frantans*, or napalm bombs tucked under its wings. In this way three 'stops' of four men each was carried by the G-cars and five 'stops' of paratroopers were carried by the ParaDak.

Most of the time there were only three Fire Forces operating at any one time throughout the whole country. This meant that each of them had responsibility for many thousands of square miles. Sightings of the enemy within the Fire Force zone could be made by anybody, whether they were civilians (often white farmers) policemen, or other regular army units, like the Selous Scouts, who often set up observation posts (OPs) in areas where terrorists were thought to be operating. Sightings could be a small terrorist column moving through the bush or may have been reported during or after a terrorist incident (such as an attack on a police post or a farm house, or a terrorist ambush on a road). When a sighting was reported, a siren sounded in the base and the troops of the first wave would rush to their helicopters. If they were paratroopers they would first hurry to the tent where their equipment and parachutes were held and get their kit on with help from the dispatchers. The troops of the second wave, or the 'land-tail' as they were known, would normally rush to their trucks.

The tactics we employed once we hit the ground were much the same as in a pheasant shoot. Some of the stops would be set down or would parachute into positions that would cover the enemy retreat, such as along a *donga* (a dry riverbed) flanked with heavy vegetation. The rest of the stops would conduct a 'sweep' in an extended line across country, with the aim of pushing the terrorists onto the guns of the others, with the circling Lynx, K-car and G-cars giving valued air support to the ground element, and three-nine directing the operation from his seat in the K-car. These tactics worked remarkably well and it was seldom that any of the enemy escaped us to fight another day.

If you were in on the sweep stage of an operation this usually meant that you would be moving forward in extended line and were spaced apart according to the terrain. Often the bush was so dense (known as *Jesse*) that you would lose sight of your comrades to each side of you. All you could do was move slowly forward with your rifle ready to fire, observing your line of sight ahead, which was often limited to only a few metres by the vegetation. When we suspected that the enemy were close we would edge forward inch by inch with our safety catches off and fingers on triggers. When we finally encountered the enemy it would usually be over in just a few seconds of rapid gunfire, though sometimes we had to use grenades to flush the bastards out of cover. Most of the terrorists were killed outright and it wasn't often that we managed to take any prisoners, even though they could be valuable to the intelligence guys. Generally it just wasn't possible to take any prisoners in such close terrain as often you would not see the terrorist until you were just feet from him, and then it was either him or you; the quick and the dead.

If your stop was placed in a position intended to intercept fleeing terrorists you could often expect a wait of several hours before sighting them, though again it would all be over within a few seconds when you did.

After a contact with the enemy it was usually down to the guys on land-tail to clear up. This would involve putting the dead bodies of the terrorists into the choppers or the ground vehicles for transportation back to base. Stuffing a number of dead bodies into an Allouette chopper was never easy, as they weren't that big. Often you'd have to break some arms and legs to get them all in.

Fire Force was my first taste of combat and to be honest none of the contacts stand out that well in my memory. There were so many of them and Fire Force was so intense at times that they have sort of all assimilated into one. However I do remember the rollercoaster of emotions that I went through on each mission. I was nervous and twitchy waiting for a call-out and damn right scared shitless in the plane or chopper. I felt the extreme high of the adrenaline buzz just before going in, was cool and sharp when we actually hit the ground, and then was as relieved as fuck when I got back to base in one piece. Initially I tried to hide my fear from the other guys on the flights out by pretending to fall asleep. I knew that everyone else was as scared as me. You would have had to be stupid not to be, but it wasn't the thing to show it to the others. Eventually this became a habit with me and I actually did fall asleep every time we shipped out. It became a joke amongst my mates that one of them would have to kick me awake just before we went in and I became a legend in my own lunchtime because of this coolness that I showed before combat.

The first person that I killed was a member of ZANLA; a terrorist. Although I didn't hesitate when it came to killing him, the aftermath for me was quite traumatic. For nights after I would wake up sweating, having had nightmares about the dirty deed. I can still see his face very, very clearly in my mind. He was turning towards me at the moment I shot him and I remember his profile very well. After this first one, subsequent killings became easier. Many of them I don't even remember now. By my real eighteenth birthday I had killed at least 48 terrorists, and I was proud of the fact.

During my third tour on Fire Force I was awarded a 'Military Forces Commendation' (equivalent to a 'Mention in Dispatches' in the British Army) for bravery during one of my ops when I saved the life of one of my mates. I was subsequently promoted to lance-corporal and put in charge of a stop. I'd begun my climb upwards to a point where I could be of use to my own country, and had already proved my usefulness as a soldier to the country I was busily fighting for under another name. Danny Brown was doing okay.

NINE

During the remainder of my time in the Rhodesian Light Infantry I was active on other operations and did not get posted back to Fire Force. Most of the time these other operations involved patrolling in the bush, not only within the borders of Rhodesia, but also occasionally in neighbouring Zambia and Mozambique. Bush patrols were bloody hard work as we usually spent between five and ten days (sometimes much longer) out in the bush, before returning to base to resupply with ammo and food. Often as not, we'd then be sent right back out again and the patrols could last anything from four to six weeks, with returns to resupply. We carried all of the essentials to keep us alive on our backs, except for water which we had to constantly search for as we could only carry a maximum of three water bottles each. Our kit weighed around 100lbs, but you've got to add to this the weight of your personal weapon and possibly the patrol radio if you were unlucky enough to be a signaller (perhaps another 24lbs in total).

Although patrols were varied and we could end up doing basically anything from setting up OPs and 'listening patrols' through to lying-up in ambush positions along tracks, they were never as action-filled nor as exciting as being posted on Fire Force. I found them personally very frustrating because I wasn't in a position to do my real job of getting good Intel back to my SIS case officer. Thus I jumped at the chance of carrying out a raid against a ZANLA training camp in Mozambique when it came up. The 'external', as we called such raids, was to involve a

56

Commando from Rhodesian Light Infantry (3 Commando) and two troops from C Squadron, Rhodesian Special Air Service Regiment (SAS), supported by two mortar troops from the Rhodesian Light Infantry. The target was a training camp located on two parallel ridge lines about 50 miles from the Rhodesian border, well inside bandit country. It had been identified by the Rhodesian SAS as a ZANLA camp supported by FRELIMO troops (who by then had become the Mozambique regular army). We were given the warning order just a few days before the operation and frantically got our kit together in readiness. I had been promoted to full corporal by this time, and as my troop didn't have an officer (our last one had been injured on a jump and hadn't been replaced yet), this meant that I was second-in-command of our troop for the attack.

Normally an external against a guerrilla camp would involve much the same tactics as a Fire Force operation, though on a much larger scale of course. There would be a 'vertical envelopment' of the camp by paratroops on one side, heliborne troops on the second, K-cars and G-cars on the third, and Lynx gunships on the fourth. However, this camp was in a difficult position as it ran for miles along two parallel ridges. The battle orders called for 3 Commando to assault one end of one ridge and then fight our way along it, supported by our mortar teams, G-cars and Lynx's, while the SAS troops did the same on the other ridge and with similar support. There would also be stop groups out to mop up any terrorists fleeing from the action.

We set out in the ParaDaks well after dark and I got my normal short snooze before being rudely awoken by a kick in the ribs a few minutes before we jumped. The drop zone was a few miles from our 'Forming up Position' at the southern end of the ridges, and we marched through a night that was totally black, so dark that you couldn't see your hand before your face, and also very hot and sweaty as it was high summer. About 90 minutes after landing we reached the forming up position and got into our assault pattern. Before we began our own attack, a few tons of bombs were dropped by Canberra and Hunter ground attack aircraft onto the target ridges, waking the guerrilla camp up to a night of terror and signalling our advance.

Things went well at first as resistance was fairly light on the ridge's lower slopes, but as we moved up higher the enemy became thicker on the ground. Normally the ZANLA guys would have legged it at the first sign of trouble, but with the regular FRELIMO troops backing them up, it soon turned into a full-scale battle. Our rate of advance slowed down as we were forced to weed out individual groups of fighters dug in behind piles of rocks on the slopes. Because it was still dark, accurate support was difficult to get from the G-cars, and for some reason we weren't getting any support from our mortar teams. It turned out later that they had forgotten their range cards and therefore they had sat on their arses all night drinking tea and watching us get fucked without giving us any supporting mortar fire. Increasingly the resistance became fiercer and our advance slowed down to a crawl. When daylight finally arrived it was hardly any better than fighting in the dark because the battle had stirred up huge great clouds of gritty dust that were whirled around by the brisk wind, explosions and choppers making visibility very poor. By now the advance was absolute chaos. Our formations had lost their cohesion and the battle turned into a right old mess. Huge clumps of rocks and boulders the size of houses provided ideal cover for the FRELIMO and ZANLA guys to hide behind, while they kept us pinned down with fire. The explosions of hand grenades and the constant crack of discharging firearms made it impossible to hear shouted orders. It was like a scene out of Hell. All we could do was to keep constantly and aggressively moving forward in short spurts, keeping our weapons pointing forward and shooting the hell out of anything that moved in front of us. You were never sure whether you would get supporting fire from your mates because of the swirling dust that would suddenly hide everything from sight, and sometimes you couldn't even be sure that your mates were still there, as you couldn't see anything around you except for a few square feet of dusty, rocky soil. It was during this point of the battle that I was hit. Me and 'Rusty', one of the best friends I had made in the troop, had found each other in the dust and were running forward into the cover of a bloody great rock in front of us. As we spurted forward some bugger poked his head up from behind the rock and sprayed a burst of automatic fire into us from an AK47 and we both went down. I felt as though someone had kicked me in the lower stomach though surprisingly there was no pain at this point. When I looked down all I could see was an expanding patch of blood around my groin. Rusty got it much worse than me. Three rounds had hit him in his left upper thigh and basically ripped his leg off. I ignored the enemy, who was still poking his head up and firing down on us, and crawled over to Rusty. He was practically unconscious so I tried to find the pressure point in his groin to stop the bleeding, but this was impossible as the top of his leg was in such a mess. Instead I grabbed the field dressing from his webbing and slapped it onto his wound. The blood was pissing out and quickly filled up the dressing so I used my own field dressing and put it on top of his. While this one filled up the blood flow showing no sign of abating, so I used Rusty's A63 field radio (he was the troop signaller) to call for a medivac (medical evacuation) from one of the G-cars. It was a wasted effort because neither they nor I knew our precise location on the battlefield. I couldn't even hear if a G-car was nearby through the noise of the shooting. I threw down the handset in disgust and whipped out a shell dressing from my webbing and wrapped it on top of the other two. This is a bigger dressing that can soak up two pints of blood. It soon filled up and I had no more dressings left. I radioed for medivac again and this time threw down a red smoke grenade to try and mark my position as well as firing off a couple of mini-flares to try and grab the attention of the chopper pilots. Meanwhile the bastard behind the rock kept firing at us and I could see spurts of dust as the rounds hit the ground around us. This seriously pissed me off. As there was nothing else I could do to help Rusty I gathered myself to run forward and chuck a grenade at the bastard. When I tried to get up my legs collapsed underneath me and that was when the first of the pain from my wound started to hit me (and it fucking hurt). I ripped the tape from the handles of the last two high-explosive grenades that I had left (I'd started out with about a dozen) and started crawling towards the rock. All the time the bastard kept sticking his head up and firing at me, so I used whatever cover I could such as small rocks and dips as I kept crawling forward, though they didn't help that much. Eventually I considered that I was close enough, rolled onto my left side, pulled the pin from the first grenade and lobbed it over the rock, immediately following it with the second. There were two distinct 'crumps' as they went off, and thankfully the bastard didn't stick his head up again. I crawled back to Rusty and felt the 'whumph' 'whumph' of rotor blades as a G-car came in to pick us up, attracted by my smoke and flares. It was too late for Rusty though, he was already dead and there was a big patch of blood-red sand around his body.

The operation was a bit of a lemon as most of the guerrillas got away in the confusion, but we did a good job of destroying the camp's infrastructure. I was shifted to an infirmary by chopper, where they sedated me heavily. I stayed there for the next three weeks. I got another Military Forces Commendation for the action, and Rusty got a military funeral.

Rusty had got his nickname because of his bright ginger hair. He was forever being got at by the Commando's non-commissioned officers for having a 'rusty' head, and the name sort of stuck. He was about the same age as me and a good bloke and mate.

TEN

Strangely, it was while I was laid up in the infirmary in Wankie National Park, that my mission to Rhodesia really began to come together. My name and growing reputation must have got around to the right people because I was visited by an officer from the Rhodesian Special Forces regiment; the Selous Scouts. He suggested that I apply for the scouts and told me that they had a selection course for the regiment coming up in a couple of months. Plenty of time for me to get fit again after my wound had healed. I didn't want to sound too eager so I thanked him and told him that I would give it some serious consideration. Inside I was elated as the Selous Scouts were involved in most of the external raids going into Zambia, Mozambique, and even occasionally into Botswana. Being involved with these raids would give me some great Intel to feed to Harry and the firm.

I was in a great deal of pain during my three weeks stay in the infirmary, and was restrained in bed to stop me from tearing off my dressings. There were two white South African doctors at the infirmary and they did a ward round every morning. This pair had a sick sense of humour. At this stage I didn't know what damage had been done to my groin and this pair of buggers thought it was great fun to keep me in the dark as to whether I'd lost any of my 'family jewels'. They would even draw a curtain across my midriff when they changed my dressings so that I couldn't see the damage that had been done. They had a great laugh at my expense.

Eventually I found out from a black African nurse that the bullet had entered to one side of my pride and joy, ripping open my bladder and lodging against a bone inside. It was a simple operation to remove it. It appeared that the round must have been 'spent' (losing a lot of its power), probably after ricocheting from a rock, because it had not gone all the way through me. If it had then I would have been 'shitting from two assholes' as the doctors had joked on several occasions. I was immensely relieved to find out that all of my bits would still work.

After three weeks I had recovered enough to be sent back to my unit on 'light duties'. The morning that I packed up my kit in preparation for leaving I asked the same nurse where I might find the two doctors to say thank you. She pointed out of the window to a bungalow set to one side of the infirmary compound and told me that they would probably have retired there, to their quarters, for a siesta. I thanked her for all her help, picked up my kit and walked out. I didn't go straight to their quarters though. First I went to the gatehouse, where I picked up a pick-axe handle. You can always find pick-axe handles in these places as they are used as a form of non-lethal defence against unfriendly visitors. The white guy on the gate asked me what I wanted it for but I told him not to worry, I'd bring it back in fifteen minutes or so. Then I went to say my goodbyes to that pair of bastards.

The day after I got back to the Rhodesian Light Infantry I left a message for Harry in my dead letter box, explaining about the visit from the Selous Scout's officer and his invitation to try for selection for the regiment. When I checked the dead-letter box again a week later, Harry had replied that this was very good news and that I should go for it. Meanwhile, I had been feted by my mates in the Rhodesian Light Infantry as a hero for what I had tried to do for Rusty while under fire, so it was no surprise when I was told that I had been promoted to sergeant. This initiated a good piss-up as I was welcomed back into the regiment. I didn't feel bad about what I was doing out there. It's hard to explain; but I wasn't doing anything that would get any of my new mates killed. I made sure that any Intel on our operations that I fed back to Harry, did not include too many details about the operation itself, just the bare essentials such as the date, time and place. I had talked this over with Harry on numerous occasions before I came out to Africa. He wasn't interested in the day-to-day stuff that we did out in the bush, not beforehand anyway, though he was always glad to receive news of how the army were coping with the bush war. It was understood that what he really wanted was to get prior intelligence about attempts to kill Robert Mugabe and Joshua Nkomo, the two leaders of the rebels. He didn't tell me as such, but it didn't take a brain surgeon to guess that these two would be informed about any planned attempts on their lives by the British government. It made sense for the British to make friends with these characters and pile up a few favours owed to us in case they ever came into power in the future, and I was happy to participate in that.

However, in order for me to gain this pre-operational information, I would have to move up higher in the echelons of the army. Getting into a Special Forces regiment like the Selous Scouts was the ideal way to do this, so I started work on getting my fitness back after lying on my back for three weeks in an infirmary bed.

I started gently as I didn't want my wound to open again. Just short marches at first, with light kit, gradually building up both the speed and distance, and then getting back into running. All of this was interspersed with circuit training, swimming, gym work, and anything else that I could think of to increase my strength, pace and stamina. I applied for the selection course and even though our medical officer didn't believe that I could get back up to battle fitness in the time that I had; I just worked at it and worked at it until I reckoned that I was about 90% ready. I also managed to fit in a couple of standard Rhodesian Army training courses on waterman-ship (river-crossings, boat-handling etc.) and demolitions (explosives) during this period to build up my skills base. Nothing in my past soldiering career could have prepared me fully for the selection course for the Selous Scouts though. It was one hell of a bastard, making basic training back in the UK and even Pegasus Company look like a picnic for the girl guides.

I've done a lot of courses in my time, most of which involved a lot of classroom work and sitting on my arse. Some have been tough, such as the Junior Leaders course and Pegasus Company that I've already mentioned. Others have been very tough; but only two that I can recall have been real bastards; one of which, funnily enough, was the Section Commander's course for the British Army which was a real bitch. The other was the selection course for the Selous Scouts. Somebody with a very sadistic imagination must have thought this one up.

The course lasted for 17 days of pure hell. From the very first moment of arriving at our drop-off point in the bush and having to run the 18 miles to *Wafa Wafa*, the scout's training camp, we were 'beasted' and antagonised by the permanent staff and worked endlessly night and day. The camp itself was just a collection of ragged straw huts surrounded by bush. There were about 60 of us in my cadre, but after only a few days, most of them had dropped out until there were only eight of us left who could stick it. Each day was the same exhausting routine. We'd get up at dawn after only an hour or two of sleep and be put through gut-wrenching physical-fitness training involving runs, circuit training, rifle PT (in the British Army we call this 'pokey drill' – holding a heavy rifle at arm's length while slowly swinging, circling, lifting it etc. - it's designed to build up strength in the arms and shoulders), and playing sports; mainly football and rugby. This would end at about 7am when we would begin training in basic combat skills. There were also long-distance 'tactical' cross-country navigational exercises. Once, or sometimes twice a day we would also have to traverse a bloody nasty aerial assault course, which was designed to build up our confidence at heights and prepare us for parachute training. I remember that the rough hemp ropes on the high obstacles would shred our hands every time that we did the assault course. We'd also complete a two hour hump (a sort of run/march) carrying a heavy sack of sand. Then when darkness fell we started on night training which would last until the early hours. During all this time there was no let-up and no rest periods; we were constantly 'beasted' and kept on the move. The worst of it was that we were issued with no food for the first five days, so we were literally starving at the same time. The first food we saw was on day six when the rotting, stinking maggot-ridden carcase of a baboon (which had been hanging in a tree in the camp during the whole time that we had been there), was dumped at our feet and the head honcho said: "Here's your grub lads, enjoy." We soon learned that you can eat even the most rotten meat if you boil it for long enough, and with no ill-effects. We also learned that maggots dissolve in boiling water, though they do add a certain after-taste to your meat! From this point on we were thrown a rotten carcase every day for our meals, most of them so badly gone that we couldn't even identify what they were. Meanwhile the non-stop physical training went on, along with the punches, kicks and screaming of our instructors. At the very end of the course, when we were just about ready to drop from sheer exhaustion, we were each given a backpack containing over 60 lbs of rocks. We had to paint our class number on the rocks in red paint. Then we carried these packs over a 60 mile endurance march (known as the 'final hump') through the bush, during the scorching heat of the day. The last two hours of the march were done at a forced pace. At the end of the march the rocks were checked and weighed to make sure that you hadn't dumped or changed any. I'm not exaggerating when I say that that march very nearly killed us. It was only pure 'bottle' or guts that kept us going right until the end. After the march we thankfully only had to wait a short while before we were told that we had passed the first phase of selection. After this we had four days off to recover. We'd dreamt about drinking ourselves stupid on cold beer when it was all over, but I think that most of us slept for the better part of our leave, and of course we stuffed ourselves with proper grub! I have never, either before or after, felt so lean and mean as I did when I finished this selection course. Every ounce of fat had been burned off and sweated out. It was a bastard course while it was happening, but afterwards, once I'd slept off my exhaustion, I felt physically and mentally on top of the world, definitely walking with a new bounce in my tread. I also felt a great deal of pride and personal satisfaction that I had not only survived the course but had come through with flying colours.

Next came two weeks of training on combat tracking (man tracking) and bushcraft followed by the 'dark phase', as it was known. This was carried out at a special base that had been built to accurately resemble a guerrilla camp out in the bush. We learned to live, eat, shit, sleep, and talk just like the rebels that we were being trained to kill. Our instructors were genuine rebels who had been 'turned' to fight on our side and they passed a huge amount of up-to-date information on terrorist modes of operation on to us. By the end of this phase we came to think and be like the terrorists in everything we did.

This selection and training regime might sound a little barbaric, but men who fight in a counter-insurgency war need to be very special indeed. We have to be very fit and resourceful to track an elusive enemy over very difficult terrain, and we have to be able to push ourselves far beyond our limits, or at least the limits that we think we have. This brutal training worked very well as the Selous Scouts was one of the most successful undercover counter-insurgency units ever formed anywhere in the world. Every man of this regiment was an expert in bushcraft, tracking, navigation, camouflage and concealment, close-quarter combat, ambushes and a hundred other essential skills. We were also very, very accomplished at the most essential ability of all - often called upon when you were many miles from friendly territory - and that is improvisation.

A week after ending my training, I was on patrol out in the bush and I'd become a fully-fledged Selous Scout. A lot of the guys in the regiment were older than me, most of them in their mid-twenties, but a few were of my age. These were guys that had been born and brought up on farms in the bush and they were known as 'junglies'. Most of them were excellent trackers and spoke the native lingos fluently. I tended to hang out more with these guys than with the older ones and made several really good friends amongst them.

ELEVEN

On my first few 'bush trips' out in the field I was posted as the second-in-command of a troop of scouts, under the command of a veteran scout. This was so that I could learn the trade from someone who was far more experienced than I was, though it wasn't too long before I became competent enough to become a troop leader with my own troop of scouts. My troop normally consisted of about 30 men on these bush trips, all of them black except me, with several of them 'tame' or turned terrorists. We acted as pseudo-guerrilla's, which meant basically that we acted as any group of genuine guerrilla's would act with the aim of infiltrating and destroying the terrorists, and gathering intelligence for the regular units of the army to act upon.

My troop would often be out on a bush trip for several weeks at a time, sometimes for months, living off the land and operating in areas that were officially 'frozen' to other Rhodesian units, so that there wouldn't be a friendly-fire incident. As we often infiltrated rural villages I spent most of the time with my face, hands, arms and legs covered with a black makeup that we dubbed 'black is beautiful' so that, at least at a fair distance, I could pass as a black guerrilla. Most of the time these operations could be very boring indeed. However on a few occasions there was a dash of action equal to anything I'd taken part in with the Rhodesian Light Infantry. One occasion that springs to mind was when we had tracked a guerrilla group into a village out by Lake Kariba. As we slowly entered the village, with me surrounded by my troopies to keep me out of sight as much as possible, we realised that something very bad was going down. An old flat-bed truck was parked in the centre of the village. On the bed of the truck a real terrorist stood shouting and gesticulating at villagers who had been rounded up by his men and who now stood with their heads bowed in front of him. We knew this group of terrorists to be a vicious bunch who had intimidated several other villages in the area into supplying them with food and women, normally by torturing or murdering the village leaders. As we pushed through the crowd around the truck, my guys laughing and shouting greetings to the real terrorists (most of whom appeared to be very drunk), we could see that the group's leader had several villagers held at gun-point and down on their knees on the truck's bed. They were obviously terrified and in fear of their lives. Then the terrorist leader grabbed one old man from amongst the group of hostages and forced him down in front of him. He was shouting and screaming abuse at the villagers and waving a panga (a type of machete) above his head. It was obvious what was going down. The villagers had either let him down in some way or had been refusing to do something that he had ordered them to do, and he was going to punish them by executing the group on the truck right in front of their eyes. I was fearful that he was going to chop off the old man's head at any moment so I took a firm grip on my AK47 and strode through the crowd to the edge of the truck's bed. I stood there looking up just long enough for the terrorist leader to realise that I wasn't just another terrorist and for his own eyes to widen with recognition and fear. Then I aimed my rifle at him, took off the safety catch with my thumb and put a round right through his mouth as he opened it to shout a warning to his men, blowing the back of his head off in a shower of blood, brains, snot and gore. General pandemonium broke loose after this but my guys knew their stuff and each of the real terrorists suddenly found themselves shadowed by one or two troopies who either shot him down dead or grabbed him and tied him up for interrogation later. In a few minutes calm had once again settled onto this little out-of-the-way community, and we were being hugged and thanked and having our hands shaken by everyone there. We settled down in the village for a couple of nights, calling in the Rhodesian Special Branch to take our prisoners away for interrogation, trial and hopefully a long detention in prison. I remember well how grateful these people were and we were treated as guests of honour and given only the best food and places to sleep. It was with real sadness that we eventually left them to get back to our patrol, though I'd hazard a guess that there are a few Zimbabweans who are living in that same village now who can only guess at who their fathers are! My guys were never shy in coming forward to comfort women in their hour of need!

Not all of my operations were bush patrols. On several occasions during my time with the Selous Scouts I joined external missions into both Zambia and Mozambique, to destroy terrorist camps and/or assassinate the terrorist leaders; Robert Mugabe and Joshua NKomo. In the case of the later objective I was able to either warn them off through Harry, or even sabotage the mission in one way or another, thus saving their lives. For example one operation that took place was an attempt to wipe out the commanders of ZIPRA, including NKomo, in Francistown, Botswana. At the time the Soviets had been sending across what were called 'suitcase bombs' to ZIPRA, to be used against targets in Rhodesia. The scouts had intercepted quite a few of these devices over the years and then someone had come up with the bright idea of using them against their former owners. Luckily for NKomo, I had access to the bombs before they were placed in Francistown and managed to sabotage their timers so that they were late in going off. I even managed to defuse one so that it didn't go off at all. Meanwhile, a message to Harry was passed on to NKomo and warned him of the attempt on his and his commander's lives, so that he was well away from the area when the bombs did eventually explode. I also took part in an external raid against NKomo in Lusaka, Zambia. Because of my warning he wasn't in his compound when we struck. The operation wasn't a total wipe-out for the Rhodesians though as we hit the main armoury in the city as we left, blowing it to kingdom come and seriously upsetting the ZIPRA terrorists, as their main supply of arms and ammo went up in the blast. On another occasion, I learned through the grapevine of an external raid to be carried out against a ZANLA training camp in Mozambique where Robert Mugabe was known to be based. This raid was militarily very successful, killing a lot of terrorists, but failed to get Mugabe as he was not there. I hadn't been involved in the raid but again my warning, passed on through Harry and London, had given the ZANLA leader sufficient time to get himself out of the kill zone.

TWELVE

It was during this stage of my deployment that Harry sent me my first direct order. In order to exert political control over the activities of Rhodesian Special Forces, especially their external raids into surrounding countries, the Rhodesians had set up an organisation known as 'Combined Operations' or 'ComOps' for short. This organisation included senior officers from all the Rhodesian armed forces, as well as senior Special Branch officers, intelligence specialists from the Rhodesian Central Intelligence Organisation and of course, several serving politicians. The main aim of ComOps was to look at the political considerations of external raids, political assassinations and other external intelligence-gathering operations in a larger context so as to ensure that any political fall-out was kept to the minimum and was in-line with current government policies. Not a bad idea really. Both Harry and I knew that I would probably never be senior enough to be invited onto ComOps, but he also knew that inevitably some junior officers and non-commissioned officers would have access to their decisions, especially those of the most respected and trusted of Rhodesia's Special Forces; the SAS. Therefore he left a message for me in the dead letter box: 'Priority: Get in the SAS and get access to ComOps'.

Of course, I already knew several SAS men through serving in the Light Infantry and the Selous Scouts, so it wasn't particularly difficult for me to get put up for selection for the regiment. It also wasn't unusual for a member of one Special Forces regiment to apply for a transfer to another regiment, so my decision to move didn't raise any suspicions amongst my comrades, though it did entail quite a bit of leg-pulling about why I would want to leave a brilliant regiment like the scouts for that bunch of 'pansies and shirt-lifters' in the SAS. All of which was just normal banter amongst soldiers of course.

The Rhodesian Special Air Service Regiment was a much smaller unit than the Selous Scouts and consisted of only around 250 all ranks. It was also an 'all white' regiment, quite unlike the scouts.

The SAS selection course, while being tough, wasn't as bad as the scout's selection, thank God. However, my continuation training went on to involve lots of things that I had never done before including High Altitude Low Opening (HALO) and High Altitude High Opening (HAHO) parachute training, which was exciting stuff, and which would hold me in good stead in later operations around the world. HALO is basically jumping from a very high altitude with the jumper free-falling wearing special clothing and an oxygen mask because of the sub-zero temperatures. At about 800 feet he opens his chute and then lands. In HAHO you jump from the same height but open the chute within 10-15 seconds of leaving the aircraft. This means a soldier can float beneath his chute for up to 30 miles before reaching the landing zone, so this technique calls for very good navigation skills. Both of these techniques are used for stealthy insertions of men and equipment by Special Forces units around the world and have the added bonus that the delivery aircraft are too high to be bothered by radar or surface-to-air missiles fired from the ground.

I joined the SAS and managed to keep my rank as a sergeant because I'd come from another Special Forces unit. I went on to be involved in several operations, including some well-known external raids, such as the attack against Chimioi, called 'Operation Dingo', and Tembue a few days later. Both of them were large terrorist training camps in Mozambique. I also took part in another raid in Lusaka, the capital of Zambia, in yet another attempt to take out Joshua NKomo at his residence there. On one occasion while serving in the Rhodesian SAS, I was one of a team of four men that undertook the first operational HALO parachute jump at night time, acting as the pathfinders to mark out a landing zone for a future operation. Only two of us survived the jump. The others were killed because we had jumped into mountainous terrain and unfortunately they hadn't opened their chutes in time. We never located the bodies of our comrades, but we did find one of their bergens, which had been smashed open and spread over a mountainside by the impact.

THIRTEEN

Operation Dingo was a classic external raid. I had been involved in the initial Close Target Reconnaissance (CTR) against the Chimioi camp in Mozambique while I was still serving in the scouts. The CTR had involved two of us infiltrating and setting up an OP inside the camp, with the aim of mapping the terrorist defensive positions and cataloguing their daily activities. We discovered that the camp had a highly effective, if unusual, early warning system of an attack by the Rhodesian Air Force – a baboon tied up at the top of a wooden tower. This baboon would go absolutely nuts when his sensitive hearing heard approaching aircraft and all the terrorists would then take cover. After days spent hiding in the middle of thousands of armed terrorists we crept out of the camp without anyone ever knowing that we had been there and gave in our report.

Before the attack by 72 SAS and 82 Light Infantry Troopers there was to be an air bombardment of the terrorist camp. However, for this to be successful and catch the terrorists in the open, the problem of the aircraft-hating baboon had to be dealt with first. This was cleverly done by regularly flying a DC-8 airliner over the camp every day, with the same aircraft returning ten minutes later. The terrorists got so used to this airliner flying over and then coming back that on the day of the attack, after the DC-8 had initially flown over, they thought nothing of the baboon going nuts ten minutes later, thinking it was just the airliner making its return trip. I imagine they were very surprised when, instead, it turned out to be a devastating air-strike by the Rhodesian Air Force, catching them out in the open.

During our following Para drop, I found myself, with a mate, surrounded by fleeing terrorists as we landed on the ground. There seemed to be thousands of the bastards, all running for their lives, and as we floated down there was absolutely nothing that we could do to avoid them. After landing we frantically released our parachute harnesses and for a few, very scary minutes that seemed to last for hours, the two of us stood back-to-back and just blasted away as they swarmed around and past us. Fortunately for us most of them seemed much more intent on getting away than turning on us, although I vividly recall the snarling faces of a few hot-heads who charged at us with raised *pangas*. It was like standing in the middle of a stampede and I must have fired at least 200-300 rounds from my rifle during that short space of time. I remember afterwards my rifle barrel was so hot that it was almost glowing red. When the wave of enemy had past us we found that we were surrounded by a pile of dead and wounded terrorists. We estimated that just the two of us had killed about 70 of them, and wounded a hell of a lot more. I was as out of breath as if I'd just run a marathon and yet the only muscles I'd used to any degree were in my trigger finger. My mouth was as dry as a *donga* and the adrenaline was buzzing around my body, making me twitchy and jerky. This was one of the scariest moments of my life, and I've had a few.

Many terrorists escaped the attack on Chimioi Camp, mainly because our 'vertical envelopment' of the camp had only managed to cover three sides, leaving the other side open for them to escape, but it was still judged as a huge success. Over 3,000 terrorists were killed and 5,000 wounded, while two of our men were killed and a handful wounded. We'd also destroyed tons of terrorist equipment and gathered a huge cache of intelligence material from the headquarters. The only downside to the raid was the escape, yet again, of Robert Mugabe. Yes, you've guessed it; he'd been pre-warned of the attack and was nowhere near the camp thanks to me and the British government yet again.

It was during the later stages of our mopping-up of the camp that I was faced with one of the funniest sights that I saw during the war. I had a mate in the SAS who was nicknamed 'Big John'. He was a really nice guy, a Rhodesian by birth, built like a brick shit-house, standing at least six feet five inches tall in his socks. However he wasn't, to coin a phrase, the brightest spark in the bonfire. John had come to my attention when a month or two earlier I'd been on another, far smaller raid with him, when he had been tasked with silently taking out an enemy sentry. Instead of doing the standard thing and slipping behind the guy before slitting his throat with a knife, he had for some reason grabbed the guy from the front and then cut his throat. This resulted in Big John being absolutely drenched in the sentry's blood. It had been a few days before we'd made it back to our base at Cranborne Barracks, and all I can remember is John walking around in the scorching heat, his combats sticky and stinking with a quarter-of-an-inch coating of dried human blood and this huge swam of flies following him at head height, a bit like the old cartoons where an individual character is followed by a rain-cloud right above them, while everyone else is in the sun.

On this occasion, whilst mopping up the camp, Big John had been issued with a 'bunker-blaster'. This device is basically a briefcase full of plastic explosive specifically designed to be tossed through the firing slits of the concrete bunkers that you often found in defensive positions around terrorist's camps. The standard operating procedure for using a bunker-buster goes something like this: Approach the bunker in question while getting covering fire from your mates to keep the bugger's heads down; stand next to the firing slit, pull the initiator on the charge to light the fuse; throw the charge through the firing slit into the bunker; then run like hell before it explodes. At Chimioi Big John did alright until he hit the 'run like hell' bit. Instead of taking cover away from the blast area like any normal idiot would have done, he decided to stay in situ and just crouched down by the bunker and put his hands over his ears. The explosion from a bunker-blaster is huge, often lifting the solid concrete tops of the bunkers many feet into the air and blowing the walls outward. Hence the need to get out of there, after delivering the package. This explosion was no different, and after the storm of dust had begun to settle, all we could see was a pile of rubble, with the huge broken slab of the ex-roof off to one side, and no sign of Big John at all. Then there was a slight shifting at the side of the rubble and a dust-caked hand pushed out followed by a rather pathetic "Shit! Somebody help me please!" We scampered over and pulled the silly twat out and miraculously he was totally unscathed except for a few minor bumps and scratches. I don't think I've ever laughed as much as I did at that moment. The whole lot of us (never mind that there was still enemy fire whizzing around through the air), were rolling on the ground in stitches, totally helpless. I can still, after all these years, hear his pathetic little voice in my head: "Shit! Somebody help me please!"

Soldiers, sailors and airmen, no matter what country they serve, often develop a very dark sense of humour, probably due to the very dangerous type of work that we do. In the heart of a war when your life may constantly be in danger, you need to find some release from the tension and developing a sense of humour is essential for your mental well-being. Looking back over my years in the forces I find that the moments that often stand out most in my memory are usually the funniest ones.

I was out on a bush patrol while serving in the SAS. We had been in the bush for a few days when we decided to set up a patrol harbour on the side of a hill. I was on sentry at the bottom of the hill while most of the patrol spread out to get some well-earned kip further up the slope. I had no sooner settled down than I began to hear a lot of grunting followed by shouting and general sounds of dismay. For a few moments I was worried that we were being attacked from further up the hill and prepared myself for a fight. Suddenly a naked man flashed past me running down the hill, soon followed by half-a-dozen others, all screaming and shouting. It turned out that we had set up our harbour on top of a colony of fire-ants and the vicious little buggers had got into my mate's sleeping bags and did what they do best, which is biting and stinging anything that they can find to bite and sting. They hurt like hell. I will never forget the sight of those tough Special Forces heroes fleeing naked through the bush, weapons forgotten and left behind in their haste to get out of there and away from the ants, their pale bodies glowing white except for well-tanned faces, arms and legs. If we had been attacked at that moment the enemy would have had one of their easiest victories ever!

On another occasion we had been tasked with blowing up a bridge in a neighbouring country (I think it was in Malawi, but can't be sure), which was a vital link for supplying equipment and weapons for the terrorists. We were approaching the bridge to lay our charges when we suddenly realised that the underside of the bridge was home to dozens of large wasp nests and we couldn't get near without being stung by swarms of the angry little buggers. We backed off and began arguing about it. It was obvious that we had to blow the bridge up but none of us wanted to risk the wasp stings. These were big black and red wasps and when they stung you it hurt like crazy for a long time. In the end, we drew lots and one brave member of our team (okay, the loser) wrapped himself in everyone's long trousers and long-sleeved shirts until he looked a bit like the 'Michelin Man', ran forward and dumped a bergen full of explosive under a bridge support, getting stung by loads of the wasps, even through the layers of clothing. Once he had legged it back, we then spent a few minutes taking pot-shots at the bergen until one of the rounds set off the explosives and luckily brought down the bridge. We then retreated with undue haste, not so much because we were worried that we would be attacked by the enemy in the area, but more to get away from the now very pissed-off wasps.

FOURTEEN

Not all of our operations were so light-hearted. The results of the war could be pretty horrific, especially on civilians. September 1978 found me at a place called Karoi, in the Whamira Hills. I was one of a team of SAS who parachuted into the scene of a civilian Viscount Airliner, the morning after it had crashed. As you can imagine the scene was one of total devastation. The pilot had tried to bring the damaged plane down in a cotton field in the bush, but it had hit a very wide irrigation ditch causing it to flip over. It had then burst into flames, killing most of the passengers and crew. This wasn't the worst of it though as a number of the passengers had survived the crash, only to be killed by ZIPRA guerrillas. We found the bodies of ten women, children and babies who had been brutally raped (yes, even the babies), bayoneted, bludgeoned and shot to death. It turned out that the airliner had been hit by a shoulder-launched surface-to-air missile fired by a group of ZIPRA terrorists who later became known as the 'Viscount Gang', after they shot down another airliner five months later, this time killing all of the passengers and crew. It's bad enough to be shot down and to survive an air crash in the first place, dragging yourself from the burning wreckage, shocked and traumatised, leaving behind dead family members and friends, but then to be treated so brutally before being killed is beyond any decency. Needless to say, with 107 civilian deaths on their hands, the Viscount Gang were vigorously hunted down and despatched.

I continued serving in the SAS for quite a while; quietly using every opportunity to collect good intelligence for the firm on one hand and not-so-quietly doing my best to kill terrorists on the other. I was involved in lots of other external raids, blowing up road and rail bridges in neighbouring countries and parachute drops into enemy-held territory. I even managed to get myself shot at on my eighteenth birthday whilst serving in the Rhodesian Light Infantry (later I was again shot at on my 21st birthday, though this was in a different war, in a different place, and facing a different enemy).

The skill that I really excelled at was CTR, the infiltration and close reconnaissance of terrorist training camps. Although CTR was supposed to be non-combative, it was also one of the most dangerous jobs going as you often found yourself right in the middle of terrorist's camps surrounded by literally thousands of well-armed men who would love nothing more than to shove a bayonet up your arse and hear you squeal. The aim of CTR is to infiltrate a position and then record everything you can without anyone knowing that you are there or have been there. In order to do this you travel light, carrying only your personal weapon, ammunition, enough food and water to last and a few plastic bags for pissing and shitting in. If you ever get discovered you are quite literally right in the crap. This happened to me only once and very nearly put paid to a promising career as both a soldier and a spy.

I was with another SAS man called Chris and we were carrying out a CTR on a ZANLA training camp in Mozambique. We had gotten ourselves right into the heart of the camp, which was spread out for miles around us, and positioned ourselves on a hill with a fine view of everything we needed to see and catalogue. On the third day in this position we caught sight of an armed guerrilla patrol coming our way up the hillside. I'm pretty sure that they didn't suspect we were there; it was just one of the many patrols that the guerrillas sent out for security. However this lot were coming straight towards us. We decided to stay put as any movement would surely give us away, so we hastily re-adjusted each other's camouflage and settled down to merge as best we could into the bush. In the event though we didn't stand a chance as the patrol quite literally walked straight over us. We got up and ran like hares, leaving the guerrillas temporarily stunned and immobile. However this didn't last long and within seconds all hell was breaking loose as a torrent of badly-aimed shots came after us and the whole camp was roused. Even in the thick of it we still followed standard operating procedure and orders, legging it towards our support group who had, of course already heard the racket and were waiting for us with their kit on, ready to withdraw. With hardly a second's stop we picked up our own bergens and slung them onto our backs. Then in good order, we began our planned withdrawal, the patrol signalman getting onto the radio to the air force for a pick-up as we moved. Pretty soon we had bad news on two fronts; the first was that there were no choppers free to pick us up as they were involved in operations elsewhere; the second was that the whole bloody terrorist training camp seemed to be on our tail. Thousands of the bastards chasing us through the bush, screaming their heads off and firing every sort of weapon that they had at us as they ran, including light machine guns and even mortars. We just legged it as there was nothing else that we could do. This chase went on for mile after mile. At first we were returning fire as we went, but as the day wore on and we saw that our fire was having no effect at all on our pursuers, we gave this up as a bad job and just kept going. The sun was up and it was scorching hot but at times the guerrillas were so close behind us that we didn't dare pause, even to get a water bottle out and to take a much-needed gulp, and all the while they were firing away at us with everything they had. More miles followed yet more miles, and eventually hour followed hour, with neither us pulling away from them nor them getting any closer to us. Our signaller kept up a constant tirade on the radio until at last he got confirmation that a couple of Bell Huey's were on the way. However, they would have to refuel first when they got back from their current mission in Zambia, so it would be a couple of hours before they could reach us. By this time we were absolutely knackered. The only thing that kept us going was the thought of what the guerrillas would do to us if they caught up with us. I had previously seen a member of a CTR support group who had been captured and had the dismembered parts of his body hung up on the thorns of several different trees as gruesome trophies. We had no illusions that the same thing would happen to us if we were captured. It would not be an easy death for any of us, so we dug in our heels and kept on running. The only things keeping our heavily-punished bodies from giving way beneath us was the adrenalin pumping through us and the hope of an airlift out. There was always the constant hail of rounds streaming after us through the bush, sending up little dust clouds when they hit the ground around our feet or whizzing by with their green tracers alight between us. Occasionally we would be blasted by the dirt from an exploding mortar as the mortar teams behind us paused in their chase to fire off a couple of bombs. It was nothing short of a miracle that none of us were hit. How can I ever put into sufficient words what this bizarre chase was like and what it felt like to be a part of it?

Eventually we got the message that we had been praying for. The choppers were at last on their way to us after refuelling and they needed to know where we were and where to pick us up. We didn't have a clue except that we were heading towards the border, but after a hoarse shouted conversation between us we agreed that we would have to go to ground and set off mini-flares and smoke as soon as we heard the choppers. This we did about forty minutes later, picking a patch of *Jesse* surrounding a natural open hollow in which to make our stand. Mercifully we threw our bergens to the ground and lay down in all-round defensive positions, sweat streaming into our eyes and our hearts pounding away as we tried to gulp in enough air, panting like dogs. The *Jesse* was so thick that we could only see a few metres into it, and it appeared to slow down the guerrillas, though it never stopped their incoming fire. When they were close enough that they were just out of sight, we opened up a blistering fire that cooled them off for a few minutes, but then they were back at us with a vengeance and their fire was terrific, scything through the trees and bushes like leaf-cutters. We only had a limited supply of ammo and there was no way that six of us could win this fire-fight, so we just kept our heads down and hoped that the storm of fire would pass over us and leave us untouched.

Then we heard the most beautiful sound in the world; the whump whump of chopper blades cutting through the air and the snarling of the Huey's machine guns as they hovered right over us and opened up on the guerrillas. This was going to be what we call in the trade a 'hot extraction'. One Huey hovered down low to the ground while we ran to it one at a time, chucked in our bergens and clambered in. The other Huey circled around spitting out death and dismay to the guerrillas. It wasn't going to go all our way though as the guerrillas were a very determined lot and they soon began to return even heavier fire than before. As patrol second-in-command I was the second-to-last to head for the chopper and my mate Chris, as the patrol officer, was the last. As I ran to the chopper and threw in my bergen the pilot was obviously getting more and more nervous about the heavy incoming fire as the chopper was drifting higher and higher above the ground. I tried to clamber on board but he was just too high so I settled on clamping half of my harness (designed for just such hot extractions) onto the runner of the chopper. Out of the corner of my eye I saw Chris run over but by then the chopper had got too high for him to even attach his own harness or to reach the runner, and we were drifting higher by the second. As I dangled there feeling useless, I could see and feel the green tracer of the enemies rounds whizzing by me, sometimes right between my legs. I could also just see the pilot's terrified face looking out of the canopy as the chopper took several direct hits. I screamed at him, though I doubt that he could hear me through the racket of rotors and gunfire, and pointed down towards Chris, who we were slowly getting further and further away from. The pilot just shook his head at me, so in sheer mad desperation I reached down and drew my Browning semi-automatic pistol from my shoulder holster and aimed it at the pilot. We were still going up so I put a couple of rounds past the canopy and I guess that when he saw my face he got the message that I'd rather shoot him and see us all crash and die than leave Chris behind to face the fury of the guerrillas. We dropped down very fast and Chris chucked his bergen into the open chopper doors and clamped himself on the runner beside me. Then with a sickening lurch we were up and away, rounds still chasing us. But then we were safe, or as safe as you can be when dangling from a fast-flying helicopter high over the ground.

Normally in this situation the chopper pilot would fly high for a few miles before setting down somewhere safe and letting us get properly on board. But this was a very pissed-off pilot and so he flew all the way back to base with us dangling beneath him with the chopper 'hedge-hopping' (as we called flying very low), going up and down to avoid trees and bushes. It was a terrifying flight home and when we eventually landed the other members of the patrol had to hold me back otherwise I'd have murdered the pilot. He quickly disappeared after landing and I presume he went straight to his commanding officer and complained that I had nearly killed him because I soon got a bollocking. Even so, I didn't much care; we had made it out of that nightmare chase and hell-hole of an extraction with not one wound between us. We had survived and I felt great. It was only weeks later that I found out that I was to be awarded the Bronze Cross of Rhodesia for my actions that day. This was the fourth highest award for gallantry in the Rhodesian Army. We made a running joke out of it that

I was the only guy to ever get a bravery award for threatening to shoot a helicopter pilot. I would laugh along with all the ribbing I got about it, but deep inside I knew how close I'd actually come to shooting that guy and killing us all in the process.

We had covered over 40 miles during the chase.

FIFTEEN

Tuesday 15th October 2013
Coventry, Warwickshire

Smith closed and locked the door behind him. He dropped his holdall onto the floor and quickly went around in the dark, closing the curtains. It didn't take long - it was only a small flat with four rooms. Only then did he switch the lights on and check around to make sure that nothing had been disturbed. This was his 'safe-house', located only a mile from where he had lived before getting arrested. Nobody knew that he rented it; there was nothing to link him or his name with the place. He had only ever visited it every three months to pick up the post and pay the bills, and he always made trebly sure that no one saw him entering or tailed him from his other, larger flat.

He went into the kitchen and checked on the stock of canned food that was stored there, mentally calculating how long it would last him before he had to buy some more. Then he put the kettle on and made himself a mug of tea with a tea bag and powdered milk. While the tea was cooling he changed out of his suit into some clean clothes from the wardrobe and chest of drawers in the bedroom, then sat on the single armchair in the tiny living room and switched on the small portable TV. He quickly flicked through the news channels on Freeview and grunted with satisfaction when he couldn't find anything relating to his escape or the killing of the two prison officers. Good, the coppers had obviously not released the news yet, so his face would not be plastered all over the TV for a while. He relaxed and sipped from his mug.

He had parked the old man's car in the city centre and bought himself the holdall from a sports shop nearby. Then he had opened the metal box that he had retrieved from the wood and transferred the contents into the holdall, before abandoning the car for the coppers to eventually find in a busy car park. His last port of call was an internet cafe, where he had logged on and downloaded the first two parts of his autobiography from a compact disc that had lain for years in the sealed box beneath the soil of the woodland. He had looked up the email address of the police HQ in Cambridgeshire and sent it onto the twat who had headed the case against him. Then he had walked the couple of miles to his flat in the fading light.

For the first time in ages he felt relatively at peace with himself. His arrest for the rape and murder of that poor young girl had been harrowing enough, even though he knew that he had not done it. But when the forensic evidence had all pointed at him he had begun to doubt his own sanity; after all he knew that he was a bit of a fruitcake by most people's standards. Perhaps he had committed that atrocious crime? Perhaps he was just denying it in his own mind? The first three days of the trial had almost convinced him that he was a complete and utter nutcase and he had just about resigned himself to the fact that he was going to spend the rest of his life in prison. Then, on the fourth morning of the trial, he had looked through the screen of armoured glass separating the dock from the courtroom and had seen Harry sitting in the public gallery, with a great big smirk plastered across his face. They had kept eye contact for a full minute and all he could see was the self-satisfied laughter in the bastard's eyes. It was at that moment that he knew that he wasn't insane; he knew that he hadn't raped and killed that girl; and he knew that he would have to get out and get his revenge on that bastard.

By the time that the court had retired for lunch he was full of rage; a white-hot rage that seared his mind. It was unfortunate that the two prison officers had decided to bait him; otherwise he might just have battered them unconscious, instead of killing them. Too bad for them. He had no regrets on that score; he'd done much worse than that in the past. They would only be the first of many who were going to pay the ultimate price.

He emptied the contents of the holdall onto the narrow bed and began to sort through it. The paperwork; mostly passports and driving licenses in different names, he put to one side to sort out later. He counted the small pile of cash; only fifteen hundred pounds as he had never been well-paid, but it would do for what he needed. The old mobile phones also went to one side while the six sets of car number plates he sorted into pairs and put away into a drawer. All of them were 'clean' fully registered plates with legitimate histories. With them he put the large set of vehicle master keys, covering a whole range of car and van makes from Skoda through to Fiat. Lastly he picked up the P226 SIG Saur 9mm semi-automatic pistol. He slotted in one of the two magazines and cocked it, slipping a round into the breach. Then he slowly screwed the short silencer onto the barrel. It felt good to hold a gun again.

Tuesday 15th October 2013
Huntingdon, Cambridgeshire

It was getting late and everyone in the squad room was tired and getting ratty, but DCI Davies didn't care. He was determined to catch that cocky bastard Smith as soon as possible. He didn't care if all of his officers had to work twenty hours a day for the next month. He wasn't going to let Smith's escape damage his career prospects any more than it had already. He had to find him.

"Have you all read through this 'autobiography' that Smith emailed in?" He was answered by weary nods and grunts of assent from his gathered team. "Okay. What did you think of it then?"

DS Price was the first to offer an answer, as always willing to share his obviously important views with anyone that cared to listen: "It's a load of old bollocks boss. Smith's just trying to pull the wool over our eyes and divert our attention away."

"Anybody else with a view apart from Price?"

"Well, it seems a bit unlikely that Smith would take the time to sit down and write, what is it - almost fifty pages of what looks like a well-researched story-line? He's only just escaped. When would he have found the time? It must have already been written." Tried Helen Wright.

"Which begs the point," said Davies, "of where the fuck did he hide it? We went through everything in his flat, every scrap of paper that he owned when we arrested him."

"Well it's pretty obvious that it was in that fucking box that he'd hidden in the woods, boss." Said Price. "He must have written it before he was arrested. Obviously he was aware that he might be done for the girl's murder so he planned it all in advance. It's like I said boss; he's just trying to cloud the issue with a load of old bollocks."

"Yeah. I agree with the DS boss." Spoke up another of the squad. "Smith's obviously a fantasist as well as a fucking pervert. He probably believes this poxy story that he was some sort of undercover spy working for MI6. Probably gives him a hard on." There was general laughter at this.

"He thinks he's James fucking Bond!"

"Or, it might be true." Said Helen, braving the sneers from a few of her colleagues. Davies looked lost in thought for a moment.

"Helen's got a point." He said. "We know that Smith is a perverted murderer. But the way that he killed those prison officers with his bare hands, and the fact that he has so far managed to run rings around the lot of us and evade capture, might mean that he's got a bit more intelligence than we have been giving him credit for. On the other hand it probably is a load of old bollocks." He nodded at Price, who smirked. "Right, I've come to a decision: Helen, I want you to follow up any possible leads that are in this story that he's sent us. See if Smith was a junior soldier, or was ever in the British Army. Put some feelers out just in case. There must be regimental associations for all these Rhodesian regiments he's mentioned as well. Find out if anybody called 'Danny Brown' ever served in them. You know the score; see if there's any bloody truth in what he's sent us. The rest of you, get cracking on your assignments. I want this bastard caught, and caught soon! Get on with it."

SIXTEEN

Wednesday 16th October 2013
Coventry, Warwickshire

Smith chose a corner of the Tesco's car park that wasn't covered by the CCVT cameras. Dressed in a dark blue jacket with the hood up, he walked quickly and confidently to the Land Rover Defender, inserted his chosen master key into the door lock, stepped up into the driver's seat and started it up. Within thirty seconds he was turning out of the car park and onto the adjacent street. Within another ten minutes he was parked up just outside the city on a lay-by screened from the road by trees. He quickly undid the screws on the existing number plates and replaced the plates with a new set. He had chosen both the vehicle and the new number plates well; choosing an older make of Land Rover to go with the newest plates that he had, which were well over ten years old. He spent another minute or two going over the vehicle and checking it for soundness. Then, satisfied, he drove off to his flat, where he reversed the vehicle into the lock-up garage that he rented with the flat.

Wednesday 16th October 2013
Huntingdon, Cambridgeshire

DC Helen Wright knocked on the DCI's office door, holding a folder full of paperwork in her hands.

"Come in!"

"Hi boss."

"Oh, hi Helen. Take a seat. Have you got anything for me?" She sat down on a chair facing the DCI's desk. She noted that he already looked worn out, and it was only the end of the second day since Smith had escaped. Mind you, the whole squad was pretty tired after hours of fruitless work.

"Sorry boss. I've checked out everything that I can so far in Smith's 'autobiography', but I haven't found anything positive yet. The British Army has had lots of Smiths enlisted, as you can imagine. They've even had lots of 'John Smiths', but unfortunately none of them fits the date of birth that we have for our man. I've asked them to fax through the physical descriptions of them all anyway, just in case, though it will take some time for them to work their way through their records as they aren't computerised. I don't know whether you know this, but luckily they have a brief physical description of each man, including identifying marks such as tattoo's etc., recorded in all of their discharge papers. I'll just have to wade through them as they send them in and see if I can find a match."

"Okay. Anything from the Rhodesian Army?"

"Nothing yet. I've managed to locate regimental associations via the internet for the Rhodesian Light Infantry, the Selous Scouts and the Rhodesian SAS, and I've sent them all priority emails requesting any information that they have on anyone called Danny Brown or John Smith. I've been thinking that we should send them a copy of the relevant bits of the autobiography, if that's okay with you? Just in case there's anything in there that might ring a bell with them, such as the supposed raids in other countries etc."

"Okay. But only the relevant bits Helen, and for God's sake don't let them know what this is all about. The chief constable has decided, in her ultimate wisdom, to give a press conference about Smith's escape and the murders tomorrow morning. It'll be bad enough without the press finding out about his bloody email to us. They'll have a field day if it gets out, so use your common sense and don't give too much away, okay?"

"Okay boss." She hesitated before carrying on "There's just one thing boss....."

"Yes?"

"What if it's all true, and Smith really did work for MI6?"

"Who cares? It was all bloody years ago. Even if he was an MI6 agent, it has nothing to do with the rape and murder of Mary Knightly. We know that he's guilty of that, and we also know that he's guilty of murdering those two prison officers. No matter what he's done in the past, when we catch him he will go down for the rest of his life. The courts will see to that."

"I know that boss. What I meant to say was: If it turns out that he was an agent of the security services, shouldn't we be getting in touch with them to find out?" It was Davies's turn to hesitate.

"Good point Helen. I'll have a word with the chief constable and see what she thinks. I doubt if MI6 would even talk to a lowly DCI anyway. Any questions to them are better coming from the top brass. Anything else on your mind?"

"No, not yet boss. Is there any news about Smith from the others?" Davies sighed and rubbed his eyes with his hands to try and dispel some of the tiredness that he felt.

"Not a bloody thing so far. Smith appears to have totally disappeared off the map. It's like he's a ghost or something." Helen tried to cheer him up:

"Ah well. It's early days yet boss. He's bound to make a mistake sooner or later. He's not superman."

"Well, for all of our sakes, I hope its sooner rather than later!"

"I'll get on then boss."

"Thanks Helen. Keep me posted."

SEVENTEEN

Thursday 17th October 2013
Coventry, Warwickshire

Smith had woken up in the morning sweating profusely with the lingering image of a nightmare clouding his brain. It had taken a good half an hour to shake himself free of the absolute terror that he had felt. Why was it always the same? He asked himself for the millionth time. It had happened nearly thirty years ago; would he ever be able to sleep without having nightmares again?

Then the rage hit him once more. A white-hot rage that made his hands tremble and his eyes narrow to slits as he snarled to himself:

"Why couldn't they just leave him alone? After all he'd done for this country and for the firm, they just couldn't let him get on with his life without fucking interfering!" He paced up and down the tiny kitchen and eventually let all of his anger and hatred flow into his fist as he smashed it against the wall, crushing the thin covering of plasterboard and leaving an impression of his knuckles in the wall. "They'll pay for this! They'll all pay for this; every one of the bastards that was involved with my arrest and trial! Fuckers!"

Thursday 17th October 2013
Huntingdon, Cambridgeshire

DCI Davies had been right about the shit hitting the fan
after his chief constable had given the news of Smith's
escape and the murders of the two civilian prison officers
in the news conference this morning. He had been ordered
up into her office shortly afterwards and had been given
the roasting of his life. Jesus Christ! He thought, any one
would think that the escape had been his own personal
fault! It wasn't as though he had had anything to do with
the security at the fucking courthouse, for God's sake!
He'd only been there to observe the trial and sentencing of
that fucking loser!

    So to compensate for his extreme bollocking, he did
what any officer and leader of men would do; he went back
to his squad room and bollocked his own team. Dog bites
cat; cat kills mouse; poor old mouse has got no one to lay
into, except for civilians; so his team were sent back onto
the streets to bully, cajole and threaten any one that had
even the remotest connection with the criminal underworld
in a bid to get a lead, any lead, on where the hell Smith
had disappeared to. All to no avail.

Thursday 17th October 2013
Perry Barr, Birmingham

Smith had driven up the small cul-de-sac twice during the
long day. Each time his eyes had taken in every bit of
information that they could about the house. The kid's toys
scattered across the tightly mown grass of the front
garden, discarded for the night by the two small boys and
their worn out mother, in her mid-thirties, that he had
earlier followed on foot to the Post Office a few streets
away. He had timed one of his drive-bys for when the
father of the children had walked home from his work (in
the Territorial Army centre) around the corner. He had

seen the man, still in his barrack-dress uniform but with a civilian overcoat thrown over it to camouflage his chosen career from casually spying eyes. Smith had watched his confident manner as he walked through a small crowd of Asian teenagers hanging out on the street corner, seeing them silently part to let him through, like the prow of an ice-breaker parting a floe of thick ice in the South Atlantic. He had noted how the man had looked around as he walked to his house, and how he had had to unlock the front door before he entered his home.

Smith was satisfied with what he had seen. He drove away down King's Standing Road to look for somewhere to park up, eat his cold can of bacon grill and take a drink of hot tea from his thermos flask while he waited for the evening to close in.

Thursday 17th October 2013
Huntingdon, Cambridgeshire

"I've had a hit boss!" Helen Wright exclaimed excitedly.

"Well, don't make me wait. I could do with some good news. What have you got?" Davies refused to get excited until he knew what she was talking about.

"I've heard back from a former officer of the Rhodesian SAS, boss, through the regimental association website." She paused to look at the dossier that she was carrying. "His name is Captain Lars van der Pol, and he claims to have served in the regiment for six years during the bush war, from 1974 through to 1979, when it was disbanded."

"Any proof that he did?"

"Not yet boss. I've contacted other people on the website to try and verify what he says but I haven't heard back from them yet. However, I did look him up on Google and there are several references to his career in the

Rhodesian SAS from a variety of sources. So far he looks kosher."

"Jesus, is this what detective work has sunk to? Using Google for God's sake?"

"Don't knock it boss! You'd be surprised what it says about you on Google."

"Really, wha.........no, don't answer that question. After this morning's bloody news conference I can just imagine what people are saying!"

"Yeah, well.....there is that. Anyway, boss, this van der Pol claims to have known a man of Smith's description during his time in the Rhodesian Army. I emailed an edited version of Smith's autobiography to the captain, just the bit dealing with his service in the SAS, and he's confirmed that everything I sent him is true, and that Smith must definitely be our man. He also added that some of those things that he wrote about are not generally known to the public."

"What does he mean by that?"

"Well, he says that only someone who had been there could have known about them. In other words, the stories are true."

"Don't jump to conclusions from the word of one man that we don't even know anything about, DC Wright." He admonished. "Firstly I want you to get some verification on this Captain van der Pol, and that what he is telling us is the truth. Then I want you to get in touch with the other Rhodesian associations and see if they have heard of Danny Brown or John Smith."

"OK boss, I'll get right onto it!"

"Don't get too excited yet Helen. This van der Pol might just be a crank. Make sure that you get verifiable facts, not just someone's twisted fantasy. Okay?"

"Okay, boss. I will." Nevertheless, as Davies watched admiringly as DC Wright's bottom wiggled away from him in her tight skirt, he couldn't help but feel a little excitement, and it wasn't all to do with how nice Helen's bum was. This might just be the lead that they had been looking for.

Thursday 17th October 2013
Perry Barr, Birmingham

Smith knocked twice on the front door of the married quarters. When it opened onto the tired-looking face of the children's mother, Smith moved fast, pushing her back into the hall, closing the door behind him with his foot and brandishing his silenced pistol into the woman's face all seemingly in one flowing movement. When her gasp of fear brought her husband bolting into the hall from the living room, Smith smiled his coldest smile and put a bullet into the soft upper arm of the woman, who fell onto the floor, as yet too shocked to feel the pain.

"Stand still and be quiet!" He ordered the man, who had discarded his uniform and was now dressed in casual civilian clothes. "If you make a sound or a move, I'll put a bullet into her throat, then I'll do the same to you, and then, before I leave, I'll do the same to your two sons'. Do you understand?" The man nodded, surprisingly calm for one faced with such a life-threatening scene totally out of the blue. Smith knew why though; he had met this man once before, a long time ago and in another place. He knew that he was a sergeant major in the 22 Special Air Service Regiment, currently posted as the Senior Permanent Staff Instructor of Headquarters Squadron, 23 SAS. He may only be working out the rest of his time before retirement from the regiment as an instructor to the Territorial Army unit, but he had always been as tough as nails and as cool as a cucumber, and by the looks of him; he still was.

"Now Mike," the use of his first name made a dent in the man's calm exterior for just a fleeting moment, "I want you to dress your wife's wound. Then we'll tie her and the boys up so that they can't get into any mischief.

100

Then, you and me are going to take a walk to the TA centre and you're going to unlock the armoury and the ammo bunker, while I help myself to some bits of kit that I'll be needing. If you do this and give me no trouble at all, you have my word that I will not harm your family, or you, any more than I have already. If, on the other hand, you fuck me around in any way whatsoever, then you'll all pay for it with your lives. Have you got that?" Again the man nodded in the affirmative. "Good. Let's move then." And with that he pulled out a small roll of bandage from his pocket and tossed it to the soldier. "Get her wound dressed; we don't want her bleeding to death, do we?"

EIGHTEEN

Friday 18th October 2013
Ely, Cambridgeshire

It took several rings of the telephone by his bed to wake DCI Davies up enough to respond and pick up the receiver.

"Yes." He mumbled.

"Make sure you're awake, boss; I've had some bad news come through." There was an unmistakable edge of glee to DS Price's voice at having woken up his superior at this ungodly hour of the morning. Davies fumbled with a light switch before registering that it was 3.30am on his bedside clock. He groaned.

"What the fuck is it Price?" He swore that he could feel the bastard smirking on the other end of the phone. He'd have to do something to sort him out soon; Price's obvious dislike for the DCI was beginning to wear thin and was beginning to infect the other, less experienced members of the team as well.

"Smith has finally turned up boss." He was wide awake now.

"Well, give me the bloody details then!" There was another smirk from down the phone line.

"The Birmingham bobbies have been on the phone boss. Smith has raided the armoury of a Territorial Army unit in Perry Barr. That's in Birmingham, boss."

"I know where the fuck Perry Barr is sergeant. Get on with it!"

102

"Apparently he shot the wife of an 'SPSI', whatever that is. Then he tied her and her two kids up and forced the husband to unlock the armoury of the local TA centre and bypass the security systems. Then he nicked a load of bloody weapons and ammo, boss."

"Jesus fucking Christ! Have we got a positive ID on Smith?"

"Yes boss. The army bloke who helped him told the Brummie coppers that he got a perfect look at his face and he'd just seen him on the news; an item about his escape, apparently. It was Smith alright, and apparently he didn't try to hide his identity at all." The cogs in Davies's brain went into overdrive and were whirling around in his head like dervishes. What the hell was this all about? Why had Smith finally showed himself after staying below the radar since his escape? Why a TA unit in Perry Barr? What weapons did he take? Jesus!

"Have we got anything on the weapons that he took?"

"No boss, not yet, the Brummies are going over the list of stores with the army bloke now, to see what's been taken."

"Dammit Price! Have we got anything? What about a vehicle? He must have had one; is there anything on that?"

"Nothing boss." The smirk was back. Davies took a moment to gather his thoughts.

"Right. I want you and Patel to get your arses down to Birmingham ASAP. Don't take any shit from the Brummies; I want to know exactly what happened and when, and I want a list of everything that's been stolen, do you hear, everything?"

"What, right now boss? I've been on duty for 22 hours straight!"

"Tough shit, Price. Get moving, and while you're at it I want you to interview the TA soldier; and I want everything on my desk in four hours time!"

"OK boss, will do." The smirk had gone from Price's voice but Davies could feel one of his own emerging as he heard the tiredness in his sergeant's voice.

"Are you still there Price?"

"Yes boss."

"Why? I told you to get moving. So move!" He slammed the phone down. Then looking at his clock again, his small moment of happy revenge dissipated as he realised that he wouldn't be able to sleep any more. He groaned as he eased his tired body out of the warm embrace of the quilt.

From: john smith (johnsmith2223@hotmail.com)
To: SOCA@Cambspolice.org.uk
Date: 18 October 2013 14:58:16
CC:
Subject: FAO Detective Chief Inspector Alan Davies, Cambs SOCA.

Hi Alan, I guess that you'll have heard about my little operation in Birmingham by now? I hope the woman is recovering okay.

Here's the next instalment of my autobiography, as promised. Any luck in finding out the truth yet? Maybe this next part will help you out a little?

I'll be in touch again; soon.

Regards

John Smith

NINETEEN

Eventually in April 1979 elections were held in Rhodesia. They were declared free and fair in the official report submitted by British observers. The majority of black Africans had voted and there were only a few isolated instances of violence and coercion reported. The United African National Council, which was an urban-based political party that had not been involved in the insurgency, won a 67% majority in this election and Bishop Abel Muzowera became Prime Minister. He was a black Methodist Church bishop who was considered a moderate politician, and was highly respected by both whites and blacks within the country. However, despite being invited to join in the elections, the political wings of ZANLA and ZIPRA; ZANU and ZAPU, had declined to take part in them.

Many people in Rhodesia hoped that this would be an end to the violence of the bush war, but then international politics raised its ugly head when President Nyerere of Tanzania and President Kaunda of Zambia objected to the elections at the Commonwealth Heads of Government meeting in Lusaka in August 1979. They demanded that Robert Mugabe and Joshua NKomo should be included in any arrangement for majority rule in Rhodesia.

The then Prime Minister of Britain, Margaret Thatcher, was placed under considerable pressure by these African leaders, who threatened yet again to nationalise British-owned mines in the Copper Belt. In the end she succumbed to this pressure and refused to recognise the new government. After this, pressure began mounting on the Rhodesians too, to hold new elections involving Mugabe's and NKomo's parties, which would be monitored by the Commonwealth. Eventually, tired of the continuing violence of the war and the depravations of economic sanctions, Bishop Muzowera agreed to the new elections and the terrorist forces of ZANU and ZAPU began to arrive openly in the country and to report to designated assembly points throughout Rhodesia. On 28th December a ceasefire came into effect.

Despite the presence of Commonwealth observers, it appears that the thousands of terrorists within the country had an almost free hand to intimidate voters, often using highly violent means such as public beatings, mutilations and killings, even at the polling stations, thus influencing the outcome of the election in their favour. Lord Soames, the temporary governor sent out by Britain to preside over the election gave Robert Mugabe several stern warnings about this behaviour, but he was ignored and nothing else was done to prevent it. The intimidation went on.

TWENTY

This is the point that the bush war in Rhodesia ended for me, and with it my successful undercover role as an agent for MI6. However, there was one more bit of intelligence that I passed on to Harry before I left to return to England, ostensibly on a well-earned leave to the 'home country', but with the intention of never returning and thus ending the career and brief lifetime of Sergeant 'Danny Brown'. This intelligence was about two operations known as 'Operation Quartz' and 'Operation Hectic'.

Operation Quartz was about placing Rhodesian troops at strategic places where they could launch a simultaneous attack, following air strikes by the Rhodesian Air Force, on the terrorist assembly points and wipe out the main bodies of the terrorist forces. At the same time Operation Hectic would involve the assassinations of Mugabe and NKomo at their campaign headquarters.

A few hours before these operations were due to begin, the order was cancelled. Presumably someone high up in the British government, perhaps even Prime Minister Thatcher herself, had warned off the attackers and applied considerable pressure on them to cancel the massacre that would surely have taken place had the operations gone ahead.

In due time Robert Mugabe was appointed as the President of Rhodesia, now known as Zimbabwe. The 23 year old bush war came to an end, and Danny Brown disappeared, as if he'd never existed.

From 1982 to 1985, it has been estimated that Robert Mugabe's men, under his direct orders, slaughtered over 20,000 of his own countrymen in cold blood. These massacres were picked up briefly by the British media when thousands of bodies were found stuffed into wells, but the story was dropped very quickly indeed. A few years later Robert Mugabe was invited to have tea with the Queen.

TWENTY-ONE

Returning to peacetime England with my own name and after years of very intense fighting in the Rhodesian Bush War, was a bit of a culture shock, to say the least. For a start it was early winter and pretty bloody cold, and I'd rather enjoyed my years in the warm sunshine of southern Africa. But it was a shock in other ways too. I hadn't had much to do with civilians during the bush war, and now I was surrounded by them. While I had spent years being involved with life and death decisions, it appeared that everything in civvy life was very petty. I mean, who really cares that much about the price of bread or who some pop star was marrying, or what was the latest gaffe by the Royals. I really couldn't care less about any of this stuff and found it so trivial and boring, like most of the people that I ran into.

Of course, it was good to visit the family again, but even here I couldn't say anything about what I'd been doing, as it was all covered by the Official Secrets Act. So such visits inevitably were less than satisfying. I had to lie to them and tell them that I had been away on tour in Germany with the Para's.

I'd managed to save a few thousand Rhodesian Dollars from my wages and changed them into pounds Stirling in Salisbury (the firm hadn't paid me a penny for the time I spent out there doing their work, so they had got quite a good deal out of me). With this money I rented a small flat in London and started to look for a job. It wasn't long before I realised that there was nothing out there in

110

Civvy Street that really appealed to me. Plus I had the disadvantage that a few years were missing from my life (I think that most people thought I'd been in prison, so again the old lie about being in the Para's in Germany was used many times, though I had no paperwork to prove it of course).

I also missed my mates in Rhodesia. Even though they'd have probably murdered me if they had found out what I'd really been doing, I still missed that sense of camaraderie and belonging to a close-knit unit. It wasn't long before I made up my mind to rejoin the British Army and to go for Special Forces again. However, I didn't count on running into a brick wall where this was concerned.

Ideally I wanted to go back into the Para's, get back into the swing of things for a while, and from there apply for selection to the British SAS in a year or two. The trouble was that officially I had left the Parachute Regiment years before with 'Services No Longer Required' stamped into my red service book. While this wasn't classed as a dishonourable discharge, it certainly wasn't looked upon favourably by the Para's, who preferred to take on only highly motivated people. In addition, officially I'd left the Para's before 'passing out' in the Infantry Junior Leaders Battalion, so I wasn't even classed as a fully trained soldier. All of this, of course was in spite of everything I had done in secret during the Rhodesian Bush War. After being turned down by the Parachute Regiment I went in despair to Harry, my case officer during the war. He was hard to get hold of, but eventually I got him to give me a call and he promised to help sort out my problems for me. To be fair to him, he did too, though I wasn't that happy about the outcome.

Apparently he arranged a brief meeting between the commanding officer of 22 Special Air Service Regiment and his own Section Head at SIS while they were both in the Capital on other business. The SIS bloke gave the commanding officer a quick rundown on my military service record in Rhodesia and explained that I had been working for the firm (without of course mentioning what my mission for SIS was out there). Then he explained my difficulty in getting back into the army and that I wanted to get into the British SAS. I imagine that the commanding officer looked upon me with some suspicion, especially as I was a former SIS agent who now wanted to join the SAS. It wasn't as if the two organisations liked or trusted each other very much. However, to his credit he did come up with a viable option for me, though it wasn't the quick fix that I'd hoped for.

To go for selection into the SAS, you normally have to have served in the regular British army, in a different regiment or corps, for a number of years beforehand. There was just no way that a guy could join the regular SAS straight from Civvy Street. However, it was possible to get accepted for selection if you went via a round-about route through the Territorial Army Volunteer Reserve (the part-time soldiers of the TA), and that's just what I did.

First of all I applied to join 3 Company, 10 Battalion, the Parachute Regiment. This was a TA unit based in Finchley in London. Luckily I was accepted for this regiment, as the TA could not afford to be as picky as the regular battalions when it came to getting recruits. I passed my initial selection weekend with 10 Para and went on to do a week's training at Aldershot followed by the TA version of 'P' company, which was, of course, followed by a brief parachute training course. Once in 10 Para as a 'badged' soldier (able to wear the maroon beret and winged badge of the Parachute Regiment) I then did what I had been advised to do by the SAS commanding officer, and immediately applied for selection to the TA SAS. In this case I applied to 21 SAS Regiment which was also based in London and easily passed the selection course. Then I applied for selection to 22 SAS, the regular British Army regiment. This was the only means open for a civvy to get himself into the regiment straight from Civvy Street. It was a load of bloody messing around and took a couple of months, but it wasn't that bad and it did help me to get back into the peace-time British Army way of doing things rather than the war-time Rhodesian way.

SAS selection in Britain was totally different from my previous experience out in southern Africa. For one thing selection took place during the winter, and the main problem was trying to stay alive in some atrocious bad weather, including snow storms and seemingly non-stop rain. It also takes place in some mean, featureless, bleak and mountainous countryside. Fully trained soldiers have died on the SAS selection course through exposure to the elements, and for a man who had grown accustomed to the African sunshine, I was somewhat at a disadvantage on a Welsh mountainside in typically British winter weather.

It wasn't long though before it became obvious to the directing staff that I had already served in Special Forces and they were more than happy with my level of skills and fitness, and my positive attitude. Discreet checking with the CO soon brought at least some of my past out into the open, and it was decided amongst the directing staff that I could be badged straight away. In this way it had only been about three months from applying for 10 Para until becoming an accepted addition to 22 Special Air Service Regiment, based in Hereford. Although I couldn't, of course, start at my previous Rhodesian rank of sergeant and was now only a trooper, I was as happy as Larry to be back in the fold and to belong, once again, to an elite fighting unit.

TWENTY-TWO

From selection I was posted straight into B Squadron, which at that time was the Counter Revolutionary Warfare (CRW) Wing of 22 SAS, and began training in the counter-terrorism role that the SAS was soon to become famous for around the world.

We trained constantly, day after day, always evaluating our progress and trying for better and faster ways of doing things. This was a new form of warfare, against a new type of enemy, but we felt that we were ready for anything. This was soon to be put to the test.

At 11.30am on Wednesday 30th April 1980, six armed men burst into the Iranian Embassy to Great Britain, located at 16 Princes Gate, South Kensington in London. The men overpowered a member of the British police forces Diplomatic Protection Squad, police constable Trevor Lock, and eventually took a total of 26 people hostage from within the building. The hostages included Chris Cramer and Simon Harris, who were working for the BBC, and several tourists and students who were all at the embassy to collect visas, as well as a range of Embassy staff, though not the Ambassador himself. Unknown to the terrorists, PC Lock secretly alerted his superiors by activating an alarm that was hidden in his lapel. He also managed to keep his own pistol concealed on his person.

TWENTY-THREE

The terrorists belonged to a little-known group calling itself the 'Democratic Revolutionary Front for the Liberation of Arabistan'. They were armed with a variety of small arms, including submachine guns, pistols, a revolver and hand grenades. They were protesting against the oppression of Khūzestān by the then Iranian leader; Ayatollah Khomeini.

It wasn't long before the Metropolitan Police were on the scene and cordoned off the area, quickly followed by Scotland Yard's anti-terrorism branch and their technical support branch. Police snipers were also quickly put into place overlooking the building.

The terrorists were led by Awn Ali Mohammed, who was 27 years old. He was the only one of the terrorists who could speak English, though not very well, so some of the hostages were used to communicate between the terrorists and the police negotiators. They sent a telex demanding the 'freedom, autonomy and recognition of the Arab people' and the release of 91 political prisoners who were imprisoned in Iran. The terrorists also demanded a plane to fly themselves and their hostages out of the UK. If their demands were not met by noon of Thursday, 1st May, they would kill all of the hostages and blow up the Embassy.

The SAS had been given the heads-up by a former SAS man who was serving in the Metropolitan Police. Thus we were already on our way to London, zooming along the roads from Hereford in our converted white Range Rovers, before we got the official warning from Regimental Headquarters.

By the time of the deadline on 1st May, the police negotiators had done a good job of calming the terrorists down. Instead of carrying out their threats they released two of the hostages unharmed on humanitarian grounds. One of these hostages was a pregnant woman, and one of them was Chris Cramer from the BBC. Apparently the English hostages had talked amongst themselves and had decided that Chris was going to play up on an old illness so that the terrorists would release him. Then he would give the police as much information as he could about the numbers of terrorists, how they were armed and where the hostages were located etc.

We were temporarily based at a nearby army barracks, where we built a mock-up of the Embassy and practiced various scenarios of entry and clearing the building, designing a 'Deliberate Action Plan' for an assault. There was also one team of our guys on constant standby next door to the Embassy at number 14, ready to commit to an 'Immediate Action Plan' if called upon. On our time off, which wasn't much, we watched the world snooker championships on TV.

On Saturday the terrorists released another two hostages, but by now, after four days, they were getting tired of the stalemate that had developed and their nerves were becoming frayed. At this point they had reduced their demands to a car and a flight out from Heathrow with the hostages. On Saturday night I was one of a small team that did a reconnaissance onto the roof of the Embassy to check out a skylight (that we had been informed by the Embassy's caretaker was in a state of disrepair). The information we'd received was correct so we forced open the skylight and one of the guys hung upside down from it to check out the room below before we headed back.

By the morning of the sixth day of the siege, the terrorists were getting seriously pissed off with the negotiations, which to them appeared to be going nowhere. They forced PC Lock to hang out of a window and shout that they were going to kill a hostage. Later, they took Abbas Lavasani, the Chief Press Attaché of the Iranian Embassy, downstairs, and at noon three shots were heard. However, it wasn't until 7pm that evening that more shots were heard and Abbas's dead body was pushed out onto the street. That was a big mistake for the terrorists. As soon as they'd killed someone on British soil, the operation was handed over to us by the police, and they'd more or less signed their own death warrants. We had been given 'a ticket to ride' as one of my colleagues joked.

At 7.23pm Operation Nimrod, the operation to rescue the hostages, began and we assaulted the building. A number of four-man teams or 'bricks' entered the building from different points, including the rear of the building on the ground floor, the front of the building via the first floor and from the roof, through the skylight. Like most of the blokes in the teams I had been pretty scared over the preceding days, thinking about the action to come and half-hoping that the siege would come to a peaceful end. But as soon as we got the order to 'go, go, go' the adrenaline was buzzing through my body and I felt invulnerable as we stormed in.

My main memories of the assault are of constant noise, not only from the exploding stun-grenades and shooting but also from my head mike which was full of the nervous voices of the police and officers outside constantly shouting for updates. There were flames and flashes, explosions and screaming. To the poor hostages in the building it must have seemed like a chaotic scene from hell, but we knew exactly what we were doing and where we were going. By 7.34pm, after just eleven minutes, we had killed all of the terrorists except for one, who was taken prisoner (and would later be sentenced to life in prison), and rescued the majority of the hostages, steering them out of the building to the rear. One hostage had been killed by the terrorists during the assault and two others had been wounded. The only wound to a SAS trooper was some minor burns sustained when one guy had got stuck on some dodgy abseiling rope and ended up swinging into a fire started by a stun-grenade. Operation Nimrod was a complete success. The lives of 19 hostages had been saved. Prospective terrorists had been shown what would happen to them if they tried an attack on British soil, and the British SAS had suddenly become the most talked about Special Forces regiment in the world. Personally, I was quite happy to join the celebration afterwards and get pissed up with the rest of the teams. The worst moment of the entire assault for me was seeing a high-explosive grenade dropped by a terrorist come bouncing down a flight of stairs towards me. There was nowhere to go and nothing that I could do to save myself if it had exploded. Imagine my relief when I saw that the daft sod had forgot to pull the pin out of it!

TWENTY-FOUR

A few days later I had my first interview with the commanding officer of 22 SAS. We talked a little about my previous combat experience in Rhodesia and then he told me that he had received nothing but praise for me from the other CRW team members on Operation Nimrod. Although he had always been a little reluctant to have me in the regiment because of my association with SIS, he had now decided that I could stay, at least for the time-being. I was informed that I would be moved from the CRW Wing into the mountain troop of G Squadron. Not because of anything that I had or hadn't done, but purely because this would be new ground for me to cover and he liked to keep 'his lads' on their toes. So I would begin training for my new role straight away. And oh, by the way, I was being promoted to lance corporal.

After a couple of weeks serving as a member of G Squadrons Mountain Troop, which involved a short, but fairly uneventful, operational tour in County Armagh, I found myself the guest of another British Special Forces unit; the Mountain and Arctic Warfare Cadre, of the Royal Marines, based in Plymouth. Here, I was to learn my new skills of arctic warfare from the most experienced teachers in the business.

Before this happened though, another, totally unrelated, but equally important thing happened to me; I met a girl and we fell in love. I was on leave and out for a drink with a few of the mates that I had made in London while serving with 10 Para, when I ran into this gorgeous young girl of Irish Protestant descent. She was 17 and I was in my twenties, but the age-difference never seemed to matter. Her name was Anne-Marie; she was about five foot ten inches tall in her stockings with lovely long blonde hair and a fantastic smile, and legs that went on forever. She was always laughing and having a good time. We saw each other constantly for the few weeks that I had off and after I travelled down to Plymouth to start my arctic training she wrote to me every day. For the first time in my life I felt that this was the real deal and that I had finally met the girl of my dreams.

The Mountain and Arctic Warfare Cadre was a small unit that trained Royal Marines to become 'mountain leaders'. These mountain leaders would then train other Royal Marines in mountain and arctic warfare and would also, in times of conflict, operate as a small but highly specialised Special Forces unit. Thus began eight months of training, which for me, was entirely different to anything that I had ever done before.

The training took place in the UK and in Norway over the autumn and winter months and covered rock, snow and ice climbing, cliff assaults, cross-country skiing, cold weather survival, patrol insertion, long range patrolling and raiding. The training was hard but fun and my fellow students were a great bunch of blokes. I don't think that I ever got fully used to the cold, especially during a Norwegian winter where the snow could be anything up to fifteen feet in depth and the air-temperature, including the wind-chill factor, could be as low as minus 60°C (76°F). But I learned to cope with it, as did with my mates, even if at times the cold seemed to pierce your body right through to your bones. The final exercise of the course started with infiltration into enemy territory, followed by a CTR and exfiltration, followed by capture and 'resistance to interrogation'. Some of the high points of this training that have stuck in my mind over the years include a so-called confidence-boosting jump from a tall cliff on the coast of

Devon onto a small 'chimney stack' rock formation nearby. The jump itself was not that hard, as the stack was lower than, and only a few metres from the top of the cliff. However I remember that it seemed bloody crazy at the time, as the grassy top of the stack appeared to be tiny and a very long way away from our vantage point on the cliff. Still, I did it with no problem at all, though not everybody on the course did, and those that failed to take the jump were binned from the course. Then there was an exercise involving a night assault on a cliff-top 'radar station' in Norway, in which I had to free-climb to the top of a very high cliff in the dark and in appalling weather conditions. Later, in the freezing Norwegian mid-winter, we had to deliberately ski into a small pool cut into the ice and then pull ourselves out using our ski-poles. The water was absolutely bloody freezing of course, taking my breath away when I initially went in. I remember that when I was struggling out of my uniform afterwards to dry myself down and warm myself up, that when I checked out my private bits my penis had shrunk to the size of a walnut and had turned a bright shade of blue! On the last leg of the final exercise, we ended up having a fight in the snow with some huge Dutch Marines who were playing the enemy. During this scrap several of our team, and the Dutch boys, ended up with nasty head and face injuries. All in all though, it was a very interesting and strangely satisfying course, and I made some really good friends in both the Royal and Dutch Marines.

After completing and passing the course with flying colours in the spring of 1981, I was posted back to the regiment. However, instead of going straight back into the mountain troop of G Squadron, most of whom were off on another operational tour somewhere or other, I ended up having yet another interview with the CO. This time I was even more convinced that I would never be fully accepted as a member of the British SAS, and it dawned on me that my posting to the Mountain and Arctic Warfare Cadre had been more to get rid of me for a few months, rather than to purely give me a new set of skills. The upshot of this interview was that it was strongly suggested that I apply for secondment from the regiment into 14 Field Security and Intelligence Company, as they were holding a selection course in about six weeks time. Although I would still be SAS, I'd be on operations in Northern Ireland for about 18 months after training, which of course would keep me out of the way again, until something more permanent could be found for me. Or at least that was how I felt.

On my next leave I proposed to Anne-Marie and we quickly got married. I was still renting the flat in North London and we spent a couple of blissful weeks setting up a home for ourselves there, before I had to go away again. However, as it turned out, I left her with more than a new husband and a new home; I also left her with a bun in the oven.

TWENTY-FIVE

14 Field Security and Intelligence Company was known by a
number of nicknames, but the one that I always used was
'the Det'. The Det was a force of highly-trained undercover
surveillance operatives, trained by a special training wing
of the SAS, led by SAS officers, and intended solely for
intelligence work in Northern Ireland. There were three
operational detachments set up across the water, one in
Londonderry, one in Belfast and one in Fermanagh, and the
headquarters detachment which was based at the RAF Base
at Aldergrove near Belfast.

The day I turned up for selection to the Det I was led
inside a Nissen hut and told to read the statement written
in chalk on a blackboard. It was a declaration that I would
be giving up my human rights; my name would mean
nothing and my rank would mean nothing; I would just be a
number from then on. I remember thinking: Yeah, what's
new about that? Then I was given a piece of paper that I
had to sign, stating that I had read and understood these
conditions.

Selection was open to anybody serving in the British
armed forces, unusually even to women. The course was
three weeks long and was, of course, physically exhausting
and similar to SAS selection except that more emphasis was
placed on mental capabilities. Working undercover requires
some unique characteristics. You need exceptional
observational skills of course, but also a lot of stamina and
the ability to think and work well under extreme stress.
You also have to have a very well developed sense of self-

confidence and self-reliance as most of the time you will be working on your own and you can expect no immediate help if a situation goes tits up and turns nasty.

After I passed selection I went on to the continuous training which was full-on for the next six months in Wales. As members of the Det we were encouraged not to tell each other our real names or to talk about our past. I learned to drive for the first time in my life, not only in cars but also in light and heavy goods vehicles. Driver training included driving at sustained high speed, skid control and controlled crashes, but also anti-ambush drills and how to use a vehicle as a weapon. I also learned the highly demanding skills that would be needed for covert surveillance. This included everything from setting up and manning OPs in wet, cold ditches and hedgerows in the countryside to doing the same in an urban situation in workshops and attics, etc. I learned to use photography as a tool and how to conceal video and still cameras in clothing and equipment. I also learned how to follow people on foot and in vehicles; how to pick locks and break into buildings in order to plant electronic bugs, video cameras and other surveillance devices, plus I was taught how to plant tracking devices on everything from people and arms caches through to vehicles.

Our instructors were men and women who had learned and sharpened their skills out on the streets. At one point we were put through a very realistic capture and interrogation scenario by team members pretending to be Provisional Irish Republican Army members. This scared us to fuck and we realised that we could expect no mercy from the real Provo's if we messed up and managed to get ourselves caught.

We then went on to receive training in unarmed combat, especially in how to disarm a knife or gun-wielding assailant, and from there we honed our close quarter battle skills even more. As a member of the Det we would always carry a personal weapon somewhere on our body and have spares in other vital places too. In my case I carried my favourite - a Browning 9mm pistol, plus a small .22 Walther PPK strapped to my ankle. Luckily flared trousers and jeans were still in fashion in those days so there was no visible bulge on my lower leg to give me away. I also carried another Browning hidden inside the door trim of my car, and another taped beneath the passenger seat. Some guys and girls used extended 20 round magazines on their pistols but I always thought that these were too prone to getting stoppages and jamming so I stuck to the standard 13 round mags. The whole idea behind this training was to encourage us to fight our way out of any trouble, because getting caught would be the end for us as we could expect no mercy. However, if we did get caught the resistance to interrogation training also showed us how to stay alive for as long as possible in the vain hope that the cavalry could come and save us.

TWENTY-SIX

After the training we were given a month's leave before our first posting across the water. This was fine by me as I felt that I had been away from Anne-Marie for much too long. She was heavily pregnant by this time and we were missing each other like crazy. She knew that I was in the army of course, and was fully aware that my commitments would keep me away from home for long periods of time. However, she never caught on that I was Special Forces. After all, there was no reason for her to know, especially as she'd probably worry even more while I was away doing my bit for Queen and Country.

I think that I was getting a bit soft at this stage, as I was thinking more and more about Anne-Marie and concentrating less on the job in hand. Going home was like reliving our honeymoon all over again every time. In hindsight I can see why of course, as we hardly ever saw each other for month after month. I guess that if we'd lived together all the time like any other normal married couple, then the gilt would have worn off our relationship a lot sooner.

Just before I was due to return to the Det and be posted to Northern Ireland my first son was born, and I was there to see it all happen. Anne-Marie's waters broke about 2am so I quickly bundled her into a taxi and shot around to the maternity hospital. I needn't have bothered hurrying though as she then kept me waiting for six hours before anything happened! Eventually she gave birth to a healthy baby boy and I held him in my arms for the first time as he gazed back with his bright blue eyes in a head that looked a little like ET. That was a magic moment that I will never forget as long as I live, and was only matched the once; when I found out that my second son had been born.

The birth went fine, there were no problems and little Robert, as we named him, was a bouncy healthy little bundle of joy. I was to leave him, to go back to work much too soon for my liking.

The Det was one of the most secretive units ever set up by the British armed forces to deal with the conflict in Northern Ireland. Hardly anybody knew of our existence at the time and even now you will find very few references. The unit has since been disbanded.

Our job at the time was to carry out surveillance on known and suspected terrorists, or 'players' as we knew them. Some team members went truly undercover on the streets and developed informers and contacts within terrorist organisations, working on their own with very little or no backup in a society that was as paranoid as it was dangerous. Other members, such as me, because of my long history and skills at CTR, were destined to spend our days and nights dug into a hole somewhere, closely observing suspected terrorists, logging their every move and contact. And I do mean closely. On occasions I actually set up OPs in the terrorist's gardens!

So this is how I was to spend the next ten months: lying hidden beneath a hedge or in a ditch, or beneath a pile of rubbish, or in an attic, watching terrorists going about their normal daily routines and waiting days or weeks for that one single moment when they would give themselves away in some form or the other. During my time I logged meetings between terrorists, taped conversations, and followed terrorists to hidden caches of weapons or stolen vehicles. I don't know how many lives I personally saved during this period. Only that the work that I and my colleagues did was making a big difference to somebody somewhere.

It was dangerous work as well as cold, wet and sometimes dirty. If I had been discovered I would have come to a very messy end at the hands of these vicious, evil bastards. But despite the dangers, many of the successful British Army operations during the conflict, whether it was the ambush of a terrorist team by the SAS, or a weapons cache being found in a churchyard, or a terrorist being arrested for a murder, had been set up by one of the Det.

In response, the terrorists increasingly used more sophisticated methods of maintaining contact with each other. They developed four-man cells who knew nothing of other terrorist cells so that if they were captured they couldn't give anything away about other groups. They sought out informers, or just those that they suspected might be informers, and dealt with them efficiently and cold-bloodedly. We, on the other hand, had to up our own game in order to continue to catch the bastards red-handed. It was a war of wits as much as it was a war of terror, and stuck in the middle were innocent people just trying to go about their daily lives.

When I started my first tour with the Det in Northern Ireland it was originally intended to go on for 18 months. Most members of the Det were operational for between 18 and 36 months at a time. Then they would return to their parent unit for a period of R & R before they were allowed, if they wanted to, to reapply for more special duties with the Det. However, in my case something happened that cut short my tour of duty: On Friday 2nd April 1982, the Argentinian armed forces invaded a little-known group of islands in the South Atlantic. The Argies called them Las Islas Malvinas. We called them the Falkland Islands, and they were British. A war was about to begin.

TWENTY-SEVEN

I didn't even know about the Argies invasion until the day after it happened. I had spent the previous three and a half weeks dug in beneath a hedgerow watching an isolated farm house in County Armagh. The person that I had been tasked to watch was a catholic girl in her mid-twenties. It was known that her boyfriend was a player who was wanted for questioning about the murder of a member of the Royal Ulster Constabulary (RUC), so my job was to wait and see whether he turned up to see his girlfriend. Anyway, to cut a long story short, her boyfriend did turn up at the farm very early on the morning of the Saturday 3rd April. I immediately got onto the net and informed South Det that he had arrived, and they let the RUC know. They arrived at the farmhouse and arrested the guy within the hour.

I followed standard operating procedure at this point and waited until the coppers had taken away the murder suspect before withdrawing from my OP and moving away, leaving no sign that I had ever been there. Even the policemen that had conducted the arrest had had no idea that an undercover operative had been based overlooking the farm. They believed that the information that led to the arrest had come from an anonymous tip-off. This was the usual way these things went down.

After returning to our base in Fermanagh, and hoping never to have to shit into a plastic bag ever again in my entire lifetime, I was greeted by a buzz of excitement and told about the invasion of the Falklands. Within minutes I was on a secure phone line to my old mountain troop commander in G Squadron SAS. I reminded him that I was a highly-trained mountain and arctic warfare specialist and about my CTR skills, and practically begged him to be included in any forthcoming SAS operation in the South Atlantic. I think that my enthusiasm impressed him because that same morning I found myself on board a plane bound for England. South Det was a bit pissed off, but I wasn't the only operative that they would lose to the war; quite a few Det guys were sent to the south Atlantic.

When I arrived at Bradbury Lines Barracks in Hereford (SAS HQ) a few hours later the place was a hive of activity. I immediately sought out G Squadron's mountain troop commander who informed me that I wasn't going to go south with them after all, but had been transferred over to the mountain troop of D Squadron, as they were short-handed. Oh, and by-the-way, I'd better get over there straight away as they were flying out the following day to Ascension Island. And that was it, I made myself known to my new troop, was issued with my personal weapons and my kit, had a few hours to grab some hot food and a bit of kip, and then found myself on a coach to the RAF base at Brize Norton. Here we boarded a Hercules and then were on our way to Ascension Island, in the middle of the Atlantic Ocean, approximately 3,700 miles away.

The Falkland Islands are located in the southern Atlantic Ocean, some 7,000 miles from Britain. They comprise over 100 islands, most of which are small and peppered around the two largest islands: West and East Falkland. There is only one town, called Port Stanley, on the east coast of East Falkland and the human population of the islands was then about 2,000, consisting mainly of staunchly British people. The main income for the islands economy was from sheep farming, and the sheep population vastly outnumbered the human population, which was probably why we soldiers came to call the Falkland Islanders 'sheep-shaggers'. The geography of the islands is fairly similar to the bleak countryside of South Wales where the regiment did a lot of its training. It is mountainous with lots of open moorland. The climate down there is notorious for being wet, cold and very windswept. Even in high summer the temperatures were pretty low.

The Military junta in Argentina claimed that the islands belonged to Argentina and not to Britain. They were having a hard time in their own country, and as is so often the case when this happens, they decided to unite their countrymen in a war that they were sure they were going to win.

The islands were defended by a small detachment of Royal Marines when the Argentinian armed forces invaded the Falklands. Despite their low numbers, they still managed to inflict serious damage on the invading forces before they surrendered along with the island's British Governor. The Argies then proceeded to transport thousands of troops (mostly young conscripts, backed up by professional marines and Special Forces), along with artillery and air force units, to East and West Falkland.

TWENTY-EIGHT

After arriving at Wideawake airfield on Ascension, we had a few days of frantic activity getting ourselves and our kit together before setting sail, along with M Company, 42 Commando Royal Marines, aboard HMS Antrim, a destroyer, and the frigate HMS Plymouth.

I realised during my short stay on Ascension Island that in the excitement of going to war, I hadn't even thought about Anne-Marie and our new child in all of the time since I had left Northern Ireland. Feeling more than a little bit guilty, I called her from Ascension and chatted for a few minutes. When she mentioned the Falkland crisis, I told her that I wouldn't be involved and that I was still carrying on with my tour in Northern Ireland with the Para's. I know it was a lie, but I didn't want her to worry unnecessarily. I was much happier with her thinking I was having an easy tour over the water than thinking about me sailing down to the Falklands and getting into a real shooting war.

We sailed all the way down to South Georgia, meeting other ships of our task force on the way, and arrived off the island on the morning of Wednesday 21st April. There, the powers-that-be decided on a plan called Operation Paraguay that would enable us to retake the island from the small Argentinian garrison that occupied the whaling station at Grytviken. The plan required the insertion of our mountain troop onto Fortuna Glacier, where we would then move forward and set up an OP at Leith, to the north of

Grytviken. At the same time, 2 Section of the Special Boat Squadron (SBS), Royal Marines (another Special Forces unit) would attempt to set up an OP to the south of Grytviken.

The initial landing by chopper on the glacier at mid-day went fine. Then, of course, it all went to pot and the weather closed in. Within an hour of landing the wind picked up until it was gusting at over 120 miles per hour. Then it turned into 'white out' blizzard conditions. We lost most of our bergens, as they were whipped away by the wind, and we found it impossible to move, the wind being so strong that you couldn't even stand up in it. We radioed in and spent the night huddled up to one another behind the relative shelter of a low ice-ridge. Just as in Norway during my mountain and arctic warfare training, the temperature dropped down to minus 60°C. It was an uncomfortable night to say the least.

The following day the weather was just as ferocious. When two Wessex helicopters came in to pick us up the next morning, we clambered on board only for both of them to be flipped over by the wind and crash back onto the glacier on their sides. Luckily no one was seriously injured during these crashes. Later that afternoon, another Wessex managed to pick up both our patrol and the crews of the downed helicopters. In blinding snow and howling wind the brilliant pilot got us airborne and safely returned us to the task force, even though his chopper was grossly overloaded.

The SBS patrol had also encountered problems, as they couldn't cross Cumberland Bay in their Geminis because there was too much glacier ice. They had to lie up before being picked up by helicopter, and then they were reinserted into Moraine Fiord.

Even though the weather had become absolutely atrocious, with 30m high waves and howling wind, by Friday both the SAS and SBS had managed to insert patrols onto South Georgia and we had both set up OPs overlooking Grytviken. The task force then received a warning that there were Argentinian submarines in the area and our ships withdrew from the immediate vicinity of South Georgia, leaving the OPs in place on the island. On the 24th April the task force was again ordered into the area to hunt for the submarines and the following day an Argentinian submarine was located in Grytviken harbour. It was subsequently attacked and disabled by the task force's helicopters. She was then abandoned by her crew.

With the addition of the submarine's crew, it was thought that the Argentinian garrison on South Georgia numbered about 140-150 men. The head-sheds decided to land all of our available troops on the island and immediately assault Grytviken. Early in the afternoon of 25th April the first wave of an ad hoc force (made up of 76 SAS, SBS and Royal Marines) was landed by chopper at a place called Hestestletten. I was among them, and we rapidly moved up to the Argentinian base under the covering fire of the naval guns from the task force ships. At 5pm the Argentinian garrison surrendered without firing a single shot.

The commander of the Argie garrison at Grytviken told us that he surrendered because he thought that we were all "Mad men. Who else but mad men would attack across a minefield?" Our reply was: "What bloody minefield?" Unbeknown to us we had run straight across it as we moved forward from Grytviken to the survey station. Fortunately no one set off any of the land-mines!

On the evening of 25th April the Union Jack and the White Ensign of the Royal Navy were once again flying over the old whaling station at Grytviken, South Georgia.

The next day, after leaving South Georgia and the Argie prisoners of war in the hands of M Company of the Royal Marines, we set sail to cover the 900 miles back to the Falklands.

TWENTY-NINE

On 1st May, the main naval task force carrying the British Para's and Marines from Ascension Island arrived within the 200 mile Exclusion Zone (a military demarcation set up around the Falkland Islands by the British government during the Falklands war). Aircraft from the British warships attacked Argentinian positions on the islands of West and East Falklands, and RAF Vulcan bombers, flying all the way from Ascension, carried out the first of five bombing runs against the Argentinian airfield at Port Stanley. Operation Corporate, the retaking of the Falkland Islands, had begun.

That same night I was a member of a four-man brick from D Squadron inserted by Gemini onto the west coast of East Falkland. In total there were ten four man patrols inserted, from both D and G Squadrons, and our task was to recce the Argentinian positions, set up OPs and generally harass the hell out of the Argies wherever and whenever we came across them. Each man carried kit weighing 130 lbs (about 60 kg), most of which consisted of ammunition and weapons (plus a sleeping bag and rations). We all knew that it would be at least three weeks before the British invasion began in earnest with troop landings, so we also knew that we would basically be on our own if we got into a fire-fight. This is what being a soldier in the Special Forces is all about; having the means and the opportunity to play footsie with an enemy force much larger than we were.

We were joined on the island by patrols from the Royal Marines, both SBS and my old mates in the Mountain and Arctic Warfare Cadre. The landscape on the islands was undulating mountainous moorland, with very little natural cover. Therefore we would only move at night and would lie up in shallow camouflaged trenches during the day. It never seemed to stop raining and every time we dug a hole it would immediately fill up with freezing cold peat-stained water. Not once did I ever feel completely dry and warm, as the incessant rain was always being driven hard by the howling wind and seemed to penetrate even the most waterproof of clothing.

Despite the number of British patrols moving around the island there was only one 'friendly-fire' incident, what we called a 'blue-on-blue'. This was between a SAS and SBS patrol when they blundered into one another one night in atrocious weather. Each thinking that the other patrol was Argentinian; they opened fire on them. Luckily only one SBS guy was injured before they realised what had happened. The thing I remember most about this brief introduction to the Falklands was the rain, the wind and the cold. We would often say to each other, with typical army black humour: "What the fuck are we doing here? Who the fuck cares if the Argies want the islands? They can have them. They're fucking horrible!" During this period we got into a number of small fire-fights with Argie forces, but nothing major. That is until the night of 14th May.

We had been called back to the task force and picked up by chopper. This took us to HMS Hermes, an aircraft carrier. There we were briefed on a forthcoming operation by our boss, Gavin Hamilton. Over the previous 13 days the RAF Vulcans had continued to bomb the main Argie airfield at Port Stanley and the enemy had been forced to disperse most of their aircraft from Port Stanley to the airfields at Goose Green and on Pebble Island, or risk them being destroyed. Our task therefore, was to carry out an assault against the Pebble Island airfield and fuck up as many Argie aircraft as we could before withdrawing.

Pebble Island is located on the northern coast of West Falkland. The main troop landings were due to take place on the beaches of San Carlos Bay in about a week's time, so this serious enemy threat had to be neutralised in order for the troops to make it safely to shore. D Squadrons boat troop had been watching the airfield from an OP since the night of the 11th, despite the fact that the island was practically bare of any natural cover.

We boarded Sea King helicopters and were joined by a naval gunfire support observer, who would give us covering fire from the 4.5 inch guns of HMS Glamorgan, a County Class Destroyer lying off the coast. We were armed with a ferocious variety of weapons, including 81mm mortars, 66mm light anti-tank weapons and M203 40mm grenade launchers slung beneath our rifle barrels. We touched down in a landing zone about four miles from the objective, protected by the boat troop boys, only to find that the night was brilliantly lit by a full moon. This was definitely not ideal for us to make a covert approach across bare terrain to the airfield. The boat troop boss gave us a short briefing and we began the tab to the airfield. Once on target we would have only 30 minutes in which to destroy all of the aircraft on the airfield.

As we approached the objective the night was suddenly torn apart by the exploding shells of Glamorgan's guns. The enemy garrison of about 200 men opened fire on us with rifles and machine guns but luckily they weren't very precise. We were very well illuminated by both the moon and the shell fire, and moved off to place our charges on the aircraft, splitting into our demolition's teams while still under fire. As soon as we'd done this we started to withdraw to the final rendezvous. When we'd all made it back the demolitions went off and Glamorgan switched her fire, hitting the Argentinian fuel dump, watchtower and ammunition stores. The whole island seemed to shake from the ferocity of the attack and the night was lit up in a fantastic display of pyrotechnics. We tabbed quickly back to the pick-up-point and both boat and mountain troops were picked up safely by the waiting choppers and transported back to HMS Hermes, where we sat down to a very welcome full English breakfast. In a classic SAS attack that lasted only about 20 minutes on the objective, we had successfully destroyed all the enemy aircraft and totally devastated the airfield. In return we had two men wounded during the extraction, one by shrapnel and another concussed when a land-mine exploded.

The war would not go entirely in our favour though. On the 19th May, while 'cross-decking' from one ship to another, a Sea King helicopter's blades were hit, probably by an albatross, and it crashed into the freezing South Atlantic Ocean. While a handful of men survived, 21 died, most of them from my troop. Luckily for me I hadn't been with them, but this loss hit me and the other survivors of the troop very hard. Although I had not served with them for very long, I had begun to class some of them as mates. Most of the other survivors of mountain troop had worked with these guys for years and they were all very close. D Squadron's mountain troop had virtually been wiped out in this one accident and B Squadron's mountain troop was flown in from Ascension to take over our missions. The show had to go on.

THIRTY

Two nights later the main British landing force of Paras and Royal Marines hit the beaches of San Carlos. To provide diversions to this landing, four SAS patrols were choppered out to various landing zones, where we then tabbed to pre-designated targets. I was in a patrol containing the remnants of D Squadron's mountain troop and our target was the airfield and garrison at Goose Green on East Falkland. It was a hard tab to our objective, as we were all heavily weighed down with weapons and ammo, including Milan anti-tank missiles and 66mm light anti-tank weapons. Having arrived, our job was to basically blast the fuck out of Goose Green, constantly moving position and letting fly with everything that we had in the hope that this would keep the Argies occupied while our guys came safely ashore. We found out later from Argie prisoners of war that they were under the impression that they were being attacked by a full battalion of around 600 men. When we'd expended all of our ammo we quickly tabbed it back to San Carlos and the relative safety of the growing British beach head, satisfied that yet another job had been well done.

After this we were at a bit of a loss and the remnants of our devastated troop eventually broke up and joined other troops, or went off to set up more OPs on West and East Falkland. I was lucky once again, as I now found myself attached to the Royal Marines Mountain and Arctic Warfare Cadre, where I had a happy reunion with a lot of the good friends I had made while doing the Mountain Leaders course. Captain Gavin Hamilton was not so lucky. On the island of West Falkland, during June, he was killed while trying to help one of his fellow troopers escape from the Argies, after their OP had been compromised. Apparently he was riddled with machine gun fire three times, but still got up each time to continue his one-man attack against the Argies. His oppo escaped at first but was later captured. The 'boss' had been a good man and an excellent troop commander. He was posthumously awarded the Military Cross, which many believe should have been a Victoria Cross. His untimely death had raised the number of dead from D Squadron's mountain troop to 19 men, the biggest loss that the SAS had had in a single campaign since the Second World War.

For one whole day we had a bit of a rest in the dryness and warmth of a sheep-shearing shed within the relative safety of the beachhead at San Carlos. It gave us our first and only chance to sort out our kit and dry most of it off, as well as get some hot food down our necks. However, it wasn't long before I found myself back out in the cold wind and rain with the cadre guys, conducting aggressive patrols against Argentinian Marines and Special Forces dug into positions on and around Mount Kent. At one point me and a mate had donned snipers 'Ghillie suits' (a one piece outfit covered with hundreds of strips of hessian and other camouflaged material to break up the human outline of the wearer) and had crept up to within a couple of metres of an enemy slit-trench in the darkness of a cloudy night. My oppo was a Spanish-speaker, so we spent an hour or so in this close proximity listening to a conversation that went on between the occupants of the trench. I didn't understand a word of what they were saying, but apparently they mentioned that 602 Commando Company (an Argentine Special Force unit) was amongst the enemy forces that we were facing. Just before we had decided to pull back, one of the Argies had removed his cap and put it onto the forward lip of the trench. My mate couldn't resist temptation and reaching forward he nicked the cap. I wondered afterwards what went through the mind of the Argie marine when he reached up to retrieve his cap and found that it had disappeared! I bet he didn't guess that a mountain leader from the Royal Marines Mountain and Arctic Warfare Cadre had nicked it from right under his nose!

A four-man OP had also been set up at a place called Bull Hill, on the route to Port Stanley from Teal Inlet, well ahead of the main British force. On 27th May they sent in a radio report stating that it would probably be their last for a while as two Argentinian helicopters were hovering right over their position. However, the helicopters moved off and a subsequent radio message reported that the choppers had dropped off troops, probably Argentinian Special Forces, on the lower slope of Mount Simon. Brigade headquarters tasked the rest of the cadre to take out these Special Forces as they couldn't be allowed to dominate the approaches to Teal Inlet from the high ground. On the evening of 30th May another patrol previously inserted onto Mount Simon, reported that Argie helicopters had just dropped off about 16 men at a deserted shepherd's house called 'Top Malo House', about 400m from their own position. They had also heard more helicopter activity nearby. As it was already getting dark it was too late to order an airstrike against the target and the area was well out of the range of the nearest British artillery units, so it was decided to launch an assault against the Argentine force early the following morning.

Nineteen of us boarded a Sea King helicopter the next morning. After a short flight we inserted in an area of 'dead ground' (not visible to the enemy) only about 1km from Top Malo House. Upon hitting the ground we immediately split into two groups; a cover group went off to the left flank while an assault group, including me, moved forward to attack the house. It was very cold; the ground was covered in snow and it was sleeting quite heavily at the time.

About two hours after dawn the cover group opened fire and the assault group charged forward. Enemy fire came at us and two of our team were hit but carried on anyway. The building caught fire and as we approached it we were almost flattened by ammunition stores in the house going up in an almighty explosion. One of the lads spotted the Argies making a break for it out the back of the house. They were legging it toward a stream-bed about 200m away, covered by the smoke from the house. We went after them and luckily the smoke also screened us from the Argies who began firing as they ran. When they reached the stream-bed and began to lay down more accurate fire onto us we also went to ground and began to return their fire. The fire-fight went on like this for about 40 minutes until eventually the Argentinians realised that we had the upper hand and decided to surrender.

The Argentine force had consisted of 12 men, mainly from the 1st Assault Section, 602 Commando Company. Some of these guys' officers had been trained by the British SBS a few years before, but fortunately for us they had not learned their lessons very well. They had decided to take cover in the house because of the bad weather and had failed to post any sentries outside because of the sleet. Two very bad mistakes. We killed two of them and wounded six during the assault. The rest were taken as prisoners, to be interrogated later at Brigade Headquarters.

Unfortunately, because of this assault, we had missed the British attack by 42 Commando and the SAS that captured Mount Kent. We took part in only one more action, a small diversionary attack on Port Stanley's defences while the 2nd battalion of the Parachute Regiment, and a troop of the Blues and Royals, took Wireless Ridge on the night of 13/14th June. The Argentinian forces on the Falkland Islands surrendered on 14th June. Their brief reign on the Falklands had lasted for 74 days.

THIRTY-ONE

Friday 18th October 2013
Huntingdon, Cambridgeshire

Every man and woman of the Cambridgeshire Serious and Organised Crime Agency was gathered together in their suite of offices on the second floor of the counties police headquarters at Hinchingbrooke. It was already well past 8pm and most of them had had very little sleep during the past four days and nights. It showed in their slumped shoulders and haggard faces, with many of the men (who formed the majority of the squad), unshaven.

DCI Davies walked out of his office to address his troops and even he realised that they needed a break if the investigation was going to drag on, and he now believed that it would.

He spent about an hour going through everything that they had learned about John Smith so far. He told them how several veterans from the Rhodesian bush war of the 1960s and 1970s had now come forward claiming to have known Smith, who had then gone by the name of Robert White, not Danny Brown as told in his autobiography. He told his team that everyone who had known this Rob White had been full of praise for his soldiering skills and personal courage. He talked about the first two parts of the man's autobiography that had been emailed to them and how nearly everything that he had written in it appeared to have been a true account, according to the other people that had served with him at

143

the same time. The only unchecked point was Smith's claim that he had been 'recruited' by MI6, the British SIS, to act as a spy against the very people that he was fighting for in southern Africa. However, the chief constable was making high-level enquiries with MI6 to see if this part of the man's story could be verified, though he doubted whether there would be a result from this in the near future, as they all knew how bloody secretive the security services could be, especially regarding 'one of their own'.

He then went on to talk about the second, and most recent part of the autobiography that had been sent to them earlier that day, in which Smith had claimed that he had joined the British SAS and had served in Northern Ireland and the Falklands War. He informed his staff that they were still making official enquiries with the Ministry of Defence but had yet to receive a satisfactory answer from them. However, 'unofficial' enquiries through the SAS regimental association had proved more positive, and several former SAS men had also come forward, and that yes, the latest 'facts' in the autobiography also appeared to be true. Furthermore there was the undisputed fact that Smith had raided a Territorial Army unit of the SAS in Birmingham displaying his knowledge of army organisation. He had known where the senior permanent staff instructor of the unit was living and his first name (although the soldier hadn't recognised Smith), and had also, according to this very experienced SAS warrant officer, known a lot about the security of the TA centre and where he could find the weapons and ammunition that he had wanted. After helping himself to a plethora of both, he had left the SAS soldier and his family tied up in their home unhurt, except for his wife who had sustained a minor flesh wound from a silenced pistol. It was only because the soldier had managed to escape his bonds after a few hours that they had been informed so quickly of Smith's successful raid. Even so, their colleagues in Birmingham had arrested the soldier and were checking him out to make sure that he wasn't in league with Smith in some way.

He summarised quickly as he could see that some of the team was beginning to drop off:

"It appears that we have been totally wrong in all of the assumptions that we have made about Smith. It turns out that he is a highly-trained and skilled Special Forces soldier, who has served with distinction in at least two wars. He is not just a van driver or a 'nobody' (a sharp look here at DS Price, who, by the look on his face didn't give a toss) and he has proved this by taking the piss out of SOCA and the police force in general. He escaped from the courthouse in Peterborough, killing two prison officers with his bare hands as he did so, and frankly he has run rings around us since then. Now he has managed to get his hands on enough weapons, explosives and ammunition to start World War Three!" He paused for effect, moving his gaze from face to face.

"We don't know where Smith is holed up or what vehicle he drives. One thing is for sure though; we will catch this bloody murderer. I don't care who he was in his past or what he has done. He abducted, raped and murdered a sweet little girl and we will catch him and make sure that he pays for his crime!" His rousing speech didn't appear to have much effect in raising the morale of his squad, who still looked like they were ready to drop off to sleep. He gave up.

"Okay. We're all pretty knackered. I want everyone to go home now and make sure that you get a good night's sleep. I want to see you all looking bushy-tailed and wide awake in the morning. We'll catch this bastard tomorrow! Okay, bugger off!"

Smith was sitting in his stolen Land Rover Defender not 200m away, as the crowd of SOCA detectives left the building. From his place in the public car park he recognised more than a few of the faces as they climbed into their own cars in the adjacent police car park, started them up, waited for the barriers to lift and drove away.

His rage grew in intensity as he watched DS Price and DCI Davies drive away. He remembered vividly the days and nights he had spent in the cells here, and the endless number of interrogations by those two wankers. He also remembered how they had paraded him, handcuffed between them, through the officers of SOCA like they were a couple of bloody war heroes with a captured POW.

Still, thanks to them he knew where the SOCA offices were located in the building. They really are a bunch of cowboys, he thought.

Half an hour after midnight, Smith finally emerged from his vehicle where he had been dozing in the driver's seat. He stretched himself to get rid of the stiffness in his body, thinking to himself how bloody old he had become, grimacing as his muscles and ligaments cracked. Then he went to the rear of the vehicle, opened the back door and took out a large holdall.

The car park was unlit at this time of night, probably to save the council a bit of money, he thought. He made his way, carrying the heavy holdall over his shoulder, through a strip of woodland bordering the road and then across the open playing field until he had a good view of the south-west aspect of the headquarters. The moon was up but it was a dull, cloudy night with a slight drizzle in the air, so he knew that he was invisible to anyone looking out of the building's windows. About 100m from his intended target he settled himself onto the short grass beneath the cover of a small clump of trees.

Working methodically he removed eight tubular items from his holdall and laid them on the ground in front of him. With the ease of many years of practice he grasped each one at opposite ends and gave them a jerk, opening them up to twice the length that they had been. There was a slight sound as the sights on each tube popped out into the firing position.

He studied the building in front of him, remembering in his mind's eye the twists and turns when he had been

146

led by Davies and Price to be paraded in front of their colleagues, and the view that he had glimpsed through the office windows as he was dragged along to the cheering and applause of all those twats. Bang on, he thought as he deftly pulled back the safeties of the weapons, noticing that only a few small desk lights had been left on to illuminate the SOCA's suite of offices.

Firing a L1A1 66mm Light Anti-tank Weapon is the easiest thing in the world. You just put the tubular launcher onto your shoulder, take aim through the simple battle sights and press down with the fingers of your right hand onto the rubber-enclosed trigger. The rocket motor ignites inside the tube expelling the 1.8kg high explosive anti-tank rocket forward at great speed towards the target, while the back-blast of the launching rocket flares out to the rear in a bright and extremely hot flash; there is very little recoil. As the rocket leaves the launcher tube six small fins automatically extend and stabilise it during its short flight. When it hits the intended target it can penetrate through eight inches of armour plating on an armoured vehicle or through two feet of reinforced concrete. When the warhead has penetrated, the main high explosive charge ignites. After the rocket has been fired the empty 'one-shot-only' launcher is discarded.

It took Smith approximately three seconds to fire each of the eight rockets that he had readied and had lying in a row on the ground in front of him. He spaced them out so that they targeted the wide span of SOCA offices on the second floor and when they hit, one after another, the dark quiet night was torn apart by the roar and flashes of the exploding warheads as they decimated everything around them. As he fired each weapon he threw it onto a growing pile of empty launcher tubes by his side.

When all of the weapons were empty, Smith calmly stood up and began the short walk back to his Land Rover, pausing only once to turn and lob a white phosphorus hand grenade onto the pile of launchers which exploded with a flash as it consumed the empty plastic tubes. Within 30 seconds he was behind the driving wheel and pulling out onto Bramcote Road.

Behind him he left a chaotic scene from hell; the entire second floor of the police headquarters was blazing intently, pouring a huge column of black smoke into the dark night; fire alarms were stringently blaring away and dozens of coughing, frightened police officers and civilians were pouring out from fire exits and running away from the building.

Smith smiled as he drove away, humming a tune to himself in satisfaction.

THIRTY-TWO

Saturday 19th October 2013
Ely, Cambridgeshire

It was 1.30am when DCI Davies's telephone rang at his bedside. He struggled to find the receiver in the dark.

"Yes, Davies here." He listened to the shaking voice of a young police officer on the other end of the phone as he relayed an account of the attack on the SOCA offices. As the voice droned on Davies felt a great weight sinking down onto his shoulders and at the same time a sharp fear began clasping his heart in a tight grip. What the fuck is happening? He thought, Why me? What have I done to deserve this? This is it; I'm well and truly fucked now!

Eventually he told the voice on the phone that he would be there shortly to see for himself. He hoped to fuck that the terrified young officer had been exaggerating about the damage, but he knew in his heart that he hadn't been; Smith was just too good at this sort of thing to fuck around.

Saturday 19th October 2013
Huntingdon, Cambridgeshire

An hour and a half later, Davies stood with a small knot of his team on the grass beneath the building that had once housed their offices. The scene around them was still chaotic and lit by the blue flashes from the fire engine and police car that were pulled up haphazardly on the grass. The police HQ looked like it had a giant open wound slashed along its side, with twisted and blackened support girders sticking out like the ribs of some dead animal. The flames that had consumed the building had been put out but columns of lung-searing smoke still snaked into the air from over a dozen places.

A white-helmeted fireman, black-faced from soot and smoke, approached the group of staring, shocked detectives.

"Which one of you is Davies?" He asked the group at large.

"I am."

"Well, I'm sorry mate, but there is absolutely fuck-all left of your offices. Whoever did this did a good job of totally destroying everything up there, in the explosions, and the fire that took hold afterwards. It was just lucky that you lot weren't in there when it kicked off; otherwise you'd all be in body-bags now."

"Yes, well thank you for that charming thought. Is there nothing usable left up there? Any computers or hard drives perhaps?"

"Absolutely not mate; fuck-all left. Your computers are just melted white blobs of plastic on the floor."

"Great. How long before we can get up there and have a look around?"

"Fuck knows mate, maybe a few weeks or so. The engineers will have to make sure that the building is safe and not structurally damaged first." Ironically, just as he said this there was a loud crash as a piece of roof collapsed in the building, sending up a cloud of dust and red-hot sparks, making the group of observers involuntarily take a few steps backward.

The fireman grinned. "As I said mate; not for a while yet!"

"Great! Just fucking great!"

"Hey, don't shoot the messenger mate. You're just lucky that our own HQ is within spitting distance, otherwise they'd probably be fuck-all left of the whole building. I reckon that you lot have really pissed off somebody?"

"Just some fucking bastard who'll get 'his' soon enough!"

"Fair play. I'm just glad that he isn't after me! Ah well, one of my minions is shouting for me. Got to go." The fireman went off into the dark, whistling to himself cheerfully. There had never been any love lost between the fire service and the police force.

The group of detectives stood there gazing up at the scene of absolute destruction above them.

"What now, boss?" asked one of them. Davies paused for a moment before answering:

"We make sure that we catch this bastard. If we don't, we'll be the laughing stock of the whole bloody police force for years!"

"Easier said than done, boss. He seems pretty smart to me and he's well and truly fucked up our investigation. Everything we had on him was in that mess up there." Davies rounded on his subordinate in fury:

"He's just one fucking man, for fuck's sake! I don't care what he's done in the past, I'll get the bastard!"

"Sure boss; sure."

From: john smith (johnsmith2223@hotmail.com)
To: SOCA@Cambspolice.org.uk
Date: 19 October 2013 10.03.00
CC:
Subject: FAO Detective Chief Inspector Alan Davies, Cambs SOCA.

Hi Alan, how are you doing?

I'm guessing that you're a little bit pissed off with me at the moment?

Well, tough titties mate; I'm having a ball.

Here's the next instalment of my autobiography.

Perhaps by now you're beginning to realise that I'm not guilty of raping and killing that little girl, and that I've been set up. Never mind; I'm just a fucking nobody anyway, so who cares, right? I bet you certainly don't, do you Alan?

I'll be in touch again, soon. Be careful out there; it's a very bad world mate.

Regards

John Smith

THIRTY-THREE

I arrived back home in London in the middle of July 1982, and had a few weeks of well-deserved leave that was owing to me. Just like the rest of my unit, there were no welcoming crowds and bands playing when I came back to England. We simply disembarked from our RAF transports at Brize Norton after a long flight back from Ascension Island, climbed into a small convoy of coaches and drove back to Bradbury Lines Barracks in Hereford. From there the lucky ones who had leave dispersed to their homes. For the vast majority it was straight back to work as usual. There were other conflicts still going on around the world that demanded the presence of SAS troopers.

Anne-Marie welcomed me back warmly, as usual, and little Robert was growing up fast. But for the first time it felt really strange to be back in the bosom of the little family that we'd made for ourselves. I found it hard to sleep at night and sometimes during the day I found that I was losing concentration. It wasn't bad dreams that kept me awake at night, although I did have a few of course. Who doesn't? It's hard to explain, but everything in Civvy Street, including my family, seemed unreal. It's as though the dreams that I was having about the army were the reality, and this life with my wife and kid was just a dream. Like I say; it's hard to explain. I put it down to tiredness, and the fact that I'd seen more than my fair share of action since I was a kid. I'd get over it. It obviously didn't affect my sex drive too much, as when I left to go back to the regiment Anne-Marie was once again in the family way.

Back at the regiment I also got the impression that things were a little strained and unfocused, especially in D Squadron. Now that the Falklands War was over, the loss of so many men from mountain troop really hit the guys hard. You could tell that the officers were trying very hard to keep everyone occupied and active, but there was a deep underlying sadness in many of the bloke's eyes, although it was hardly ever spoken about. As a surviving member of what was left of mountain troop, even though I hadn't been with them for long, the mood still affected me strongly and I found myself becoming listless and unenthusiastic. After a week or so of this though, I got a grip of myself and decided to get back into the flow. I approached my squadron commander and talked to him about my future and what it might hold. I suggested that I should get on some courses and away from Hereford for a while and he agreed with me.

As was usual with the regiment, things happened pretty quickly after this and within days I was whisked away to Sennybridge in South Wales. Luckily a sniper course was just about to begin and the senior instructors agreed that I could become part of it. The course lasted six weeks and at the end of it I became a qualified sniper instructor.

Next up was a short two week assault pioneer course run for the TA by the Royal Engineers. The course covered demolitions, field engineering, mine-laying and mine-clearing and waterman-ship. The instructors were excellent and the TA guys were a good and very enthusiastic bunch, so I had a good time as well as learning a few new skills and practising some old ones.

After this I had another ten days leave before the next course came up. Anne-Marie and I had spoken about the need to move home, especially as the family was growing in size. The flat that we rented only had two-bedrooms and was beginning to feel a little pokey, so we shopped around and decided to rent a three-bedroom house with a garden. We talked about the possibility of Anne-Marie moving into married quarters, but she was keen to stay in London, close to her family and friends. I didn't mind this at all; especially as we both knew that my job would take me away from home for long periods. It didn't seem fair to leave her entirely on her own while I was away, although I'm sure that she would have been quick to make new friends among the other wives, as she was an easy-going and happy-go-lucky sort of person. The time flew by as we looked at new places to live, found one that we both liked, and then moved in.

THIRTY-FOUR

The next course set up for me by my squadron commander came as a bit of a surprise, as it also came with a promotion to full corporal. This was the Section Commanders Battle Course, known to most soldiers simply as 'Junior Brecon'.

It was one of the toughest I've ever done, and it's the course that every junior non-commissioned officer in the British infantry has to go through and pass if he's to be considered for promotion. It was based in Brecon in south Wales; a place that I knew very well indeed and one of the toughest landscapes in the UK to train in.

I had enjoyed this peaceful period of training. However I knew that it wouldn't last. After a second short leave with my wife and son I reported back to Bradbury Lines barracks in January 1983 having volunteered, and been accepted for another tour in Northern Ireland with the Det.

I had a couple of weeks of retraining to remind me of the skills that I had used so often in the past. Then it was back into my role of keeping close observation on known and suspected terrorists. I learned to hone my skills in following targets, rather than spending all of my time in hedges, but basically this period was similar to my last tour across the water, and not very exciting.

THIRTY-FIVE

It was only later that year in April that things began to look more interesting again. My team was called off operations and ordered back to our HQ at RAF Aldergrove for a briefing. After arriving from our various separate operations across Armagh, we were led into the Det commander's office. There were six of us in the team, five men, and one woman, who had volunteered for the Det after serving in the Royal Military Police. As I've no doubt mentioned before, under no circumstances were we ever encouraged to talk about our past lives with each other, so I never really learnt much about the other members of my team, apart from the fact that they were all exceptionally good at their job. We were joined in the CO's office by a couple of guys in smart civilian suits. The CO introduced them as members of the SIS and then promptly left the office.

The briefing that followed was long and detailed, and during it the two spooks referred constantly to a pile of paperwork, most of which we could see had been stamped with 'Top Secret'. The gist of the briefing went something like this: Information had been flowing into the offices of MI5 (the sister intelligence agency of the SIS that dealt with internal security within the borders of the UK) for quite some time. Some of the information had been gathered by MI5, some by the SIS, some by military intelligence sources such as the Det and SAS, and some from civilian sources such as Ulster Special Branch and the RUC. Taken separately all of the little bits of data did not mean much. However when collated and put together like a giant jigsaw, they had all suddenly started to make sense to the analysts at MI5. It appeared that SIS agents had photographed members of the Irish Republican Army getting off a commercial airliner in Morocco who had gone on to hold a clandestine meeting in a hotel room with senior members of the Libyan 'Military Intelligence Force' (Libya's main intelligence agency). This could have been about anything of course, as it was acknowledged that Colonel Gaddafi's country often aided, and sometimes even funded, terrorist organisations like the IRA throughout Europe and the United States. It was also known that there were terrorist training camps located in remote areas of Libya where foreign terrorists, including members of the IRA, learnt their skills. However, other information had come in, both from the Republic of Ireland and Northern Ireland, that suggested that the IRA were looking to up their game, principally by getting hold of more sophisticated weaponry. In addition, the IRA had recently been increasing their level of funding through high-profile fund-raising in the States, and a higher than normal number of bank and post office raids both in Northern Ireland and south of the border. To top all of this off, a senior IRA player (who was also a double agent being run by the Det), had informed his handler that the IRA was negotiating for a massive arms delivery from Libya which included shoulder-launched surface-to-air missiles, rocket-propelled grenade-launchers, heavy machine-guns, sniper rifles and significant quantities of Semtex (a Czech-produced plastic explosive) and detonators.

Further intelligence gathering had been specifically targeted on this significant new threat bringing to light an arms shipment that would be leaving Libya within the next few months. Furthermore members of an 'Active Service Unit' of the IRA had recently left the UK for the island of Cyprus and set up a base in a remote farmhouse there. It therefore seemed reasonable to assume that the shipment and the IRA unit would meet up somewhere in the

Mediterranean. In order to keep track of the IRA unit the SIS wanted us to use our skills in covert surveillance on the island. Meanwhile other agencies would be trying to identify and track the shipment. Back in Northern Ireland the UK border forces would be on the lookout for the shipment in case it got through the net.

We agreed that this would be a good idea and immediately started to draw up our plans. Great stuff!

When we finally left Det HQ to return to our billets it was with mixed feelings of excitement and fear. We would be travelling to Cyprus within the week, and who knows what would await us when we got there.

THIRTY-SIX

After an intense couple of days getting ourselves and our kit ready for air transfer to Cyprus, we eventually took a civilian airliner to Nicosia International Airport. Here we were met by one of the Royal Military Policemen on attachment to the UN forces who drove us to the British Contingent HQ in Nicosia itself. Two of our team members went straight down to the 'British Sovereign Base Area' at Limassol to collect our vehicles, as they had been flown in by RAF Hercules aircraft.

The next day we donned our combats and bright blue UN berets for an official tour of the UN-maintained buffer zone between the Cypriot south of the island and the Turkish north. We were also presented as new personnel to the commanders of both the British Contingent and the UN Peacekeeping Force. It was essential to operational security that we maintain our cover as UN peacekeepers throughout the mission. We needed to make sure the IRA didn't learn that we were there, and to prevent any bad political ramifications that may have arisen if it became known that British undercover military personnel were using the UN Peacekeeping Force in Cyprus as cover for clandestine operations against suspected terrorists.

The next day our job began in earnest. Together with another team member I drove out of Nicosia in one of our Q cars. It was a specially adapted civilian car as used by the Det in Northern Ireland. On the outside it looked perfectly normal but it had several modifications, including lightweight Kevlar armour incorporated into most of the body work (except for small areas which would allow us to fire our own personal weapons from inside them if we ever needed to). The windows were bulletproof and the tires were 'run-flat'; self-inflating in case of a puncture or bullet hole. There were also hidden compartments inside for various weapons and other equipment.

We had been briefed that the IRA base was located about a mile and a half south of a small town called Akak, a few miles from the capital Nicosia. Dressed in civilian clothes we parked the Q car on the edge of Akak and set off on foot towards the isolated farmhouse that was the IRA base. We then spent the next few hours doing a thorough reconnaissance of both the farmhouse and the approaches to it, including taking dozens of photographs, before making our way back to our own base and briefing the rest of the team on what we had found.

After holding what we called in the SAS; a 'Chinese Parliament', which is basically all of us sitting in a room and figuring out what we were going to do and how we were going to do it, the whole team set off once again for the IRA base. This time we took all the kit that we would need to set up an OP overlooking the farmhouse. We arrived at the location just after last light and two of us began digging a hole in an overgrown patch of olive trees about 100m from the building on a slight hillside. This position had been chosen by the team as a perfect location for the OP, with an unobstructed line-of-sight on both the front door of the farmhouse and the rough vehicle track that led up to it. The rest of the team split into two cover groups, one group moving forward to within 30m of the farmhouse and the other covering the rear of the digging party by climbing further up the hillside. We didn't want to be surprised by anybody. Soil was dug out and thrown onto a large green poncho laid on the ground, until a hole two feet in depth had been made that was long enough and wide enough for two people to lie down beside each other inside. Once the digging was completed, a roof made of triple-thickness chicken wire was laid on top. This was covered by a sheet of thick green polythene, and this in turn was covered by a substantial layer of the excavated soil. The last job was to camouflage the whole OP with local vegetation, including the original turves that had grown where the OP was located. Once it was finished it would contain two of the team and no one would be able to spot it, even from just a few feet away. Facing the farmhouse was a slit just four inches deep, hidden by the stems of vegetation growing in front. The operatives inside would watch the IRA base through the slit. At the rear of the OP was a small trapdoor, again well camouflaged with growing vegetation, which would allow us to have ingress and egress to the OP.

When we had finished constructing the OP, we set a booby-trapped explosive charge on the trapdoor and all of the teams withdrew. The booby trap was our insurance. If the IRA had seen or heard us during the night and came to investigate while we were away, then at least one of them would die in the ensuing explosion and we'd know that the operation had been blown, if you'll excuse the pun.

The next night we returned to the area and this time set up a hide about 500m farther back from the OP. This was larger (and more comfortable) than the OP and hidden in a dense stand of trees amongst thick undergrowth. There was no direct line-of-sight to the farmhouse from this position but that was okay. Nearby we also set up a hiding place for a Q car, close to the track that led to the farmhouse.

The following night the entire team closed in on the farmhouse itself. As each team member was covered by a colleague, they placed tiny transmitters on the glass of every ground floor window, and using lightweight extendable ladders, on the glass of the first floor windows as well. These tiny, almost unnoticeable bugs were a great piece of kit. What they did was to convert the smallest of vibrations on the window panes caused by people talking inside into an audible radio signal that was transmitted to a listening device located in the OP. This allowed us to listen in on conversations that were held anywhere inside the farmhouse. Prior to this we had tapped the phone line to the farmhouse, so now we would hear every word that was said inside and be ready to react when we were needed. The last thing that we did before leaving was to place a tracking device on the old beat-up pickup truck parked by the house that the IRA was using.

We were ready now to begin our surveillance. The team was split into three pairs. The first pair would lie inside the OP watching the house and listening in on the conversations inside. They would lay together side-by-side, drinking from plastic bottles (which they would then use to piss in) and eating cold rations. It was always good to try and hold your shit in while you were in an OP, but if you got caught short then you did it in a plastic bag which then went back into your bergen. These two alternated the duties, with one person watching and listening for two hours while the other person slept. 500m behind these guys were the second pair of the team. They were located in the larger hide and were there as an immediate armed response in case anything went pear-shaped. They were in contact with the OP team by radio but otherwise they spent their time relaxing and resting. The only time they got called upon was if the IRA went for a drive. Then they would jump in the Q car and follow them at a distance using the tracking device to see where they were going. Luckily this only happened once or twice during the operation, when the terrorists drove into Nicosia to buy food. The third pair of the team was based at the British Contingent HQ in Nicosia, where they slept and watched TV most of the time. This team was also in radio contact with both the OP and the covering group's hide, and had the use of our second Q car. Daily updates on the operation were sent via secure communications to the SIS in London. Every 48 hours, during the middle of the night, the teams would swap around, the OP team going back to Nicosia to rest and clean up, the cover group moving into the OP to take over the surveillance duties, and the team that had been resting moving into the hide as the new covering group. This way every member of the team got their fair share of rest and the IRA was covered by alert people at all times.

The operation went on for about eight weeks, and it got slightly boring and repetitive, as surveillance work always does. Apart from information that directly related to this mission, we also managed to pick up and record for posterity some interesting information about the activities that these particular IRA active service members had been involved with in Northern Ireland. The IRA unit consisted of two men and two women who were normally based in Belfast. They never knew that they were being watched by the British security services and felt pretty much at ease in their Cypriot base, relaxing sufficiently enough to talk over old times and about people that they knew; something that they probably never would have done back in Belfast, where they would have been as paranoid as everyone else. It was almost as if they were treating this trip as a sort of holiday away from it all. Maybe it was the warm sunshine, or the large volumes of local wine that they drunk during the evenings, or maybe it was the sex that the two pairs seemed to have every night. We didn't care much either way because we were picking up enough solid information to see them all locked up for a very long time when this particular mission was over.

At the beginning of May I received some very good personal news. My wife, Anne-Marie had given birth to a healthy baby boy, my second son. I managed to talk to her for a long time on the telephone. I was sad that I had missed the birth but happy that he had all his toes and fingers etc. We decided to call him Alan.

THIRTY-SEVEN

It wasn't until the beginning of July that we realised that the operation was coming to a head. The IRA received a telephone call from their contact in mainland Britain informing them that they had to be ready to leave within 36 hours. The shipment of arms had left Libya and was heading towards Cyprus. We instantly went on standby, preparing ourselves to follow them when they left their base to meet the incoming ship. We also informed the SIS in London. We didn't know whether the firm had managed to identify the ship carrying the arms but they did tell us that a British frigate, presently at the Sovereign Base Area in Limassol, was to be used for the mission and was also going onto standby.

Twelve hours later, in the early hours of the morning, a second telephone call was received by the IRA. They were to immediately vacate the farmhouse and drive down to the harbour at Larnaka, on the south coast, where they were to meet a Libyan contact in a cafe by the seafront. They would then be taken by small boat out to the Libyan ship. This was it.

When the IRA left the farmhouse for the last time, another team member and I, who had both been on 'rest' in Nicosia, followed them in one of the Q cars, while the other teams withdrew from the OP and hide and followed on behind us, in constant contact by radio. By the time we had driven the thirty or so miles to the port, the other team had overtaken both us and the IRA vehicle, and were already in place watching the cafe in Larnaka. Everything went smoothly and as we had expected. The IRA abandoned their vehicle in the town and with the two of us following at a discrete distance, they made their way on foot to the cafe where they were met by a tall, thin man who appeared to be of North African origin. They had a cup of coffee together and then walked down to the harbour. There, they clambered into a small boat powered by an outboard motor and cruised slowly out of the harbour, to all intents and purposes looking like tourists setting out for a day along the coast. Our surveillance was at an end, as there was no way that we could follow them out to sea and remain unnoticed. However, our job wasn't over. We recovered our Q cars and set off at speed to the nearby Sovereign Base Area, where we were due to board the British frigate that was waiting for us.

Within an hour we were safely aboard the frigate and being welcomed by a young lieutenant commander who was obviously impressed by all the cloak and dagger stuff. As the ship prepared to set sail we were led to the inner sanctum of the operations room where we were introduced to a team from M Squadron SBS (the maritime counter-terrorism squadron), a naval bomb-disposal officer (who was going to check the cargo ship for booby traps) and the SIS officer who was in charge of this part of the mission. We didn't know any of them and despite inter-service rivalries that might have raised their ugly heads at any other time, the excitement of the chase was obviously getting to everyone and we instantly hit it off with all of them.

A Lynx helicopter from the frigate was in the air, watching the target boat's progress on their radar and relaying the information back to the frigate. We found some chairs and sat down in a big group around the SIS man at his designated consol. The adrenalin rush of the last few hours began to wear off and I found myself yawning, along with a couple of the other members of my team. It wasn't long before I begged the use of a cabin and went to get my head down, as it was obvious that things were going to be fairly quiet for a while and I wasn't really needed at this point. I wasn't the only one either, as the rest of my team, barring our female member, who was fairly new to the game and still wide awake, also retired for some well-earned kip.

This was a good move on our part as very little happened for the next 14 hours or so. The Lynx tracked the small boat as it left the harbour and headed out to sea, and also as it rendezvoused with a cargo ship a few miles offshore. The helicopter returned to the frigate, which then took up the chase at a relaxed distance using its longer-range and state-of-the-art ship-to-ship radar to keep contact with the slow-moving cargo ship. It then became a waiting game, as it had been decided a long time in advance that we would not make our next move until the target ship was well out in international waters.

A 'fast rope' assault on the ship could have been carried out by using the Lynx, but it was thought that the danger of an explosion, either accidental or self-detonated by the terrorists, was a real and present danger. It was therefore decided that a clandestine mission carried out by the SBS guys had the best chance of catching both the terrorists and the ship's crew by surprise.

THIRTY-EIGHT

We started our next action in the wee small hours of the morning, when we would be hidden from any prying eyes on board the target ship by the dark moonless night. Two Gemini semi-rigid inflatable boats crewed by the SBS team, three to a boat, with myself, as senior member of the Det team, on one of the boats and the SIS field officer in command of the operation and the bomb-disposal guy on the other, were lowered down from the huge bulk of the frigate. Both then motored out into the dark, fairly calm waters of the Mediterranean. This was going to be an interesting operation, I knew, as boarding a moving cargo ship in the dark was not going to be easy. Especially as we wanted to do it without the ship's crew seeing or hearing us. I wondered how the SBS guys were going to handle this. We hadn't been told how they were going to do it, as the securing of the vessel was their bit of the operation. As far as they were concerned, we were just along for the ride. Our bit would come later after they had done all the hard work.

The two Gemini's motored along close together for about an hour or so, until eventually the head honcho of the SBS, who was in my boat, waved us to a halt. In the dark he fished a GPS from out of his webbing and briefly scanned it, the green glow of its screen hidden from prying eyes beneath a poncho. He signalled to the other boat to join us and the two rubber hulls bumped together. A large coil of thick rope lay in the back of our boat and the SBS commander proceeded to pass one end of it to the helmsman of the other boat. Checking his GPS readout again he held a quick whispered conversation with the other helmsman and pointed off into the dark. The second boat then began to slowly move away from us in the direction that had been indicated, playing the rope out as it went. A few minutes later there was a slight jolt as the full length of the rope, which I guessed was about 150m in length, had been reeled out between the two boats. Our end was already tied off to the bow of our Gemini, so now the two boats were about 150m apart and joined together by the rope, which I could see was floating just beneath the surface of the sea. It was so dark that I couldn't see where the other boat was; just the line of the rope snaking out from us.

That was it for a while. Both boats kept position with low revs of their motors, while the SBS commander checked our position on the GPS every few minutes or so. He also held whispered conversations over his personal radio, presumably with the radar operator of the frigate, which by now was a fair few miles away. It was very dark and very quiet. The only sounds were the gentle slapping of the mild swell against the side of the boat and the steady breathing of the SBS guys as they made themselves comfortable for a long wait. Although it was quite warm, our enforced inactivity and the constant breeze began to cool my body down. I decided to wrap myself tighter in my combats and settled down in the bottom of the boat for a snooze.

I don't know how long I dozed for, probably not for longer than an hour, as it was still very dark when I was woken up by a hand shaking my shoulder. I slowly sat up and stretched my cold muscles. Things were just the same as they had been when I had dropped off, except in the distance I could hear a very low rumbling sound. The SBS commander pointed into the dark and grinned, his white teeth flashing in contrast with his camouflaged face.

"Here they come" he whispered to me. I stared out into the dark, seeing nothing at first. Then it hit me; there was a slight glow in the direction that the SBS man had been pointing. He lowered his head to mine and whispered again: "That's the phosphorescence from their bow cutting through the water. They don't seem to have any running lights onboard, but that's not surprising considering what they're up to." He grinned again. "Shouldn't be more than 30 minutes now".

Sure enough, he was right. Gradually the phosphorescence grew brighter and the rumbling sound that I had heard grew in volume until I could discern that it was an engine; a big engine. Then all of a sudden the hull of the cargo ship emerged from the darkness and was steaming down on us. For a moment I felt real panic as thousands of tons of metal, looming huge against the sea, seemed to be coming straight for us on a collision course. I glanced at the SBS guys, who were slightly illuminated by the churning phosphorescence around the bow of the approaching ship, but they seemed to be well in control and relaxed, as though they did this sort of stuff every single day (which of course they probably did). I felt their confidence and tried to relax myself, but it wasn't easy. I'd never done anything quite as unsettling as this, and my mind kept flitting to the thought that the sea probably went downwards for hundreds, if not thousands, of feet beneath the flimsy rubber hull of our boat. We were a long way from help and an even longer way from any shore. If we went under then that was probably it. We'd be dead for sure.

Then, just as this cheering thought was swimming around my head for the umpteenth time, all hell seemed to break loose. The huge bulk of the cargo ship charged past the Gemini right through the position where our line was floating, and suddenly our boat was snatched violently from the bow and hurled towards the side of the passing ship. Then the ship's bow wave caught us and tossed the small boat around as we all held on grimly for our lives. I thought that this was the end and that everything had gone tits up. No way could our tiny rubber boat survive the pounding that it was now receiving.

Then there was the solid but quiet thump as our boat swung into the side of the ship. Suddenly the violent surging and bouncing about stopped and we were held steady and tight against the cargo ships hull. It was only then that I realised what had happened and it was very hard to stop myself from laughing out loud.

The two Geminis, attached together by the length of floating rope, had been positioned directly in front of the advancing cargo vessel. The ship's bow had caught the rope as she passed over it and dragged both of the boats along until they were held up tight against the side of the ship, one on each side. It had all happened so faultlessly and so quickly that I could only marvel at the navigational skills of the SBS. To place us exactly in the path of the cargo ship on a moonless, dark night in a featureless sea was no mean feat. I wondered how many lives had been lost in the past to perfect this technique. I was well impressed.

We stayed in this position for several minutes, with everyone clutching their personal weapons and very alert to the slightest sign of alarm from above us on the deck of the ship. There was nothing. Next the SBS team slowly pulled the Gemini forward on its rope until we were aligned with a series of steps ascending up into the darkness on the hull of the ship. Then they were off and going up. I was quietly told to stay where I was in the boat. They didn't want me in the way as they got on with their work.

I sat there for what felt like hours, getting colder by the minute as the dawn began to light up the eastern horizon. At last I heard a shout from above and looking up I could just make out the silhouette of a man leaning over the deck rail high above me. I couldn't hear what was shouted but I presume it was: "watch out", as the next second a heavy rope ladder was slung over the side and nearly took my head off as it banged against the hull. I didn't wait to complain; I was up the ladder like a monkey

171

in just a few seconds, I was so glad to move. Then I was clambering over the deck rail to be thumped on the back by a grinning SBS commander.

"We've done it!" He said. "The crew is secured below decks and the ship is ours." He was in very high spirits and I wasn't surprised. The SBS had yet again showed their professionalism and skill. He had a right to be proud of a job well done. I couldn't contain myself either and grinned along with him. Then a thought struck me: I'd been stuck in that little Gemini for a long time.

"Where's the toilet mate?" I asked.

It was two days before I left that cargo ship. Two days of clambering about in dark holds, moving crates and prizing them open to reveal their contents. And what a cargo there was. There were hundreds of assault rifles, sniper rifles, semi-automatic pistols, dozens of rocket-propelled grenade-launchers, a dozen machine-guns, and even a few heavy machine-guns. There were also literally tens of thousands of rounds for the above weapons and hundreds of hand grenades. Most chilling of all though, were the hundreds of pounds of Semtex plastic explosive, with various types of detonators, and the two dozen shoulder-launched surface-to-air missiles that we found. I could easily imagine the destruction that the IRA could have caused with these lightweight missile-launchers if they had made it onto the streets of Northern Ireland. I had already seen what these weapons could do to a civilian aircraft back in the Rhodesian bush war. I've no doubt in my mind that by seizing this arms shipment we had saved the lives of hundreds, perhaps even thousands, of ordinary men and women.

After we had catalogued the contents of the cargo, we were taken back on board the accompanying frigate, and we left the cargo vessel in the hands of a Royal Navy prize crew. I have no idea what happened to the ship, the ship's crew, the IRA members, or their Libyan contact after that. I do know what happened to the cargo though. More of this later.

As for us guys from the Det, we were taken on to Gibraltar by the frigate, where we caught a civilian airliner back to the UK. Apart from a long debriefing, our part in the operation was over. I was looking forward to being reunited with my family and seeing my new baby boy for the first time.

THIRTY-NINE

I pleasantly surprised my wife by returning home on leave earlier than expected. I didn't know how long we were going to have together this time, so we decided to do as much as possible as a family, and quickly. There were visits to the zoo, to the park, and walks in Epping Forest; the type of things that normal families get up to all of the time. It seemed my new son was putting on weight and getting bigger by the minute. During these times I tried to forget the army, but the affliction that had got hold of me on my last leave, was hitting me harder than ever. My mind kept wandering back to my work, and I had this feeling that everything at home was unreal. It was very unsettling for me and I think for Anne-Marie too, as I'm sure she picked up on my mood. It was almost a relief when I received a call from Regimental HQ after two weeks:

"You've had plenty of experience in Africa, haven't you?" asked my squadron commander on the other end of the phone.

"A fair bit, sir." I replied.

"Fancy a trip to Chad?"

"When, sir?"

"Well, as soon as possible would be good. I know that you're on a well-deserved leave, but I could get you picked up at the train station in Hereford if you could catch a train within the next hour or so."

"Okay, sir. I'll see you in a few hours."

"Excellent! Good man!" I put the phone down. There was no hesitation about going off again, no question that I would do whatever it took to get back into the field again. I loved my wife and sons, don't get me wrong; I loved them more than life itself. But the job was real to me and life in Civvy Street wasn't. I needed to get back out there again.

I quickly said my goodbyes, citing that I'd been ordered back to duty because a colleague had fallen ill. This was a lie, perhaps a white lie, but a lie all the same. I couldn't bear to look into the eyes of my family as I hurried away from home, bound for God knows what. All I knew was that it was better than being here.

FORTY

Chad is quite a large country in North Africa. The north of the country is mainly sandy, wind-blown desert and lies adjacent to the equally sandy and wind-blown desert of south Libya. There had been an intermittent war raging between Chad and Libya for nearly 20 years, from 1978 through to 1987, and at least 8,500 soldiers had lost their lives during this conflict so far.

My small, but very active and bloody part in this war came about because the British SAS were asked to send somebody there by a French Special Forces unit called the 'Commandos de Recherche et d'Action en Profondeur' or 'CRAP' for short (Deep Action and Reconnaissance Commando). Yep; I was dropped into the crap at the request of the crap! Wonderful.

The war originally started because Libya decided to support anti-government rebels in Chad during the early 1970s. Then in the mid 1970s Libya occupied and annexed a 45,000 square mile strip of land in northern Chad adjacent to its southern border. As is often the case when one country wants some land that belongs to another country, there's a hidden agenda. In this case the strip contained deposits of uranium, and this was needed by Libya to develop their own atomic energy programme. Eventually, after a lot of fighting and intense diplomatic pressure Libya withdrew from the strip in the early 1980s. There had been more fighting in the area since then, with first one side and then the other gaining the upper hand.

When I arrived in August 1983, the Libyans were supporting a significant incursion into the strip and had amassed a huge ground force of 11,000 men. They launched an assault on a key city in northern Chad, defeating the Chadian forces that were based there.

This action severely worried the French, who were the former colonial masters of Chad and were still closely allied to the country. They sent in a force of around 3,000 men, warning the Libyans that if there were any further assaults on northern Chad, then they would face the full force of the French forces now based there. One of the units that had been sent to Chad was 2 REP, the Second Foreign Parachute Regiment of the French Foreign Legion. CRAP formed a small part of this regiment and they were tasked with the close reconnaissance of Libyan forces in the area. My job was to help them.

I had originally been worried that I might not be able to communicate with the guys in CRAP, as I could hardly speak a word of French. But I needn't have worried as quite a few of them were British guys. After all it was the *Foreign* Legion. Although there was a lull in the fighting over the next few months, I still found myself busily engaged with my new playmates. The terrain was harsh and it was a lot hotter than any other theatre of war that I had served in (even compared to southern and central Africa), but I was still young and extremely fit, so it presented no major problems for me. Acting as small independent groups, we were tasked with the reconnaissance of Libyan ground forces operating in northern Chad and southern Libya. We also carried out longer-ranged missions into Libyan territory where we would set up OPs overlooking their military airfields to give early warnings of air attacks and the deployment of troops. We were also tasked with putting together aggressive patrols and spent many happy nights laying ambushes and conducting fighting patrols against the outlying enemy forces. We saw a lot of action during this period, although some of my time was spent training the French commandos in CTR techniques.

I also made a lot of good mates and learnt a lot about the French Foreign Legion too. One particular friend that I made was a Scottish guy, originally from Glasgow, who went by the name of Andy. At the age of fourteen he had run away from home and a violent, alcoholic father. After getting into trouble several times with the local police and ending up serving a short period in a London jail, Andy eventually wandered onto the continent and had; "in a drunken stupor", as he put it, decided to join the French Foreign Legion at the age of eighteen. He had presented himself at the Legion's recruitment and selection centre in Aubagne, Paris, and "never looked back". At the grand old age of thirty two, he had already served just over fourteen years in the Legion when I met him, and held the rank of sergeant chef (senior sergeant). He had become an airborne commando two years previously. The only real action that he had seen during his service in the Legion had been at the Battle of Kolwezi in Zaire. In 1978 this small African mining town was occupied by armed guerrillas from Angola. They had murdered and tortured the town's inhabitants, and had also taken lots of hostages, including some French nationals. 2 REP parachuted in to rescue the hostages and had had a good shoot-out with the guerrillas, saving many innocent lives. Andy loved it in Chad and I worked with his team many times, including a CTR of Al Kufrah airfield in south-eastern Libya. During a few heavy drinking nights back in our operational base in Chad, Andy told me how tough the training had once been in the Legion. He had a particularly battered nose that looked like it was squashed flat on its side onto his face. He told me that at one time, when Legionnaires used to stand on parade; if they were out of line by as little as 1cm, the drill instructor would smack them across the face with a big length of wood. That was how he had got his nose. Then he would go into a long lament about how soft the Legion had become compared to the 'good old days'. I can still hear his French, spoken with a harsh Glaswegian accent, in my head.

178

In the middle of December the powers-that-be decided that I had spent enough time running around the mountains and deserts of Chad and Libya, and I was ordered back to Britain. For the first and only time during my whole career in the army, I spent the Christmas holiday period at home with my wife and sons, which was great. I spent the whole of Christmas playing with my kids and having fun, for once in my life without having to look over my shoulder all of the time and dodging bullets. I remember this as one of the best times of my life. I loved my family.

However, all good things must come to an end, and in early January I was again posted overseas on a training mission, this time to the United States of America.

FORTY-ONE

My job for the next couple of months was to cross-train with the Green Berets of the US Special Forces at Fort Bragg in North Carolina.

Fort Bragg is situated to the west of Fayetteville and is one of the largest and busiest military complexes in the world. I had been invited along by the US Army because of my CTR skills, what else? I joined the 3rd Special Forces Group at Bragg, training Green Berets, along with some personnel that I later learned were from the Special Operations Group of the Special Activities Division of the Central Intelligence Agency (quite a mouthful, but basically these were the guys that did most of the 'sneaky-beaky' 'black ops' stuff for the CIA). The 3rd Special Forces Group's regional area of responsibility was sub-Saharan Africa, so there was a lot of locally-based knowledge that I could pass on to them. The guys from the CIA were going to put their new skills to use against the drug barons in central and southern America. I was a bit cheeky and managed to get myself invited along on a couple of the short operations in Columbia after befriending this group of quietly-spoken and highly-skilled men. I liked the 'yanks' that I met over there in the US. They were sometimes a little more 'gung-ho' than soldiers I had previously met and worked with, and I think that they found my English sense of humour a little weird, but we got on like a house on fire and if the truth be told I was treated as a bit of a celebrity because I was with the British SAS.

After this I was posted to Bavaria in West Germany, this time as a trainee rather than as a trainer. This was my second posting to the International Long-Range Reconnaissance School at Weingarten, near Ravensburg. The course that I attended was the 'Patrol Insertion' course and involved honing skills in HALO and HAHO parachuting, not only from fixed-wing aircraft but also from helicopters, and patrol insertion by boat and vehicle. I spent a few fun evenings in the Special Forces Club at the school, drinking with US, Dutch, German and Italian Special Forces soldiers, as well at Brits. Inevitably the bar-men, who were German conscripts, were nick-named 'Hansel and Gretel'.

After this course I was allowed home on leave again, but not before learning that I had been promoted to sergeant and had earned a 'Mention in Despatches' for the operation in Cyprus. Apparently it was quoted on my citation (though I never actually saw it) that I had 'led my team from the Det in a very calm and professional manner during difficult circumstances'.

This time when I got home, especially as I'd had a few months of mostly non-tactical and non-combative activities as well as a good Christmas, I was well relaxed at home. I had a great time with my family, especially my little boys who were growing up so fast. Little did I know that this would be my last such leave. I was about to be dropped into the meat-grinder that was called the Soviet invasion of Afghanistan, and things were never going to be the same for me, or for my family, ever again.

FORTY-TWO

In May 1984 I returned to Hereford and to duties with the re-formed mountain troop of D Squadron. I had only been there for a few days, trying to settle in amongst a group of blokes that I didn't know when I got a call to get my arse over to the COs office in Regimental HQ. What now? I thought as I made my way there.

When I entered the office I was surprised to see my old case officer from the firm; Harry, sitting having a cup of tea and a chat with the colonel. He stood up, and with a big grin on his face, pumped my hand up and down.

"It's great to see you again John." He said, "It's been a long time!" I agreed with him. But I'm afraid that I couldn't raise as much enthusiasm as Harry could at our meeting again. Harry was SIS, so I knew that something was up. It was beginning to look like I'd never get a chance to settle into some sort of normal routine within the SAS (if there ever was such a thing).

I sat down with Harry and the boss and was told about an exciting opening that was coming up in the next few weeks. Apparently MI6 was joining forces with the various Special Forces; including the SAS, the Det, SBS and Mountain and Arctic Warfare Cadre. They were forming a small but highly skilled force that was going to be called the 'Increment' and this small, clandestine and highly secretive force would take over all covert operations that were presently run by various agencies in the SIS. The Increment would recruit its members solely from British Special Forces. Oh, and by the way Sergeant Smith, you've

182

performed a sterling job with both the firm and the Det in the past, as well as with the SAS of course. Would you like to be a part of this new initiative?

Do I have any bloody choice? I thought, as I looked at the smug smile on the CO's face. He'd never fully accepted me within the regiment and was always trying to palm me off to somebody or other.

"I'd be delighted to." I said to Harry and that was it. The very next morning I packed my things up and left the SAS barracks behind me forever.

The Increment is the most secret outfit in British intelligence. As a rule members of the Increment only normally serve a specific time-span within the unit, usually the length of the particular job that they have been recruited for. For example, if you're a serving member of the Special Reconnaissance Regiment (the Special Force that has taken over from the Det in the modern British Army), you may be asked to work for the Increment on just one job, say a covert surveillance of a politician in some hostile country. Once the job has finished you'll find yourself back in your regiment. All of the jobs that are carried out by the Increment are deniable. In other words, if you get caught on such a job, the British government will completely deny that you were there in any sort of official capacity. You will have no backup whatsoever. This is similar to the work carried out by the Special Activities Division of the CIA. The missions could be anything from surveillance through to assassination and are known variously as: 'Black Ops' or 'Wet Jobs', or in other words, the crap jobs that no one else wants.

FORTY-THREE

Harry had clearly done well for himself since he had been my case officer back in the Rhodesian Bush War, as he was now the section head of the Increment. He had also apparently spent some time out in either Afghanistan or Pakistan, because it was Harry who briefed my new team on our first mission together, and he appeared to have had personal, first-hand experience of dealing with Afghans.

There were four of us in this team. The boss was called Mike, and it was pretty bloody clear from the moment that I heard him first speak that he was a bloody officer. He had the biggest plum in his mouth that I'd ever heard in my life. As you can guess I soon let him know, in no uncertain terms, that although he was nominally the officer in command, it was me who would be making all of the important decisions (to be fair to the bloke, he actually turned out alright once we got out into the field).

The second member of the team was a sergeant from the SAS who I had never met before. His name was Phil and he was a quiet sort of a chap who just got on with the job, without any fuss. He had served for a number of years in B Squadron's mountain troop. We eventually became good mates and he was a good bloke. The last member was already a mate of mine. His name was Ricky and he was a sergeant from the Mountain and Arctic Warfare Cadre of the Royal Marines. A fully trained and thoroughly professional mountain leader with a wicked Liverpool accent and a sharp sense of humour to match it. We had known each other since I had taken my own

Mountain Leaders course and we had served together in the Falkland's War as well. He was the salt of the earth and as good a soldier as I've ever met (even if he was a Royal Marine!).

Harry started off our briefing by saying this of the Afghans: "Don't ever trust them. Your typical Afghan will say one thing, think another thing and do something else entirely different. He would sell his own grandmother for a few Afghani's (that's their currency out there). He's never heard of the concept of 'honour' and he would happily kill you for the boots on your feet. On the other hand, he is most likely to be a Muslim, and Muslims are without a doubt the friendliest people in the world. If an Afghan came across you in one of their numerous deserts and you were naked and dying of thirst; he would take you into his home, feed, water and clothe you at his own expense, and pray to Allah for his mercifulness in letting you be found and saved. In short, gentlemen, Afghans are a confusing mixture of contradictions and you just never know what they're going to do next."

This was good advice that I would remember time and time again over the coming months.

Our mission was to meet up with a shipment of arms that were on their way to northwest Pakistan, and then deliver these weapons to a particular group of *Mujahedeen* (Muslim rebels) in the Panjshir Valley, about 100 miles north of Kabul, on the edge of the Hindu Kush mountain range in Afghanistan. In addition to the weapons, we were to escort a group of so-called 'Afghan Arabs' into the country. They were foreign fighters from other Muslim countries who were joining in the *Jihad* (or Holy Islamic War) against the *Kaffirs*; the Soviet oppressors of their Muslim brothers. Once we had delivered the weapons and the fighters then we would attempt to win the heart and mind of the rebel commander in the Panjshir Valley, a certain Ahmad Shah Massoud, known as the 'Lion of Panjshir'. If we were successful in this then Mr Massoud might allow us to train some of his 10,000 rebel fighters in classic guerrilla-style, unconventional warfare techniques, and we could eventually lead them in attacks against the Soviet 40th army which was based in Afghanistan. It sounded like a bloody great challenge and a lot of fun, and the arms that we were going to deliver to the Afghans were the very same arms that I had helped to capture in the Mediterranean. Funny how these things turn out.

FORTY-FOUR

After an intense week of briefings, delivered by a variety of different people (from serving officers of Pakistani intelligence agencies through to academics from British universities), we knew (or at least we thought that we did) just about everything there was to know about Afghanistan, and the Soviet armed forces that occupied the country. The Soviets originally 'occupied' the country at the request of the Afghan government back in 1979, at a time when the government had been fighting a losing battle against armed rebels for several years. Once in position the massive numbers of Soviet troops (as many as 115,000 at any one time) began to attempt to quell the 2 million or so rebels through a mixture of artillery bombardments, air strikes, and division-sized infantry attacks. Since their invasion four years previously they appeared to have done very little harm to the *Mujahedeen*, but had succeeded in killing tens of thousands of Afghan civilians.

The *Mujahedeen* (known by the Soviets as *Dukhi*), were giving an excellent account of themselves (despite the fact that at this stage of the war they were mostly a bunch of uneducated peasants armed with very old bolt-action rifles or in some cases, even muskets!). They were not, as you might imagine, a single organised group of rebels, but consisted of lots of different groups, distinguished by their tribal and ethnic origins. As often as not, these groups would end up fighting each other as often as they would fight the Soviets. The *Dukhi* tended to live normal lives during the daytime in their *Kishlaki* (villages), going out and tending their crops in the fields or holding down jobs. But come the night-time they would take up their rifles and attack the occupiers of their country as they had been doing for centuries before, from Alexander the Great through to the British. They were basically a very war-like people, and you had to admire them for refusing to take any shit off anybody.

The idea was that our team was going to help to change this state of affairs by first of all giving the *Mujahedeen* better weapons, and secondly by improving their tactics and enabling them to inflict higher casualties upon the Soviets. There was no doubt at all that this was going to be the toughest mission of our lives.

FORTY-FIVE

Saturday 19th October 2013
Huntingdon, Cambridgeshire

"Good morning mam."

"Forget the pleasantries DCI Davies. I am not a happy bunny at the moment." The chief constable of Cambridgeshire constabulary indicated the plastic chair in front of her desk. "Sit down and tell me exactly just what you're doing to catch this maniac."

"Everything that we can, mam, considering that our entire suite of offices has been blown up and we have almost no resources left."

"Dear me, that sounds like a reproach against me, Davies. I hope that you're not going to be tiresome and blame this situation on your superiors?"

"Of course not, mam. I was merely pointing out that SOCA now finds itself without any computers. We're presently working out of the back of a police incident van in the car park."

"You'll just have to make do for the time being! This attack has left almost half of our personnel without an office, or a computer, until the engineers let us back into the building. You may have noticed that even I am working out of the gymnasium."

"Yes, mam, of course mam. I do apologise."

"Good! This whole fiasco has lowered our standing with just about everyone in the county and the press are having a bloody field day! We might all find ourselves out of a job if we don't catch this character Smith, and catch him quickly. I want your squad to drop everything else that you are involved with and concentrate solely on Smith's recapture. Do you understand?"

"We've been doing that since he escaped from the courthouse, mam. My team has worked almost non-stop on this case and we're no more forward now than we were at the beginning."

"Don't tell me that, Davies! That's not what I want to hear from you. What I *want* to hear is that your team is doing everything in its power to apprehend this man and that an arrest is imminent! This is what I am going to say at the press conference that I'm holding in an hour's time, and I want to be sure that we are all reading from the same page."

"Yes, mam, of course mam. I think that you'll find that all of my team is doing everything humanly possible to catch Smith, and I'm sure that we'll get him soon; we have some very good leads on him, mam."

"That's better, Detective Chief Inspector, *much* better. Now, what did you want to see me about?"

"Have you heard anything from the security services, mam?"

"Yes, I have. The official government line is that Smith is nothing but a deluded fantasist and that he has never served in the SAS, or been recruited by MI6."

"I see mam, and the unofficial line?"

"Unofficially you will be contacted by a senior member of MI6 in due course; he will fill you in on the details."

"May I ask when he will be in contact?" The chief constable glanced at her watch.

"I believe that he is driving here from London even as we speak, Davies; he should arrive about the same time that I am being grilled by the media. Now, if you don't mind, I have a press release to write?"

"Of course mam, thank you."

"I don't want your thanks, Davies. What I do want is for you and your team to pull out all the stops and catch Smith!"

"Yes mam, of course mam."

"Good! Now go and do what you do best Detective Chief Inspector. I'll look forward to hearing from you soon that this incident is closed."

"Yes mam, of course mam."

Saturday 19th October 2013
Coventry, Warwickshire

Smith grimaced as he looked at his reflection in the mirror. Bloody Hell, he thought, I look like some sort of aging porn star! After four days on the run, his lower face and top lip had grown a fine covering of fairly long white stubble (like father bloody Christmas!) but he had now dyed the stubble, his eye-brows and his cropped hair a bright blonde. The addition of two large pads of cotton wool stuffed into his cheeks and the donning of a pair of quite-heavily rimmed spectacles (with plain lenses) had completely changed the shape of his face.

He glanced through the door of the bathroom at the small flat-screen TV in the living room; his face was once again being flashed up on the lunchtime news, as it had been since the coppers had first told the press about his escape from court. He noticed that there was still no mention of his raid on the TA centre or his rocket attack against the police HQ; the former had been ignored and the latter had been put down to a gas explosion. Obviously, they didn't want to cause a panic or look too stupid on national TV.

Even so, his face was still on every news programme on TV and probably on the front page of every newspaper as well (though he hadn't bought one to check as it was far too risky). He stayed away from people as much as possible, keeping his head and face covered as much as possible on the rare occasions when he did. So far he had not been recognized.

Most of this morning he had spent in the lock-up garage putting a dozen explosive charges together. He had also had a quick trip to an internet cafe to send his latest email. However, it was time to venture out into the big bad world again; he had an appointment to keep back in Peterborough......

Saturday 19th October 2013
Huntingdon, Cambridgeshire

It was closer to an hour and an half before the man from MI6 turned up at Hinchingbrooke. DCI Davies sat opposite the senior security service officer and for the second time since the man had introduced himself as "Harry; please call me Harry," he thought to himself: Jesus Christ, he looks absolutely nothing like a spymaster is supposed to: He's short, obese, balding and sweaty, not at all like James Bond.

They were sitting in his new temporary office in the back of a large police incident van parked up near the still smouldering remains of the HQ. Harry had just finished explaining that he was sort of 'semi-retired' from 'the firm' and only acting in a 'consultancy role' these days. Davies didn't buy it at all.

"So, er...Harry, what can you tell me about Smith and his service in the Increment?" Harry chuckled quietly to himself.

"First of all I would like to set the record straight; there never has been, and never will be, a unit called 'the Increment'. The British security services would never even consider setting up such a unit."

"So you're denying that Smith was ever recruited by MI6?"

"I'm denying no such thing Detective Chief Inspector."

"So Smith did serve in MI6?"

"You don't mind if I call you Alan, do you?"

"Not at all."

"Good, we are on the same side you know, Alan."

"I'm glad to hear it, because so far we've had very little cooperation from MI6."

"Well that's not too surprising really. We are the *Secret* Intelligence Service, after all." He chuckled again and Davies began to feel his temper rising.

"I understand that, but Smith is a very dangerous killer and he's on the loose. You've seen what he's done so far. God alone knows what he'll do next!" Harry pursed his lips.

"Everything that I am going to tell you now is covered by the Official Secrets Act, Alan. You realise that you must not disclose any of this information to anyone? And this includes the other members of your team?"

"Of course, that's not a problem."

"Good, because it could be very detrimental to your health if any of this got out to the press."

"Jesus! Are you threatening me?"

"Not at all old chap. The thought would never cross my mind. As I said before, we are on the same side." Harry chuckled yet again. "Listen to me carefully Alan. John Smith is not just a 'dangerous killer' as you call him: He is an exceptional man in many ways and is endowed with a very impressive array of deadly and not-so-deadly skills. He is intelligent, tough, courageous and has a very big axe to grind, not only with the SAS and SIS, but now also with the police force, especially the Serious and Organised Crime Agency. It would be very dangerous to underestimate him."

"I'm beginning to realise that."

"Good."

"Now will you stop farting around and tell me what I need to know to catch this bastard!" Harry looked hurt at Davies's sudden outburst.

"Look at it from our point of view Alan; the more that is known about Smith by the civil authorities, including you, the harder it will be for us to deny that he ever worked for the firm. Do you understand what I'm saying here?"

"Jesus Christ! Am I ever going to get a straight answer from you?"

"Probably not old chap."

"Great! Just fucking great!"

FORTY-SIX

Saturday 19th October 2013
Peterborough

Snatching the barrister from the car park at Peterborough Crown Court had been child's play for Smith. Surprise, speed and controlled, extremely focused aggression were the keys to conducting the most successful kidnappings. He had found this out a long time ago, in a country a long way away. The be-suited civilian had never faced a man like Smith before; at least not when he didn't have a crowded courtroom between them. Now Steve Mackay, the chief prosecutor of Cambridgeshire's Crown Prosecution Service was sitting in the drawing room of his own extremely opulent country house on the edge of Holme Fen, a few miles to the south of Peterborough. His ankles were secured firmly to the legs of an antique, and obviously expensive, chair by plastic plant ties, and his arms were secured painfully behind the chair by a length of electrical cord that was also wrapped around the chair and his chest. He was helpless and couldn't move. He was gagged by a piece of oily cloth that Smith had found in the back of his Land Rover, which he had shoved firmly in his mouth.

Smith had done a quick recce of the house and it was obvious that MacKay lived alone. He had found an extension cord and a brand new electric drill in the garage next to the house and now he dangled the drill by its cord as he re-entered the drawing room, followed by Mackay's terrified eyes.

"You do remember me, don't you?" Asked Smith pleasantly, crouching down before the helpless man and smiling. "Just nod if you do." He added. Mackay nodded. "Good, that's the way. Do you live in this big old house all by yourself?" Another nod. "Divorced?" There was another nod, but this time with a hint of snot dripping from his aquiline nose.

Smith moved away, searching for a wall socket. When he found one behind the expensive leather sofa he plugged in the extension cord and began to unwind it in the direction of Mackay. Finally he attached the short cord of the electric drill to the extension and crouched down again.

"I want you to understand something from the very beginning Mister Mackay: I'm not a very nice guy; in fact, I'm a nasty bastard. Nod again if you believe me." The piece of snot dripped onto Mackay's lap as he nodded vigorously. "Good." Smith lifted up the electric drill and looked closely at the drill bit, touching it gently with one finger. "A long time ago I served as an undercover soldier in a little conflict in Northern Ireland. The enemy over there was a bunch of pasty-faced wankers who called themselves the IRA. Do you remember them?" Another nod. "Good; you're doing very well indeed. Keep it up. The problem with the IRA was that they were riddled with informers and double agents and even undercover policemen, so in time they developed a very effective way of getting these people to talk very quickly when they managed to identify them. Can you guess how they this did this?" This time a quick shake of the head. "Well; it was by drilling into their kneecaps with an electric drill, just like this one." Smith smiled again. Then he triggered the drill and the sound of the whirring bit cut sharply into the air.

Mackay screamed soundlessly into his gag.

An hour later Smith climbed into his Land Rover. Behind him the yellow glow of flames showed at the windows as they began to take hold of the old house. He absently scraped a fleck of dried blood from his blonde-bearded cheek with a finger and waited calmly as a window exploded outwards and flames leapt out. When he was satisfied that the isolated building would be gutted by the fire before a fire appliance turned up, he reached across to the sat nav and switched it on. After the few moments that it took the device to warm up he typed in his new destination: London; Hendon; Aerodrome Road.

From: john smith (johnsmith2223@hotmail.com)
To: SOCA@Cambspolice.org.uk
Date: 19 October 2013 18:01:37
CC:
Subject: FAO Detective Chief Inspector Alan Davies, Cambs SOCA.

Hi Alan, I hope that you've still got your job after all that's been happening?

I'm afraid that I've been busy again; poor old Steve Mackay of the CPS is feeling a little bit crispy at the moment. At first I thought that he might be difficult and not answer all of my questions, but he soon got the point, if you'll excuse the pun (you'll understand later).

He told me some very interesting things and I've made a lovely digital recording of our little conversation, but more of this later hopefully.

I guess that you've met Harry by now. Be careful: Harry's a snake and is proud of it.

Please find attached the latest instalment of my autobiography.

Speak to you again soon.

Regards

John Smith

FORTY-SEVEN

We arrived separately at Islamabad in Pakistan at the end of May, and then proceeded in pairs to the city of Peshawar. This is one of the oldest cities in all of Asia and lies at the eastern end of the famous Khyber Pass.

Summer starts at the beginning of May here, and the temperature was already soaring over 40°C (104°F). It was very, very dry and dusty.

To reach our final destination in the Panjshir Valley we had to travel by caravan across several provinces of Afghanistan that were commanded by other Afghans. To facilitate our journey we first had to meet up with Sayyid Ahmad Gailani, the leader of the 'National Islamic Front of Afghanistan' at his headquarters in Peshawar to discuss a deal. He was the leader of the rebel forces that occupied the provinces we would have to cross first. *Pir* (His Supreme Holiness) Gailani turned out to be a very well-educated man who had a razor-sharp mind and could speak flawless English. He was also a direct descendent of the Prophet Muhammad and the upshot of this was that he was a very, very important man in both Pakistan and Afghanistan. After much intense discussion the deal that we ended up striking with him was very much in his favour. It was decided that he would be given one third of all of the weapons and ammunition in our shipment. In return he would provide us with an escort through the provinces of Nangarhar and Kabul, and guarantee us safe passage through the land that was occupied by his own forces. Surprisingly he didn't want anything to do with our Afghan

Arabs – since he lived at the gateway to Afghanistan he was constantly being inundated with requests from such foreign fighters to join his forces. Most of them turned out to be less than useless when it came to actual fighting, and he had had enough of them to last him a lifetime.

Although *Pir* Gailani probably thought that he had got the better of us in this deal, he had no way of knowing that this was exactly the way we had planned it. We were more than happy to give him so many weapons and ammunition, as we knew that they would be put to good use against the Soviets by the rebel groups that he commanded. Liberating ourselves from a third of our weapons meant that we could keep our caravan to a modest size, thus giving us more of a chance to slip through Soviet-controlled territory without being ambushed and killed.

We set off into Afghanistan at the beginning of June. Our caravan had over 200 donkeys heavily-laden with our shipment of modern Soviet weapons. We were escorted by about fifty tough-looking Afghans provided by *Pir* Gailani, plus nearly a hundred Afghan Arabs. About a quarter of the Arabs would fall by the wayside on the long march through the mountains and deserts to our destination, unable to carry on in the intense heat with very little water and food to sustain them. Personally, each of our four-man team carried about 140 lbs of kit on their backs, in a bergen that was as big as a small person, plus their personal weapons of an AKM assault rifle and a Makarov PM pistol each. In our bergens we carried everything that we were likely to need over an extended period, from boot polish to keep the leather of our boots supple and partly waterproofed, through to mess-tins, hexamine stoves and rations for the journey. In addition I also carried a SVD Dragunov sniper rifle in a soft case, to keep the dust off it, across the top of my bergen. I was the team's sniper, as well as its second-in-command.

As you can probably imagine, this was a nightmare journey. We travelled only at night, lying up in any cover that we could find during the day. The landscape gradually got harsher as we made our way from the flat floodplains surrounding Peshawar across the Afghan border and into the foothills of the Hindu Kush. These hills were as dry as a bone and speckled with barren deserts. We tried to avoid the deserts of course, making our way mainly along the drying river beds and letting the donkeys graze on the green vegetation that lined the routes and gave us much-needed cover during the day time. The heat during the day was very intense and seemed to suck all of the moisture from our bodies. There were times that the spit in my mouth turned into dry foam, and when I pissed my urine was so condensed that I almost had to squeeze it out of my cock like a tube of toothpaste. During the nights the temperature would plummet to well below freezing and we were glad of the *bushlats* (padded Soviet Army jackets) and *ushanka* (furry Soviet Army hats with ear flaps) that we had been given as a gift by *Pir* Gailini. We avoided Soviet outposts along the way of course, but we also avoided *Mujahedeen* encampments and fortified positions, as well as most of the *Kishlak* (village) the length of the route. In a land where you can trust very few people we deemed it safer to avoid them all as much as we could. Occasionally we would bed down for the day in the *Kishlak* of one of our *Mujahedeen* escort, but for the most part we spent our days sleeping beneath whatever shade we could find.

This is a massive country and though we had been briefed to expect to see a country ravaged by warfare, with the smoking ruins of bombed villages and the dead bodies of murdered civilians littering every valley, we were pleasantly surprised to see very little evidence of such famed Soviet atrocities. For the most part the countryside was quiet except for the howling of the wind through the hill tops and mountain peaks, sounding like some strange sort of pipe music, and the occasional call of an eagle gliding way up in the air. We did have a few moments of excitement when Soviet planes or helicopters passed overhead, but nothing that threatened discovery or impeded our progress. The trek was about 160 miles as the crow flies, but with the ups and downs of the mountains and the constant detours that we were forced to make, I reckon that we covered about 260 miles in the end, and we did it in about three weeks. Even with our high levels of fitness, we still found the going tough. The shoulder straps of our bergens cut into the nerves and blood vessels of our shoulders and sometimes we would suffer from mild paralysis of our arms and shoulders. Our legs and backs burned from the steep inclines and when going downhill our calves would scream with agony. Our final destination, the Panjshir Valley, was set in breathtaking scenery; a river bed bordered by lush green vegetation meandered its way through the valley bottom overlooked by vast snow-capped mountains. All on such a huge scale that you can barely imagine it.

When we finally made contact with the *Mujahedeen* forces led by Ahmad Shah Massoud, it was with extreme caution. We kept our caravan well hidden in the vegetation at the valley's bottom while I and a couple of our escorts approached a small fortress-like encampment constructed from rocks, high-up on one of the slopes. This was a very dangerous time for us, for not only were my escorts of a rival rebel force, but they were also of a completely different ethnic group. They were *Pashtun* while the *Mujahedeen* of Ahmad Shah Massoud were mostly *Tajiks*. At least both groups were Sunni Muslims, otherwise the meeting would have been impossible and would have ended in bloodshed.

After we had approached the fortification with our hands up and weapon-less (though I still kept my pistol in a shoulder-holster beneath my *bushlat*), we were roughly pushed inside and there was a lot of jabbering in a lot of different languages and dialects and a great deal of pointing of rifle barrels at us. Finally a consensus appeared to have been reached among the rebels inhabiting the rock fortress and one of the *Mujahedeen* went off, presumably to go and get someone more senior. We were pushed into a corner and told to sit down and wait.

About an hour later another *Mujahedeen* arrived on the scene which resulted in even more arguing. Then he left too. Finally, as the sun was going down behind the towering peaks and my backside was going to sleep after sitting on a rock for hours on end, another *Mujahedeen* turned up. I was extremely surprised when this one spoke to me in perfect English. I explained the whole deal to him at which point he and his mates herded us outside and down the slope towards the hidden caravan. This was a really tense moment. As soon as we arrived at the caravan the first thing that the rebels did was to round up our escorts and take all their weapons off them. This resulted in a heated debate with the escorts and for a while I was afraid that there was going to be a massacre. Then, as some of the *Mujahedeen* looked through the huge packs that had been removed from the backs of the donkeys and were now lying on the ground, things began to get lighter and the two groups even made a few jokes and laughed together. Eventually the escorts were turned loose and allowed to go on their way, minus their weapons (which really pissed them off). Then the packs were once again loaded onto the donkey's backs and we continued on and up the valley in the darkness.

FORTY-EIGHT

It was a further two nights of travelling before we met up with the 'Lion of Panjshir'. We learnt that there was a huge Soviet offensive taking place further up the valley resulting in a constant accompaniment of artillery in the distance and flyovers by Soviet aircraft every ten minutes or so. When we were finally led into Massoud's presence in a heavily bombed-out *Kishlak*, he was in the middle of some sort of judgement, as there were three dishevelled Soviet soldiers kneeling before him with their hands on their heads. They had clearly been beaten pretty badly because their faces were covered with swellings and dried caked-on blood. Ahmad Shah Massoud himself was a surprisingly gentle-looking young man, with a short beard and a very intense expression. He spoke English fairly well and welcomed us to his 'kingdom' as he called it with a smile and a laugh. His eyes were lively and he was obviously very intelligent.

He dismissed the 'court' with a wave of his hand, and invited us to sit down with him and drink some 'green tea'. We proceeded to talk for quite some time, explaining our purpose in coming to his stronghold and what we hoped to achieve in the area with his help. It appeared that he wasn't very impressed by our words and promises and though he was happy to receive the 'present' of weapons from Her Majesty's government, he could really see no use in our remaining, as his *Mujahedeen* warriors were doing very well, thank you very much. He explained that they were such a thorn in the Soviet's side that the current attack was the seventh by the Soviets on the Panjshir Valley since the war had begun four years beforehand.

Mike, our boss, did his very best to try and persuade Massoud that we were highly-skilled soldiers and that we could really help him in fighting the Soviets, but this didn't seem to impress him at all. He proceeded to tell us that some of his neighbouring rival *lashkars* (fighting forces) had been receiving training from American CIA operatives and that this had got them nowhere. He wasn't very impressed by westerners, whom he thought were just too soft, and that was that; the end of it. This was where I had an idea and stuck my nose in. I asked him why the Soviet prisoners, who were still kneeling nearby under heavy guard, were here and what would be happening to them.

At the mention of this, Massoud seemed to brighten up and launched into an explanation of what was happening to the *Kaffirs* and why. Apparently the three soldiers were airborne troops who were based in an outpost at the top of one of the mountains off the valley. A couple of nights previously they had got very drunk (and probably also stoned on *Chars*, which was an opiate consisting of a mixture of opium, horse sweat and horse shit). They had then decided to go down to a local *Kishlak* and have some sport. They started their night of fun by breaking into and robbing several shops of their goods and had then carried on by kicking the door of a house in and killing the parents of three young girls with the butts of their rifles. Then they had gang-raped the girls, who were aged from six to eleven years old. After a few hours of fun they had then beaten the girls to death so as to leave no witnesses behind and made their drunken way back towards their outpost. Unfortunately for them they had been captured by local *Mujahedeen* on their way back. It turns out that they had done a poor job of killing the girls because the eldest of them had survived and had told her story to the *Mujahedeen*. Massoud had them interrogated by some Soviet Army deserters that were living with his forces and they had admitted everything, showing no remorse, except that they should have done a better job of killing the witness and not getting caught. Massoud went on to say that he was trying to decide what to do with them, with the help of some local *Mullahs* (Holy men), as by *Sharia* (Islamic) law they should really be stoned to death for child-rape, but he couldn't make up his mind.

I saw my opportunity here. As casually as I could I stood up and approached the Soviet soldiers. I bent over and looked each of them in the eyes and they stared back at me through their swollen eye-lids, obviously as scared as they ought to be, considering why they were here. They looked liked rough buggers though, and I was utterly convinced that they would happily rape young children. With their round, well-tanned (and battered) features it was hard to tell exactly which part of the Soviet Union they came from, though there was more of a hint of central Asian than European about them. I moved slowly behind them and then very quickly I drew my pistol and put a bullet into the head of each one of them, splattering their brains over the rocky floor. The bang of the three shots echoed loudly around the room. I had acted so quickly that everyone was taken aback as the Soviet's bodies flopped forward onto the ground, lifeless and with a good part of their heads missing. Suddenly I found myself surrounded by furious *Mujahedeen* pointing their rifles at me, jabbering away angrily. To be honest I half expected to be shot dead right there and then, and for my body to join the Soviets on the ground. I was pissing myself at this point but managed to keep the fear out of my voice as I said, as calmly as I could: "I hate fucking child rapists and I hate fucking *Kaffirs*." And then slowly put my pistol back into its holster.

Massoud looked at me for what seemed a very long time, and then he burst into laughter, instantly relieving the tension in the room as he was joined by the other *Mujahedeen*. I was suddenly being pummelled on the back amidst a group of laughing and grinning Afghans as I was invited to sit back down with their leader and more green tea was pressed into my hands.

"Perhaps you are not so soft after all, Englishman." Massoud laughed. "I like you, so I will let you train some of my very best men! The 'Lions of Panjshir' are yours!" With that we were in.

FORTY-NINE

The Soviet's prisoners had already confessed to child-rape
and had been identified by one of their victims. The truth
was that they were going to die anyway; there was no way
out of it for them. At least I gave them a quick and clean
way out, a lot more than they would probably have had at
the hands of the *Mullahs* and the *Dukhi*. Being stoned to
death is not a very pleasant way of dying. You are tied up,
shoved into a hole that will later become your grave, and
then a couple of hundred very willing people chuck brick-
sized stones at you until you're dead. They had already
murdered innocent Afghans, including children, and had
gang-raped the young defenceless girls before killing them.
In my book, they deserved to die. If I had used this act of
merciful revenge as a way to get us accepted by Massoud
and his men, then so what? We had a job to do and I was
prepared to do whatever it took to get that job done.
That's why my country had spent an awful lot of time and
effort and money training me up; to get a job done that
most people back home would never have conceived
themselves doing.

    Mike was not too pleased with me and the way in
which I had killed the Soviets though, and he let me know
of it as soon as Massoud and his warriors left us, giving me
a dressing down in a very shocked voice. I told him to fuck
off. Ricky and Phil just laughed.

The next few months were extremely busy.

A couple of months earlier the Soviets had launched a massive attack against Massoud's *Lashkars* in the Panjshir Valley. Over 11,000 Soviet troops supported by Afghan army soldiers were involved and they were supported by tanks, artillery, mortars, multi-barrelled rocket-launchers, helicopter gunships and over 200 ground-attack aircraft.

The first thing that they did was to bomb and shell the fuck out of every *Kishlak* and rebel fortification in the valley. The aim of this bombardment was to either kill the local civilian population or at least to drive them from their homes. To the Soviet way of thinking, civilians were either rebels or were rebel sympathisers, and so were legitimate targets. At the same time as these bombardments took place they landed battalion-sized groups of troops at all of the smaller valleys leading out of Panjshir, in an effort to catch and kill the fleeing *Mujahedeen*. Then they put down more troops in the valleys and on the mountains around the Panjshir and gradually began to close in on Massoud's *Lashkars*, like a noose tightening around a neck. These troops were spear-headed by their elite soldiers of the airborne battalions.

But Massoud was a clever bloke. He had learned about the attack long before it had actually started from disaffected members of the Afghan government, and so he had ordered the civilians that were living in the Panjshir Valley to leave and to head into the mountains. Then he had planted tens of thousands of land mines in every *Kishlak* and possible helicopter landing zone and prepared himself for a massive confrontation. Our shipment of arms and ammunition could not have come at a better time for him, as his forces were engaged constantly with the Soviet ground forces, and our shipment of superior arms for his troops was very welcome.

True to his word Massoud placed us in charge of one of his best *Lashkars*, known as the 'Lions of Panjshir'. They were a group of about 300 veteran rebels who had been fighting the Afghan government a long time before the Soviets had turned up in 1979, and had been fighting the modern might of the Soviet Army since. They were a hard-bitten crew of killers and I grew to love them. At first we didn't have too much time for training the 'lions' in our ways of unconventional warfare, and anyway, they already had their own highly successful methods. We just got stuck in with them.

Day after day we would launch successful attacks against a range of targets. Sometimes this involved straightforward simple sabotage of power-lines, pipelines, temporary airfields and road bridges etc. At other times we would lay ambushes for armoured vehicle convoys that were travelling up and down the Panjshir ferrying troops or supplies. Eventually we forced the Soviets to surrender the wider countryside to the Afghans and to take cover inside large fortifications dotted up and down the valley. Then we started to attack some of the smaller police posts or sentry posts that they had left behind. In one particularly successful incident, we almost wiped out a whole battalion of airborne troops on patrol in a spectacular ambush in a small river valley leading off the Panjshir. We basically never gave the *Kaffirs* a chance to rest and re-group; we were at them all of the time like a pack of hunting dogs wearing down a bear by constantly snapping at its heels.

With the new weapons that we had brought in, especially the heavy machine-guns and the surface to air missiles, we even managed to bring down a few of their precious helicopters and a couple of bombers.

We gradually acquired more and more sophisticated weaponry from the Soviets and Afghan Army themselves through our ambushes and other tactics, until we were one of the best-armed rebel groups in the whole country.

FIFTY

By September 1984 the Soviets had had enough of fighting in the Panjshir and retreated from the valley. The Afghan rebels had lost hundreds of men during the campaign, but so had the Soviet Army, despite all its might. They withdrew their forces and left the Panjshir firmly in *Mujahedeen* hands, naturally claiming an outstanding victory against the rebels in the Soviet media.

This would have been a time of rejoicing for me if I hadn't suffered a very personal loss during the fighting. Just a couple of weeks before the Soviets had withdrawn their forces, Ricky and I had been leading a more or less routine attack against a small police outpost in the north of the valley. We had crept into position during the early hours of the morning and had waited until dawn before launching an attack on the fortified building. Our own intelligence on the outpost indicated that there were only about twenty or so Afghan policemen based there, and so we had decided to attack with a small force of about 80 Mujahedeen. We were armed with our usual light mixture of assault rifles, machine-guns, rocket-propelled grenades and hand-grenades. When we went into the assault, I was leading a fire-team of twenty men on the right, and Ricky was leading the second fire-team of twenty men on the left, with only ever a few metres between us. Our two fire-teams were leap-frogging forward, one team laying down covering fire while the other moved forward, and then the second doing the same while the first team moved forward. Meanwhile, the other forty men of our fighting force were lying on the right flank of our assault and letting loose with everything they had at the police post, in order to keep the policemen's heads down as we advanced. It's a classic tactic called 'fire and manoeuvre' and 'winning the fire-fight'.

Everything was going according to plan until we reached a point about 50m from the outpost. Suddenly we came under very heavy fire, not from the policemen, but from hundreds of Soviet Spetsnaz (Special Forces) troops dug in on the hill behind the outpost. Heavy machine-gun fire splattered our covering group, killing a few of them outright. Several more heavy machine-guns also opened up on our advancing fire-teams, along with a few grenade launchers. I was in the process of jumping up and running forward, to leap-frog past Ricky's fire-team, at the precise moment that the Soviets opened up on us. Ricky was just to my left and slightly in front of me, and was in the process of flinging himself to the ground to give covering fire. He never made it; a rocket-propelled grenade from a Soviet RPG hit him in the chest and exploded on impact. Normally one of these things will just pass straight through you, leaving a gaping hole in your body, as they are designed to detonate when they hit a hard target, not a 'soft' one like the human body. However, Ricky had a bergen filled with hand-grenades and plastic explosive that we were going to use to blow an entry into the police post, and I guess that this blew when it was hit by the RPG. Everything just exploded at the same time and Ricky disappeared in a flash of bright red as his blood, snot, gore, bones and brains were blasted all over the place. There was nothing left of him afterwards, absolutely nothing except this big red stain on the hillside. I must have been shouting a warning as the grenade hit him because my mouth was wide open. Apart from being covered from head to toe in the splattered remains of my best friend, I had a large amount of him inside my mouth as well. No matter how much I tried to scrape the mess off with my fingers, I couldn't; it was in my eyes, ears, hair, hands, and clothes – everywhere.

I didn't succumb to the shock of it right away. I stayed calm and focused, and gradually withdrew all of the *Mujahedeen* fighters away from the Soviet ambush, fighting our way out in good order. It wasn't until several hours later and after we had covered a lot of miles to put some distance between ourselves and the ambush site, that it hit me fully. I had lost the best friend that I had made in a long time and in the process had managed to swallow some of him. I couldn't get rid of his taste out of my mouth for weeks after.

Ricky had been a bloody good soldier and a great mate. I'll never forget his Liverpool-accented voice or the stupid look he'd have on his face when he was making a joke. We'd shared an awful lot together, and it was a shit way for anyone to go. I didn't even have enough left of him to scrape into an envelope and send home to his loved ones. He'd just gone. I was left with yet another large hole in my life at the loss of a valued comrade.

FIFTY-ONE

We found out a few days later that the Soviets had been tipped off about our impending attack on the police outpost by the commander of one of our neighbouring *lashkars*. Even though his group and ours were both under the command of Massoud, and we were supposedly on the same side, this man had still been jealous that it had been the lions and not his lashkar that had been chosen for the successful British soldiers to lead. He was also jealous about our spate of victories over the enemy, and so he had sold us out to the Soviets for a few hundred Afghanis, and had got my best mate killed into the bargain.

When I found out about this, I set off with Phil and my Dragunov sniping rifle down the valley to extract some revenge. Mike wasn't best pleased about this, but he sensibly kept his mouth shut, and when we returned back to the lions a few days later he knew better than to ask us how it had gone.

I'd put a 7.62mm round right into the traitorous bastard's belly, just above his groin, from a range of 600m. We then lay on the hillside, watching through my snipers brass telescope, as the bastard had taken hours to die, and in great pain. His own men had sat around him on the hillside, drinking green tea and watching him while he died. Even though he must have begged and pleaded with them, as he must have been in a hell of a lot of pain from the gut wound, they had not lifted a finger to help him. They knew that if they had done anything, a bullet with their name on it would have come flying out of the air to make them suffer as well. We didn't hide ourselves while we watched and they knew who we were and why we had shot the bastard.

Three weeks after this incident, Phil bought it. He was leading a unit back to the Panjshir after a successful ambush of an Afghan Army convoy when he triggered an anti-personnel mine by walking through a trip-wire. Phil was basically cut in half by the mine and died instantly. I liked Phil, even though he could be quiet and taciturn at times. He also had a very dry sense of humour and was a total professional.

At least we had enough of him left to bury, unlike Ricky. Now there was only Mike and I left.

After the Soviets had withdrawn their troops from the Panjshir Valley during September, Mike and I had a short period of relative calm in which to fully train up our troops. Then we unleashed them against an array of *Kaffir* targets.

When I had been a younger man, back in my Rhodesian army days, I had completed a course on demolitions, including the setting of booby-traps. The main idea behind booby-traps is not to kill your opponent, but rather to injure him. This is because it ties up more enemy personnel to look after an injured soldier than to bury him or to stick him in a zinc coffin and send him home. So booby-traps are generally made up of a small explosive charge that is more likely to blow off a foot or a hand, or other bodily extremity. Sometimes they are made up of 'shaped charges' that direct a molten globule of gunk, rather like a bullet, in a specific direction, causing particular wounds.

In the British Army we have various means of getting booby-traps to explode, but the most common is a lovely little bit of kit called the 'M142 combination switch'. This is a small tubular switch with a tiny blasting cap that can be set to detonate using pressure or a trip wire. A pressure detonation can be set for either pressure added (such as someone stepping on it or driving over it) or pressure released (such as someone lifting a weight off it). The tripwire can be set to detonate the switch by someone pulling it (for instance by catching it with their foot when walking through it) or by releasing it (for example by opening a door inwards to which the tripwire is connected, thus releasing the strain on the wire), or in some cases by a smart-arse who finds the wire and cuts it, thinking that he's solving his problem, only to find the switch detonates a shaped charge positioned directly beneath his bollocks. A shaped charge is literally that; a cone shaped explosive that when it detonates fires a molten lump of metal upwards at high speed similar to a bullet being fired.

Anyway, the upshot of this was that we found ourselves in charge of several hundred pounds of Semtex plastic explosive that we had brought into Afghanistan, with hundreds of combination switches, plus other niceties such as hundreds of metres of detonation-cord, safety-fuse, timing detonators, electrical detonators and initiators. We also, of course, had access to a whole range of soviet mines and explosives that we had managed to acquire from the Soviet Army during ambushes and attacks etc.

The Afghan *Mujahedeen* were very willing students learning about the art of booby-trapping. We also had the perfect targets – over a hundred thousand Soviet soldiers who just loved to pick up anything that looked bright and shiny, and were forced by rebel activity to drive or march along a limited number of well-protected roads and tracks.

Of course at the time, I had no idea that the same skills I was passing onto my willing Afghan students were going to be put to such devastating use against our own forces in twenty years time, when the term 'booby-trap' would no longer be in general use and would be replaced by 'Improvised Explosive Device' (IED).

Over the next few months I personally taught hundreds of the *Dukhi* how to use explosives, not only as booby-traps but also in more normal circumstances, such as blowing up bridges, power pylons, telegraph poles, etc.

You name it – I taught them to blow it up or knock it down. The Soviets soon learned that if they came across an abandoned *Mujahedeen* position, that they should touch nothing in it until it had been cleared by their own demolition experts. We booby-trapped anything that we possibly could; from thermos flasks through to stacks of Russian pornographic magazines. There would always be some mug that forgot about the danger and eagerly picked something up, thinking to shove it in his pack for later, only to find that he would be missing a hand for the rest of his life.

Travelling by road became very dangerous for the occupation forces as well, even in their armoured vehicles. We planted thousands upon thousands of stolen mines along the most heavily used roads during the nights. It became a common sight to see a de-tracked or de-wheeled armoured personnel carrier stuck by the side of the road. This must have been a logistical nightmare for their engineers to cope with.

The Afghan summer passed and the winter set in with a vengeance. Even the Russians, who were used to sub-zero temperatures and several metres of snow lying on the ground, complained that the winters in Afghanistan were much colder than those at home. To an Englishman like me, whose only real experience of blinding snow-storms had been a few months spent in Norway and the Antarctic, this was a white nightmare of freezing toes, fingers, nose, ears and lips. The rivers all froze over so deeply that you could drive a 60 ton tank over them (and the Soviets often did) without even cracking the ice. The constant howling wind would drive the falling snow into huge drifts causing you to sink up to your arm-pits if you stepped in the wrong place. In some spots the snow would be packed solid and frozen so that you could safely and fairly easily walk over it. Then the next second you'd sink up to your knees without any sort of warning and have to fight your way forward through deep snow that sapped your strength and your will to carry on. Outside your extremities would be freezing while inside your clothing your body would be soaked in sweat from your exertions.

I didn't spend all of my time teaching Afghans how to blow things up during the months that followed the failed assault by the Soviet 40th Army on the Panjshir Valley. A lot of my time was also taken up training our *lashkar* in ambush drills and assaults against strong-points, and then actually putting the skills to use in the field. Sometimes we would march through the snow for miles to some God-forsaken point on a map, then lie for hours in the freezing conditions before spending a few hair-raising minutes blasting the fuck out of some poor un-expecting convoy. Other times we would march for miles into the high passes of the Hindu Kush and launch an attack against some poor bloody Soviet soldiers who had spent the past year holed up in a tiny outpost miles from anywhere.

We didn't have it all our own way of course. I'll say this about the Soviet Army; it is full of tough and highly professional soldiers, especially the airborne battalions and the *Spetsnaz*. We weren't fighting some half-arsed amateurs here. These guys were good, and I mean really good. We often found ourselves out-manoeuvred and out-fought by these guys, especially during the winter months when they seemed to be at home in the sprawling whiteness. The Afghans are a tough bunch of course. They live here all of the time and are well used to the foul weather, but the Soviet Special Forces are also a tough breed of men and they often-as-not gave as good as they got from the *Mujahedeen*, if not more so. Several times I and my men would escape capture or death only by the skin of our teeth.

This was a bloody hard-fought war; probably the hardest I had ever operated in, but I was about to face the hardest test of my life. A test that would change me forever, and not in a good way.

FIFTY-TWO

If there was one thing that really pissed us off about the Soviet forces in Afghanistan, it was their total and unremitting air superiority. We would have to march for hours, if not days, carrying our obligatory heavy bergens, demolitions kit and personal weapons over rough terrain to reach our destination. The Soviets on the other hand would simply have to climb aboard a helicopter, spend a while reading a book or falling asleep, and then alight at their chosen landing zone, fully refreshed and almost perfectly safe from interdiction on the part of the rebels. Admittedly we did try to make it as hard as possible for them to do this without sustaining some losses. We would lay land-mines and booby-traps at every likely-looking landing spot to give them an unexpected surprise when they dropped off their troops. Occasionally we would get lucky and put a round or two through the fuselages of the choppers speeding along high above us. But it was still an annoying fact of life in the war that they could move almost anywhere they wanted to, at any time they wanted, with impunity. Then, when they arrived at the place they wanted to be, they could call upon awesome fire-power to back them up, provided by the Mi-24 'Hind' helicopter gunships that tagged along 'riding shotgun' with the Mi-8 'Hip' transport choppers (which were capable of ferrying up to 24 troops) wherever they went. The Hind was a bastard of an enemy, nicknamed the *Shaitan-Arba* (Satan's Chariot) by the *Mujahedeen,* and almost impossible to shoot down unless you had carted a heavy machine-gun along with you, and even then, not that easily. They were armed with a deadly and extremely effective array of 80mm rocket pods (sometimes armed with flechette warheads, which would air-burst into hundreds of small, pointed steel projectiles that had vaned tails to give them a stable flight and were quite capable of penetrating a human body with the force of a bullet), and a 23mm gun in the nose turret. They also usually had a couple of light machine-guns placed in the window ports on each side, fired from inside the troop compartment. They could carry normal bombs for attacking strong-points, but seldom carried troops, even though they were capable of ferrying up to eight fully-equipped soldiers.

Not only were these Soviet helicopters employed to transport men and supplies, but they were also used to 'spot' for Soviet artillery and mortar strikes, to medivac wounded troops and to escort large convoys. They were the bane of our lives in all of their many different roles.

Then, as if this were not enough, the Soviets could also call down pin-point air-strikes on our positions from an array of fighter/ground attack aircraft or organise carpet-bombing of large areas by dedicated bombers.

Mike and I decided that we would have to do something, anything, to disrupt the Soviet air-superiority, and the only logical way forward appeared to be a ground attack against a Soviet military airfield. Thus, in the middle of January, 1985, I went off to carry out a CTR of the airfield that was causing us the most problems in the Panjshir Valley, at a place called Bagram.

Bagram Airfield is located in a valley some thirty five miles to the north-east of the city of Kabul and played a key role throughout the Soviet invasion of Afghanistan. Apart from operating large numbers of military helicopters and aircraft, the airfield was also home to at least two battalions of airborne troops and several units of *Spetsnaz* as well. To have any success in an attack against this well-defended airfield we would have to get some very good intelligence about troop disposition and the layout of the airfield itself, but first of all I would have to get there. This would involve a trek of about sixty miles over some very rough mountain terrain, and then an approach through a relatively densely populated area of farmland, dotted with dozens of *Kishlaki*.

I decided against going it alone; at least not until the actual CTR part of the operation, because of the danger of attack, not only from the *Kaffirs* of course, but also from the rival groups of rebels whose territory we would be passing through. So I travelled south with a platoon-sized group of *Mujahedeen*, many of whom were hand-picked because they had either lived or worked around Bagram at some time in the past and therefore had some knowledge of the area. The plan was to get the whole force over the main road that snaked north from Kabul, then find somewhere for them to lie up before I moved on, with a smaller covering group, towards the airfield. Then I would drop this group off at the outskirts of the airfield before penetrating the airfields defences on my own and conducting the CTR.

The first part of the trek went well and we managed to get over the mountains without having to fire a shot, travelling only at night and lying up during the day anywhere we could find cover.

We had crossed the main Kabul road without being spotted, and were about a mile across the other side, going downhill. It was a dark, moonless night and the snow lay deep, with more snow falling. I had had to make the stark choice of either walking away from any existing tracks and leaving a huge swathe of disturbed snow in our wake that would have surely given the game away (no way can thirty guys walking through thigh-deep snow leave no trail behind them), or using a well-established track that was already pounded by a lot of feet and where a few extra footprints would make no difference. I decided on the latter, which is against all the rules of patrolling at night. This turned out to be a bad mistake in judgement that would cost us dearly.

It was a well-laid ambush by *Spetsnaz* troops that took us, and we didn't know anything about it until we walked right into their 'killing ground'. Then all hell broke loose. First of all my two scouts, who were about 30m in front of the main body of my men, walked through a trip wire and set off an anti-personnel mine, which with a very loud 'pop' jumped into the air to waist height before detonating its main charge and literally cutting them down where they stood. Then I heard the unmistakable sound of mortar shells being dropped into their tubes and being fired. That is basically all I can remember of the actual ambush. I don't know exactly what happened as I must have been blown off my feet, probably by a mortar blast, and was concussed. I was out of it.

FIFTY-THREE

The first time I woke up, I was in the back of a Gaz truck, lying on the bare metal floor between four Soviet troopers who were sitting on benches to either side, and I remember two things very clearly. The first was that I hurt like hell all over and was bloody freezing. The second was the smug smiles on the Soviet's faces as they laid into me with their boots and rifle butts. Then I was out of it again.

The second time I woke up was probably the most terrifying moment of my life. My arms were bound behind me, I was hatless, and I was being dragged by the same troopers towards a building which I couldn't see very clearly because of the falling snow. A door was thrown open and light spilled out into the darkness. Then I was dragged along a bare concrete corridor and into a room where I was thrown to the floor before the Soviets gave me a yet another good pounding with their booted feet, fists and rifle butts. This time though I didn't black out immediately and I remember every bone-crushing blow as though it was yesterday. I was sure that they were going to beat me to death right there and then. I did my best to double up and try to protect myself but it was useless. They smashed me in the face and the head, in the gut, on my back and in my bollocks and there wasn't a thing that I could do to stop them. All that I could do was lay there and soak up the blows. This wasn't a bloody *Rambo* movie; I wasn't going to jump to my feet and fight my way out. My arms were tightly bound behind me and my body was so battered that I wouldn't have been able to stand up

223

unaided, never mind fight my way out of there, and there were four of the bastards beating me non-stop, kicking my head like a football and battering every square inch of my body. I don't know how long I stayed conscious this time. It could have been only ten minutes or it might have been an hour: All I remember is the pain – pain like I'd never felt before, and the fear. I thought that this was how it was all going to end for me; I was going to die right here and now in this poxy bloody country, and no one would ever know what had happened to me. I was a dead man.

The third time that I woke up my first thought was that I had died and gone to hell. I couldn't see a thing because my eyes were crusted together with dried blood and I couldn't open them, but I knew that there was bright light because I could see this reddish glow through my closed-up eyelids, looking for the world like the glowing light from large hell-fires. My body was burning fiercely, but it wasn't from the flames that I feverously imagined; it was from all the pounding that I had taken, and from the bloody freezing temperature.

When I groaned and moved I was suddenly blasted by a jet of freezing cold water that smashed my head and body against a wall. This at least cleared some of the bloody grime from my eyes, and when the blast stopped I found that I could open them, at least into tiny slits, and see where I was. It didn't take long before I it dawned on me exactly where I was, and what was going to happen to me. If I could have, at that point in time I would gladly have swapped the halls of hell for what was coming; no contest.

I spend every day of my life doing my best never to think of this episode in my life, mostly unsuccessfully, as hardly a day goes by when I don't think of it in some form or another. I spent the next three months being 'interrogated' by the Soviets. Some people would say that it was torture, not merely interrogation. I think it was worse than that: In the next three months I would be reduced from an extremely fit, healthy and basically happy man into something that was less than alive; a thing that couldn't walk or talk; a broken less-than-human piece of shit that was scared of its own shadow; a nothing. And it was all courtesy of the GRU; the 'Foreign Military Intelligence Directorate' of the Soviet Army General Staff.

During this period I didn't know who my interrogators were. I didn't know exactly what they wanted, I didn't know how much time was passing and I didn't know whether I was going to get out of there alive or dead. The only thing that was certain in my life at this point was that I was going to experience pain and more pain. Pain like you can't imagine. And I hate to admit this; I was scared most of the time, and I mean shit-scared.

The GRU, which no longer exists, had not been a part of the infamous KGB, or 'Committee for State Security'. In fact the GRU had hated this rival intelligence organisation and vice versa, and they had been fiercely independent of both the KGB and the communist party. The GRU were responsible for the collection of all military and political intelligence outside of the Soviet Union and they also had 25,000 *Spetsnaz* troops under their command. When it came to interrogation techniques, the GRU had been practicing their skills since they were first formed back in 1918 under Trotsky. They made the KGB look like a bunch of boy scouts at a tea party. These guys were the professionals.

Apart from the first brief glimpse that I had, as I was dragged into it, I never actually saw the exterior of the building I was interrogated in, and I had no idea of where it was located in Afghanistan. All that I saw of the place was the cell where I 'lived' (existed would be a better word to describe it), the corridor outside my cell and the other cells that lined it next to mine, the room at the end of the corridor where the 'softening up' took place, and the room

225

beyond that where the interrogation itself took place. Though I was once taken into a courtyard to see a number of executions, all I saw there was an empty square of concrete surrounded by concrete walls that were pock-marked with bullet holes.

My cell was approximately five feet by five feet in size; too small for me to lie down, even if I'd ever been given the chance, which I was not. It was tiled with five-inch square white ceramic tiles on the floor, walls and ceiling, and lit by a single very bright light-bulb behind a protective wire mesh on the ceiling that burned constantly for 24 hours a day. There were no windows and so there was no source of natural light, and there was no door, just an empty doorway. There was no furniture either, not even a bed. In fact there wasn't even a pile of straw on the floor. The floor itself sloped gently down from three corners of the cell to a small six-inch wide pipe outlet in a far corner which was my toilet. Because of the lack of natural light, and the fact that the artificial lights never went out in this place, I had no idea of the passing of time except that each minute of pain could and would last a lifetime.

Through the open doorway and just outside in the corridor, a GRU guard was permanently stationed. He had a clear view of me the whole time that I was in the cell and would watch me like a hawk. As soon as I relaxed or closed my eyes or tried to fall asleep, he would be on me, either laying into me with his boots and fists, or throwing a bucket of freezing cold water over me or blasting me with a powerful jet of freezing water from a hose pipe permanently at hand, whichever took his fancy at the time. The idea behind this was of course to make sure that I would get no sleep whatsoever.

I would sit curled up in the farthest possible corner away from the guard, my back leaning against the wall and my legs drawn up in front of me while I hugged them with my arms. I was permanently naked and it was bloody cold in this place. There was no heating of any sort and it was the middle of an Afghan winter.

The GRU guards were all of the same ethnic background, which I imagine is somewhere in the far east of Siberia. Every one was fairly short and stocky; they had wide flat faces and cold, slitted eyes. Their faces never, ever, showed any emotion at all apart from cold hatred, and they were vicious, brutal bringers of pain who I guess enjoyed their work immensely.

Although I was never allowed to go to sleep, it's amazing what the human body and mind can do when it is forced to. I learned to 'cat-nap', just for a few seconds at a time, without closing my eyes. When I was in the cell for extended periods my mind would drift away into a sort of trance, where I would think about and feel nothing at all. I suppose in this way I managed to get some sleep or at least to switch my mind off, and to fool the ever-present bastard at the door that I was actually wide-awake. I never got anywhere close to getting enough sleep though, even with lots of tiny 'cat-naps', and the lack of sleep (known technically as 'sleep deprivation') worked away at my mind all of the time that I was held captive. At first my mind went sort of hazy, as though it was wrapped in cotton wool, and I couldn't think straight. My already battered strength of mind and purpose plummeted into the depths of despair, and my body became so weak that I couldn't even stand without the guards holding me up. All that I wanted to do the entire time I was held captive was to fall asleep. It's difficult to explain but sleep became the thing that I most desired in the entire world. Even the gnawing hunger on account of the lack of food was nothing to compare with this desire to fall asleep. As time went by and the lack of sleep became more and more acute, I found that I was suffering from hallucinations as well. In many ways these were the hardest to deal with, as sometimes it became impossible to sort out real events from those I was experiencing in the hallucinations.

The lack of proper sleep was aggravated by the paucity of food. I was fed, of course, but I have no idea how frequently (it could have been three times a day or once a week for all I know). Every now and again another guard would turn up at the door with a metal tray holding a metal bowl of what looked and tasted like lukewarm washing-up water. I guess that it was some type of soup but God knows what it was made of as there was never anything in it like lumps of meat or vegetables, and it really did taste like shitty washing-up water. It was accompanied by a small piece of horrible-tasting Russian black rye bread, which was always mouldy and stank. I would wolf it down regardless, even though the grinning guard would often gob in the soup. I knew that to survive I had to eat, no matter what the food tasted or looked like. There was never enough food to even remotely satisfy my hunger and the desire to eat my fill was second only to my desire to fall asleep.

This then, was my daily routine during the entire period of my captivity at the hands of the GRU. What amazes me is how quickly a human being can adjust to such a brutal regime so that it does, even over a short length of time, become purely routine inside your head; normal almost.

Every now and again this miserable fucking routine would be broken by the sound of boots marching down the echoing corridor; a sound that I grew to fear. Two more guards would appear at the open doorway, laughing and joking with each other. They would grab me under the armpits and haul me up and then drag me away down the length of the corridor and past the mainly empty cells adjacent to my own. Sometimes I would get a glimpse of another pathetic-looking creature curled up naked in the corner of his own cell as I was dragged past, with his own personal mother-fucker of a slant-eyed shit-eating guard posted outside.

I would always try and fight the guards who were dragging me, not because I was a brave Special Forces hero who wanted to be like John Rambo, but because I knew what was waiting for me in the room at the end of the corridor. It never made the slightest difference as I was so weak I couldn't do anything more than a starving kitten could and the guards just laughed at my pathetic attempts, slapping me painfully around the face and head whenever the fancy took them.

FIFTY-FOUR

The room at the end of the corridor was bare concrete with only a few chairs for the guards and a small table on one side. On top of the table was a small music-centre, much like those that you can buy from any electrical shop or supermarket in the world. There were also plastic buckets filled to the brim with icy-cold water lining the wall. This was what I called the 'softening-up room' and I hated the fucking place even more than I hated my fucking cell.

I would be dragged into the room and one of the guards would pull a rough black hood over my head and tie it off tightly around my throat. Then the guards (I guess) would put ear-mufflers over their ears and the music centre would be turned on to full volume. It wasn't music that it played though; it was 'white-noise'.

White-noise sounds like the static you get on your car radio when you can't find a channel. It was played very, very loudly (so that it hurt my ears it was so loud), and it seemed to penetrate even the remotest part of my brain as though someone was constantly sticking red-hot needles through my skull.

I would be placed into one of two different 'stress' positions for this softening-up, depending, I guess, upon the choice of the guards. One of these positions was standing up against the wall with my arms and legs spread out wide, so that my full weight was just on my outspread fingertips and toes. In the second position I would be forced to my knees with my hands on my head with my fingers interlocked. In this second position my thighs and

230

my back would be in a straight line so that the weight of my entire body would be directly above my knees. I don't know which position I hated the most; they were both extremely painful to maintain even after a short period.

Once I was in one of these positions, I would be made to stay there for God knows how long. If you think it sounds easy – try it yourself on cold concrete. If you can last more than ten minutes in either one without getting a shit-load of pain then you're either a superstar or brain-dead. Now imagine doing it with a black hood over your head, so thick that you can't even see the light shining through, and add a mind-numbing and never-ending blast of white-noise. Then, just for fun, imagine that there's a burly sadistic fucking guard behind you who every now and then will either pour a freezing bucket of water over your head (which soaks into your hood so that you have difficulty breathing and it makes you feel like you're drowning), or batters you with all his strength using a truncheon (I'm guessing here as I never knew what they actually belted me with as I couldn't see it) across your naked buttocks, the backs of your thighs, or your lower back. I never knew when something like this was coming as I couldn't see or hear a thing except for the blackness and the white-noise. I never knew how long these sessions actually lasted; all I know is that it felt like years.

This was just the 'softening-up' period for the real stuff that was to follow.

FIFTY-FIVE

Somehow or other, during this process, I would sink into a world of nothingness. Perhaps it would even be a deep sleep, I don't know which; it's amazing how humans can cope with shit like this (I keep saying this – but it's true). In spite of the constant pain, the darkness and the noise, I would drift off, only to be periodically snapped out of it by a bucket of water or a searing stab of pain as I was battered un-expectantly. Then I'd drift off again. Then the time would come when I was grabbed roughly and I'd feel the sharp stab of a needle somewhere on my body (I'm guessing that this would be a hypodermic full of some powerful mind-bending hallucinatory drug or other) and I'd know with a sinking feeling in my guts that this was the end of the softening-up and the time for the real pain to begin.

Almost sobbing with fear I'd be dragged into the next room.

I never got to see this room as I was always hooded, but in my mind's eye I can clearly see where all of the implements of my interrogation were placed around the room. I know that over to the left was the bath full of water and the wooden chair near to it that I would sometimes be strapped to. Over to the right was the big concrete slab that I would be fastened to, and the electricity generator that I'd be clamped to. And in the centre of the room was the space that they'd use to throw me to the ground and kick and beat the shit out of me. Beyond this on the far side of the room was the other chair that they'd strap me into when I would sit right opposite *him*.

I never got to see *his* face either. All I'd hear would be his ever-so-soft voice with its heavily Russian-accented English. But I would know that voice even if I heard it amongst a room full of thousands of loudly-shouting people, and I swear to you now; if I ever do hear that voice I'll kill the bastard before he gets a chance to say more than three words. I dream about killing this bastard. If there is a God and any justice at all, then one day I'll get my chance.

This is the setting for my world of fear, pain and humiliation endured a hundred times. This is the world that still inhabits my fucking nightmares nearly thirty years later.

This is how it went:

Sometimes I'd be strapped into the chair on the opposite side of the room. Here I'd be battered around the head from behind, or sometimes they'd take my fingers one by one and snap the bones in them, or they'd take my toes one by one and snap the bones in them. Whenever they did this the doctor/medic in the room (there was always one present and I could distinguish him from the others by the constant 'tch tch' sound he'd make with his tongue whenever he treated me) would reset and splint my fingers and toes, only for them to be broken later, again and again. Sometimes they'd cut me on my chest or shoulders, and sometimes they would burn me as they stubbed out cigarette butts on my flesh.

Sometimes I'd be deposited in a heap on the floor in the centre of the room and there the guards would kick my head around like George Best on a scoring spree. Their boots would also slam again and again into my ribs, my back, my arms, my legs, my guts, my head, my face and my groin. They could go on for what seemed hours with amazing enthusiasm and stamina.

Sometimes I would be strapped upside down to some sort of wooden plank and lowered face-first into the bath that was full of ice-cold water. I would struggle like crazy, but it wouldn't help as I was always tightly bound and could hardly move. As I was lowered into the water I would try to hold my breath for as long as possible, but eventually I'd have to open my mouth and gasp for air and then I'd suck in nothing but water. At this point I would feel the painful constriction as my throat closed off to stop any more water entering my body (this is an involuntary bodily reaction known as 'laryngospasm'). Usually then the whole plank, with me strapped to it, would be pulled out of the water and put on the floor so that the medic could do his stuff and revive me. Sometimes, just for a bit variation, the bastards would hold me down under the water for longer until my thrashings died down and I became unconscious. Then my throat would relax and the water would enter my lungs and fill me up. When they did this I'm guessing that the medic would have a tougher job of reviving me, because I'd hear him muttering *govno* ('shit') under his breath as he pumped away on my chest as I came around. He would then call the guard in charge of my drowning a *sraka* (an 'asshole'). The guards just laughed at him.

Sometimes they would strap me into the other chair, the one closer to the bath. Here they would force a metal pipe into my mouth. I'd always try to fight this by clamping my jaws shut but they would just shove their filthy fingers into my mouth and prise my teeth apart. They would always win this contest of strength, and the pipe would be harshly pushed down into my throat until it passed my larynx. This was fucking painful and scraped my throat raw. Then cold water would be pumped into my stomach using a stirrup pump (or at least that's what it sounded like) until I'd be in agony from my stomach bloating up like a balloon and feeling like I was going to burst. Eventually I'd feel the water rising higher into my throat as it filled my body cavities up and then it would start to get into my lungs. The medic would usually stop them at this point by desperately shouting "Stop! Stop!" in English. Sometimes they'd stop and at other times they'd just carry on, laughing at him. If they did stop here, then they would un-strap me, flip me onto the floor and smack me in my bloated belly, which was excruciating, before forcing the water out of my stomach by kneeling on me with their full bodyweight, while I would gasp and flounder, spewing the water and whatever food I'd recently eaten from my mouth. Then they'd strap me back to the chair and start all over again, and again. If they didn't stop at this point then I'd become unconscious and literally drown as the water entered my lungs, and then the medic would have to revive me and I'd have to listen to his bad language all over again.

Sometimes they'd drag me across to the right hand side of the room and strap me down onto the big slab of concrete. If they strapped me down on my back then I could expect the electrodes to be clamped either onto my ear lobes (they'd pull up my hood for this), or onto my nipples, or onto my balls, or onto my foreskin. If I was strapped face down then they'd push an electrode up my arse. Then they would throw a bucket of ice-cold water over me (I'm guessing that they did this to improve the flow of the current) and shove a piece of padded wood into my mouth to stop me biting my tongue off (after all, I wouldn't be able to talk if I bit my tongue off, would I?). Then I'd hear this whining noise right by my head, getting higher and higher in pitch as the electricity generator charged, until it bleeped, once, and then I'd be hit with it, and by fuck did it hurt. My body would go into spasms and my hands and feet would curl up into claws (after a session of this it would take a long time before they could relax and straighten out). My throat would spasm and I wouldn't be able to breathe, so the medic would stick his fingers down my throat in between each shock to get my airway open again. I don't know whether I screamed during the shocks but my throat would feel as ragged as fuck, and my voice would be hoarse for a long time afterwards. On four occasions, always when the electrodes were clamped to my ear lobes, one of my teeth exploded inside my mouth. Although this hurt a lot I wouldn't notice that particular pain until the shock had stopped, and only then could I feel the bits of tooth embedded in the roof of my mouth and taste the blood. Then I'd hear the whining of the charge building up again, and again.

Sometimes, just for a bit of variation, they would beat the soles of my feet with their truncheons while I was strapped onto this slab, before the electrocutions began.

And all of the time his fucking voice would be softly whispering in my ear:
"Tell me what I want to know and I'll stop it John."
"Tell me what I want to know and the pain will go away John."
"Tell me what I want to know and you can go home to your family John."
"Tell me what I want to know and it'll all end John, it'll just be a bad dream John."
"Tell me what I want to know John."

Sometimes a session in this room would consist of one of the above methods being carried out again and again and again. Sometimes they would vary my interrogation by mixing a couple of them up. Sometimes they would go from one to another and then back again and then onto something else. It didn't really matter as each one of them held its own particular terrors for me. I've no idea how long each of these sessions would last, as time would stretch out into infinity for me anyway; a second can seem like a day when you're having your genitals fried. I've no idea how many sessions I faced in the end either, but I'm

236

guessing it must have been at least thirty to forty. They all seem to merge into one awful and terrifying period in my memory.

I humiliated myself all of the time. I would cry like a baby and scream as soon as they touched me, and I would vomit and piss and shit myself. What I never did was to stand up and tell them to "Fuck off". This wasn't a movie.

FIFTY-SIX

During my career as a soldier I have been given training two times in what the army euphemistically calls: 'Resistance to Interrogation' techniques. These were good courses and I learnt a lot on them, especially on how to conduct myself if captured by an enemy. During these courses we would be put through a quite life-like interrogation and shown some of the tricks that the interrogators could use to get us to talk. But of course, it could never be the same as a real interrogation. During these courses you always knew that the interrogators would never go too far and that you would walk out of it alive and unhurt at the end. The real thing is entirely different.

On the training courses they also emphasised that your interrogators would never actually beat you or hurt you, because, as they would point out; this would be detrimental to them getting any information out of you. According to the organisers of these courses, as soon as a person is physically hurt they will begin to clam up and not to talk. No, they said, interrogation is much easier for them and they get much better results when they only use psychological means.

I wish that someone had told this to the fucking GRU.

I had also learnt during my time with the British SIS that you always had to have a good 'cover story' when on an operation. I had been supplied with what I thought initially was a fairly good one for Afghanistan. My particular cover story went something like this: I was a freelance journalist in Afghanistan writing about the Soviet invasion. I carried a camera with me everywhere I went in Afghanistan and had taken lots of photos of *Mujahedeen* rebels and mountains and rocks etc., and I had a stack of paperwork with me too; old articles that I had supposedly written for newspapers and magazines but which had been supplied courtesy of the firm. The only trouble was that both I and the GRU knew that this was a load of old crap. They are, after all, a thoroughly professional intelligence-gathering agency with huge resources; they had known all about me and the other British guys for months, through their network of Afghan informers, and had been actively hunting us down. My cover story lasted all of my first session of interrogation before it was ripped apart. From then on I had reverted to answering his questions with 'name, rank, army number and date of birth' and the phrase: "I cannot answer that question." (this used to be "*Sorry*, I cannot answer that question," but the psychologists back home had thought that the 'sorry' bit was detrimental to the whole psyche of trying to remain positive while being interrogated, so it had been changed). So this is what I answered to every single question that he asked of me.

"Smith, John, Sergeant, 244*****, 10th ***** 19**, I cannot answer that question." A million times over.

One of the worst moments of my interrogation was when I was dragged outside into the courtyard of the building. There was a line of tough-looking *Spetsnaz* troopers standing and facing a bullet-holed wall, and all of them were armed with 7.62mm AKMs. My first thought was shit; they're going to kill me! Then, as a naked Afghan was dragged out of a door to one side, his body covered in cuts, bruises and open sores (just like mine), I realised that it wasn't me that they were going to kill; it was the Afghan. I'm ashamed to say that I felt intense relief. Even when I realised that he was one of the *Mujahedeen* fighters that I

239

had lived with and had been training for months and that he must have been captured during the same ambush as me. He was unceremoniously thrown against the wall and his escort backed away, before I heard the *Spetsnaz* officer in command of the firing squad shout "Ready! Aim! Fire!" and the poor fucker was blasted by ten rounds in the head and chest and slumped down dead. This was followed by the officer strolling over to the recumbent figure, putting a round into the back of the Afghan's head from his pistol – just to make sure. These executions went on for ages. I lost count of the number of my former comrades who were shot by the firing squad, but there must have been at least ten or eleven of them.

They all reacted in the same way to their own executions; with relief. At least they were confident that they would be going to paradise as warriors of Islam. I didn't have any such delusions.

Then I was dragged out and shoved against the same wall. There was no blindfold for me, no last cigarette and no last chance to talk or confess my sins. The officer again shouted: "Ready! Aim! Fire!" and then the sound of the shots echoed loudly in my ears and I collapsed against the wall, brown adrenaline running down my legs along with a stream of steaming piss. I'd thought that this was the end.

They had used blanks and were all pissing themselves laughing at me as I half-lay against the wall sobbing my fucking eyes out. It was all a big joke and I was dragged back into my cell.

I held out for a long time. It was only after it all ended that I could calmly sit down and try to work out exactly how long I had endured the interrogation without breaking. My best guess is that it was for around 90 days; three fucking months. Do you want to know why I held out for so long without breaking? Well, it had nothing to do with Queen and Country, and sadly it had nothing to do either with trying to save the lives of my Afghan compatriots or Mike, and give them a chance to get the hell out of where they were. It's simple really: I survived and held out for three months because of hate and anger. That's what did it for me. Every moment of every single day and night I was literally consumed by hate. I hated *him*, the GRU, the *Kaffirs*, the Afghans, the country, the war, the regiment, the British Army and the SIS; basically I hated everything and everyone that I knew, especially myself and the way that I cried and sobbed and screamed and pissed and shitted myself. Then there was the anger: I was angry at all of the above and more. I wanted to tear out the throats of the GRU bastards with my teeth and rip out their hearts with my hands. I fantasised about it all of the time. This is what kept me going throughout those 90 days and nights of pure terror, of pain and of deep humiliation; hate and anger. I still feel it now; sometimes it consumes my inner self like a white-hot flame. Sometimes my dreams are filled with the hate and anger that kept me alive all that time. This rage kept me from breaking; there was no way on fucking earth that I was going to give into them, no matter how bad it got!

It couldn't last, of course. No one could go through what I went through without breaking at some point or other. No one is that strong. No one.

FIFTY-SEVEN

I didn't just 'break'; I broke with a capital 'B' for 'Big time'. When I had finally had enough of being beaten, drowned and electrocuted - when I just couldn't take it anymore, I practically got down on my knees and begged them to let me tell them anything and everything that I knew, from the name of my section head in the Increment to the nickname my wife had given to our dog. I talked and talked and talked, and while half of it was probably a load of old waffle, the other half wasn't. I put more lives into danger than I can remember, and I didn't give one fucking hoot at the time. I just didn't give a shit. When I broke, I really broke.

I'm not going to tell you what happened to make me finally break: That's a secret that I'm going to take to the grave with me.

When those bastards broke me they also killed something inside of me, something that I've never gotten back. It's like a part of me died on that day well before the rest of me has had time to catch up. I know that this sounds like a load of old codswallop, but it's true. I'm only half the man that went into that interrogation room for the first time.

Things got easier after I broke down of course. I was still kept in the same cell, but I was given an old pair of trousers and a shirt to wear, and the guard on duty didn't soak me every time I fell asleep, which was wonderful - I could, at long last sleep. Even the food was better and there were actually things floating in my soup (I don't know what they were though) and although the bread was still stale and mouldy and stank; there was more of it.

I was in such a poor physical state by this time that it was weeks before I could even stand on my own, so I was still dragged down the corridor for interrogation. But this time it was in the opposite direction from the softening-up room and I was sat in a chair in another, much more pleasant room, and asked questions for hour after hour after hour. One new difficulty was that I could hardly speak, and when I did I had to think very carefully about the words that I wanted to say before saying them. This was not because of what I was saying (I didn't give a shit about what that was any more), but because I was slurring my words terribly and the stenographer writing everything down couldn't understand most of what I said.

The interrogator (who thankfully was not him by the way) had to ask me the same questions time and time again before they could understand my answer. Eventually this improved, as did my bodily strength, but it was slow work and I would tire very easily. I had lost a lot of weight and my ribs stuck out grotesquely from above a pinched and drawn-in stomach. My legs and arms looked like stick insects on hunger-strike. My body was very pale where you could actually see the skin, but for the most part it was covered in cuts, burns, stinking open sores and a kaleidoscope of variously coloured bruises. In short, I looked like a very battered anorexic whippet.

It was around the end of May that I heard the only good news that I had in months; I was going home. The GRU was doing a swap with the SIS: me for some lowlife Soviet operator that had been caught doing naughty things in the UK. During the following two weeks I was given better and better food. I was moved to another building and allowed to sleep in a metal-framed bed. It had a smelly old mattress but to me it was pure heaven. I was also given a thin woollen blanket, again pure bliss.

243

I was also given a series of check-ups by a Soviet Army doctor and slowly my wounds began to heal, at least the ones that you could see anyway. It was obvious that they were doing everything they could to repair me as much as possible before my big day.

Every day I would try to stand and walk around my room unaided, until I could do so fairly confidently. I would have been proud of this achievement if a piece of shit like me could have felt any pride. Instead, I just got on with forcing myself to get better, just like I'd always done.

All of the time I knew that I never really would though, would I?

FIFTY-EIGHT

Saturday 19th October 2013
London

Everything had gone according to the plan that Smith had been outlining in his head for the past few days. He had driven down to London, stopping at a number of petrol stations along the way to buy small 5 litre plastic petrol containers and filling them with fuel. He had not worried at all about CCTV cameras or number plate recognition cameras (ANPR) in any of the stations. The registration plates on the stolen Land Rover Defender were old SIS plates that were still operational and therefore perfectly kosher, even if checked by a police traffic officer. He also didn't worry about being recognised, as his simple disguise had changed the shape of his face so much.

After arriving in the city he had searched and found a computer-manufacturing company that was located fairly close to his intended target in Hendon and had sat in their car park until all of the staff had left at the end of the day. Then he had stolen one of their vans with the company's logo stencilled in big letters on the side. He hadn't needed to change the registration plates on this one as he was only intending to use it for the next few hours or so. He left the Land Rover parked next to the computer company offices and set up one of his special 'fuel-air bombs' inside it, timed to detonate 15 minutes before he expected to leave his prime target of the coming night. The resulting explosive conflagration would not only cause a nice diversion for the local fire service and delay them from reaching his prime target before that also exploded, but would moreover eradicate any physical evidence that he may have inadvertently left in or on the vehicle. The fuel-air bomb would obliterate everything, including the number plates, and would almost certainly set fire to the computer company's premises as well, causing even more of a diversion. Before leaving he put his bomb-making kit inside empty cardboard computer boxes that he found inside the van, and donned the hi-visibility jacket with the company's logo on its back that he had found in the van's cab.

Finally he drove off towards the site of his primary target.

He drove up to the main entrance at Gate J of Hendon Police College and spoke with the civilian security guard on duty, who just happened to be a black African. They chatted amicably for a few moments about Africa, Smith telling him that he had lived and worked on the African continent for a few years. Then Smith drove the van around to the loading bay at the rear of the huge Data Centre building, ostensibly to deliver some computers. The security guard was not suspicious in the least; after all Smith was in a computer company van and hi-vis jacket, and he obviously knew the site well, knowing exactly where to go without having to be told. What was there to be suspicious about? Computer and IT guys were always delivering to or visiting the data centre at all times of the night and day; there was nothing unusual.

Smith was met at the loading bay doors by another security guard who had been alerted to meet him by the gatehouse. This guy was big and fat and spoke with a cockney accent. Smith smiled pleasantly at him and said:

"Hello mate; how yer doin'?"

"I'm alright mate. What yer deliverin'?"

"Computer monitors. Got to leave them in the basement."

"Basements got a lock on it. Yer need the code to get in."

"I know mate, I've been here loads of times. Trouble is I always forget what the bloody code is."

"Okay. Well I'm gonna have a sly fag while I wait for yer. Don't tell no one I told yer; but the code is CX297Z."

"CX297Z? Cheers mate; I'll only be about 10 to 15 minutes. That alright with you?"

"Fine mate. I'll have a couple of fags then. Bastards won't let yer smoke anywhere on site so yer have to grab a sly one when yer can!"

"They're all bastards. I'd have one with you but this is my last job of the night and I wanna get home!"

"Fair enough."

Smith borrowed a small sack truck from the bay and loaded it with the boxes from the back of his van. The security guard raised the roller door just enough to let him inside the building, and then lit his fag, cupping it with his hand. Smith pushed the sack truck along a corridor to an internal lift and went down to the basement level. Once he had keyed the code into the basement door's keypad he quickly went into the main room and closed the door firmly behind him.

This main room housed the massive server of the Police National Computer database, otherwise known as the PNC. The PNC is a computer system used extensively by all of the law enforcement organisations in the UK; it holds millions of records on people, criminal convictions, vehicles and drivers and even buildings. It's the original 'big brother' computer system. The computer server in the basement consisted of huge black and silver cabinets, filled with whirring, buzzing hardware that almost filled the big room; and there were dozens of cables snaking over the floor between the cabinets. Smith quickly emptied his boxes, taking out four large 5kg charges of PE4 (plastic explosive). He placed each charge in a corner of the room, accompanied by a red plastic 5 litre container of petrol next to it. He then unrolled four lengths of pre-measured detonation cord; a white cord that looked much like a washing line but with a core of high explosive running through the middle of it. He knotted one end of each of the lengths of det cord and pushed the knots into the four charges so they were firmly embedded within the PE4. Finally he clipped the other ends of the det cords together; clipped a single detonator to them and pushed a long length of safety fuse (this was similar to the det cord but black in colour and filled with a core of slow-burning explosive) into the detonator. Finally he placed a smaller charge of 1kg of PE4 adjacent to the room's fire-exit door which was located a level below the main floor, reached by a short flight of concrete steps and sheltered by a low internal brick wall. To this charge he added a longer length of det cord, made sure it was knotted and well-embedded in the charge, and attached the other end to the clip that held the detonator and other cords.

Before leaving the basement room he looked around, checking that everything was correctly set up. Then he lit the free end of the long safety fuse and casually took the empty sack truck back up to the loading bay. The whole job took him less than ten minutes to complete.

On his way out of the data centre he took a cylindrical smoke grenade from his jacket pocket, pulled the pin and rolled it into the empty corridor behind him.

It was another five minutes before he pulled the van out of the college grounds onto Aerodrome Road. As he drove away he could hear the strident siren of the college's fire alarm going off and saw the first of the college's staff pouring out from the building's exits and rushing to their various fire assembly points. He'd missed hearing the 'crump' of the Land Rover bomb going off while he was busy in the data centre, but he didn't miss the huge explosion of the college bomb going off when he was a mile and a half away. It was enormous and lit up the night with a flash bright enough to be seen above the street lights. The Police National Computer was no more.

The safety fuse had burned for 12 minutes before igniting the detonator, which in turn had instantaneously exploded the five lengths of det cord. These in turn had ignited the four 5kg plastic explosive charges simultaneously. Each explosion had caused a huge shock wave that had obliterated the petrol containers next to them, dispersing the petrol as vapour into the air; as the separate shock waves hit each other in the centre of the room they had forced the explosion upwards and outwards with immense force, fragmenting and destroying everything in their collective path. The fifth length of det cord, which had been longer than the others, ignited the smaller 1kg charge of plastic explosive by the fire-exit door a fraction of a second later than the other charges and the flash from this explosion ignited the petrol vapour that had mixed with the air of the basement and turned the blast into a huge fireball that burned at several thousand degrees for a few microseconds. This simple 'fuel-air bomb' totally destroyed not only the PNC server but also brought down the whole data centre building in the blast. The explosion was so big it could be heard fifty miles away.

Smith smiled to himself as he drove away. He had one more visit to make in the south; to the PNC backup server located at Buncefield in Hemel Hempstead. Then it would be a long drive north to the Forensics Science Service HQ at Solihull in Birmingham, home of the National DNA Database. It would be a busy night but one full of mischief-making and mayhem. Just how he liked it.

FIFTY-NINE

Sunday 20th October 2013
Huntingdon, Cambridgeshire

At 8am DCI Davies sat in his temporary office, his head in his hands. DC Helen Wright sat opposite him.

"Are you OK boss?" She asked softly. Davies groaned and looked up at her with bleary, defeated eyes.

"This is my worst bloody nightmare come true." He said. "Not only has Smith totally destroyed the PNC; he's also blown up the only bloody backup server, the location of which was supposed to be a secret; and he's blown up the computers and server that held the National DNA Database. We're totally blind! On top of this the chief constable is demanding updates on Smith's case every hour; SOCA HQ is on my back all of the time and the press are going to town on the story!"

"But most of the information on the PNC and NDNAD is also held by local police computers, isn't it? That's what I heard."

"True. Most of the ongoing criminal cases will have their information stored on their local police computers, so the damage he's done nationally is minimal, but that doesn't help us. He destroyed our bloody computers the night before last, every single bloody one of them!" He felt his temper rise at the bloody audacious cheek of Smith. "There is now no information held anywhere on any police computer regarding John bloody Smith. He's left us with absolutely nothing that we can use in a court of law; no statements; no evidence, including his DNA profile; absolutely bloody nothing! Jesus fucking Christ! I wish I'd never heard of Smith!"

"But what about photographs and fingerprints? Even I know that the PNC is – was - a text-only operating system and that all the images etc, are stored separately. Can't we still use those against him boss?"

"You just don't get it, do you Helen?" The police force has millions of photographs and fingerprints on file, absolutely fucking millions. But they were all coded through the PNC. Without the relevant codes it would take months, perhaps even years to locate Smith's among them. Even then they probably wouldn't be of any use because without Smith being here in person we cannot possibly verify the authenticity of the photographs or prints so that they can be used in court! Sure, we had a few hard copies of everything but they were burned up with everything else when he blew the fuck out of our offices. He's shafted us big-time! Like I said; this is an absolute fucking nightmare!"

"Christ boss. I didn't realise it was that bad. I'm sorry."

"You don't have anything to be sorry about Helen; it's fucking Smith who has destroyed everything we ever had on him, not you." His hand slipped across the desk and gave one of hers a squeeze, causing her face to take on a hint of redness. She squeezed him back.

"What now then boss? Where do we go from here?" Davies visibly pulled himself together.

"Well at least he didn't kill anybody this time. Smith set off the fire alarms in every building before he blew them up, so everybody managed to get out. The only casualty of the night was a have-a-go-hero security guard in Birmingham that Smith shot in both legs. It's a miracle that there weren't any deaths."

"But why? Smith doesn't seem to be the merciful kind. Look at what he did to poor Steve Mackay."

251

"God knows why Smith does anything. His acts appear to be random but they're not; he obviously has a plan. The full pathologists report on Mackay is still to come in but it appears from the initial findings that Steve was probably tortured before he was murdered, though mercifully it seems that he was already dead when Smith burnt his house down around him. From what Smith said in his last email he managed to get some information from Mackay that he wanted, but we don't know what that info is. It's pretty clear that Smith thinks there was something dodgy about his trial and that he's innocent, but with the amount of physical evidence we had amassed against him, I just don't believe it. Still, just in case Smith has a go at any of the other solicitors or the judge, I'm going to assign them with 24 hour security. I'll put Price onto the judge as his close protection; that should keep him busy and out of my hair. He's beginning to seriously piss me off. I want you to continue looking into Smith's past. There must be something there that we can use. I'll assign DC Hart to give you a hand. I'm going to have another go at this bloody Harry and see if I can get anything from him that we can use. He must know something, the bastard! At the moment, even though the biggest manhunt in the history of this country is looking for Smith, we have absolutely no leads on him at all."

The telephone rang on the desk.

"DCI Davies. What? You're a bit bloody late aren't you? Okay, get them here as fast as you can." He turned back to Helen with a wry smile on his face. "That was procurements. Our new computers have arrived. Not much bloody use now, are they?"

From: john smith (johnsmith2223@hotmail.com)
To: SOCA@Cambspolice.org.uk
Date: 20 October 2013 12:39:06
CC:
Subject: FAO Detective Chief Inspector Alan Davies, Cambs SOCA.

Hi Alan, I'll keep this one short as I'm bloody knackered and need to get some kip mate. It's been a busy few days!

Please find attached the latest instalment of my autobiography.

Speak to you again soon.

Regards

John Smith

SIXTY

When the time to go home eventually came, in late May 1985, it happened so quickly that I blinked and almost missed it. One day I was still being coaxed back to health by the GRU and the next I was being whisked away. There was a confusing mixture of sights and sounds as I was bundled into the back of a Gaz truck, driven to an airfield, shoved on board a helicopter, and then flown south for an hour or so. When we landed, in a veritable sand-storm thrown up by the helicopters rotors, I was bundled once again into the back of a truck and driven at high speed to the Pakistan border.

The actual swap wasn't at all like you see in the movies. For a start there wasn't a bridge involved and I didn't even get to see the Soviet spy that I was being swapped for. It was all rather mundane; I was helped out of the Gaz, walked about six feet and helped into the back of a rather more comfortable car. Then we were off, and that was it.

I don't know how long we drove for as I must have fallen asleep with the strain of it all (I hadn't physically done this much in a long time and I was still as weak as a kitten). When I was shaken awake, it was just to walk a few feet directly from the car, parked in the middle of a Pakistani airport, up some boarding steps and onto a small airplane. Inside the plane was a medical team that immediately set upon me with a barrage of tests. All I wanted to do was curl up in a corner and die; I didn't want anyone seeing me like this as I was deeply ashamed of myself and of the way I looked and the way I stunk. I was stripped naked and given a bed bath with luxuriously warm water, but ended up screaming and pissing myself when they tried to wipe my face with a wet face-cloth, much to the medic's shock and obvious disgust.

Eventually, after a lot of weak struggling on my part, and a lot of sticking-in of needles and the taking of blood samples on the part of the medical team, I was allowed to go to sleep. I didn't wake up once until we landed in the UK at RAF Brize Norton. There I was bundled into a Range Rover and whisked away to a safe house for my debriefing.

The intense debriefing by a team from the SIS lasted three weeks and was, in many ways, very difficult for me. As you would expect there were questions about the GRU interrogation methods used on me and about the GRU personnel that I had seen. I guess that they wanted to learn as much as possible so that they would know what their agents could expect to face if they were ever unfortunate enough to be captured by the Soviets. This was particularly hard for me as I had to relive the months of interrogation all over again and this was the very last thing that I wanted to do. All I wanted was to forget about everything that had happened to me over the last 4 or 5 months.

Then the debriefing centred on to the subject that I really dreaded, which was the information that I had given to the Soviets when I had broken. This was deeply humiliating for me and I could see in the debriefing officer's eyes exactly what he thought of me – that I was the lowest form of pond-life he'd ever met. But I told him everything; no matter how ashamed of myself I was, as I was desperate to reduce the damage that I had caused by my terrified blabbing to the Soviets. The more that the SIS knew of what I had said and therefore what the Soviets now knew the more remedial action they could take to change things. Or so I hoped anyway.

The whole time that this was going on I was also being tended to by a small army of medics and

255

physiotherapists who did their best to repair my body. I ate like a man possessed and soon started to put some weight back on. Quite soon I was capable of standing completely unaided and was even allowed outside the house to walk around the grounds in the sunshine. I even had access to a speech-therapist who helped me to talk more clearly. Despite all the lovely attention that was paid to my physical well-being though, not once did I see any sign of a psychiatrist. It was as though it didn't even occur to the SIS that I might be suffering psychologically. The only thing that I did during this whole time that could be construed as anything to do with 'mental health' was to take a standard British Army psychological test (a PT45). I found out the reason that I was given this test just before leaving the safe-house to go home to London and my family. It was delivered to me by Harry, the head of the Increment, on the day before I was due to leave.

SIXTY-ONE

Harry invited me into the library of the safe house for a 'little chat', as he called it. We were entirely on our own as he poured me a cup of tea from a tea-set on a tray that looked like something out of a costume drama on the Victorian gentry. I hadn't seen him since I had left for Afghanistan the previous year, so there was a lot of catching up to do between us, but we got the formalities over pretty quickly. He asked how I was feeling. I said "Fine", and that was basically it. The conversation that followed went something like this:

"I have to tell you John that the 'powers-that-be' are not best pleased about you getting caught by the Soviets."

"Really? That's tough."

"Now don't be like that, John. We both know that your capture could have caused quite a sensational scandal for the firm, never mind for HM's government."

"Yeah, sure. What do you mean 'could have'?"

"Well, luckily for us the Soviet chap that we swapped for you was also caught in the act of a particularly sensitive operation against us, so we and the Soviets have both come to a mutual understanding."

"Why? What was he up to?"

"Sorry old chap, but that's on a 'need to know' basis and you don't need to know. Let me just say that neither us nor the Soviets will be publicising what we have been up to, so the damage that could have been caused by your capture has been negated. Thank God."

"Super." I really didn't give a shit anymore.

"We have also been through the information that you gave to the Soviets, and fortunately it appears that the damage you've caused may be minimal."

"How?"

"Well, you were never in possession of that much sensitive information old chap. A lot of the stuff that you gave away is in fact quite old and out of date. It's also thought that the Soviets had probably been aware of much of it even before your capture."

"So I might as well not have held out as long as I did then; if all the information that I gave them was so old and bloody useless?"

"No; I'm not saying that at all. What I'm saying is that the problems you have caused can be minimised. We've already moved a few people sideways so that they cannot be compromised, and we have also changed some of our Standard Operating Procedures on a few of our ongoing operations as well."

"Super."

"Of course, this does mean that you personally will no longer be able to undertake operations against the USSR."

"Now that is good news. Does that mean that you still want me to work for the firm then? I thought that I'd be shelved after this?"

"Well, in the normal run of things, you would be shelved of course. You probably wouldn't even be allowed to return as a serving member of the Special Air Service. However, and this is why I really wanted to talk to you today, there may be an opportunity for you to continue on as a member of the Increment, if you still want to, that is?"

"Go on, I'm listening". At this point Harry leaned across to me and lowered his voice conspiratorially.

"I have been instructed from very high up to put together some very special operations."

"How high up and what 'special operations'?"

"From very high up; in fact as high as you can go; this is the PMs very own idea. Apparently dear Maggie is very, very pissed off with the Provo's and their like after the Brighton Hotel bombing last October: They very nearly got her, don't you know. She has spoken to 'The Chief' at Century House, and he in turn has spoken to me, and now I am speaking to you. The operations will be very, very top secret, with only the four of us knowing about them. Not even the Joint Intelligence Committee will be aware of our existence. Are you still up to it?"

"Sounds interesting. Carry on." Harry hesitated, looking at me closely.

"Are you sure you're still up to it? After all, you didn't do so well in Afghanistan, did you?" This really pissed me off.

"Just get on with it! You know better than anyone that I can cope with all sorts of crap."

"Okay then. But what you hear now must never, ever be repeated to anyone. Do you understand?"

"I understand perfectly. Tell me."

"Okay. I have been tasked to undertake 'wet jobs', as our cousins across the pond like to call them."

"Oh, I see."

"Do you understand what I mean by 'wet jobs'?"

"Of course I do. You're talking about knocking people off; assassinations."

"Technically yes, though of course HM's government could never be seen to be involved in anything like this and it will remain entirely within the Increment's domain."

"Super. Count me in."

"You're not worried about killing people in cold blood?"

"Are they good people or bad people?"

"Well, that rather depends on whose side you are on, I suppose." He chuckled at this one.

"Like I said, count me in. I don't care who are they are."

"Perfect, that's just what your psychiatric test indicated you would say. You're in."

"Super."

"By the way, I do have some good news for you."

"Go on."

"Your Commander in Afghanistan, Mike was it?"

"Yeah; what about him?"

"Well, you'll be happy to know that when the news reached him that you had been captured, he did the only sensible thing, considering that the rest of his team had either been killed or captured, and he packed up and came home. We picked him up at the Pakistan border and returned him to the regiment."

"So?" I hadn't actually liked Mike that much.

"Apparently he was very impressed by your service in Afghanistan, and as the officer commanding you over there he has been able to put you forward for a medal; the Distinguished Conduct Medal in fact. Of course, due to the sensitivity of your mission, it will never become gazetted, and therefore will never be official."

"Super." And that was it.

SIXTY-TWO

After all of this, I was finally allowed to go home to London and my young family. I had guessed that this reunion was going to be difficult after everything that I had been through, but I had no idea exactly how hard it was going to be. Anne-Marie still had no idea what I did for a living and was therefore blissfully unaware of what I had been through and the changes that this had wrought in me.

This was in the days before such technology as mobile phones or emails were in wide circulation. In fact I remember being issued with one of the very first models of a mobile phone for my SAS Land Rover just a year or two before I went to Afghanistan. It was basically a normal telephone handset on top of a black box the size of a car battery. We called it the 'bat phone' for some obscure reason that I can't remember now, and this was the latest mobile phone technology at the time!

I often told Anne-Marie that I was posted overseas during my frequent extended sojourns away from home, and in those days even calling on a land line from many foreign countries was bloody difficult. She believed, quite reasonably, that I was in such unexciting places such as Germany, Belize, Cyprus, Gibraltar or Hong Kong, along with many other soldiers from the British Army. The only reliable method of communication between us was through the post using the British Forces Post Office; or BFPO. Before embarking on an operation I would write several post cards and letters to my wife, which would then be slowly drip-fed to her over the period that I was away. The

BFPO naturally played a big part in this by stamping my mail with the relevant overseas stamp and date. This was the normal way of doing things in the regiment, most of the time anyway. A lot of the guys' wives and families knew that they were in the SAS, though they were mostly kept in the dark about precisely where their loved ones were posted, when they went off to one conflict or another around the world. But then the majority of them lived just off camp in Hereford, in married quarters, and they had the mutual support of all the other wives and families when the shit hit the fan. Anne-Marie had chosen right at the beginning of our relationship to stay away from the army and had continued to live in London, close to her family and friends, where she wanted to be. Therefore I thought it was best to keep her in the dark about what I actually did for a living, especially as so much of my work was ultra-sensitive, even by SAS standards.

Anyway, this all meant that when I returned home after nearly a year away, Anne-Marie expected the man that she loved and had chosen to spend the rest of her life with to return to her. Instead she got the new me; a twisted, bitter, angry bastard who was as cold as ice and didn't give a shit about anything at all anymore. As I was to learn much later, after I finally left the army for good, my last psychological test had revealed that I was suffering from the initial stages of Post Traumatic Stress Disorder, or PTSD. The British Army recognized this disorder at the time but did nothing to counteract it.

I now had a mixture of emotions, sometimes conflicting, that would get much worse as time went by and would thoroughly confuse and upset me, making my anger turn to pure rage and hatred at times. Sometimes this rage and hatred would be directed aggressively at others but often it was turned inwards towards me. I would often have intensive and terrible flashbacks to my torture. These flashbacks could be brought on by anything from a seemingly innocent smell to seeing a news piece on the TV. In fact anything that reminded me of my experience in any way whatsoever. Then there were the nightmares when I would wake up screaming and sobbing, often with a sweat and piss-stained mattress. These nightmares occurred every single night for years on end. I avoided talking about my experiences or indeed, anything at all to do with the army, at all costs, especially with Anne-Marie who was, quite naturally, extremely disturbed at the changes in my personality. I became totally convinced that no one could ever understand me or what I had been through and I felt increasingly disconnected from everyone and everything around me. At times the shame and guilt of my breaking under torture would engulf me and I would totally withdraw into myself. I was deeply depressed yet at the same time I was very irritable and I often became aggressive. In short, I was a total and complete fucking mess.

Even worse was the fact that I took it out on everyone around me, especially Anne-Marie and my kids. I became violent and abusive towards them, and this gradually got worse as time went by. I also started to turn to the bottle to try and numb my feelings when they threatened to engulf me.

When you think of it, Harry must have wet himself with glee when he became aware of this change in my personality. He found himself able to use a man who genuinely didn't care about anything anymore, with no sense of guilt about killing people, and with no emotions except cold rage and hate. I also happened to be a very highly-trained individual in hand-to-hand combat, an exceptional sniper and very skilled at using explosives. I wasn't a complete psychopath, as even the Increment would not be able to use a psycho, but I was the next best thing; basically I was a killing machine that could be pointed in any direction they chose to take out any target with the minimum of fuss. This, of course, is exactly what they needed and wanted.

SIXTY-THREE

I began my new career in Central and South America. During the 1980s Britain saw the illegal drug problem as one of the major modern crisis facing our country. Cocaine, and to a lesser extent marijuana, were being produced in vast quantities in many Latin American countries, especially Columbia and El Salvador. They were then shipped to the Caribbean, Turkey and North Africa, before finally ending up in the UK. Here the rate of drug-related crimes, especially violent crimes, was rising to an all-time high and it was widely recognized that the British police and Customs were losing the war against drug smuggling and drug abuse.

Illegal drugs from Latin America were also becoming a big problem in the US, and the US government had authorised the CIA to investigate and take any action that they deemed necessary to stem the rising tide of drugs being smuggled into America.

Illegal drugs were very lucrative as a 'commodity' and this gave rise to a vicious war between the people who were struggling to gain control of the trade in Latin America. There was a lot at stake in these drug wars; not least the billion-dollar profits that could be made out of the misery of others. Often these wars were fought between corrupt politicians and their armies on the one hand and the growing number of drug-barons on the other, each vying to gain control over the trade and prepared to go to any lengths to protect and increase their profits. This increase in the use of extreme violence in turn led to an increasing need for men who were trained in violence and not scared of using it. Mercenaries from the US and Europe were offering their services to the drug-barons, in return for huge wage packets. A lot of the mercenaries recruited in the UK were failed soldiers or wannabe's from county infantry regiments trying to live out their fantasies. But there was also a significant and growing number of ex-Para's, Royal Marines and SAS soldiers joining the ranks of the drug barons. This new problem was being carefully monitored by the CIA, who in turn was kind enough to pass on the information that it gathered on involved British citizens to the Increment.

So after just a few weeks returning home to the bosom of my family, I was whisked away overseas, to the relief of everyone involved with me back home. Harry and I, occasionally supported by members of the Increment, began a whistle-stop tour of Latin America. We travelled on false papers, normally posing as tourists or students. Using the intelligence supplied to us by the Americans, we would first of all locate the British mercenaries and where they were staying, which was usually in very expensive hotels. Then Harry and I would make ourselves known to these guys, often as they were enjoying a nice quiet drink in the hotel bar. We would approach them and Harry would address them by their real names, which would usually be enough to get their attention, as many of them were using aliases to try and maintain their anonymity. Harry would do all of the talking while I remained silent and brooding; something which I do very well when I want to; I can be a real frightening bastard when I try. Harry would inform them that we were from the British government and that we were aware of what they were up to. Although he was careful to never give the game away and tell them that we were from the firm, it didn't take a genius to work out who we were, and a lot of these guys were highly-trained and experienced soldiers who soon figured out the score. Using carefully-veiled threats Harry would basically give them an ultimatum; either they leave the service of the drug-barons and find employment somewhere that would be less embarrassing to the British government, or they would have to face the alternative. I could see by the look on many of their faces that they realised that the alternative was me.

We personally visited over a hundred of these guys in half a dozen countries, and luckily for them, most of them saw the light and withdrew from their nefarious occupations. However, you always get a few who are either too stupid or too proud to back down. Where this happened I got rid of them, permanently, with a bullet in the head as they slept peacefully in their hotel rooms. Getting hold of weapons was made easy because all of the British Embassies and High Commissions on the continent held small armouries on their premises, smuggled into the countries concerned inside diplomatic pouches. We would simply visit the relevant consular employees (normally attachments from the SIS) to pick up the weapons. Then we would drop them back when we had finished with them. We didn't have to cross any borders carrying weapons.

We would leave the bodies where they were as a deterrent. There was never a problem with the local authorities as they simply put the killings down to the growing number of casualties in the escalating wars between the drug barons. It wasn't long though before the rumour mill got into full swing and the action dried up for us as the mercenaries began to quit their lucrative jobs. Towards the end of this period they would often get out before we had even got near to them for a little 'chat'.

In total this phase took just a little over six months to clear up, though I would have to make a return journey on a few occasions over the next couple of years, when some of the guys thought that they were in the clear and returned to their former masters. They only ever got the one warning; just the one chance.

What did I feel about killing these guys? Nothing at all is the answer. The guys that stayed there after we had warned them off were just plain stupid and the majority of them were the wannabes and not the real professionals. They didn't care about the misery and loss-of-life caused by the drug barons that they were supporting. As far as I was concerned they took their chances and they lost. I didn't give a shit about them.

SIXTY-FOUR

By this time I was a bit of a lost cause and I really didn't care much about anything or anybody. I began a long period living at home, the first time since I had joined the army more than twelve years ago. On the outside I was almost the perfect husband and father. I would get up in the morning and help the kids to get washed and dressed, then take them on the 15 minute walk to their school. During the day I'd do a bit of housework such as the washing up or vacuuming, but mostly I'd either read or watch TV. Then come the afternoon, I'd go back to the school and pick the kids up. In the evening, after tea, I'd watch some more TV until it was time to go to bed.

On the outside I was as nice as pie and seemed perfectly normal. On the inside I was a burning turmoil of rage and hatred, mostly addressed at myself, that would occasionally explode into anger and violence. I tried to control myself and succeeded most of the time, but there were the occasional moments when I just couldn't. It was at these times that I was very, very lucky not to badly hurt or even kill the people that I loved the most. To be honest, Anne-Marie didn't help at all. With her Irish blood she had a fairly volatile temper of her own, and once she got going she just wouldn't let go. There were plenty of times when she lost her rag with me and started throwing things, or screaming and hitting me, and she was a big-boned lass who could put some weight behind a slap or a kick. I really don't know how I didn't end up killing her at times like these.

I don't blame her though; don't get me wrong. She knew that something was terribly wrong and that I'd changed completely from the bloke that she had married. I wasn't that happy-go-lucky man anymore. I was now a complete stranger who just happened to be the father of her children, living with her. I sometimes think that the shouting and screaming fits were just her way of trying to get through this immensely thick wall that I had set up between us, and when she couldn't she would just get more and more frustrated. This period was definitely not easy for her at all. The kids were even more difficult for me to cope with in a way. Deep down inside I loved them immensely, and still do. Anne-Marie said to one of her friends once that loads of fathers say that they would die for their kids, but she knew that I really would die for them, because I loved them so much. The trouble was that I couldn't show my love, either to my kids or to my wife. It was bottled up deep inside of me and I just couldn't let it out. I was cold and hard and that's all that they could get from me. One evening I was at home with my wife and kids and we were watching a nature programme on the TV. This programme was about bats and at one point, when the presenter was talking about hibernation, he mentioned that bats lower their body temperature during hibernation until they are very cold indeed, and also slow their bodily functions. He went on to add that hibernating bats have only one heartbeat per minute. Anne-Marie had turned to me and said:

"Those bats are just like you John."

"In what way?"

"Isn't it obvious? They're as cold as ice and have no heart."

"Super."

Ever since then, that's how I've always thought of myself; as having only one heartbeat a minute. It was a very bad time for all of us.

Did I get any help from my employers during this time? You're kidding; I got nothing from them. Even though they had my psych evaluation; even though it must have been obvious to anyone that I was cracking up under the strain and even though they were perfectly aware of the awful events that I had been through; nothing was done at all to help me. I was the perfect killing machine and they were determined to get as much use out of me as they could before I burned up completely, and this they did.

SIXTY-FIVE

This was all happening back in middle of the 1980s. Islamic fundamentalism had not really come onto the world's radar at this point in time and most terrorism was home grown. In Europe a lot of countries had their own problems with terrorists. For example Spain had the ETA; Basque separatists who were carrying out assassinations, kidnappings and bombings. Germany had the 'Red Army Faction' who had taken over from the 'Baader-Meinhof Gang', and carried out similar atrocities. The 'Red Brigades' was a terrorist organisation that operated within Italy and the rest of Western Europe, and of course there were Palestinian terrorist groups such as the PLO, PLF and Abu Nidal, that, apart from a few well-known occasions remained local and had not become an excessive menace. In the UK, of course, we had the Irish terrorists who were fighting for a united Ireland and an end to British rule in Northern Ireland. Chief amongst these Irish terrorist organisations was the IRA (or the 'Provos'), and its political wing, Sinn Fein.

The IRA had been carrying out assassinations, bombings, robberies, shootings and general intimidation, mostly in Northern Ireland, for years, but in the 1980s they branched out their activities onto the UK mainland; culminating in the 'Brighton Bombing' of 12th October 1984. An IRA member, Patrick Magee, had planted a bomb in the Grand Hotel in Brighton. This bomb was intended to kill not only the British Prime Minister, but also all of her government cabinet staying in the hotel during the Conservative Party Conference.

The bomb exploded at 2.54 am and although it failed to kill Thatcher or any of the Cabinet, it did kill five other people (including a Conservative Member of Parliament) and injured over thirty others. It was a close call and must have left a very sharp impression on the Prime Minister and the other members of her government.

After returning from Latin America, my time was spent between living a normal life at home with my family, occasionally training other Special Forces at the 'International Long-Range Reconnaissance Patrol School' in Bavaria in West Germany, training recruits in my local TA unit in London in basic infantry skills and going across to Northern Ireland and sometimes other countries, and causing as much mayhem and confusion amongst the ranks of the various Republican terrorist groups as I could. The latter I did in a very simple way: I killed the bastards.

I also attended a number of training courses that were intended to make me even better at my job of killing people. The Close Protection or 'Bodyguard' Course, run by the Close Protection Unit of the Royal Military Police (RMP), is one such course. After all, as I was probably going to face the bad guy's bodyguards in combat, it would be extremely useful to know what they knew and how they would be operating. The 'monkeys' (a nickname used by British soldiers for the RMP's - probably because their knuckles tend to drag on the ground as they walk along) had originally been trained in close protection techniques by the CRW Wing of the SAS. They had gone on to develop a very good course of their own in VIP protection and trained many other British Army units. I also attended a short course at the French Marines School in Lorient, Brittany. Here I was taught some very interesting and original fighting skills by members of the Naval Commandos of the French Navy, such as silently taking out sentries with a crossbow. Interesting, if not very useful. They were very good at teaching close quarter combat with knives though, something that I would later find to be very useful.

Other courses I attended during this period included the Special Operations Target Interdiction Course and the Special Forces Sniper Course, both at the John F. Kennedy Special Warfare Centre at Fort Bragg in North Carolina. In addition I attended a short demolition's course hosted by the Dutch Marines with instructors from the Dutch Special Forces, in Rotterdam.

My assassinations were not like those that you see in the movies or on TV; nothing quite so glamorous. I was licensed to kill, not to thrill. Most of them went basically like this: First the terrorist would be identified by one of the intelligence agencies, and then investigated until either a case was proven without a shadow-of-a-doubt against him or her, in which case they would be arrested, charged and tried. If they were really slippery bastards, and it was certain in everyone's minds that they were terrorists but there just wasn't enough evidence to take to Court and get them convicted, then their case files would be handed on to the Increment.

Harry would sift through these files, and having chosen which terrorists we could safely take action against, he would then clear things with his bosses. Then he would give me a call and I would meet up with him and travel into the province under false identification given to us by the SIS. Harry would then take me to a location and physically point the intended target out to me. He'd give me my instructions and then he would bugger off and leave me to it.

Normally, I would simply stay on the tail of the target until an opportunity arose and then I'd kill him or her (one prominent woman that I killed was the ex-wife of an IRA terrorist who was known to have also been involved in the murders of several British security personnel; I shot her dead at her home). Some of the time I would be given instructions to make the killing look like an accident, so I'd take the targets out by running them over with a car or a truck, or I would push them under a train or a bus or a lorry. Sometimes I'd knock on the front door, get inside their house and make their death look like a suicide or a simple accident. Some of the time I would be ordered to make a mess of them as a warning to others. Then I would do just that; taking them out in a particularly brutal and bloody way, usually in public, but not always so; some of the time I would just beat them to death and leave their bodies where they would be easily found. I learnt that the only way to be successful in this kind of job is to be even more vicious than the person you faced. I went in first, I went in hard and I didn't let up until the job was done and he, or she, was dead.

One of the big successes of my time with the Increment came about quite by chance. In 1974, the Irish National Liberation Army (or INLA) was founded by Seamus Costello and other paramilitaries who had broken away from the official IRA feeling they were way too soft. It wasn't long before INLA came under attack from their former colleagues in the IRA, who wanted to destroy the organisation which they viewed as too hard-line, before it could fully get off the ground. There followed several years of feuding between the two organisations, resulting in the death of several members on both sides, including Seamus Costello himself in 1977.

INLA became quite a well-known terrorist organisation during the late 1970s and early 1980s, although it always remained relatively small. They were responsible for several attacks against the British Army and RUC, and were based in West Belfast. Their most famous assassination during this period was the killing of Airey Neave (a Conservative Member of Parliament) in a car-bomb in the House of Commons car park in 1979. Neave was a good friend and staunch political ally to Margaret Thatcher at the time. Another well-known INLA operation was the bombing of a bar in Ballykelly, County Londonderry in 1982. Eleven British soldiers and six civilians were killed when the bomb exploded in a crowded disco.

In 1983 an INLA volunteer, Harry Kirkpatrick, was arrested and charged with the murder of five people. He decided to become a 'supergrass' to save his own skin, and gave evidence against many other members of INLA, who were themselves arrested and subsequently convicted. This sudden drop in the number of active INLA members almost led to the end of the organisation. The distrust and suspicion that was sown during this period also led to yet another faction splitting from INLA. This was the IPLO, the 'Irish Peoples Liberation Organisation', which was founded by Jimmy Brown and Gerard Steenson; both of whom had been convicted on the supergrass's information. The IPLO was formed by people who had either resigned or been expelled from INLA, and their initial aim was to destroy INLA and its political wing, and replace it with their own organisation. In 1987 this feud began with the killing of the INLA leader, John O'Reilly, and another leading INLA member, Thomas 'Ta' Power, by the IPLO.

Harry saw this sudden internecine warfare as an ideal opportunity, not only to knock off a few more Irish terrorists, but also to further sow seeds of hate and distrust amongst the various Republican factions. I was immediately mobilised and bloodily murdered a couple of INLA members followed by an IPLO member for good measure. These murders led to an immediate increase in the violence between the factions, which resulted in the total deaths of 11 INLA and IPLO terrorists before a truce was eventually called between them. I have no sympathy for these bastards as INLA killed over a hundred people by the end of the troubles, including almost fifty British service personnel. As far as I know, to this day neither of the two organisations even suspects that it was actually the British who added fuel to the fire of their rivalry. This was a mastermind of an operation to my way of thinking. Getting INLA and IPLO to do their own dirty work was very clever.

Good old Harry. In 1992 the IPLO was in turn wiped out by a massive operation put into place by the IRA, who believed that the IPLO was heavily involved in drug trafficking. Although this was well after my time, I often wonder if this feud had also actually been set up or helped along by the Increment, perhaps by Harry himself. Nice one if they did.

SIXTY-SIX

I didn't keep tabs on exactly how many people I killed across the water in Northern Ireland, but it was quite a few. Some of the best targets were acquired by the Increment, via SIS, from double agents and spies actually working within the IRA and other terrorist organisations, often in high positions. We even managed to get some of the killings passed off as sectarian assassinations that were carried out by loyalist paramilitary death squads, such as the UFF or PAF.

The best of the British spies was a man known by the code-name 'Stakeknife'. This guy had volunteered to spy for the British after he had been badly beaten as a youngster by other IRA members. He then joined the IRA and slowly worked his way up the ranks until he became the guy who was in charge of the IRA's 'Internal Security Unit', which sought out and eliminated informers within the organisation. He brutally interrogated over 40 suspected informers before murdering them and was privy to almost everything that went on in the IRA during this time.

There were several assassinations that I carried out that were obviously intended to protect Stakeknife as an important source of high-value intelligence. However, during a particularly tense period when Deputy Chief Constable John Stalker (formerly of the Greater Manchester Police) was causing concern in the British intelligence community with his investigation into the British Army's so-called 'shoot-to-kill policy' in Northern Ireland, I was actually given Stakeknife as a target. Presumably this was because it would have been very bad for all concerned if he had ever been exposed. Luckily for him though, the order was revoked before I could carry it out. Harry also mentioned to me his wish to kill John Stalker, but apparently the 'boss' wouldn't sanction it, which really pissed Harry off. He obviously hated Stalker and what he was doing. It would have been a waste of effort anyway, as other intelligence forces got to work on Stalker and his investigation was called to a halt in 1986 when he was accused of corruption.

One of the targets that I killed was involved in an attempt to take out Stakeknife. He was a protestant member of the Ulster Defence Regiment of the British Army, but was also a member of an illegal Loyalist terrorist group. I killed him by setting off a remote-controlled bomb, which I'd hidden in a telegraph pole, while he was passing it during a foot patrol.

In May 1987 Stakeknife proved his worth by giving us intelligence of a carefully planned IRA attack on the police station in Loughgall, in County Armagh. The SAS dealt with it in their typically robust way and ambushed the attackers, killing all eight of them. I was attached to the 20-plus SAS team, but unknown to the others, I was there to make sure that the IRA team was wiped out. In the event I didn't need to.

The IRA team that was involved in this operation included the guy commanding the East Tyrone Brigade of the IRA, Patrick Kelly. The Provos drove a stolen JCB digger straight through the police station's perimeter fence, followed in by a blue van full of armed men. In the bucket of the JCB was an oil drum packed with 200 lbs of explosives. Once the men left the vehicles they lit the fuse of the bomb, and then opened fire on the police station with semi-automatic and automatic weapons. The SAS ambush party, which included me, were hidden behind a line of trees and a fence on the other side of the road from the police station. As soon as the IRA team began firing we returned fire on the attackers with our G3 assault rifles. It only took a matter of seconds before the IRA team was wiped out to a man. Then the explosives went off and decimated the police station in a huge ball of flame and noise. We had of course, evacuated all of the RUC officers well before the IRA arrived, so no good guys were even injured. If we hadn't evacuated the police station and taken out the IRA team then dozens of policemen and women would have died or been wounded.

This was a good, clean operation but of course, like cowardly terrorists everywhere, the IRA bleated about the 'unlawful killing' of their members by an SAS 'hit squad'. The European Court of Human Rights later said that the SAS had denied the dead men their fundamental human rights. One of the IRA men killed at Loughgall was a guy by the name of Jim Lynagh. His nickname was 'The Executioner' and he was believed to have killed at least twenty eight people during his illustrious career. Did anyone ever ask about his victim's human rights being violated? I doubt it somehow.

Other targets that I took out in Northern Ireland between 1985 and 1988 included a civil-rights lawyer who was an active member of the IRA and who had successfully defended a number of them in court. I shot him to death in front of his family. Another was one of two IRA men who were lying in wait to ambush an army patrol when an SAS team, of which I was a part, ambushed them instead, wounding them both. I quickly interrogated one of them before putting another bullet into him, ending his life for good. Another good 'kill' of mine was an IRA man who died (when his hand grenade went off 'prematurely') while attacking a British Army patrol in Londonderry. Harry had given me access to an IRA arms dump a few weeks before and I'd used my extensive skills with explosives to sabotage a few of the cached weapons. One of these weapons had been a hand grenade, which I had shortened the fuse on. Anyone pulling the pin and releasing the handle would be caught in an explosion that was almost instantaneous,

279

rather than the usual delayed one three-to-seven seconds later.

Not all of my targets in Northern Ireland were Republicans of course. The Loyalists also had several terrorist organisations, such as the UDA and UVF, which were fond of killing anyone that opposed their own views. Their victims included members of Republican terrorist groups, but also innocent catholic civilians as well. One such Loyalist was a politician who had become well known for his extremist and out-spoken views and was an active member of the UVF. In his case though, I didn't kill him because of his personal views, but because he had agreed to become an informer for the opposition. I took him out as he sat in his car about to pass on sensitive intelligence to the bad guys. Unusually for me I didn't manage to kill him outright but he did die of his wounds a couple of weeks later, so all was not lost. I got a bollicking from Harry over this lapse.

During the troubles in Northern Ireland about 4,000 people died as a direct result of terrorist activity, and many more were mutilated or crippled for life. Some of these victims were Republican terrorists, Loyalist terrorists, or British security forces, but the vast majority were innocent civilians murdered while going about their normal everyday lives. Innocent men, women and children were blown up by bombs, caught up in the crossfire, or even deliberately murdered. Many were murdered just because they belonged to the opposing religion.

The terrorists didn't give a shit about these innocent people who died or were injured. They didn't care about the loss of life that they caused or the intense family tragedies that were played out in countless homes across both Northern Ireland and mainland Britain.

If I had been caught on one of my operations, I would have faced brutal torture and death. Favourite torture methods of the IRA included forcing their victim's hands onto the electric rings of stoves or using an electric drill on their knee-caps. Not all of the people that I assassinated were unprepared or unarmed. Often I would have to disarm a target before killing him as these were vicious murdering thugs who were quite adept at killing others. On a few occasions I even had to take out their personal protection (bodyguards in other words) to get at them. These bodyguards were always armed and were themselves vicious and violent men. This was not a job for the faint-hearted.

I had been constantly involved in one war or another for years, with no real breaks from the constant fear and tension that this entails. I had also undergone a lengthy and extremely brutal interrogation at the hands of the Soviet GRU; an interrogation that I believed I would not survive. My mind was empty of almost everything except rage and hate and I did everything on a form of 'autopilot', not feeling anything at all towards my 'victims', or anyone else for that matter. My personal life was in a complete mess, and I was even denied the normal soldier's comfort of being among his mates, as most of mine were either dead or had left the army. Even the SAS, to whom I still belonged in name at least, were still very wary of me and had never fully accepted me as one of their own.

Over the three years from 1985 to 1987, most of my 'wet jobs' were carried out either in Latin America or in Northern Ireland. However, I also undertook several jobs in other parts of the world.

One such job was in Scandinavia, where I killed a prominent politician with a bullet in the back (I also shot his wife for good measure, but I believe that she survived).

My last major job during this period took place in March 1988 in Gibraltar, and is also one of the most well-known; this was called 'Operation Flavius'.

SIXTY-SEVEN

Operation Flavius began months before my involvement, when high-level intelligence was passed to the British security services about an IRA plot to plant a bomb in Gibraltar.

The intelligence had come from a number of very highly-placed sources within the IRA, including our very own Stakeknife. Confirmation had also come from other less usual sources, such as the Garda (the police force of the Irish Republic). Even in the early days of the surveillance it was considered to be good, robust intelligence, and the operation soon became a high priority when a female member of Sinn Fein, who was also a close associate of Sinn Fein's leader, Gerry Adams, was photographed carrying out what we believed was an early reconnaissance of the island.

The IRA was in a bad way at the time, having had at least twenty of its active service unit members killed during the previous year. They were out to make a point by conducting a big operation that would grab the attention of the world's media. If a lot of innocent civilians were going to be killed by their actions, then this was not going to put them off at all; in fact it was an important component of their plan that lots of civilians would die. My part in all of this started when three well-known members of the IRA were observed gathering in Spain by the Spanish authorities. There were two men; Daniel McCann and Seán Savage, and one woman; Mairéad Farrel.

Just for a change, I became involved right at the start of the operation. It was obvious that there was going to be a very real need for careful undercover surveillance. My former experience with the Det, as well as my more recent experience with the Increment, made me a prime candidate to help with this surveillance.

For several weeks I and a small team from the Increment worked in Spain with our counterparts from the Operational Support Unit of the Spanish intelligence agency; 'CESID'. We wanted to carry out the surveillance ourselves of course, but their Spanish bosses wouldn't allow it, so the CESID guys carried out all of the surveillance on the three IRA terrorists. They passed on the information that they gathered to us, but they never managed to get full 24 hour surveillance in place on all of the terrorists. The Spanish guys were professional enough at their job, but they seemed to lack a sense of real urgency and motivation and this led to the terrorists dropping off their radar from time to time. It also helps to explain why the IRA unit managed to give them the slip on the morning of 5th March and more importantly, why they didn't inform my team that they had lost contact with them. It wasn't until later that morning when Savage had been spotted parking a white Renault car in the small square next to Inces Hall, in Gibraltar itself, that we realised that the IRA were already making their move. We hadn't even known that the car existed until this point in time and were mortified when we got the call from our own guys on the Rock.

My team shot across the border from Spain as fast as we could and we managed to pick up Savage's trail just as we heard over the radio net that McCann and Farrel had also been seen crossing the border into Gibraltar and were heading towards us.

The place where the Renault car was parked was right next to the assembly point that was going to be used for a scheduled military parade in a couple of day's time. The parade was going to include the band and soldiers of the 1st Battalion of the Royal Anglian Regiment; men who had just finished a tour of Northern Ireland. This parade was very popular with the local population and usually many thousands of civilians gathered to watch it, especially as the participants formed up in the square to begin the parade. If this was a car bomb, and if it was due to go off as the men mustered for the parade, then the blast would cause many hundreds of casualties and fatalities in the fairly confined area of the small square, surrounded as it was by lots of tall, solidly-built buildings.

We finally caught up with all three of the terrorists shortly afterwards when they met up, and we began watching them from a distance. We were soon joined by the three-man SAS team that was tasked with attempting to arrest the terrorists. As previously planned (well in advance of course) by Harry, I shifted over from the surveillance team to join the SAS team (after all I was still a fully serving member of the regiment), and the surveillance guys withdrew from the immediate area to a standby position.

The three IRA terrorists were looking decidedly agitated at this point and kept on returning to the square and looking at the car, then wandering off again. We managed to get an army ordnance guy to walk past the Renault and give it the once over during a period when the terrorists weren't present; his report was ambiguous, saying that he didn't think it contained a bomb, but that it did have a dodgy-looking radio aerial that might be used to detonate explosives remotely. The head-sheds (bosses) of the operation decided to be cautious and informed us over the net that the car probably did contain a bomb and we were asked to confirm the identities of the IRA trio over the radio. When we did this the control of the operation was officially passed over from the local police to the SAS.

The terrorists split into two groups, with Savage heading into town by himself, and McCann and Farrel heading back towards the border crossing. The SAS team also split into two teams of two to follow them at a distance of about 10-15m. A nearby police siren going off (this was totally unconnected to our operation) made McCann look backwards as he drew near to the Shell petrol station along Winston Churchill Avenue. As he did so he made eye-contact with one of the SAS guys following him. The SAS trooper knew that the game was up and quickly drew his Browning pistol from beneath his civilian clothing. He was about to issue a challenge when McCann moved his hand across the front of his body. Fearing that he was going to grab either a weapon or the remote device to detonate the car-bomb, the SAS guy didn't hesitate and shot McCann several times in the chest. At this point Farrel also made a move towards her handbag, so the SAS man switched his fire onto her, joined a split second later by his colleague, who also began to pump rounds into the two terrorists. Meanwhile, Savage, who was further down the same road, turned as he heard the gunfire behind him. The other SAS trooper and I, who were shadowing him, drew our pistols and shouted a warning at him to stand still and keep his hands away from his body. He stupidly made to put his hand inside his jacket so we put a volley of rounds into him. He was dead before he hit the ground, as were McCann and Farrel, but we kept on shooting anyway. We weren't going to take any chances that civilians were going to get hurt or killed, either by the terrorists themselves or by the car-bomb being detonated remotely. McCann was shot five times, Farrel eight times and Savage eighteen times.

A sudden silence enveloped the road as the shooting stopped, but it only lasted for a couple of seconds, and was soon replaced by the screaming of civilians who were nearby and the wailing of police sirens as they stormed towards the bloody scenes of mayhem on the street. We quickly pulled out our SAS berets from our pockets and put them on so that the cops could tell who the good guys were.

Two days later I was back home with the wife and kids.

The white Renault didn't contain a bomb, and the IRA terrorists were not carrying remote-detonators. However, a few days later our CESID colleagues did find a car and explosives just over the border in Spain. The car was set up as a bomb, to be detonated by a timer-device, and contained 140 lbs of Semtex plastic explosive. As more intelligence was gathered the true story of what the IRA was up to began to emerge. It appears that the three terrorists had been informed that it was quite hard to find a parking space next to Inces Hall. So they had decided to park the white Renault in an available space a few days beforehand. Then, on the morning of the parade, they would collect the real car-bomb from Spain, drive it across the border into Gibraltar and park it in the space taken up by the Renault. In this way they would guarantee that the bomb was in the perfect position to cause the most damage and loss of life.

At the official inquest to the shootings a few weeks later, we were absolved of guilt and the coroner's jury found in our favour by a majority of nine to two. It was judged as a 'lawful killing'. During the inquest we had been hidden behind curtains as we gave our evidence to protect our identities, and our real names were never used; we were known simply as Troopers 'W', 'X', 'Y' and 'Z'. It was a pretty solemn occasion except for one moment when I was asked the question:
"...and why did you shoot Mister Savage fourteen times?" My answer was quick and to the point:
"Because I ran out of bullets, sir."

In the mid 1990s the shooting was taken to the European Court of Human Rights. Once again the court found that we had denied the IRA members their basic human rights, even though they were involved in a terrorist plot that would have taken many innocent lives. It sure is a nutty old world.

SIXTY-EIGHT

Monday 21ˢᵗ October 2013
Thorney, Cambridgeshire

Smith had left his newest acquisition, a grey Ford Focus, parked off the road and hidden from casual passers-by, about half a mile away. In the early hours he approached the big house on foot, the darkness and heavy rainfall helping him to go totally unnoticed. He circled the house like a ghost in the darkness, easily avoiding the basic security system of infrared-activated lights. Satisfied that he could break in if he needed to, he backtracked along the driveway and onto the public road running past the house. This is bloody perfect, he thought. One road in and out with lots of cover and sharp bends, and best of all, even though it was a public through-road, it was only just wide enough for two cars to pass each other and looked like it was hardly ever used. Perfect.

He walked back to his car to wait until daylight.

Detective Sergeant Henry Price was well-pissed off. He was a very experienced street copper; a detective for fuck's sake, not a bloody nursemaid to this poxy, stuck-up, son-of-a-bitch judge who thinks he's the most important person in the world. And if anything, his podgy unattractive wife is even worse than her husband; she's a royal pain-in-the-ass with her plum-in-the-mouth upper-crust accent and condescending way of talking down at Price. Price cursed DCI Davies under his breath as he opened the front door and walked into the garden to check that the area was clear. That twat Davies had used the excuse that Price was a qualified firearms officer who had served in Scotland Yard's Specialist Firearms Unit for a couple of years to post him as the close-protection officer for the judge. But Price knew it was just to get rid of him and keep him as far from the investigation as possible. Suddenly he laughed; that might not be such a bad thing for him, as Davies had completely fucked everything up from the moment that that bastard Smith had escaped during his trial. Davies wasn't going to last; the bosses were on his neck all of the time and it wouldn't be long before the media started to bay for blood. Then someone's head would roll and it would more than likely be Davies's. For the time being the further Price could distance himself from that wanker, the better!

There was the roar of an over-powered V12 engine as the judge drove his brand new top-of-the-range metallic-silver BMW 760Li Sedan out of the garage and parked up in front of Price. Price got an instant hard-on as he gazed with love-filled eyes at the car. This was a beautiful motor with a price-tag of at least £150,000; it was absolutely bloody gorgeous.

The judge waved impatiently at Price, indicating that he should climb into the passenger's seat. This was another thing that pissed off Price. He should be driving the car not his bloody principle. After all he was an advanced driver, an emergency response driver and had been trained in defensive driving during his close-protection course. The problem was that the judge refused to let anyone else drive his sparkling new car and he always got what he bloody wanted. Fucking bastard judge!

Price asserted his manhood by pulling his 9mm Glock 17 semi-automatic pistol from his shoulder-holster and checking there was a round up the breech in full view of the judge, before climbing into the passenger seat.

The car roared off.

Smith watched the BMW pulling onto the road from the judge's driveway through a pair of binoculars. He picked up his silenced MP5 Heckler and Koch sub-machine gun, flipped off the safety catch with his right thumb and walked to the spot that he had carefully chosen beforehand for the ambush.

As the BMW started to slow down to negotiate a ninety degree right-hand turn, Smith stepped out from behind a big tree and fired a couple of short bursts from the MP5. The 9mm rounds ripped through the offside tyres of the car, causing it to rock violently and begin to swerve out of control.

Not being sure of which direction the heap of metal was going to come off the road, Smith stepped back behind the protection of the tree until he heard the crunching crash of the BMW smashing into the deep ditch running alongside the road on the other side. He had chosen the ambush spot well; this was a typical country road in the fenland, raised a metre or so above the surrounding farmland with deep water-filled ditches on either side. Perfect.

The BMW had slewed off the road and buried its nose into the ditch while travelling at about 40mph. The once beautiful car looked a complete mess with the front smashed in, the windscreen and side windows shattered and the air-bags inflated. Smith walked to the car and looked down through the smashed driver's side window. The judge and his passenger were both conscious, saved by the now-deflating airbags, but it was obvious that they were trapped in the wreckage and would have to be cut out by the fire and rescue services. Smith leaned in to identify the passenger and when he saw the battered and blood-smeared face of Detective Sergeant Henry Price he grinned.

"Hello Pricey. Hi judge. It's nice to see you both again!" Price was struggling to reach his Glock and pull it from his shoulder-holster but was still dazed by the crash. Smith calmly poked the barrel of his MP5 through the window and shot Price once in the upper right arm. He screamed in shock and pain.

"Now, now, Pricey. That's not nice; is it?" Price started to blubber in fear as the realisation of his predicament started to hit him. The judge on the other hand just scowled up at Smith.

"What's the meaning of this?" he snarled, "Do you know who I am?"

"Oh yes judge, I know exactly who you are and surely you remember me from that farce of a trial you presided over?" The judge scowled again as Smith walked back to his tree and picked up a small red plastic petrol can, unscrewing the top as he walked back to the car. He started to pour its contents through the car's window, liberally splashing the judge and Price. Price was in tears now and the smell of his own urine soaking into the crotch of his trousers mixed with the harsh throat-burning stink of the petrol.

"Please!" He begged, "Please don't!"

Smith grinned again, throwing the now-empty container onto the back seat behind them. As he walked away he pulled the pin from a white phosphorus grenade and lobbed it in after the petrol can. There was a loud whoosh as the grenade went off and caught the petrol alight, followed by the loud screams of pain from the judge and the detective as they burned alive.

Smith sauntered back to his own car.

From: john smith (johnsmith2223@hotmail.com)
To: SOCA@Cambspolice.org.uk
Date: 21 October 2013 10:40:09
CC:
Subject: FAO Detective Chief Inspector Alan Davies, Cambs SOCA.

Hi Alan, I do hope that you and the other members of your team are not missing DS Price too much? Though somehow, I doubt that you are.

Please find attached the latest instalment of my autobiography.

I am going to give you a phone call at 6am tomorrow morning. I want to explain some of my actions but I will only talk if Harry is there; I have a few things that I want to ask Harry.

Regards

John Smith

SIXTY-NINE

The rest of 1988 is just a blur to me now. I took to the bottle in a very big way and became even more abusive towards my wife and kids. Finally, even Harry could see that I was falling apart and that he had to do something to help me, or risk losing his star operator. In December he arranged for me to see a psychiatrist at the Queen Elizabeth Military Hospital in Woolwich, East London.

My first appointment at the hospital was eventful as I turned up drunk and got quite abusive towards the junior staff. I didn't even manage to see the 'trick-cyclist' and I was turned away with a flea in my ear, told to make another appointment and to make sure that I was sober next time.

A week later I went back. This time I was stone-cold sober but as angry as ever. I noticed that there were a couple of big 'monkeys' hanging around in the waiting room as I entered to see the psychiatrist, and I guessed that they were there in case I caused any trouble. Obviously I was already gaining something of a reputation in the hospital.

The psychiatrist turned out to be a lieutenant-colonel of the Royal Army Medical Corps. Right from the moment we met I could tell that he was a no-nonsense sort of chap who would give me short shrift as a probable malingerer. I wasn't far wrong and at points during the appointment he got quite angry at me. As the interview progressed, I could feel the rage building up inside of me, reaching boiling point. Then, after one particularly thoughtless question directed at me about my family, my anger broke loose.

"Listen you silly twat. One more stupid fucking question like that and I'm going to put you through the fucking window." I've never been known for my diplomatic skills.

"Don't you talk to me like that, young man! Remember who you are!" was his peevish reply. "Now answer my question!"

Needless to say, about thirty seconds later he found himself outside his office window, hanging onto the ledge by his fingers tips. The look on his face was so funny that my anger quickly evaporated. However, his screams soon brought the two monkeys bursting into the room where they found me laughing my head off as I pounded on the colonel's fingers, trying to get him to let go of his frantic hold on the sill. We were only a couple of storeys up and there was grass beneath the window so he would have been alright, but he was bloody petrified and I thought it was the funniest thing that had happened to me in years. The monkeys were surprisingly gentle with me as they pulled me away from the window, obviously reassured that my laughter meant that they were okay. They got me to sit in a chair while they retrieved a very grateful but very flustered colonel from the open window.

I was taken immediately to the nearest guardroom and locked up. I think the colonel probably had to take the rest of the week off from work.

Two days later I was released and a car arrived to take me to Hereford. I don't think that Harry had been informed of the incident; otherwise he might have protected me from what was about to happen. However I might be wrong, of course. Perhaps he knew all about it but had decided that I was no further use to either him or the Increment. Either way, as soon as I got back to SAS HQ I was taken in to see the CO.

I got an almighty bollicking from the CO and was given a simple choice: I could leave the British Army of my own free will, in which case I'd get a reasonable reference from him. Or he would personally see to it that I was kicked out immediately with a 'Dishonourable Discharge' on my service record. And that was that. After years of faithful service to my Queen and Country I was being kicked out of the army with nothing to my name except a single month's pay and a little red service book with a lukewarm reference from my commanding officer in it.

My military career was suddenly over.

SEVENTY

I found myself in my early thirties, suddenly thrown into a world that I hardly knew, with a family to support. The bastards didn't even give me a rail permit to get home to London. I had to delve into my last month's wages, which I'd been given in cash to buy a rail ticket for myself. Cheers guys. Fuck you, too.

I was still in a daze when I got home and broke the news to Anne-Marie. We had an almighty argument that ended up, as usual, with her screaming and throwing something heavy at me, and me slapping her down. Then she dashed into the kid's room sobbing her heart out and screaming her head off that "Daddy is trying to kill me!" At this point I came to my senses a bit, found a bottle and started to drink myself into a stupor. I felt that life just couldn't get any worse than this.

Over the next month or so I could easily have gone over the edge and topped myself, but it was my kids that saved me. Suddenly forced to be at home all of the time, because basically I had nowhere else to go, at least meant that I could spend more time with Robert and Alan.

Anne-Marie would find any excuse to get out of the house to get away from me. This suited me just fine too, and meant that I spent more and more time alone with my sons. Little Robert wasn't quite so 'little' anymore. He was now seven years old and getting to be quite tall for his age. Alan was five years old. Even at these tender ages it was obvious that they were developing very different personalities. Robert could be quite emotional at times and was also very artistic, while Alan was a stubborn little lad who would never give up trying, no matter what.

Being with them most of the time was the best tonic that I could ever have had. Though I was still suffering from PTSD (and in some ways it was still getting worse), at least I managed to quit the bottle (to be honest this was probably because I couldn't afford it any more) and to keep my anger locked away deeper inside me. It was also an immense relief to know that I wasn't going to be called away at a moment's notice to face a situation from which I might never return. The stability of home and the laughter and smiling faces of my kids, who still loved me of course, despite all of the shouting and arguing over the last few years, was great. I could feel normality returning to my life for the first time since I'd left my own home to join the army all of those years ago at the tender age of sixteen.

I spent about a month just playing with my kids and getting to know them. And do you know what? They are the best sons that a man could ever ask for.

I didn't miss the army one little bit, especially the uncertainty of what I might be doing or where I might be going, but there was one part of army life that inevitably left an empty hole in my existence, and that was the comradeship of other soldiers. I had made some great mates during my career, and though a lot of them had died during active service, or had succumbed to some sort of unidentifiable tropical disease or injury, or had simply had enough and left the army behind them, I missed them all. Most of all, I guess, I missed the earthy good humour of my mates that might well have helped me to pull through the bad days far quicker and less painfully.

Often I'd find my thoughts turning back to the 'good old days' and my old mates, but eventually real life would always bloody intrude; where was I going to get some money to pay the rent and the bills; just what was I going to do with the rest of my life now that I had been abandoned not only by the army but also by the Increment? I'd heard nothing at all from Harry. So I went out and forced myself to get a job in Civvy Street. It wasn't a great job, just driving a van and delivering stuff all day, but it was a real job where I wasn't living in fear of getting killed or maimed at any moment. Anyway, with all the holes in my past that I couldn't explain, it was the only job I could get where the boss didn't really care about my past as long as I turned up for work each morning and got on with it.

Gradually, as the months went by, I began to adjust to my new life and things slowly started to get better. I was still angry and full of hate most of the time. I still woke up several times a night screaming and wetting myself, as some memories just wouldn't go away. But the gaps in between these negative vibes began to get a little more frequent and to last a little bit longer. My bodily scars began to fade a little more each day and my mental scars became duller and duller as time went by. Even my relationship with Anne-Marie began to get better. We still had the occasional fiery row, but at least it didn't usually end up with us hitting and throwing things at each other.

Other strains were still there of course, such as surviving on my poor wages and the long hours that I had to spend at work. But on the whole life was beginning to look up at last. After a year I got myself a better-paid job working fewer hours, and we spent more time together as a family.

I even did the unthinkable and told my civilian doctor about the way that I felt. For me, this was a big breakthrough and a huge step forward. The doctor referred me to a psychiatrist and for the first time ever I was able to talk to someone about how I was feeling inside. He wasn't a great help. In fact some of his first words to me were that I would never, ever get over these feelings that I had and get better (thanks mate!). But for the first time I could understand a little more clearly what was happening to me, and more importantly, why it was happening. Just to have this knowledge was an enormous relief in itself, and to also realise that I wasn't by myself in how I felt and that there were tens of thousands of other PTSD sufferers out there as well. It meant that I didn't feel quite so alone in my pain.

Then, out of the blue, my whole world went to shit again. On 2nd August 1990, a bloke named Saddam Hussein invaded Kuwait.

SEVENTY-ONE

The Persian Gulf War, or the First Gulf War as it came to be known, began the moment that the Iraqi Army, under the command of their infamous President, Saddam Hussein, invaded the neighbouring country of Kuwait. The Kuwaitis were caught off guard and were unprepared when the initial invasion occurred, but put up a strong fight. In the end however most of the Kuwaitis that had not been captured or killed by the first invasion force eventually fled south to Saudi Arabia.

Saddam cited many reasons as to why he had initiated the invasion of Kuwait, including a very long-running argument that Kuwait was actually a part of Iraq. Kuwait had apparently been created as a separate entity by British imperialists in 1932, in order to stop the newly independent Iraq from having access to the sea, thus reducing any future threat from them. Iraq also accused Kuwait of exceeding their agreed quotas for oil production and thus waging 'economic terrorism' against their larger neighbour because the international price of oil was subsequently driven down. Saddam even accused Kuwait of 'slant' drilling across the border into one of Iraq's oil fields and stealing oil that was rightfully Iraq's.

However, as with most wars, it is probably true to say that the war began because Iraq was in a mess internally and had been driven almost to bankruptcy by the previous eight-year long war that had gone on between Iraq and Iran, which had only ended two years before. The rest was just an excuse with which Saddam hoped to pull the wool over the eyes of the rest of the world and claim some sort of legitimacy for his actions.

Almost as soon as the US learned of the invasion of Kuwait they requested, along with other delegations, an emergency meeting of the United Nations Security Council. The council subsequently issued Resolution 660, condemning the invasion and demanding the withdrawal of Iraqi troops from Kuwait. Following this, the Arab League passed their own resolution in which they called for a solution to the problem to be found within the Arab world, and warned against intervention from the 'outside'. Then the UN passed more resolutions, placing economic sanctions against Iraq and authorising a naval blockade to enforce the economic sanctions.

The US began to build up their armed forces stationed in Saudi Arabia and called upon other nations to join them in an international coalition. On 29th November the UN passed another resolution which gave the Iraqis a deadline of the 15th January 1991 to withdraw all of their forces from Kuwait. The coalition continued to grow in size as other countries pledged their support and armed forces to Operation 'Desert Shield', which was originally set into motion to protect Saudi Arabia from an Iraqi invasion.

On the afternoon of Christmas Eve, 1990, while playing with my sons in front of the TV, and looking forward to a peaceful and relaxing Christmas holiday in the bosom of my family, there was a knock on my front door. Anne-Marie answered it. Her face was furious as she led a uniformed police constable into our front room, probably thinking that I had been up to no good. The policeman didn't even bother to introduce himself. He simply asked who I was and then produced a thick envelope and gave it to me when I had confirmed my identity. I had no idea what was going down and was as confused as my wife was. When I opened the envelope and pulled out a sheaf of papers, my heart sank as I recognized the pink form on the top of them. I read the form with a hollow feeling growing in the pit of my stomach. Why now? After all this bloody time?

The form stated that I was being called up for active service in the British Army. I was to present myself at so-and-so police station by seven o'clock that evening, where I would be provided with my kit and picked up.

It was like being shot in the bollocks all over again.

SEVENTY-TWO

The police station was empty except for a bored-looking woman behind the desk. When I passed her my call-up papers through the armoured glass screen, she perked up a bit and smiled briefly at me as she pressed the buzzer that opened the door to the back of the station. I passed through and was shown into a bleak looking room by a male copper and told to wait there.

After about half an hour of sitting there looking at the wall I thought that I'd been forgotten and was about to go and find out what was happening. Then the door opened and standing there in the open doorway, looking as smug as a kitten who'd found the cream, was Harry. Fuck it! My stomach did a flip and my heart sank to the floor.

Harry didn't bother to say sorry for not saying goodbye after everything I'd done for him and the SIS. He just closed the door, slung a sheaf of folders onto the table and, pulling up a chair, sat down heavily.

"I've got a wet job for you'. He said. I was fucking furious with him for tearing me away from my family after all this time.

"Hello to you as well asshole. Since when did you start talking like some fucking yank?" I spat out.

"Now don't be like that John. Your country needs you." I almost wiped the smirk off his face with my fist, but somehow I managed to keep my temper from erupting into violence. I think he realised that he was treading a thin line: "I know, I know." He said, holding up his hands in front of him. "You thought that all of this stuff was over.

Well, we're going to be at war soon, and I'm afraid that we are in need of your particular skills again John."

My temper passed as quickly as it had flared up. What else could I do given my position? Harry and the Increment had me by the short-and-curlies, as ever. It was as though the last year was fast receding into a nice dream and reality was back.

"Haven't you found anyone else to do your dirty work for you?"

"No one who is as good as you are John".

"That's a load of bollocks. There must be hundreds of guys out there and in the army who are younger, fitter and fucking keener than I am!"

"Well, you're right of course, there are. The problem is that there's no one who is as good a shot as you are. On top of which, none of them look as Arabic as you do, or speak the lingo as well as you do."

"You're joking aren't you? I haven't held a gun in a year! And as for speaking Arabic, which I guess is the lingo you're talking about? I never ever knew more than a few phrases, and you know that. After all you know more about me than I do myself, as you've told me often enough." I couldn't get my head around all this. It was happening too quickly. "What's the real reason Harry?" He started to get that pissed-off look on his face that I knew so well. The look he got when something was not going according to his meticulously-conceived plans. "I get it." I said, suddenly getting a flash of brilliant insight. "You need someone expendable? Am I right? You need someone who will go out there, do whatever you need doing, and if they get their silly arse caught up in a meat-grinder, tough shit. You'll be able to stand up and say that they're nothing to do with you. Am I right?"

Harry sighed and I knew that I had hit the nail on the head.

"So you need a dirty job doing and if it all goes tits up you'll be able to wash your hands clean. You're a total piece of shit Harry, fuck you!"

"No, fuck you John. You either do what I want or I'll make sure that your comfy little life with your wife and kids is over! Remember that I'm the head of the Increment John, and I can do whatever I like with you! I could make you and your family disappear for good and no one would ever be the wiser!"

"Are you threatening me, you little shit? Remember what I am, Harry! What you made me! Do you really think that you or the Increment could make me disappear? You want a war mate; I'll give you a fucking war!" I was up and in his face at this moment, and I could see the fear in his eyes. He knew exactly what I was capable off. He backed off.

"Look John, this arguing is getting us nowhere. You've been called up and there's nothing that you or I can do about it. As of half an hour ago you became a member of the armed forces again. There's a job to be done, and we need someone like you to do it. So let's just settle down shall we?"

Even in my anger I knew that he was right. I was caught between a rock and a hard place. He knew it, and he knew that I knew it. I was fucked if I did, and fucked if I didn't, whichever way you looked at it.

"Okay. Tell me what you want me to do."

SEVENTY-THREE

Two days later, after a gruelling six-hour journey from RAF Lyneham in Wiltshire in the back of a heavily-laden and bloody noisy Hercules transport aircraft, I found myself stepping off the plane's ramp into the heat of the Arabian sun.

For the next two weeks I joined the British SAS in the Saudi's 'empty quarter', known as *Rub' al Khali*. This is a massive area of sand desert, about a quarter of a million square miles in size, located in the southern part of the Arabian Peninsula. Almost the whole of the SAS regiment had been committed to the coming war, except for one and a half squadrons who were unlucky enough to have already been deployed on active service elsewhere. The 'empty quarter' was a perfect place to acclimatise and practice the skills needed for desert warfare away from prying eyes, and both the SAS and Special Force units from other coalition armies were busy doing just that.

I had two main priorities; to get my fitness levels up, and to practice my shooting skills. The first wasn't so hard, as I had kept myself fairly fit, even during my civvy days. It just meant that I had to turn the pressure up and work at it a lot harder. I joined the rest of the regiment guys as they went for runs and did physical training in the desert heat and it wasn't long before I began to get back into combat shape again.

Getting my shooting skills back was a lot more difficult. Maintaining your skills as a marksman isn't like riding a bike; if you don't practice constantly then you gradually lose your ability to hit a target. Another problem that I had initially was trying to get used to unfamiliar weapons. The old bog-standard Lee Enfield L42 sniper rifle was gradually being phased out of the British Army and being replaced by more modern weapons. The increased accuracy and range of these weapons should have been a major boost for me, but I knew that I only had a very limited time to get my skills back on-line, and learning how to handle a completely new weapon system would take me a lot of valuable time that I didn't have. So I moaned and groaned a lot to Harry, and eventually, after a couple of days an L42 was grudgingly procured for me by an SAS armourer, complete with its sniper case and brass telescope.

When I wasn't running or doing some other sort of physical training, I was down on the ranges. The first job was to 'zero in' the telescopic sights. This took me a day and a half of constantly firing at different ranges and minutely adjusting the sights until they were as near to perfect as I could get them. Then it was simply a matter of time and practice. Over the next couple of weeks I must have fired over a thousand rounds a day into targets ranging from 100m to over 1,500m away. At the end of each day I'd tumble into my pit with a sore shoulder and trembling limbs brought about by the constant recoil of the heavy rifle, but gradually I began to 'get my eye in' again. By the time that I began my second week in the 'empty quarter' I was very nearly as proficient as I had been in my early sniping days. At the end of the next week I was even better.

In the middle of January I was given the warning order to prepare to move. It didn't take me long as all I had was my desert combat kit and my rifle. A few hours later I began the long flight by chopper to King Khalid International Airport at Riyadh. I surprised myself by falling into my old mode and sleeping for most of the flight. I guess that old habits die hard.

It was dark by the time we landed at Riyadh. I got nothing more than a quick glimpse of the impressive and distinctly Arab architecture of the airport buildings in the distance before I was whisked away in a Land Rover over to the central administration complex. My briefing was given by a SAS officer in a small air-conditioned office and was short and to the point. I had a few questions to ask at the end but not many as most of the operational details had been covered well by the Rupert. Then there was a long wait of several hours before anything else happened. I got some scoff down my neck and had another kip. After all, from now on I didn't know when, or even if, I'd get another chance to do either.

In the early hours of the morning I was awoken by a subdued conversation between the Rupert and Harry. I was issued with some civilian clothing; not your traditional Arabic *thobe* or *bisht*, but more contemporary stuff including an old and dirty T-shirt and a worn denim jacket and jeans, though I did have a *chmagh* to wrap around my head and face. This typical dress of a poor, working Arab in the modern world was topped off by a pair of ornately decorated yet worn leather sandals. I swapped my rifle case for a long and battered sports holdall. Then it was back into the Land Rover and a quick drive through the darkness out onto the airfield.

The helicopter that was waiting for me was an old Soviet Mi-8 'Hip'. This was the workhorse of the Iraqi army at the time and apparently this one had been captured at some point and was still regaled in its Iraqi Army Aviation markings. I hadn't been in one of these bloody things since Afghanistan and I had a rush of old memories come flooding back at the sound and sight of it. The rotors were already turning as I started to climb on board, but surprisingly Harry stopped me before I was fully into the cabin and solemnly shook my hand. He said something which I couldn't hear before turning away. Then I was strapping myself into a cargo seat as the chopper lifted off into the night. The flight from Riyadh into Iraq was long and

308

uneventful, although the constant dipping and swaying motion of the chopper as we flew low over the ground meant that even I couldn't get any more sleep. The aircrew were so engrossed with their mission that they barely seemed to notice me and they didn't say a word until the dispatcher tapped me on the shoulder and shouted over the noise of the rotors that we were approaching the 'Drop-off Point'. I gathered my thread-bare kit together, unstrapped myself and suddenly we were on the deck and I was piling out the cargo-bay door onto the ground. I couldn't see a thing through the combination of darkness and the dust-cloud thrown up by the chopper's rotors, and then the chopper was pulling away into the night. It had been on the ground for about five seconds in total and I was left standing there all alone and nervously clutching the butt of my pistol in a sweaty hand as I pointed its barrel into the darkness.

As the chopper disappeared I was assailed by the absolute peace and silence of an Arabian night. It was bloody cold in the night air but that wasn't the only reason that I felt a shiver go down my spine.

Then, out of the silence boomed the voice of a man that could have only been born and brought up in the Black Country of the English West Midlands:

"Yam alright mate?" I almost laughed out loud at hearing his broad accent.

"Yeah mate. Are you Nobby?"

"Sure am. Come and get in the car mate, we've got a long ride and the fucking roads are shit!"

'Nobby' and his team were from A Squadron, SAS. They had spent the last two weeks living in a hide in the desert just a few miles outside of Bagdad. Their patrol harbour was hidden amongst a pile of rocks and contained everything that they needed for a protracted stay behind enemy lines, including a huge stash of weapons, ammo, food and water. They had 'borrowed' a couple of beat-up vehicles from Iraqi civilians, which they hid during the daytime under camouflaged nets. The four man patrol spent their down-time during the day doing sentry duty, sleeping and playing cards. Then each night they mounted up and drove into the city to search out and check the locations of key military installations. If the Iraqi's decided to be stupid and not withdraw their invasion forces from Kuwait, then these boys would be 'lighting' up their targets with laser-designators so that the coalition could take them out with pin-point accuracy in air-strikes.

Before the air war began though, they had one other job that they had to do, and that was to guide me into Bagdad and provide the cover group for my mission. The guys welcomed me with big friendly grins. They seemed a little bored with their job so far and I guess that I was a bit of a pleasant change from their routine. They were also full of questions about how diplomatic efforts were going to sort out the situation, and were very happy when I told them that it looked as though this was going to turn into a real shooting war. Starved of information from the outside world, as they had been for the last two weeks, I think that they had begun to despair that it was all going to be for nothing. The thought of actually getting to grips with the Iraqis in a full-blown war was like a wet-dream coming true for these guys.

SEVENTY-FOUR

At the beginning of the First Gulf War the Iraqi Air Force or IQAF was the largest air force in the Middle East, with over five hundred combat aircraft on its books and an establishment of over 40,000 men. The vast majority of the aircraft were of Soviet origin, but there were also several French-built aircraft, some of which had been 'acquired' by the IQAF from the Kuwaitis during the invasion. This was not a force to be trifled with, especially as many of the pilots and commanders had been battle-hardened during the long war between Iraq and Iran, and had developed their own very effective air combat techniques.

On the other hand, the IQAF had suffered in one major way since the war with Iran had ended in 1988. Saddam Hussein, as paranoid as ever, had decimated the senior ranks of the IQAF in several major purges of the higher ranks, removing officers that he believed were treasonable. Therefore, the considerable threat to the coalition forces gathering in Saudi Arabia was not as worrying as it could have been. US intelligence, passed to the British, suggested that there were only a few senior officers who would have the backbone and skills to be a potential thorn in the side of the allies. Chief amongst these officers was a character that I only ever knew by the codename 'Muzahim'.

During my operational briefing in Riyadh, I had been informed that this senior officer was considered to be the leading 'hawk' of the IQAF. He was a veteran of the Iraq/Iran War, where he had served as an ace pilot. Since the end of this war he had risen quickly through the ranks, surviving the many political purges, and it was now believed that he held the rank of air vice-marshal. The yanks and the Brits were so worried about this Muzahim that they felt it was imperative that he be removed from the game before the allied air attacks started, as he had the potential to hold the IQAF together and to form them into an effective defensive and possibly even an offensive force. This could not be allowed to happen.

Muzahim was the reason that I had been called up; it was my job to assassinate him.

At the time that I landed behind the lines in Iraq I had no idea what my target looked like, as I hadn't even seen a photograph of him. However, Nobby and the boys from A Squadron had been fully briefed on Muzahim and were very familiar with his image. They had spent several days conducting reconnaissance on the IQAF headquarters buildings in Bagdad in an effort to locate him. They had done sterling work, beyond all expectations, locating both his office and a very handy firing position with a good sight-line overlooking the target's office windows. The only problem was that both the target's office and the firing position were in adjacent tall blocks (one an office block and one a housing block), about 800m apart and aligned slightly obliquely to each other. There were no other options available to us as security around the target was very tight. Muzahim never showed himself in public and was driven around in an armored limousine with lots of close protection personnel in support. He even alighted from the limo in a covered area in the basement car park of his office block, so it was not possible to get him there. It would take a very, very good shot to take out Muzahim from the chosen firing position, having to deal with the high winds that were found at such a height and through an office window at an oblique angle. Added to this there would only be the one chance. If I cocked up and missed the target, then undoubtedly the security around Muzahim would be beefed up, and I'd never get another chance to take him out cleanly. If the operation failed then the allied air forces would be facing a highly-motivated and effective enemy in air combat over Iraq, with the potential that many more allied servicemen would die. Talk about pressure.

SEVENTY-FIVE

We held a Chinese Parliament in the patrol harbour to work out a plan of action for the following day, and once we had all agreed on the best course, we ate and had a good night's sleep in preparation.

Early the next morning we set out in the two battered civilian cars, Nobby and I in one vehicle and the other three members of the patrol in the other. We split up before we got into the outskirts of the city and drove to our RV point along different routes. For such a big city, Bagdad was surprisingly quiet. I suppose that this was because of the coming war, and although everything appeared normal on the surface, you could feel the tension that lay underneath. There were vehicle checkpoints everywhere in the city, both military and police, but by now Nobby and his team had become familiar with the routes that held the fewest and had also become familiar faces to the personnel on those few checkpoints that we had to pass through. There was no trouble getting to the RV and meeting up with the rest of the team. Then we set off on foot to the housing block where the firing position was located, spacing ourselves out so that we wouldn't draw undue attention to ourselves. We were just a few of the tens of thousands Iraqi civilians in Bagdad setting out for work after the nights curfew was over.

Once we were in the block we made our way up flight after flight of dirty, smelly stairs until we reached the required floor. The room that had been chosen for the firing position was unoccupied, but Nobby still insisted on going in first and checking it out in case someone had moved in since his last recce of the place. He signalled the all clear and we entered a rubbish-strewn apartment with stains on the walls and a bare concrete floor. I used my small brass snipers telescope to get my first glimpse of the target building through the grimy window glass of the apartment. Shit, this was going to have to be the best shot of my life!

One of Nobby's team found an old rickety formica-covered dining table in one of the other rooms and I placed it in front of the window, making sure that the legs were secure with wedges of folded up paper so that it didn't wobble. Then I set up my shooting stand to support the rifle on the table. The rounds that I'd brought along with me were especially hand-made and of perfect weight, to give me the best shot possible. I carefully loaded them into the rifle's short magazine while Nobby set up his own high-powered telescope on a tripod to my side. Nobby was going to be my observer and spotter as he knew the target's face, while the rest of his team spread out as the cover group for us. One was stationed inside the slightly open door to the apartment, one was just outside the door and the third was down the hall at the head of the stairwell. They were all in communication with each other via short-wave radio mikes and hidden ear-phones, and were all armed to the teeth with an array of weapons from fighting knives through to AK47s, smuggled into the apartment block in a variety of bags and holdalls.

I withdrew my rifle from its holdall and carefully unwrapped it from the soft cloth that I hoped had protected it and its "painstakingly zeroed-in" telescopic sight from stray knocks and bangs. Then I slotted in the magazine and placed the rifle securely onto the rifle stand. I looked through the sights and through the apartment's window at the office block opposite. Then I let Nobby look as well to make sure that I was lined up on the correct window in the IQAF headquarters. Finally I operated the bolt mechanism on the L42, putting a round into the chamber, and opened the apartment window just enough so that I could see clearly, jamming it open with another bit of paper.

With the window open it was suddenly apparent that the wind outside was pretty strong and blowing from right to left. I searched outside again through my brass telescope until I found a small *Ba'ath* Party flag flying on another building, which at least gave me a pretty good indication of wind speed and precise direction. Then we settled down to wait.

Despite the fact that we had to wait only about thirty minutes or so, it seemed like a life-time. Luckily the apartment building was pretty empty, and we were never in danger of being compromised. Even so, the tension inside that small apartment was immense, and every little noise in the block jangled my nerves, which felt like they were stretched to breaking point. Nobby kept his eye glued to his scope, only withdrawing every few minutes to wipe the sweat from his eyes and rub some life back into them. His concentration was intense.

When he finally spoke I almost missed it as his voice was so quiet:

"There's action. There are people in the office." I gently gripped the stock and butt of the rifle, bringing my eye into line with the sight. My vision blurred for half a second then the office window came into focus. I could vaguely see movement through the pane of glass, but the sun was shining onto it and I couldn't see clearly into the room beyond. Shit!

Nobby obviously had a clearer view than I did:

"There're at least two people in the office, both in uniform."

"I can't see fuck all, the suns reflecting off the window."

"That's okay, I'm polarised. I'll let you know when the target comes to the window. There's a coffee jug just in front of it, and he loves his morning mug of coffee."

"Okay. Just let me know where he is exactly and I'll take the shot."

"Willco."

There were another few minutes of tense waiting then Nobby said:

"Here he is, he's at the window."

"I still can't see clearly. Where is he, left, centre or right?"

"He's slightly left of centre. His head is two thirds up, facing you full on."

Looking through the telescopic sight I could vaguely see the shoulders and head of a man standing beyond that window 800m away. My unconscious mind must have calculated the wind speed and direction without my conscious mind even knowing and I 'aimed off' the target the correct amount. My index finger slipped into the trigger guard and gently gripped the trigger, squeezing it ever so gently to take up the first pressure. I took one or two deep, slow breaths, then took another breath in, slowly let half of it out and very, very gently squeezed the trigger, the cross-hairs of the sight slightly off to the right but on a dead level with the man's head.

I don't even remember hearing the shot or feeling the rifle bucking in my grip. I just saw a hole suddenly appear in the window exactly where the target's head was. Then I slowly let out the rest of the breath.

"Fucking brilliant!" Nobby blurted out. "Spot on fucking target! Fucking brilliant!" For just a second or two we stood there, each rooted to the spot, feeling the tension flow away in waves. Then we were moving; me unloading the rifle and shoving it into the holdall; Nobby packing up his scope and tripod. Within seconds we were out of the apartment and following the cover group down the stairs, along the street, round the corner and into the vehicles. Then we were driving slowly away in different directions again.

317

It was over; I'd done it. Muzahim was no more.

SEVENTY-SIX

Nobby and his gang were well chuffed with me, and kept
going on about what a perfect shot I'd taken. When we got
back to the hide and radioed in the good news, they even
broke open a few cans of beer that they had somehow
smuggled in with the rest of their kit and we had a small
party. They had no idea who the target had been or why he
had been taken out but they guessed correctly that he
must have been pretty fucking important otherwise the
army would never have spent so much effort in getting
him.

That evening Nobby took me off to the pick up point
where I got back onto the chopper and flew back to Riyadh.
I left him and his team to go back to their work with quite
a bit of sadness, as they were great guys, and for the first
time in ages I had really enjoyed the good comradeship of
fellow soldiers.

When the chopper arrived back at Riyadh it was to
the blare of the publicity machine, as every reporter and
news crew in the world seemed to be gathered on the
airfield. Even though we landed at night-time right in front
of them in a captured Iraqi helicopter, and that it was
blatantly obvious that we must have been on some sort of
clandestine mission, I've never seen a single report
anywhere in the world's press that mentioned us.

Harry was well-chuffed and went as far as to slap me
on the back during the debriefing, especially when it was
confirmed through other independent intelligence sources
that I had definitely killed Muzahim with that one difficult

shot. I'm guessing that Harry took a shit-load of credit for the operation; probably got a medal for it, even though he wasn't even there.

I was shipped back to rejoin the regiment, who were still training in the 'empty quarter' and were still without a clearly defined role in what everybody knew by now was going to be a full-on proper shooting war.

On 17th January 1991, two days after the deadline that had been set by the UN, the coalition forces began a massive air campaign against the armed forces of Iraq, who still had not withdrawn from Kuwait. This was the beginning of Operation 'Desert Storm'.

SEVENTY-SEVEN

It was while we were all gathered around a battered old TV set one evening, listening with eagerness to the news of the air-strikes into Iraq that Harry came to visit me again. We walked out into the desert as the sun began to set.

"You did a very good job for us in Bagdad. The firm is very pleased."

"Oh goody. That makes me feel very warm inside."

"Now, now, John, don't be bitter. I've come to offer you a deal."

"What sort of a deal?" He'd got my curiosity peaked and he knew it.

"Well, we should be sending you home right now, now that the job you were brought over to do is over, so to speak. But....."

"What? Don't tell me you've got another fucking job up your sleeve?"

"No. It's just that I thought you deserved a choice about what happens to you next." I could hardly believe this; Harry, giving me a choice. To say that I was sceptical was vastly underrating how I felt at this moment.

"What sort of choice?" I was expecting the worst.

"Well old chap, I know that we dragged you away from your family, and I guess that you really want to get back to them and your comfy life in Civvy Street. But....."

"Just get on with Harry. Who do you want me to kill this time, Saddam sodding Hussein?"

"I've already told you, it's nothing like that. I just thought that you might want to stay on in the Middle East

321

for a while, especially as you seem to be enjoying working with your old pals again."

"I haven't got any 'old pals' left. You saw to that when you and the Increment turned me into a killer. SAS guys don't like assassins, and the rumour mill is in full swing out here; no one will even talk to me. Anyway most of the guys that I knew in the regiment are either dead, been invalided out or have left. I don't know any of these fuckers."

"But they're your kind of 'fuckers' aren't they. In spite of what they may or may not feel towards you, you do enjoy their company and no doubt you'd like to see some proper action again, wouldn't you?" I had to concede to him on this point, so I just nodded.

"Good. The war is about to take on a very different perspective and you and your chums are going to be in very high demand soon. It'll do you good to be at the sharp end again. Civvy Street doesn't suit you at all."

"So that's my choice is it? Go home to the wife and kids or stay out here and play at soldiers?"

"Quite. You've got it in a nutshell old boy."

Harry wasn't stupid; he knew what floated my boat only too well. I chose to stay on and fight.

SEVENTY-EIGHT

It was with extremely light hearts that the SAS learned that
we were going to go into Iraq at last. Both A and D
Squadrons were each tasked with putting two heavily
armed half-squadron fighting columns behind enemy lines,
to cause as much mischief and mayhem as we could.

I set off with one of the fighting columns from A
Squadron. I had not worked much with this squadron in the
past and I hardly knew anyone within its ranks, though I did
recognize the faces of some of the old-timers. Nobody
recognized me though, and despite my rank (I had kept the
same rank of sergeant that I'd had when I'd been booted
out of the army), all that they knew of me, apart from the
rumours, was that I had been called up with about 14 other
blokes into R Squadron (the reserve squadron). Therefore I
was offered the chance of being a motorcycle outrider;
obviously a position where the rest of the guys thought I
wouldn't get in the way too much. I didn't mind one bit, as
it gave me a little bit more independence and I wouldn't
have to spend so much time fielding awkward bloody
questions from the rest of the guys, who were naturally
very curious about me.

Each fighting column consisted of eight to twelve
Land Rovers with a four-wheel drive Mercedes Unimog
truck in support carrying most of the supplies, and around
thirty SAS soldiers. The wagons were very heavily armed
with a mixture of Browning heavy machine-guns, general
purpose machine-guns, Milan anti-tank guided missile
launchers and belt-fed 40mm grenade launchers, plus all of

the guy's personal weapons. With each column there were a couple of outriders riding Honda XR 250 off-road motorcycles. It was our job to scout ahead of the columns, looking for trouble and picking out targets.

We did most of our travelling at night and lay up during the day under camouflaged netting. Our targets were everything from individual vehicles, communications centres, anti-aircraft batteries and air-fields to weapon dumps. You name it, we hit it. Sometimes we would call in air-strikes and sometimes we would just mallet the fucking target with everything we had. Other jobs we carried out included surveying targets that had been hit by coalition air strikes. Occasionally we'd capture enemy officers who were then choppered back to Saudi to be interrogated. We generally made a very big nuisance of ourselves in the enemy's rear and thousands of troops that should have been placed in the Iraqi front line were kept instead in their rear areas, trying to find and eliminate us. We did what we were very good at: being a pain in the enemy's arse.

A few times we ambushed vehicles travelling at night along the Iraqi Main Supply Routes (MSRs). We would approach the MSR just after dusk and park our vehicles up in a line along the side of the road. When an enemy convoy passed by we would open fire and all hell would break loose. The quiet of the desert night would explode with the sound of Milan missiles and grenades hitting their targets, and the dark sky would be illuminated by the lines of tracer rounds from the SAS machine-guns and rifles snaking into the convoy, soon followed by the whumph of exploding fuel tanks and munitions. After malleting the bastards for a couple of minutes we'd get the order to bug-out and make for our RV, before the Iraqis had time to put together any sort of co-ordinated defence. We'd leave behind a line of mangled and fiercely-blazing enemy vehicles.

It wasn't long though, before the focus of our mission began to narrow significantly.

When the coalition air strikes into Iraq began, Saddam did his best to try and draw Israel into the war. He knew that if the Israelis could be pushed into joining the allied forces that were set up against Iraq then there would be a very real possibility that the coalition would break down. He recognized the fact that there was not an Arab government in the world that would agree to its troops fighting alongside those of Israel, especially against another Arab country, even Iraq. He tried to do this by targeting Israeli cities with his Scud missiles.

At the time of the first Gulf War, Iraq was armed with the Soviet-built Scud Ballistic Missile System. These missiles had been used successfully by the Iraqis against Iran during the Iraq/Iran War and they had developed several local variants with higher payloads and longer ranges than the standard versions supplied by the Soviets. Some of the missiles were based in fixed firing sites, but of course these had already been targeted and blitzed by coalition air strikes, so they weren't a problem. However the main missile force was operated from mobile Transporter Erector Launchers (TEL for short) on soviet-built trucks. The TELs were highly mobile and had the ability to hide during the day, only to emerge at night when they would lob a missile into an Israeli city from close to the Jordanian border.

It became a priority for the coalition forces to seek out and destroy these missiles and their launchers, but this was not easy as the Iraqis had been previously well-trained by the US in how to avoid satellite and aircraft reconnaissance. They hid beneath road bridges, in warehouses and barns etc, where they were out-of-sight and relatively safe from being spotted from above. Despite hundreds of sorties flown against them by coalition aircraft, not one single TEL had been located and missiles continued to fall with impunity into Israel.

Although the Israeli government showed remarkable restraint, it was obvious that this couldn't last forever. Things were becoming desperate until someone suggested to the head-sheds that perhaps Special Forces teams on the ground would be more effective in taking the Scuds out. So it was that the SAS fighting columns were diverted into an area of western Iraq that was soon to become known as 'Scud Alley'. US Special Forces, who operated in columns very similar to the SAS fighting columns, were at the same time tasked with taking out the Iraqi Scuds in the area to the north of us, which they called 'Scud Boulevard'.

From the day we moved into Scud Alley not one more Scud missile was launched into Israel. When we located a Scud TEL we would assault it from the ground, using plastic explosives to knock out the guidance systems on the vehicles, while shooting up their launch crews. We also targeted a few well-protected communication sites in the area, driving our wagons right up to them in the dark and blasting them to fuck.

On one occasion both of the A Squadron fighting columns were brought together for an attack on a communications centre that was code-named 'Victor Two'. The installation boasted a tall communications tower that was a major link in ordering and targeting Scud missile launches. The plan was for my assault team to enter the facility on foot without being detected. We would then lay our demolition charges and get out before detonating them. The wagons were split into two groups to give us fire support in the event of the plan going wrong. The wagons with the bigger and longer-ranged weaponry would give us support from a distance while the ones with only light machine-guns would give us close fire support from nearby in the event it all went tits-up and we were bumped by the Iraqi's on our way in.

Before the attack, intelligence had informed us that the installation was manned by a small number of Iraqi troops, but as it turned out there were literally hundreds of the bastards and they laid down a withering fire onto our small assault team.

The wagons blasted back at the defenders with everything they had, giving us a chance to carry on moving forward and to lay our charges. We did so, and then made a fighting withdrawal; some of the guys laying down covering fire while others moved back, went to ground and then provided covering fire while the first guys moved back. 'Leap-frogging' like this we eventually extracted ourselves from the contact and everyone bugged out back to the final RV. Amazingly we didn't suffer a single casualty during the operation. Once again, the explosions as the demolitions went off lit up the desert sky like a huge firework display.

At first light in the morning I went back as a member of a small reconnaissance party to see what damage we had done in the attack. We reported back to the head-sheds that we had achieved our objective; the installation was destroyed and there were still dozens of Iraqi bodies littering the ground.

At the end of February the ground assault by coalition forces into Kuwait and Iraq begun, and a mere 100 hours later President George Bush declared that Kuwait had been liberated and declared a cease-fire. The war in the Gulf was over, at least for now.

It had been predicted that the mobile fighting columns of the SAS would suffer high casualty rates during our operations but in the end, after 42 days of fighting behind enemy lines, we only had four of our guys killed. We had won the war in style, but now it was time to go home and face the music, or at least, so I thought at the time.

SEVENTY-NINE

A sense of normality had returned to the Cambridgeshire Police HQ at Hinchingbrooke for the first time since the rocket attack by Smith. The structural engineers had given the all-clear the day before. SOCA, however was still working out of temporary offices in the incident van parked in the car park. The huge scar in the HQ building that marked the location of their old offices was covered by a series of large blue tarpaulins, while civilian contractors worked inside to clear up the wreckage and begin repairs.

In the chief constable's rather large and plush office (which had remained untouched by the attack) DCI Davies, DC Wright and Harry were sitting together with the chief constable, her assistant and half a dozen police technicians. Smith had promised to phone and everyone in the room, with the exception of Harry, was looking forward to receiving the call. The technicians were there because they were ready to put into motion every technical resource that they had for rapidly tracing the phone call. The scene was set for the capture of John Smith, at long bloody last.

The office's large picture window overlooked the car park and the strip of woodland beyond it. Outside the sky was dark grey and the rain was pelting down. It was a bloody miserable early morning. They had the lights on in the office.

The phone rang; the single green light flashing on it meant that it was from an outside call that had been put through from reception. Everyone in the room tensed; a technician hissed at Davies as he reached out his hand to pick up the receiver: "Not yet sir, let it ring a few times......now, sir." Davies answered the call:

"DCI Davies."

"Hello Alan."

"Hello John."

"Put me onto speaker Alan, I want everyone there to hear."

"Done."

"Hello everyone. Are you there Harry?"

"Yes I am, hello John."

"Move closer to the phone Harry, I can't hear you very well and I want to." Harry reluctantly did so.

"How's that, better?"

"Super."

"Where are you John?"

"A long bloody way away; the further away from you the better!"

"Now, now, don't be like that John. This is rather like old times."

"Bollocks, you prat. Why Harry? Why did you set me up?" Harry glanced around the others in the office, then making a decision he gestured at the technicians.

"Get out!" He ordered. They looked for confirmation from the chief constable, who nodded at them, and then they trailed out of the office. Harry bent closer towards the microphone. In a low voice he said: "Because you know too much John, and you're unstable." The others in the room looked at each other in surprise.

"Unstable? Of course I'm bloody unstable! It was you who made me this way with your bloody missions, you bastard! What did you expect? Did you think that you could just wind me up and point me in the right direction and that I wouldn't bloody well be affected by all of the sodding wars and the killing?"

"Now, now old boy, don't get upset!"

"Upset? You set me up to face a life sentence for something that I didn't do and you didn't think I'd get upset, you bastard?"

"I am sorry John. But you've got to understand that I couldn't just leave you as free as a bird to tell your story to whoever wanted to listen."

"You stupid twat. In all those years I'd never said a word to anyone."

"Ah, but you're wrong John. We knew about your visits to psychiatrists and the writing of your autobiography. For therapy wasn't it? Do you know what would have happened to HM's government if that had fallen into the wrong hands?"

"More to the point, what would happen to you? That's what you really mean, don't you Harry?"

"Not at all, old boy; I'm just a tiny cog in a big machine."

"Bollocks Harry, you're the head of the Increment. You've always believed that you were above the law, but you're not Harry; you're not untouchable." There were a few moments of silence in which everyone in the office craned forward, waiting for Smith to say something else. Instead there was an audible click as the connection was closed. Only Harry reacted:

"Shit!"

During the night Smith had taken a long time to slowly and carefully move into position. He had guessed, correctly as it turned out, that such an important call would only be taken in the chief constable's office, where else? So he had crawled into a perfect fire position with a good view of her office window. His camouflaged ghillie-suit blended perfectly with the glossy leaves and deep shadows of the tall, sturdy holly tree in which he was perched at a height of about forty feet. When he saw Harry move closer to the phone in the light spilling out from the office window, he had had to pause for a few moments to quell the rage that

330

threatened to eat him up. Even worse; it threatened to put him off his aim. Harry's justification for setting him up just made him angrier, but he forced down the pure hatred that he felt for his former case officer and section head and centred the cross-hairs of the L42's scope on the spot right between Harry's pig-like eyes. He controlled his breathing as he had all of those years ago in Bagdad when he assassinated the Iraqi air force officer, and, as he saw Harry's mouth form the word "Shit" gently squeezed the trigger. He saw Harry's head literally disintegrate as the high velocity round struck him. Smith had filed a deep cross onto the tip of the bullet that he had used, so that when the round hit and penetrated Harry's skull, the force of the impact had split it into four independent pieces that carved their own paths through his soft brain tissue and exploded out of the back of his head, splattering the office walls and everyone near to him with blood, brains, snot and gore.

In seconds Smith had dropped to the ground beneath the holly tree and sprinted away. A minute later he was climbing into the cab of the Scania truck parked near the wood in a lay-by. He turned the engine on and set the heater to demist the windows as he rapidly stripped off the ghillie suit and used a wet cloth to scrape off the soot that he'd used to cam-up his face. He slipped the truck into second gear, indicated and pulled out into the quiet lane. No one took any notice of the huge heavy goods vehicle liveried in the ever-familiar green, red and white of the 'Eddie Stobart' haulage company as it drove down the road. Who would ever guess that it was being driven by an assassin?

From: john smith (johnsmith2223@hotmail.com)
To: SOCA@Cambspolice.org.uk
Date: 22 October 2013 16:41:37
CC:
Subject: FAO Detective Chief Inspector Alan Davies, Cambs SOCA.

Hi Alan, I really must apologise for using you the way I did to get at Harry, but what the hell; I enjoyed it after all.

Please find attached the latest instalment of my autobiography.

Not much longer to go mate; you'll have my entire life story up until the point you forced your way into it. Maybe you'll have some answers as well; who knows?

Speak to you soon.

Regards

John Smith

EIGHTY

It wasn't simply a matter of packing up and going straight home after the ceasefire in the Gulf was declared. We were still operational and had a lot of clearing-up operations to perform, including rounding up prisoners of war and disarming them, and making sure that various Iraqi military installations were secure.

However, by the end of May things had wound down and we eagerly looked forward to getting out of Iraq and back to the UK, though some of us (namely me) weren't looking forward to this as much as most of the guys were. We eventually moved south back to Saudi and this is when I was approached by Harry once again, whilst having a coffee in the regiment's makeshift mess.

"Before you bugger off home again....." He began, indicating that we should take a walk outside, away from prying ears.

"As I was saying, before you get discharged, do you fancy another quick job for the firm?"

"I hate it when you ask that. What's the job this time?" I was pretty mellow at this point.

"There's a problem in Eastern Europe, in Bosnia, to be exact, in Yugoslavia. We need a team on the ground to give us an update on developments there."

"What? You don't want me to knock anybody off?" He actually smiled at this point.

"I'm afraid not. It's purely intelligence gathering this time."

"Bloody hell, Harry, things must be quiet."

"Not that quiet old boy. We believe that a civil war is about to kick off in Yugoslavia. Let's just say that it's getting a little tense out there."

"Okay. I'll do it. When do I start?" He smiled again.

"Today; I'll get both of us on an aircraft back to the UK this afternoon. We'll be met at Brize Norton and taken to join the rest of the team for a detailed briefing."

"An Increment team?"

"Not strictly, old boy. More of a standard SIS operation. There'll be four of you in the team. You'll be the team's operational commander, with one ex-SAS, a serving marine with SBS and a serving case officer from SIS, who will be the team's overall commander. Your job is to provide protection for the case officer while he goes about his intelligence gathering and recruiting new intelligence sources amongst the locals."

"Okay, sounds good to me. Have I got time to finish my cup of tea?"

Harry was true to his word and we were on a flight back home within a few hours. I felt a fleeting moment of guilt about not seeing my family since Christmas and volunteering for yet another mission, but to be honest I also felt a great deal of relief at not having to face them yet. I had enjoyed the last few months too much; it had been great working with the regiment again. Perhaps over the years I'd become addicted to the danger and the adrenaline rush that I got from being operational? It's very true to say that I never felt happier or more at peace with myself than when I was in a war or a conflict somewhere in the world, though it does sound like a contradiction in terms. All of those years of being constantly on the alert to danger or actually in the thick of the action must have affected me in some way. Why else would I have volunteered so readily for yet another potentially dangerous operation? It's not as if I actually cared about what might happen in Yugoslavia, or how it might affect the UK; I still didn't give a shit and had a chip on my shoulder the size of a mountain about the way I had been treated since Afghanistan.

The team, apart from the SBS guy, were a bunch of wankers as far as I was concerned. The ex-SAS bloke turned out to be a slightly paunchy and balding reject from 23 SAS, one of the TA SAS regiments. His name was Tom and he was nothing but a former part-time hero who had never seen action in his life and was, as far as I was concerned, a bloody liability. He also had a problem with authority, which wouldn't have been so bad except that in this case, as the operational commander of the team, I was the authority concerned. From the beginning our relationship got off on a bad foot as he started trying to tell me how to do my job when we first met. It was only a matter of minutes before I told him to "shut the fuck up". He sulked after that. Jesus! I could only think that the Increment had been short of potential recruits from the Special Forces units with most of the blokes still in the Middle East.

The SIS wallah wasn't a surprise to me. His name was Michael and he was typical of the firm; a self-serving twat in a suit who thought he was superior in every way to any simple soldier in the British Army. He was young and obviously very ambitious. I decided the moment that I met him that I didn't like him one little bit, but that he would go far in the SIS; it was full of wankers like him already, so he'd fit in perfectly. Probably make section head if this job went well; just like Harry had. Whenever I asked this guy about his experience and how long he had spent out in the field, he would always answer with a finger tapping the side of his nose and the phrase:

"Need to know, old boy. Need to know." This, of course, led me to believe that he didn't have any field experience at all.

On the other hand, Bill, the SBS guy, was okay. He was also young, but full of pride in his job, the Royal Marines and the SBS, yet still reacted well when I started taking the piss out of all of the above, and gave as good as he got. It's standard operating procedure amongst members of the British armed forces to take the piss out of each other's units. I had an instant rapport with Bill, even though he was a 'bootneck' (marine) and I had a feeling that he would get on with the job and do it as well as he was able.

All in all though, I was a little pissed off that the team was so young and inexperienced. It dawned on me that I would have to carry half of them during the upcoming operation. Not an ideal prospect in a potentially dangerous theatre.

I really got pissed off though when I found out that the only small arms we'd be allowed to carry on the job were pistols. I prefer to have something a little heavier in the ordnance department if the shit might be hitting the fan, but Harry was intent on keeping us as low-profile as possible and I suppose he had a valid point when he said that four guys carrying assault rifles might stand out in a crowd. As operational commander, and with this limited choice in mind, I chose the P228 SIG Saur semi-automatic pistol as our personal weapons and was again pissed off when I found out that neither Tom nor Michael had ever handled one. I had to give them a brief training session before we hit Yugoslavian dirt.

I could tell that this operation was going to be fun.

Our cover for the job was as a television news crew from New Zealand; chosen as a suitably neutral country that would hopefully be above suspicion. I was the producer, Michael the reporter and Tom and Bill the sound and camera men. We were issued the relevant dog-eared passports and paperwork through the firm and our weapons were hidden amongst a mountain of equipment on the short flight to Sarajevo from Brussels. This was a good cover story that would allow us to move more-or-less unhindered throughout Yugoslavia, and as one of our primary objectives was to recruit potential informants and agents from amongst the locals, we could interview and talk to whoever we wanted to on the ground, without raising undue suspicions. After all, that's what TV news crews do.

We arrived in Yugoslavia to find that the country had gone to the dogs after the death of the Yugoslavian President, Marshall Tito, in 1980. After a couple of weeks of moving through the country and 'interviewing' dozens of people, from local politicians through to ethnic religious leaders, it became clear that Harry's initial assessment of the situation was sound; things were indeed getting a little tense. It was also a very complicated situation. First of all there were the different states; Bosnia and Herzegovina, Croatia, Serbia and Slovenia, some of which were vying for independence while others didn't want to see Yugoslavia break up. Then there were the different religious factions consisting mainly of Muslims, Orthodox Christians and Catholics. The trouble was that the religious factions weren't evenly divided into the geographical boundaries of the countries that wanted independence. For instance Bosnia was comprised of mainly Muslim Bosniaks, but there were also large populations of Orthodox Serbians and Catholic Croats. In short, the whole area was a powder-keg just waiting to explode.

We kept moving from one area to another, finding potential recruits in almost every corner of the country. Michael would then wean them onto our side with gifts of money and promises of more to come. I didn't like the little prat but I've got to admit he was very good at his job, and pretty soon he had begun to set up a network of informants and agents throughout the country. Our cover also held up well and there was never a moment when I thought that we might be blown.

It couldn't last, of course, and at the end of June we received a coded message ordering us to leave Bosnia and travel immediately to Slovenia where the situation was deteriorating badly.

We hitched a ride in the back of a truck and arrived in the Slovenian capital of Ljubljana in the early morning of

26th June, the day after Slovenia and Croatia had announced their independence and a day before Slovenia and the Yugoslavian Army would go to war.

EIGHTY-ONE

The Slovenian War of Independence, also known as 'the Ten Day war', lasted from 26th June until 4th July 1991, when a ceasefire was declared. Basically it was a fight between the Slovenian Territorial Defence Force (or 'TO'), who wanted an independent Slovenia, and the Yugoslav People's Army (or 'JNA'), who wanted to keep Yugoslavia as a single entity. Less than a hundred people died during the ten days of fighting and around 300 were wounded, but for our small team it was a tragic conflict.

Tom, the part-time SAS soldier, had been a pain-in-the-arse from the moment that I'd met him. He had a real problem with obeying orders and would often go off on his own when we were supposed to be working together as a team. He even got a bit too drunk on occasions when we were keeping our cover as a news team together, hanging around the bars frequented by other members of the world's press. Occasionally he almost dropped us right in it by opening his mouth a bit too much. I blame myself for what happened to him in the end, as it was my job to keep the team together and make sure that everyone did their bit. The fact that he was a drunk and big-mouthed and had a problem with authority didn't cut it as an excuse with me. He was one of my team and I should have kept him in order. I was responsible for what happened.

In the early hours of the 27th, we heard that a column of JNA tanks was leaving its barracks near the capital and heading towards the main airport at Brnik. We spent some of our hard cash on a beat-up old four-wheel drive car and hot-footed it to the airport, arriving shortly before the JNA, who then proceeded to take over the airport without a shot being fired. We decided to stay on along with a bunch of other foreign journalists, as this looked like it was going to be a likely flash-point if there was going to be any significant fighting.

During the night we regretted our decision as there were reports flooding in, via our media colleagues, of fighting between the TO and JNA breaking out all over the country and unfortunately it was quiet where we were. Michael really wanted us to move out as he wanted to witness some of the fighting first hand for his superiors in the firm. I told him we were staying put and not moving until first light as I didn't want us being mistaken for combatants in the darkness; he reluctantly agreed.

Meanwhile Tom was hanging around with a couple of Austrian journalists, even though I had ordered him to stay close to the team in case we had to move out quickly. I suspect that the Austrians had a ready supply of *schnapps* handy, and that was why he was being so friendly towards them.

The following morning an attack was launched by the Slovenians against the JNA forces holding the airport. We positioned ourselves in relative safety behind a brick wall as there were rounds flying about in all directions. I called over to Tom to come and join us and for once he obeyed me, scuttling away from the Austrians and taking cover with the rest of us behind the wall. The fire-fight went on for an hour or so, and more than once I had to yell at Tom to keep his fucking head down. He was overly excited by all the commotion (and probably a little drunk too) and kept looking over the wall to see what was going on. He was pushing his luck, and eventually it ran out; he got a bullet in the head and we were showered with his blood and brains. It was probably only a stray round as we weren't being targeted at the time. It didn't kill him instantly and we did our best to help him, but after a few minutes he died.

The team was in shock, as I'm sure that none of them had ever seen a real casualty before, especially one that they had known personally. They just sat with their backs to the wall, getting that 'thousand-yard stare' that's talked about so much. Luckily for us the Yugoslavian Air Force picked that moment to launch an attack against the Slovenian ground forces and all hell broke loose. 20 or 30mm cannon shells laced the ground close to where we were taking cover, and ripped into a number of parked airliners behind us. They were instantly set on fire, to be followed by a thunderous blast as their fuel tanks exploded amid vast clouds of thick, black, choking smoke.

I took the opportunity to shake the team out of their shock, with a few choice phrases like: "Get your fucking asses together!" I also launched a few well-aimed kicks into backsides. We used the temporary cover of the smoke clouds to throw Tom's corpse into the back of the car and to get the fuck out of there. We drove away from the airport and the fighting as fast as we could; only stopping when we were about ten miles or so away, and the sound of fighting had receded behind us. We disposed of Tom's body by hastily burying him in a wood by the roadside. We didn't want to have to explain a dead body to the authorities and it would also have been very difficult for us if they had decided to repatriate Tom's body back to his home country, which they believed to be New Zealand. There would have been all sorts of difficult questions being asked of us.

It was only later that we learned that the two Austrian journalists at the airport had been killed by the air-strike.

We stayed on in Slovenia for the rest of the war, with Michael making some very good contacts amongst both the Slovenians and the Yugoslavians, and were recalled to the UK during the middle of July.

Our subsequent reports on the situation in the area proved to be right. A three-year-long war broke out in the following April between the Bosnians, Serbs and Croats, leading to the deaths of over 100,000 people from all sides. The difficult ethnic and religious situation that we described would lead to the indiscriminate shelling of cities and towns and their civilian populations, systematic genocide, massacres and mass-rape, and some of the most bitter fighting that Europe has seen since the Second World War.

I'm glad that I was only there to see a small part of it.

EIGHTY-TWO

After returning to London via a roundabout route through Europe, we were put up in a safe-house in the centre of London. There we were separately put through a number of long and intensive debriefings by the firm, who picked apart our reports and the events leading up to Tom's death in Slovenia.

Several days later I was dumped by the firm yet again, quite literally; by being shown the front door and told to make my own way home. The SIS stooge laughed at me when I told him I had no money on me.

"I guess you'll have to walk then mate. The exercise will be good for you."

My eventual return to my married home was no better. When I let myself in through the front door, it was to find a tearful Anne-Marie and her mother sitting in the front room.

"Where the hell have you been?" Were the loving words for the returning hero, home at last from the war.

"You know where I've been. I was called up, remember?"

"The fucking war has been over for months! I've not had a phone call or a letter to say that you were alright! Nothing from the bloody army, either! So where have you been?"

"Like I said, I was called up!"

"Bollocks! You've been with another woman, you bastard!" And so the argument went on, with me unable to answer her questions and she unable to believe that I had not been having it away with some other woman since the war in the Gulf had ended. I was finding myself getting angrier and angrier, and Anne-Marie was getting more and more upset, with her bloody mother sitting at her elbow and adding fuel to the fire by whispering in her ear about how I must have been shagging another woman. The boys just sat in one corner of the room crying their eyes out as the argument got even more loud and intense. Eventually I reached breaking point. I knew without a shadow of a doubt that I was on the edge of lashing out in my rage and hurting someone that I loved, and as I realised that something within me went 'click'. Just like that I knew that I couldn't do this anymore; I couldn't settle down to married life again after all that I'd been through. This was the end of my marriage and I knew it.

Without saying another word I picked up my wallet and the car keys from the sideboard and walked out of the front door. I strode over to where the car was parked on the other side of the street and got in. Just as I started the engine, my kids came running out of the house crying for me to come back. I choked back a sob, kept my eyes on the road and pulled away, my insides churning up and my mind spinning with the injustice of it all. I could very easily, at that point, have just driven my car at full speed into a brick wall and ended all of the pain. Why I didn't, I'll never know.

After spending a few nights at my parent's house, I bought a newspaper, found an advert for a cheap bedsit, called the rental agency and went to view it. It was a tiny room with nothing in it but a single bed, a chair, a wardrobe, a sink and a two-ring gas hob, but it would do and I paid for a month's rent in advance. Next I went to the company that I had worked for before being called up, only to find that I'd been sacked in my absence and someone else was doing my job. After that I went back to the bedsit, via the nearest off-licence where I bought a bottle of cheap brandy and a four-pack of beer. I lay down on the bare mattress, opened a beer, took a slug of brandy and drank myself into oblivion.

EIGHTY-THREE

For the next few months I lived on my own in that tiny room. I couldn't get a full-time job as I was in a drunken state most of the time. The few part-time jobs that I managed to blag my way into, such as serving in a MacDonald's, lasted for only a few days at a time, as I was angry and rude and a pain-in-the-arse, and soon found myself sacked.

I went onto Social Security, the Dole, which just about paid enough for my rent, food and booze, and I sat in my room drinking, all day and every night.

At one point I went back to see Anne-Marie and my sons, only to find that she had put almost everything that I had ever owned on to a big bonfire in the back garden and burnt it. I put up with her screaming at me as I searched through the ashes and saved what I could. Then I went around the house, shoving the clothes and personal items that she hadn't burnt into a black plastic bin-liner before leaving without a word. She could have the house and everything else in it; I wasn't interested. From the day that I'd walked out of their lives I'd known that I'd never go back; it was over.

Occasionally I'd visit my parents or talk to my brothers on the phone, but mostly I kept my own company. I didn't know it at the time but this was my first bout of severe clinical depression. I didn't hear anything from the army or Harry or the regiment; I was totally on my own.

Depression has been likened to being in a deep, dark pit where no light shows through. You feel useless and in despair, and nothing matters to you at all. Coming out of depression is akin to suddenly seeing a small chink of light in the darkness, which gradually, over days or weeks, gets brighter and brighter, until the brightness overwhelms the darkness and at last you can feel your spirit lifting. Sometimes this depression can be with you for years, and sometimes only for a few months. On this occasion I was lucky and it was the latter. By the end of October I could feel myself getting better. I dragged myself out of it, cleaned up my act and for the first time in ages, began to think of the future.

Unfortunately, this is when Harry turned up yet again in my life. He had one last job for me.

EIGHTY-FOUR

"I've got one last job for you." Were the words that he said as I opened up the front door of the block of flats. Not: "Hello" or "How are you?" or "Nice to see you after all this time." Just "I've got one last job for you."

My reply was:

"Fuck off Harry, I'm not interested."

"I don't really care whether you're interested or not, old boy. I've got a job for you and you're going to do it."

That was that.

Harry stayed with me for about 15 minutes, sitting on my bed and looking distastefully around my tiny room.

"You stink." He said. "Have a wash and clean yourself up."

"Fuck you."

"You're also drunk. Sober up and go out for a run."

"Fuck you. You go for a run."

"You've got a week to sober up and get relatively fit. You're going to need to be fit for the job."

"What is the job?"

"It's an Increment job."

"I didn't expect it to be a job playing Father fucking Christmas! Of course it's an Increment job! That's why you're here fucking bothering me!"

"Yes, well, if you can understand with that alcohol-drenched brain of yours, an Increment job means that you don't find out what it is until I'm ready to tell you!"

348

"You're a complete arsehole Harry."

"Of course I am, I work hard at it. Now you must work hard on getting yourself cleaned up and fit. This is an important job and I don't want it fucked up."

"And what if I don't want to do it?"

"Then you will be the next job on my list, *comprende?*"

"Shit-head."

"Just do what you're told. I'm going now but I'll be back in touch in a few days."

I'm one of those lucky people who doesn't have to spend months getting fit. I don't know whether it's a result of all the training I've done over the years or whether my body is just built this way. What I do know is that I can get reasonably fit without too much hard work and over a relatively short period of time. Four days after Harry's visit, a couple of dozen miles run and a few hundred sit-ups and press-ups done, and I was as right as rain. I wasn't as fit as a serving member of the SAS would be, of course, as that would take a lot longer to achieve, but I was at least as fit as anyone of my advancing years is likely to get in such a short time.

Harry was lucky that he approached me after I had begun to climb out of my depression. If he had done so while I had still been in its full grip, I might very well have taken him up on his back-handed offer of getting knocked off by the Increment. Thoughts of suicide had often been on my mind during this time.

Or perhaps it wasn't entirely luck on his part, as I have little doubt that he had been keeping tabs on me since I'd finished my debriefing three months before. Or then again, maybe I'm just a little paranoid, but then who wouldn't be in my position? And remember, just because you're paranoid, it doesn't mean that every bastard isn't out to get you.

Either way Harry turned up again at my bedsit four days after his initial visit. He didn't seem to be a happy bunny and merely grunted when he saw that I was back on my feet again. Within minutes I was whisked off in the passenger seat of his old and battered BMW.

"Okay, what's the job then?"

"It's probably the most important job we've ever taken on John."

"Really?" That got my interest, for sure. "Who have I got to kill this time, the Prime Minister?"

"Not quite; but you're not far off the bloody mark old boy!"

"So who is it then?"

"I'm afraid that I can't tell you that John. I've no doubt that you'll recognize the target when you come face to face though."

"Prince Philip? Margaret Thatcher?" Dear old Maggie was no longer the Prime Minister by this point, having been given the old heave-ho by the Conservative Party, in favour of her former confidant John Major.

"Stop asking, you'll find out soon enough. That's if we can keep tabs on him and find a good spot and time for you to take him out."

"Well, at least I know that it's a he, anyway." I said, relaxing back into the pseudo leather seat.

"This is going to be a very difficult job John."

"In what way? Has he got protection?"

"None at all. The difficult bit is that we're going to have to work with other people; people that I don't know and I don't trust."

"Spooks?"

"Yes, but not ours."

"Are you going to tell me who they are Harry?"

"Believe me John; you don't ever want to know the answer to that particular question!"

"Super. Just what I fucking need." I turned away from him. "I'm going to get some kip. Wake me up when we get to wherever it is that we're going."

EIGHTY-FIVE

Our destination turned out to be Heathrow Airport. Harry provided me with yet another set of false documents. This time I was going to be a tourist going on a two week holiday to the Azores. We separated at the airport, Harry parking his car up and me going directly to check-in with a suitcase full of touristy things provided by the SIS.

After checking in, I sat in a bar in the departure lounge, sipping on a half-pint of cold lager, while I waited to board the flight to Lisbon, where I would transfer to another flight to the islands. I was going to fly economy of course, and I have no doubt that Harry was flying business class.

I didn't see him at Heathrow again, so maybe he caught another flight or just did a very good job of steering clear of me. It was almost second-nature to both of us to avoid being seen together in public, especially where there were CCTV cameras. Deniability was always the watchword of any operation by the Increment. The flights were uneventful, and when I arrived in São Miguel Airport I caught a local taxi to the tourist hotel where a room had been booked for me.

Once there, I spent a lot of my time by the hotel pool, sunbathing, until the inevitable contact was made. It paid to be as invisible as possible in this type of work, and the easiest way to do this was to act as a typical tourist would and blend in. I stayed put and read an old paperback novel that I'd found in my luggage, only leaving the poolside to get something to eat and to enquire at reception if I'd received any messages.

It was two days before I got the expected message from Harry.

"Meet me at the Ponta Delgada Marina at 2pm, today." This was it then. It sounded like the job was going to happen and happen soon. I'd finally get to meet my target face-to-face and find out who he was.

After meeting Harry at the marina, we sauntered down to the port and climbed on board an old and worn-out fishing trawler that was tied up at the quay. The captain of the boat, who also looked old and worn-out, gestured for us to hurry up and get out of sight below, which we did. We were in for a surprise as this old-looking wreck was nothing of the sort. Below deck it was all gleaming chrome and glowing computer and radar screens. This was obviously one of our 'spy' vessels, used in times of peace to trail enemy shipping and collect electronic intelligence on them. The old captain turned out to be an ex-Royal Navy officer.

"Your cabins are down below. I expect you to stay in them until we call you up for your briefing. We'll be sailing in a few hours after your colleagues arrive. Hopefully, we'll be on the target's tail within a couple of days or so."

Harry wasn't happy about being bossed around like this and only went below after grumbling a bit. I didn't give a toss and went below for a kip.

I didn't get to meet my 'colleagues' for three days as it turned out; three days of motoring along south-eastwards through the Atlantic at a surprisingly high speed. This spy tub might look like an old wreck on the outside but she certainly had some very serious horsepower in her engine room. I spent my time finishing off the old paperback I'd had the sense to bring along, and sleeping of course. Harry and I shared a cabin, which really seemed to piss him off.

He was forever grumbling like some old maid and had nothing to do except sit on his bunk and stare at the bulkheads. I simply ignored the miserable git as much as possible. We had never had much in common. He was the long-term career-orientated spook and I was just a tool that he used when he needed me. We didn't even like each other.

When we were finally called up into the cabin for our briefing, things got very tense. Our two new colleagues were slightly dark-skinned Mediterranean-looking guys, who looked as tough as nails and about as much fun. When I offered my hand for a hand-shake it was ignored and the two of them sat there throughout the whole operational briefing without saying a single word. It wasn't hard to guess who they were and where they were from; they had 'Mossad' (the Israeli 'Institute for Intelligence and Special Operations') written all over them.

The gist of the briefing was that I and my two colleagues would be leaving the trawler in a semi-rigid inflatable and making for a set of co-ordinates off the Canary Islands. We would set off at dusk on 4th November and approach the target vessel, which was described as a fucking big white yacht by Harry, in the early hours of the morning, before dawn. There was no need for a strictly covert approach, as apparently the target was expecting us to arrive. He was under the impression that we would be delivering a 'very important' package to him. We would pull up alongside the vessel and I would then climb onto the yacht's lower rear deck, confirm that whoever met me there was indeed the target and kill him. I was to make it look like a suicide or an accident and drop the body overboard. Then I'd return to the boat and we would get back to the trawler as soon as possible. If all went well the whole operation should be done and dusted just after dawn the next day.

Then I was shown a photograph of the target. Harry had indeed been right; this was the most important job I'd ever taken on. The target was none other than Robert

Maxwell; a very famous media mogul and one of the richest men in the world. He was a war hero, an ex-Member of the British Parliament and the friend and confidant of some of the most important politicians in the world.

In the event all went as planned. We arrived on location at the allotted time and I clambered on board the yacht to come face-to-face with the target. When he realised that I was not bringing him the package that he was expecting, I could see a look of calm resignation come onto his face and into his eyes. He guessed what I was there for, as it must have been pretty obvious to him. He could have fought me but he must have realised that he wouldn't have stood a chance when he looked into my eyes. He just pulled himself up to his not inconsiderable full height and stood there very calmly. Unlike some of my former targets, he didn't beg or plead with me to spare him, and he didn't show any fear to me. It didn't stop me from doing my job though. I punched him hard on the bridge of the nose, and while he was disorientated from this blow, I grabbed him and used a small syringe to inject into his neck. I don't know what the substance was in the syringe, but I guess it was something along the lines of *Ricin*, or perhaps a fast-acting anaesthetic. Whatever it was, he began almost immediately to get 'rubbery' legs, so I quickly whipped off his night-robe and pushed him over the rail. I distinctly heard his head collide with the hull before I heard the splash of his body hitting the sea. Then I did a quick final check of the deck, climbed back down to the semi-rigid inflatable, and we were off into the night.

A few days later we arrived back in São Miguel. Harry and I and the two Israeli bastards went our separate ways. I returned to my hotel, enjoyed a few more days lazing around the swimming pool and drinking, then caught my return flight home.

This was the last time that I ever had any contact with either the SAS, the firm, the Increment, or with Harry. But the aftermath of all that I had done for them over the years and all that I had become, will stay with me until the day I die.

EIGHTY-SIX

Monday 28th October 2013
Epsom, Surrey

Smith had spent several days in a perfectly-camouflaged OP watching the house of Sir Thomas Sewell MBE, former head of the SIS during the 1980s and early 1990s. The close protection team that was permanently assigned to the firm's former chief was very professional and Smith was impressed with their business-like attitude. They were a tough-looking bunch and didn't make mistakes. He didn't know which unit they belonged to, but it was probably in the military rather than the police; they looked and acted like army guys.

Smith had tentatively tried to penetrate the security around the house one night but hadn't been able to find a hole in it. There were sensors, pressure pads, trip wires, you name it, and it was deployed around the large grounds surrounding the house, making it into a veritable fortress.

In the end he decided to keep it simple. Smith knew what all professional security men around the world knew; that you could never fully protect a principle no matter how good your security was if the assassin was determined to get him. You could do your best and hope to catch him at it, but you could never, ever guarantee your principle's total safety.

In the early afternoon, after a full day's tiring work by the security team and in a natural lull in the day's activities, the ex-SIS chief made a fatal mistake and took a stroll with his wife in his garden to catch the last waning sunshine of the autumn. Smith put a hole in his head with the L42 sniper rifle from an unbelievable range of 2,200m.

It was the shot of his life and the end of his campaign of revenge. The last person who had known his real identity was now dead. He knew that there would never have been any computer or paper files on the work that he had carried out for the Increment.

It was over at last for Smith, at long last.

From: john smith (johnsmith2223@hotmail.com)
To: SOCA@Cambspolice.org.uk
Date: 30 October 2013 9:22:33
Subject: FAO Detective Chief Inspector Alan Davies, Cambs SOCA.

Hi Alan, I hope that you are well?

Please find attached the final instalment of my autobiography; you'll be pleased to know that I will be out of your hair forever after this.

You may have wondered why I have left you alive during all of this while I have killed so many others. Well, the answer is fairly simple. As far as I know you were just doing your job when you arrested me for the rape and murder of Mary Knightly. I will be sending you a recording of my interrogation of the CPS barrister; Steven Mackay. In this recording (try to ignore the screams and the sound of the drill) Mackay admitted that I had been set up by Harry in collusion with Mackay, the judge and Detective Sergeant Henry Price of SOCA. Harry had given the orders, Price had planted the evidence and Mackay and the judge had manipulated the trial and the jury; all of it in order to permanently get me out of the way and discredit anything that I may have said about my time in the SAS or the Increment. I don't know why Harry just didn't have me knocked off, except perhaps that he would have known that I would have put away some sort of insurance in case I was killed (which I have of course; all the documentary evidence that proves my story to be true).

I could forgive Harry even this; after all I have done much dirtier jobs myself in my time. The one thing that I cannot forgive is the rape and murder of that beautiful little girl, Mary. Who actually murdered her, whether it was a paedophile employed temporarily by the Increment and now lying at the bottom of a river somewhere feeding the fishes, or whether it was Harry himself (who had always struck me as a bit of a paedo), I guess that we'll never know for sure. Either way, justice has now been done.

I guess that all of this hasn't done your job prospects much good, has it Alan? Take the advice of one who's lived a long time in this fucking awful world and find yourself another job mate. You're not too good at this detective lark, are you? At least get a transfer out of SOCA. They are a bunch of useless fucking cowboys mate; just look at the fiasco they're creating in Afghanistan trying to stop the opium trade!

One last thing. Don't bother to continue looking for John Smith; he doesn't exist any more. Smith is just the name I chose when I came back to the UK from Rhodesia, and the SIS suggested that I should take on an alias as protection; just in case any of my former colleagues from Rhodesia had ever found out about my real purpose there. You'll never know my real identity. I'm not even sure that I can remember who the fuck I am now.

358

With any luck you will never hear from me again.
Regards
John Smith

EIGHTY-SEVEN

On my return to England the depression came back to me with a vengeance. For months I could do nothing at all and lived in a very poor state, drinking myself senseless and staying indoors for most of the time. I thought of killing myself, often visualising how I would do it. My favourite method was to put a noose around my neck, tie the rope to a lamp post, get in my car and drive away as fast as I could.

Eventually I began the long hard climb back to normality. I got myself another driving job and managed to keep it; I began to contact my family again, though it was always difficult whenever I tried to see my sons, as Anne-Marie never forgave me for having my 'affair' and leaving her. It got to the stage where she refused to let me see Robert and Alan, and I was forced to take her to court to fight for visitation rights. However, during the subsequent meetings with the social services, I was branded by Anne-Marie and her mother as a complete nutcase. The outcome of these meetings inevitably went against me, not helped at all by the fact that I couldn't explain to the welfare officers why I was like I was, or what had turned me into such a violent and often drunk depressive. I decided to do the decent thing and withdrew from the court case, only to then be blamed by Anne-Marie for time-wasting and trying to get at her by starting the court action in the first place. I just couldn't win no matter what I did.

This forced separation from my sons was the hardest of all the things that I had to go through. In spite of the fact that I had not seen that much of them during my life, due to the commitments that I had had during my military career and afterwards with the Increment; I missed them very much. I spent a lot of my time thinking about them and was only slightly consoled when my family all assured me that my sons would no doubt get back in touch with me once they had come of age and could make their own minds up.

Things came to a head when Anne-Marie applied for a divorce, naming some poor girl at my workplace that I barely knew as my 'lover'. I didn't contest it though, as I felt that I would never be believed.

During this period Anne-Marie changed completely from the lovely girl, full of laughter that I had married, into a vindictive and spiteful bitch. She used our children as a weapon in the 'war' between us and I will never forgive her for that. When our divorce finally came through and she remarried some Polish bloke, things still did not change and she was forever trying to turn my sons against me. Letters and birthday cards that I sent were never given to them, and my phone calls were intercepted with shouted exchanges in which she called my sons 'wankers' for wanting to talk to me. In the end I just gave up, thinking that I was doing my sons more harm than good by trying to stay in contact with them.

I never have and never will lay all of the blame at my ex-wife's feet. It was my behaviour and my career choices that had led to our breakup. She had never wanted me to leave her in the first place; this decision was totally my own. I had made my own bed and I would have to now lie in it. I was a nasty bastard at the best of times, but after my experience in Afghanistan I was as cold as a fish towards my close family and my friends. That episode and the period after it, when I spent so much time killing people in cold blood, and not giving a damn about it, were the beginning of the end as far as our relationship went.

I still think that I did the right thing though. If I had stayed with Anne-Marie and my sons, with my depression, my drinking, and suffering from PTSD, God knows what might have happened. I could change from coldness into blazing rage at the drop of a hat, and though I had never seriously hurt any of them, there was always the very real possibility that I could have. I was also right to withdraw from the court case as well. The last thing that I wanted was for my sons to be drawn into a long bitter dispute between me and their mother, with them acting as 'pig-in-the-middle' and being torn both ways. I loved them far too much to allow that to happen and Anne-Marie was always a good mother to my sons, despite our differences.

There were other things, apart from my divorce and the forced separation from my sons that constantly brought me down. I missed my days in the army, and particularly in the SAS with a passion. My old mates in the regiment had often helped me to get over my own problems, just as I had helped some of them. This deep comradeship, forged as it had been in the fire of conflict, had always been a large part of my life, and one that I missed a lot. I also missed the sheer excitement and adrenalin rush of combat. The old saying that you 'never ever feel as alive as you do when your life is in mortal danger' is very true. In addition, the responsibility that I had held, not only for operational matters but also for the very lives of my comrades, had been a constant challenge which I had always strove to meet head on with all of my personal resources. Even the fact that I had taken part in events that had changed history, such as the Falklands War, the Iranian Embassy Siege and the halting of the Scud missiles being fired into Israel by the Iraqis, made me feel that my present life had little or no real meaning to it. After all, how can you compare delivering parcels to offices and factories with some of the events that I had been such a large part of? There is no comparison of course.

Possibly the worst part of it all though, was that I could not even talk about my past, not to family or new work-mates; not to anyone. Even if I did, who would ever have believed it all? I'd have been tagged as a boastful wannabe if I'd owned up to even half of what I did during my long and eventful career, especially as I could never prove any of it. Most of the operations that I had taken part in were totally deniable. My time with the Increment had been unaccountable, except to the highest people in the land, and there had never been any paperwork involved, or any record of what I had done. Very, very few people even know about the existence of the Increment, never mind its role. I'm a ghost, as simple as that.

EIGHTY-EIGHT

During the next five years or so, my life became a roller coaster of ups and downs, with the downs; the 'depressions' getting longer and more severe. I don't really want to dwell too much on these years, as even now, nearly thirty years after Afghanistan, I can easily find myself slipping back down if I dwell on my past too long or too deeply. Simply writing this autobiography has been a nightmare for me, with all the images and memories that it has evoked, even though my trick-cyclist thought it would be good therapy for me.

One of the worst moments was when Anne-Marie went to the police with a totally made-up story about me. It was nothing to do with sex or violence, but it did end up with me being arrested, charged and convicted of a crime that I never committed. I then spent four and a half months in prison. I've never had a satisfactory answer from her about why she did this to me, but I guess that this was her way of getting back at me for all the hurt.

It happened at a time when I was feeling really low. Two policemen came to my bedsit and I, like a bloody fool, invited them in. Before I knew it, they had arrested and carted me off to the local police station. You can imagine what it was like for me being thrown into a cell after my experiences in Afghanistan; I just went to pieces. Eventually, after several interviews during which I couldn't prove my innocence, I was charged and released on police bail.

The old maxim of 'innocent until proven guilty' doesn't appear to exist in Britain any more. These two policemen bullied and cajoled me, and it didn't seem to matter at all to them whether I was innocent or not, so long as they got a conviction. I was in such a poor state during this period that I couldn't defend myself at all. This experience has led to me having a deep dislike and distrust for the police. I don't suppose for one minute that they are all like the ones that I have come across. After all, there are good and bad people in every organisation. It was just my bad luck to have to deal with the bad ones.

I appeared in Magistrates Court and was then referred to Crown Court, as the charge was too serious for the Magistrates to deal with. Despite having no physical evidence against me at all, and even though I pleaded not guilty, the jury found me guilty at my trial and I was given an 18 month sentence with nine months of that suspended. My dad was at the trial and I can still see the look of shock that was on his face when the sentence was passed on me by the judge.

I was escorted to prison in a coach with six prison officers sitting around me; I guess that they believed I was as dangerous as the police accused me of being.

Surprisingly, prison wasn't so bad. After two weeks of being cooped up in a two-man cell in Winston Green with an ex-burglar for twenty-three hours a day, I was transferred to Sudbury Open Prison for the rest of my sentence. Here I was in a room with five other prisoners; a pawn-broker who had been done for handling stolen property, a con-artist in for fraud, two cousins who had been caught stealing cars and selling them on to order, and an Australian who had been caught smuggling ecstasy tablets from Holland. We all got on fine and had a few small adventures, such as going over the fence a few times to collect booze and even Kentucky Fried Chicken that a friend of one of the guys dropped off; brewing our own booze made from apples, oranges, sugar and yeast; and getting into a scrape with an ex-armed robber from another room. This latter event started when the armed robber tried to intimidate the pawn-broker into smuggling him some dope in when he was allowed out on 'day-visits'. The pawn-broker refused, so the armed robber began to visit him in our room and would just sit there staring at him. He was a big black guy and nasty looking, but I got fed up with his intimidation tactics one evening, took one of the metal legs off my bed and told him that he had five seconds to get out of the room or I'd beat him to death. I think he could see that I was serious and disappeared by the time I got to 'three'. There was no more trouble from him after that.

We all became good friends during our incarceration, and even though I was totally innocent and should not have been locked up, I've got to admit that my time served at Her Majesties pleasure did me some good, and my depression had lifted by the time that I was released.

The good moments could be very good indeed. I gradually worked myself up from job to job until I found myself in a really good and relatively well-paid position; though I was still only delivering parcels and driving. Then, I decided to take the plunge into something that I'd always wanted to do, even though it was quite a financial risk for me to do so, and I got myself into University to complete a post-graduate degree course alongside a bunch of much younger students.

This led to a chance discovery that shook my life to its very foundations. During my course I became quite ill, and found myself periodically suffering from partial paralysis, particularly when I found myself under pressure or stress. I contacted my family doctor, who in turn referred me to a specialist in neurology. I undertook a barrage of tests, including an MRI scan of my brain.

When the results of the tests came in I was given an appointment to visit the specialist and I found out that I had extensive brain damage, estimated at 40% of the volume of my brain! The specialist consultant could not believe that I was actually on my feet. He had envisaged me as basically being a drooling idiot in a wheelchair, unable to do anything for myself. When he found out that not only did I seem comparatively unaffected by my injury, but that I was actually taking a degree course at a university, he could hardly believe it.

It turns out that when I had undergone my interrogation in Afghanistan; the constant beatings, drownings, electrocutions and the mixture of powerful drugs that I'd been given, had caused massive injuries to my brain, some of them due to oxygen starvation; others due to physical injury. When I relayed the story of how I had had to teach myself to talk and walk again, he nodded his head sagely as if he now understood. The one thing that really made him quite angry was that I'd never been told about the injury by the army on my return to the UK. He told me that they must have known about it, as even army doctors were not 'complete idiots'. If I had been told about the damage straight away, then I could have taken some remedial treatment that would have helped my recovery immensely. Now it was far too late. He advised me that I should put in a compensation claim to the forces.

I didn't tell him that I knew them much better than that. I had been on a deniable mission in Afghanistan, and no way would either the army or the spooks ever admit to my being on that mission, or even to its existence. At best I would be laughed out of court. At worst, I'd end up beneath a bus or a train somewhere, a victim of my old unit: the Increment.

I have damage to most areas of my brain, including my long and short term memory, my senses and my motor areas. I decided that I had no option but to carry on as though I didn't have the injury, and that is what I've done ever since. Even my family have never found out, and never will.

367

EIGHTY-NINE

After I successfully completed my Masters degree I went into business for myself and was doing pretty well, when suddenly I was overcome by the need to give something back to the world at large. I immediately got in touch with several charities that carried out humanitarian activities overseas. Armed with my Masters degree and a life-time full of experience, it wasn't long before I hooked up with a charity that needed a new Executive Director in a third world country. There wasn't much competition for the job, especially as the pay was at local rates, in other words hardly anything at all by British standards. This was no doubt the reason for me getting it. Not that I cared; money had never been something that motivated me that much.

Before I gave up my life in the UK, however, I had some really good news; my sons had been in touch with my parents and wanted to visit them. My dad told me this over the phone and suggested that I come by their house before Anne-Marie turned up to drop the boys off. Then I could hide myself away so that she didn't know I was there, and I'd get to spend the whole day with Robert and Alan before she picked them up again. This I duly did, and all five of us spent a great day together.

Over the next few months we would do this every couple of weeks, and my ex-wife never guessed that my sons were actually spending time with me and not just with their grandparents. It was hard at first as I hadn't seen my sons for such a long time, but we gradually got used to each other again. At one point I thought about giving up the new job and staying in the UK because I enjoyed these visits so much, but I didn't.

This was one of the better periods of my post-army life and I really enjoyed my visits with Robert, Alan, my dad and mum. The lads were getting older and were proper teenagers, talking about computer games and movies. Thankfully, they didn't seem to have been damaged too much by having dysfunctional parents, which was a real blessing as far as I was concerned.

Eventually though, as all good things do, it came to an end. I packed up my gear, left my flat, and flew out of the country on what I thought would be a short two-year posting. In reality I ended up leaving all of my old life behind me for the next eight years.

I helped to tackle appalling poverty and abject misery amongst the local people of a developing country with the same intensity of purpose that I've always shown, no matter what I did for a living.

I am happy to say that, although I never got any richer, I do believe that I made a real difference to the lives of a lot of poverty-stricken people who would never have got the chance in any other way. I helped to give hope to people where there had not been any hope before, and I'm bloody proud of that. I also had a few more adventures along the way, and even dodged a few more bullets too.

Since I've returned to the UK life has not been easy for me. You would think that a person with all of my experience and life-skills, not only from my time in the army but also as a charity worker overseas, would be snapped up by a company and given a decent job full of responsibility. Unfortunately this is not the case: many potential employers, offering good jobs, could not see the qualities that I would bring to their workplace. So I'm back on the road now, driving and delivering parcels all over the UK.

I've had an interesting life. Never a dull moment. But it's been a life that not many people would have liked to live. It's also been a hard life, but I'm a hard bastard and I've coped.

Over the years I've put my body and mind through some bloody tough ordeals but luckily they still seem to be functioning okay most of the time. I bet that even at my age I can still out-march, out-run and out-fight at least 95% of people, and probably out-shoot almost all of them.

I can live in the harshest terrain and survive for as long as required. I can strip, clean, assemble and fire just about every weapon that's known in the world; from pistols through to anti-tank weapons. I can navigate by the stars or the sun, and I can drive just about any vehicle that's ever been made. I can even fly a helicopter, though I wouldn't want to be a passenger of mine! I'm fully qualified as an instructor in a whole range of subjects from map-reading through to sniping, and I'm fluent in half a dozen languages including Russian, German, Pashto, Shona and Matabele, and I can also get by in another half a dozen, such as Arabic, French and Spanish. I've parachuted out of airplanes and helicopters and operated undercover in lethally-dangerous situations. I've tracked that most dangerous of animals, man, through bush and deserts, and I've killed around four hundred people with every type of weapon from hand grenades to my own two bare hands.

More than all this though, what really makes me proud is that I have led and motivated some of the bravest and most honourable soldiers in the world on dangerous missions, and I have brought them out alive.

These days I live on my own, with very little contact with anybody outside of my workplace. I don't make friends easily, if at all. My parents have passed away and I seldom talk to my brothers; normally just a short phone conversation every month or so. I don't have a partner, and I doubt that I ever will; not now that I'm grey-haired and getting on a bit in the age department.

I keep a watchful eye from afar on my now grown-up sons, but again have very little contact with them and none at all with my two grand-daughters. Thankfully they all seem to be leading very normal and uneventful lives.

I still suffer from PTSD, just as my psychiatrist said I would all of those years ago. I still have awful nightmares, though not as regularly as I once did and thankfully I don't piss my bed anymore, but I still scream in the night at least once or twice a month. My brain injury doesn't cause me too much aggravation, except for the odd terrifying occasions when I wake up not being able to remember what my name is or where I am. These episodes never last for too long though, so I should be grateful for that. I worry that one day I'll wake up and my memories will never come back, but that wouldn't be too bad a thing, all things considered. There is a lot of my life that I wish that I could forget.

None of the dreams that I had as a teenager will ever come true. I will never be rich and live in a big house with lots of land. I'll never fall in a love with a beautiful woman and live happily ever after. I'll never have a happy loving family around me. I guess that I'm not really the happy-families type though, am I? What is more than likely going to happen to me is that I will die in the same old flat I'm living in now, on my own, and it will probably be weeks before anyone even notices that I've gone. I doubt that there will be many people who will turn up at my funeral.

But, and in spite of the severe clinical depressions that hit me hard every now and again, life is not so bad. It could be a lot worse. I might have died on any of a dozen or so occasions, or worse, I could have lost a limb, or two, or four, and been left a cripple for the rest of my days.

I've done some good things in my life and I've done some bad things. I've given new life to the world in the form of two sons, and I've taken life away from a whole lot of people, most of them bad people, but not all of them. I've travelled the world and lived in hard conditions in harsh places, and I've had the best of friends. But, and I'd

371

like to emphasise this, there are hundreds, perhaps even thousands of good, decent, everyday people who are walking around today, getting on with their lives, who might not have been able to if I had not risked my own life and killed those murdering terrorist bastards. You could be one of them, or a member of your family, or a friend of yours.

I'm proud of this fact, and when I finally go, I'll die a happy man knowing this to be true.

I really did make a difference.

As for the Increment, I've no doubt that they still operate. Will they ever come gunning for me? Who knows? One thing is for certain though; a man like me does not go through life without taking certain precautions.

As Dylan Thomas once said:

"Do not go gentle into that good night." Don't worry; I don't intend to.

EPILOGUE

Friday 31st January 2014
Brussels, Belgium

The man sat in a departure lounge at Brussels Airport,
waiting for his flight to Banjul International Airport, in The
Gambia, West Africa. His hair was long and mousy-brown in
colour, with just a faint hint of grey to show his age,
gathered into a ponytail held by an elastic band. He sat
comfortably on his plastic seat watching his fellow
passengers with obvious amusement as they sat around him
or walked by. He was smiling at Dutch, English and Swedish
tourists who were dressed in a range of brightly-coloured
shorts and T-shirts despite it being bloody freezing outside.
Everybody there seemed to be full of the holiday mood
already and their bright smiles and laughs filled the room.

The man opened his dog-eared British passport and
stared at his own long-haired photo looking back at him. He
read the name on the passport to himself once more: Paul
Gray. It would be the only name that he would be known
by from now on so he had better get used to it.

The call for boarding came loud over the tannoy.
Paul Gray picked up his small travel bag, smiled and
winked at a teenage African girl that was giving him an
appraising look up and down, joined the other passengers
that were walking to the departure gate, and began his
new life.

Authors note

Anyone who knows me will know that there are certain parallels between the 'autobiography' of the main character in this book, John Smith, and my own life. However, I would like to emphasise that I am not an assassin working for the Secret Intelligence Service, nor have I ever been, or ever will be. So please, don't send me any 'job' offers!

This novel is a work of fiction. However, many of the incidents mentioned in it are in fact true and did take place. The Rhodesian and British Army units highlighted in this novel either exist today, or have existed in the past. They include the Rhodesian Light Infantry, Selous Scouts and Rhodesian Special Air Service Regiment (which all fought with distinction during the long bush war in Rhodesia). The Parachute Regiment and 22 Special Air Service Regiment of the British Army, the Mountain and Arctic Warfare Cadre and Special Boat Squadron of the Royal Marines do exist, and all of them have long and distinguished histories. I hope that my use of these units in the context of this novel has not offended any past or serving members, whom I greatly admire. 14 Field Security and Intelligence Company also existed throughout the troubles of Northern Ireland, though very little is published about the work they carried out or the people that served in this unit.

Other parts of this novel are pure speculation, though again they may be grounded in fact. For example persistent rumours exist that there was a British 'spy' who was ranked highly in the Rhodesian Army's Combined Operations. It is thought that this unknown person did pass back information regarding operations that were targeting either Joshua NKomo or Robert Mugabe, and that warnings were then given by the British government to these rebel leaders. There is also a persistent rumour that the British Secret Intelligence Service (MI6) employs a small number of

Special Forces operatives to undertake 'deniable' operations, and that this unit is named the 'Increment'. However there is no firm evidence that this is true, even if it does seem likely.

The Police National Computer and the National DNA Database both exist in real life and both are sited at the locations that are given in this novel. Neither of these are secret locations, and both can be easily found by trawling the internet. However, the locations of their backup servers are secret, so I took the liberty of using the old location for the PNC backup server at Buncefield, which became publicly known when it was in danger of being destroyed by a fire in a nearby oil terminal.

Any names of real people that are used in this novel are purely to place the story into a believable context, and I do not intend to denigrate the memory of any of these individuals.

As for the remainder of the story, it is down to you to imagine how true any of it may be.

Craig William Emms
April 2012

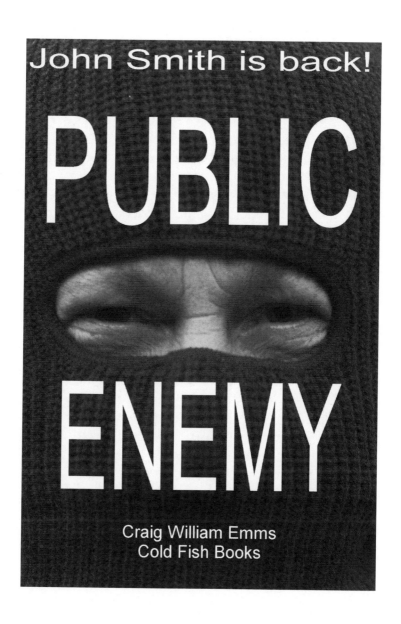

John Smith is back!

PUBLIC ENEMY

Craig William Emms
Cold Fish Books

The second novel in the saga of John Smith is
PUBLIC ENEMY

John Smith is an ex-Special Forces soldier,
spy and assassin who killed on the orders
of the British government.

He is wanted for waging a war against his former masters that left a swathe of destruction and dead bodies behind him in the first book in the series: ***One Heartbeat a Minute.***

Now the Special Intelligence Service has been ordered to bring John Smith to justice, but they don't want him to go on trial.
He knows too many of their dirty little secrets.
They want him dead.

They're not the only ones;
John must also fight for his life against a group of fanatical terrorists
Survive a face to face encounter with an ex-IRA hitman who wants bloody vengeance for the murder of his brother
Face a life sentence for a crime that he did not commit
And rescue two members of the Royal Family kidnapped by a gang of vicious thugs

Will John Smith survive against all the odds?
Or will his luck finally run out?

Currently available as an ebook on Amazon

4044250R00210

Printed in Great Britain
by Amazon.co.uk, Ltd.,
Marston Gate.